D0333563

HEREWARD

Wolves of New Rome

www.transworldbooks.co.uk

Also by James Wilde

HEREWARD
HEREWARD: THE DEVIL'S ARMY
HEREWARD: END OF DAYS

For more information on James Wilde and his books,
see his website at www.manofmercia.co.uk

HEREWARD

Wolves of New Rome

James Wilde

BANTAM PRESS

LONDON · TORONTO · SYDNEY · AUCKLAND · JOHANNESBURG

TRANSWORLD PUBLISHERS
61–63 Uxbridge Road, London W5 5SA
A Random House Group Company
www.transworldbooks.co.uk

First published in Great Britain
in 2014 by Bantam Press
an imprint of Transworld Publishers

A CIP catalogue record for this book
is available from the British Library.

ISBNs 9780593071830 (cased)
9780593071847 (tpb)

Addresses for Random House Group Ltd companies outside the UK
can be found at: www.randomhouse.co.uk
The Random House Group Ltd Reg. No. 954009

The Random House Group Limited supports the Forest Stewardship Council®
(FSC®), the leading international forest-certification organisation.
Our books carrying the FSC label are printed on FSC®-certified paper.
FSC is the only forest-certification scheme supported by the leading
environmental organisations, including Greenpeace. Our paper procurement
policy can be found at www.randomhouse.co.uk/environment

To Elizabeth, Betsy, Joseph and Eve

PROLOGUE

Palace of Boukoleon, Constantinople, 28 May 1072

Death waits in silence.

When he took the axe-oath in the ringing chamber deep beneath the house of Hormisdas, that had been the first thing Wulfrun was told.

Death waits, everywhere.

More than honour, more than duty, it was the lesson he had been supposed to take away from that rite. Never rest. Be always vigilant. Death waits for all.

Now, cocking his head, he listened.

Silence.

As he stood in the shadows at the back of the vast, sunlit hall, Wulfrun felt his heart slow, his breath still. From under heavy lids, he looked up into the golden glow that suffused the chamber. The air here was fragrant. The perfume of the pink mullein flowers tumbling down the white walls of the palace drifted into the hall on the warm breeze. Through the great window, light twinkled across the swell of the Marmara Sea.

Soon.

Wulfrun looked across the heads of the throng waiting to hear the words of Elias Cephalas, wise counsel to the emperor. Here were representatives of the greatest families in Constantinople. Gold spilled from their coffers. Their lands stretched to the misty horizon. These were the ones who wielded power like a sword, who commanded armies, who controlled the strength of the church, and the cutting tongue of politics.

And here he was, Wulfrun of Barholme. An English dog with the mud of the fens under his nails, now risen to the heights of a captain in the feared Varangian Guard, the emperor's right arm. Here, in the greatest city on earth, at the heart of an empire that stretched from sea to sea. Aye, he had power too, of a kind. A quiet power. No one would look him in the eye unless bidden. His choice to leave behind England and its miseries had been the right one. Now he could be the man his father had always hoped he would be.

His smile faded, and anger flickered across his face at the loss he had endured. The grief was still raw.

Wulfrun shifted his stance, feeling the comforting weight of the hauberk he wore. His leather breastplate, oiled and scented with sandalwood, creaked as he flexed. Steel vambraces protected his forearms, and on his flank, under his crimson cape, he carried his broad, circular shield, painted red and white with his raven sigil black in the centre. His fingers closed around his long-hafted Dane-axe. As always, he was dressed for battle.

A man cleared his throat and the spell was broken. Across the hall, necks craned as the emperor drifted in.

The slight figure clambered up on to the throne. In the sunlight, his jewelled *loros* gleamed with all the colours of the rainbow. The ruby at the centre of the crown shone, a pool of blood surrounded by gold. Though Michael had seen twenty-one summers, he still had the face of a child. Unlined, cheeks permanently flushed, eyes too wide, too innocent. Wulfrun sensed the crowd's odd mix of awe and contempt. Did the emperor know that he was so despised? Did he care?

Michael had been seventeen when his father, the old emperor, had died. He was of an age to rule, but even his mother Eudokia had recognized that her son had no interest in politics, no desire for anything but to continue his studies. Yet Eudokia did not want to lose her grip on power and had conspired to establish herself as the young emperor's regent alongside his uncle John Doukas. Wulfrun turned up his nose. Politics in Constantinople was little more than a pit of snakes. When Eudokia's fingers had eventually been prised off the throne and she was dispatched to a monastery, the ineffectual emperor was left at the mercy of anyone with ambition, and in this city there was no shortage of that.

Never had there been a worse time for such weak rule, not in all of the empire's glorious history. Less than a year had passed since that crushing defeat at the battle of Manzikert. The Turkish hordes had decimated the ranks of the professional soldiers from the western and eastern *tagmata*. For centuries, the empire had been feared. Now its authority had been destroyed. The borders could no longer be defended, and the Seljuks moved closer by the day.

War was coming, anyone could see that. Bloodshed the likes of which Constantinople had never known. While the emperor hid away in his chambers, everyone else marched towards doom.

A tall man with burning eyes loomed behind the throne. This was the architect of so much of Constantinople's misery, Nikephoritzes, the finance minister, the man who held Michael in thrall. Wulfrun narrowed his eyes. He had sworn no oath to protect that viper.

But then Elias Cephalas stepped before the throne. Tall and strong and draped in many layers of the finest embroidered silk, Elias radiated a potency that the emperor lacked. His kin had built their power-base in the green northern lands, and he towered over the imperial court in every way.

Wulfrun eased a path through the crowd, unnoticed by all as they hung upon every word. Would the counsel dare tell the emperor of the sour mood across the city, here, in such a public setting? Elias would dare anything, the warrior decided.

'A storm sweeps towards us all.' Elias' voice boomed off the marble walls. 'A storm of steel, a storm of blood. And this greatest of empires falls into shadow. We have stayed silent for so long in hope that the fate we all foresee could be averted by strong actions and a will to lead us back into the sun.' For a moment, he bowed his head as if a heavy sadness weighted his shoulders. ''Twas not to be. I can see that now, as can we all. You are too weak.'

A shocked murmur rustled around the chamber. On the throne, Michael leaned forward, frowning. Even then he did not have the strength to speak out in anger.

'As long as you sit there, always a child, the empire is doomed to fall.' Elias' voice hardened. 'The candle of hope must be lit before the darkness consumes us. There must be an ending . . . now.'

Steel flashed from the folds of Elias' tunic. His face twisting in fury, he lunged towards the emperor.

For Wulfrun, the world was calm. His heartbeat was barely a whisper, his features peaceful. The screams that erupted around him were as nothing. The commander stepped forward, and with an effortless swing of his axe he took the counsel's head.

Blood showered across the imperial court.

Without emotion, Wulfrun watched the shrieking women staring at their red hands in horror, the men reeling in disgust. Never had these cosseted nobles been witness to such slaughter. They were soft, in spirit as well as muscle. They never took up arms, never fought for what they believed in. That was why the army withered and the Varangian Guard was filled with English and Danes, the fiercest warriors in all the world.

Wulfrun could have spared the court this sight. He had known of Elias' plot for days now. How easy it would have been to drag the snake out of his bed and leave his head upon his doorstep. But a lesson was needed, and here it was.

10

And it was not yet over.

When he raised his arm, the men under his command flooded through the doors leading into the hall. Helms and hauberks flashed. Silent they were, eyes cold, jaws set. Only the heartbeat of their leather soles upon the flags announced their arrival.

A wave of steel broke upon the crowd. Plunging among the churning, terrified aristocracy, the Varangian Guard swept towards the remaining plotters. Elias' allies clawed their way towards the doors, crying for mercy. There would be none.

Wulfrun watched, unmoved, as the short swords stabbed. Arcs of ruby droplets shimmered in the shafts of sunlight. Women slipped and fell on the slick, ruddy floor. Men stumbled over them, sprawling. The highest in the city, now stained by the mire of life that they had sought so long to avoid. The captain gave an approving nod.

Finally, the stabbing blades stilled. The Varangian Guard retreated to the edges of the hall, their swords dripping. Wulfrun looked around the scarred faces of his men and saw no emotion. That was good. He raised his left fist, then flexed the fingers forward. The warriors ghosted away into the depths of the palace.

'You do your duty well, Wulfrun. Once again I owe you my life.'

The captain turned at the sound of the reedy voice. Someone had handed a cloth to the emperor and he was dabbing at the splatters on his tunic. Wulfrun bowed his head. Michael forced a wan smile as Nikephoritzes took his arm and guided him out of the chamber.

Lessons had been learned here, the commander thought, but none by those who most needed them.

Stepping over the bodies littering the crimson lake, the captain marched past the ashen aristocrats without giving them a second glance. Outside the door, he inhaled a familiar fragrance, as sweet as those flowers cascading down the palace walls. He saw her, half hidden in the shadows of the entrance to an antechamber. With a sweet smile, Juliana Nepa beckoned to him. She fairly glowed in the half-light, her fine dress the colour of amber, her blonde hair covered by an ivory headcloth. On her breast was the gold brooch, the token he had given her months before.

'You should not be here, Juliana—'

'You are so stern.' Grasping his hand, she dragged him into the room. Once they were out of sight, she stood on her tiptoes and kissed him upon the right cheek. 'Wulfrun the warrior!' she teased, reaching out to his iron helm. With a frown, he jerked his head back, but he could never resist her. Bowing, he let her take the gilded helm. His hazel hair tumbled free. For a moment, she caught her fingers in it. Her face grew serious, her thoughts flying away he did not know where. But then a smile lit her face once more and she murmured, 'You are two men, Wulfrun, did you know that? Two men, and I know not which is the true one.'

He laughed at her playfulness.

'There!' She pressed the tip of one finger against his lips. 'When you wear the helm of the Guard you never smile and never, never laugh. Your face is like stone, your voice so grim. Yet when you strip it away you are warm and caring, and gentle.'

'You do not like the captain of the Guard?'

Juliana hesitated. 'He scares me.'

Wulfrun flinched. But he understood what lay behind her words. The rite deep beneath the palace had changed him; remade him. The choking smell of the cloying smoke from the torches, the stink of fear-sweat on the naked men, the reek of the urine that they all would drink to usher them across the threshold to their new life. The blood of the lion, and the bull. To stand under the banner of the Varangian Guard meant being a man no longer. All weaknesses, all flaws, aye, and all kindnesses too, had to be put aside. Now he felt as if he were carved from stone. There were days when he could feel the heart of the person he had been begin to crumble, become dust, drift away. He peered deep into Juliana's face. She was the last bond that connected him to that fading man. Without her, he truly would be lost.

Beyond the doorway, the aristocrats began to trail out of the hall. Amid the hubbub, a familiar creaking echoed. Wulfrun glanced at Juliana and saw a shadow cross her face. The Nepotes had suffered much during the last two years, but in Constantinople the price for failure was always harsh.

Juliana eased past him to spy on the throng. Sure enough, there was her father, Kalamdios Nepos. Four slaves carried his chair at shoulder-height on wooden poles. Wulfrun felt a pang of pity. Kalamdios too had lost the man he used to be, but his loss was not by choice. His face was fixed in a permanent scowl, and though his eyes swivelled in his head, seeing everything, he was cut off from the world like a ship adrift in stormy seas. His mouth could not form words, only the mewling of an infant. Drool dripped from the edge of his lip. He could not lift his arm to wipe it away, nor feed himself, nor walk. Wulfrun had seen his fingers flex, and his wrists had some movement, but that was all that remained of the once-powerful Kalamdios. On the side of his head, a large patch of hair was missing where the blade had cut through the skull and into his brain.

Beside him walked his wife, Juliana's mother. Simonis Nepa was still slender, still beautiful, though silver streaked her auburn hair. Wulfrun thought she had the saddest face he had ever seen. When he first arrived in Constantinople in the stream of English refugees fleeing the devastation wrought by William the Bastard upon their homeland, he remembered Simonis laughing as she welcomed the wealthiest merchants in the city into her house.

He glanced down at Juliana, frowning as she watched her kin pass by. Did she believe her bloodline was cursed, as many said?

13

Juliana must have sensed him looking at her, for she glanced up and smiled. 'All is well,' she murmured.

A small figure pushed through the blood-spattered aristo-crats like a rat swimming upstream. The head turned this way and that, searching, until Wulfrun glimpsed the thin face.

'I must go,' he whispered. 'Ricbert looks for me.'

'More news from your spies in the city? Or your scouts across the empire?'

'Both, I would wager.'

Her eyes flashed with affection and she breathed, 'Keep well.' She kissed him on the cheek once more and then slipped out into the flow of bodies.

Wulfrun hailed. His aide grinned and elbowed his way through the crowd, caring little how many of the high-born snapped with irritation. In the anteroom, Ricbert pulled off his helm and ran his fingers through his lank brown hair. 'You gave the great folk of Constantinople a fright,' he said, showing his crooked teeth.

'Aye. They will not be so quick to plot for a while. Until they start to wince under Nikephoritzes' taxes again.'

The smaller man snorted. 'A little blood makes them afrit? They have too many comforts here. They would not last a day in England.'

'They pay us well for our hardness, Ricbert.'

'Long may they refuse to get their hands dirty.'

'You have news?'

Ricbert shrugged. 'Seljuks to the east, Normans to the west. So many enemies to the north, I would not know where to begin. But all is as it was. No movement towards Constantinople as yet.'

Wulfrun shook his head, feeling the weight of his responsi-bilities. 'These soft people can lose themselves in the endless rounds of who-is-doing-what, but soon enough they will be forced to face up to the reckoning that is coming their way. Till then . . .' He paused, sensing a hesitancy in his aide. 'There is more?'

'The scout has returned with news of England.'

For a moment, Wulfrun let the words settle on him. Then he removed his helm from under his arm and slipped it on his head. The world closed in around him.

'The rebellion is over. In the fenlands, the English have been defeated. William the Bastard is victorious.'

'And Hereward?' *Dead.* He heard the word in his head before the other man spoke.

But Ricbert shook his head. 'England is rife with tales of what happened to the rebel leader after Ely fell. The Normans claim he ran like a whipped cur and threw himself upon the king's mercy, betraying his own men in the same breath.'

Wulfrun set his jaw. He knew Hereward too well. 'More Norman lies.'

With a sly smile, Ricbert threw his arms wide. 'Perhaps he flew away 'pon the wings of an angel. In the inns, they call him Bear-killer . . . Giant-killer . . . wielder of a magic sword which can cleave whole mountains in two, so the scout tells me.' He chuckled to himself. 'I would pay good coin for a sword like that.' His smile faded when he saw Wulfrun's cold face. 'A ship set sail from Yernemuth with the last of the English rebels upon it, and, so it seems, Hereward among their number. It is said they come here, to Constantinople, to seek their fortune.'

Wulfrun felt a heat deep in his bones. He had thought himself stone, but it seemed there was a part of the old Wulfrun that still lived on, even under the colours of the Varangian Guard. 'Then let him come,' he said, trying to keep the tremor out of his voice. 'If he dare walk through this city, his days will soon be ended. My axe will see to that.'

CHAPTER ONE

The warriors watched the ship drift towards them across the green swell. With faces like winter, they took in the billowing amber sail and the cracking lines, the freshly painted shields lining the side and the tiller swinging at the mercy of the currents. For this was a ship of ghosts, they could see that now. The vessel looked as if those who sailed it had only just set its course, but no man walked upon that deck. And all that rolled out was the groaning of the hull as it flexed against the waves, a sound that seemed to come from beyond the grave.

'Pull alongside,' Hereward commanded. In the sultry heat, he was stripped to the waist. The tattooed blue-black circles and spirals of the fighting man flexed across his tanned arms. Placing one foot upon the side of his own ship, Hereward studied the deserted vessel. Though he could sense his men urging him to leave well alone, instincts honed on the field of battle demanded that he know more.

Overhead, the sail swelled as his men took to the oars. Their vessel was a warship, just large enough to accommodate the thirty men upon its benches. But some would say they were ghosts too, dead men all, stripped of their lives, their home, their loved ones, their hope. Outlaws, exiles, condemned to wander the earth for ever.

'This is bad business,' the Viking growled under his breath. Kraki was his name. Wild of hair and beard, his face was cleaved by a jagged scar. He scowled, trying to hide his unease. On land, he was a seasoned warrior, a former leader of Earl Tostig's deadly huscarls, and axe-for-hire, trailing death behind him as he trekked from his cold northern home. But here on the whale road he seemed as superstitious as any drunken ceorl in the dark midwinter. Ghosts and portents and curses. He needed dry land under his feet to find himself again, Hereward knew. But he was not alone there.

Only one of those aboard was not a member of the war-band. Red Erik was long seasoned by the salt winds and, unlike the others, capable of navigating to distant shores. In the five days they had been upon the waves, the warriors had started to learn to be seamen under his command. Until the exile, many of them had never left the well-trodden paths of their villages in the fenlands of eastern England. Then they had been forced to venture into open water with waves as high as towering cliffs. But England was gone for good, of that there could be no doubt. The comfort of the winter hearth, the care of kin, the joyful feasting after the harvest, all gone, never to be seen again. King William had seen to that.

Hereward gritted his teeth. These good warriors had fought the Bastard long and hard after he had stolen the English crown that day at Senlac Ridge. And for a brief time, it had seemed the hated Norman invaders might be driven back into the sea. But betrayal came lightly to some, and while they had been looking out over the walls of their fortress at Ely they had not been paying heed to their backs, and the blades of their own.

He swallowed his bitterness. On the Isle of Eels, their forces had been strong. They had weapons aplenty and the walls stood firm. The secret paths through the treacherous bogs and dense woods and flooding watercourses were unknown to the enemy.

Once they had destroyed King William's camp at Belsar's Hill, it had seemed the invaders were on the brink of collapse. But the monks of Ely, who had offered sanctuary to the rebel band, began to fear for their gold and power. And so they showed the Bastard the secret ways and led his army to the gates. In the face of such vast numbers of Normans and mercenaries, it was then only a matter of time until the hopes of the English crumbled.

In the end, his leadership had amounted to naught. He winced. To save England from the brutal retribution of the king, to save his birthland of Mercia, to save all the desperate men and women who had rallied to his standard, he had been forced to take the Bastard's deal: leave the shores of his home for ever, and do so in secrecy so that the people for whom he had fought so hard would think he had abandoned them. What choice did he have? If he had stayed the king would have killed and maimed and starved the English until he had wiped out all trace of them. He had accepted that final twist of the knife; it was the only honourable course. And his most loyal warriors had followed him even then. He owed them everything. Now their fate lay on his shoulders alone. He could not, would not, fail them again. But there was hope. Though England was forbidden to him, he had heard there was a need for fighting men in the east. Perhaps there they could find a new home.

The ghost ship drifted closer still until his men could throw their hooks into the wood and drag it alongside. Before Hereward could peer into the vessel, cries rang out all around. Men crossed themselves or clutched the lead hammers that hung round their necks.

Leaning over the side, the Mercian saw what had dismayed them. Blood sluiced along the deck from prow to stern, a lake of it, gleaming darkly in the midday sun.

'Still wet,' Kraki mumbled, moistening his lips. Thirty pairs of eyes flickered towards the horizon, searching for whatever had brought about this curse.

19

'You have waded through a sea of Norman guts on the battlefield,' Hereward called to his crew. He pushed scorn into his voice, trying to cut through their superstition. 'Are you afrit of a little blood?'

Kraki heaved himself off his bench and leaned in. 'Now it is not ghosts that trouble me.'

Hereward stared into the distance. They had sailed without incident past Normandy and Brittany, Guyenne and Navarre. But then they had put in to the rocky shore of Leon and Castile to replenish their food and water and there the fearful fisher-men had issued their warning. A vast fleet of sea wolves was laying waste to the coastline, searching for one of their number who had robbed them of some great prize.

A cry rang out from the prow.

Hereward whirled. A figure was standing on the side of the ship, arms outstretched, ready to throw himself into the waves. The Mercian glimpsed the red hair, the pale skin, and realized it was Sighard, the youngest of the war-band. Men scrambled over the benches. They knew as well as Hereward that a black despair had eaten its way into the lad's heart since his brother had been slain by the Normans.

For an instant, Sighard teetered on the brink. But just as he lifted one foot to take a last step on to the green fields of the whale road, a huge figure rose up and strapped his mighty arms around the lad's chest. Guthrinc was an English oak who towered over every man there, with a heart just as big. He wrenched back, and the two men sprawled across the deck.

Hereward thrust his way through the circle of warriors that had gathered around them. Guthrinc kept his arms wrapped around the lad, just in case.

'Let me die. I am no use to anyone,' Sighard mumbled, one arm thrown across his freckled face.

'You are a brother to us all,' the Mercian said, crouching down. 'You have proved yourself in battle a hundred times.

20

There is not a man here who would not give up his life for you. Do you hear?'

'Let me die,' Sighard repeated.

As Hereward stood up, Alric caught his arm. The monk's brown hair was lank from salt spray, his sodden tunic clinging to his slim frame. They had been friends for long years now, and knew each other better than any men there. Alric pulled the Mercian to one side and whispered, 'You cannot leave Sighard to his own devices. I have seen this affliction before. There will be smiles, and kind words, but the blackness will gnaw away at him, and sooner or later he will take his own life. He needs hope.'

'Every man here does.' Hereward felt the weight of his burden. All of his spear-brothers had lost so much during the long war against the Normans. Exile had left them with nothing, and they looked to him, as their leader, to give them that hope once more. 'All will be well when we reach Constantinople.'

The monk nodded. 'Aye. Gold and glory. That promise keeps them going. Without that—'

'They will get their gold and glory. I will see to that,' Hereward said curtly.

As he pushed his way through the warriors towards Kraki, the Mercian knew that nothing less would do. He had to deliver them to Constantinople. Only then would they be able to put the past behind them. Only then could their lives begin anew.

Though the Viking hid his own loss better than most, the Mercian knew it still consumed him. Kraki was a fighting man. He lived for battle. But then he lost his heart to a woman, and when he was forced to send her away to save her life the agony had cut deeper than any blade. Hereward weighed his choice, and realized it was the right one.

'I need your aid,' he said.

'You always need my aid.'

'Sighard must have a wise head to guide him. I cannot find one, so I have chosen you.'

21

Kraki snorted. 'Am I to wipe the snot from the noses of babes?'

'He mourns his brother still. More . . . that loss is turning his heart black.'

Kraki looked away, understanding.

'He is a good man, you know that. And he has always given all for his brothers. But now he needs us,' Hereward continued. 'Watch over him. He is wounded, and this battlefield is no less dangerous than any other.'

After a moment's thought, the Viking grunted his assent. Though he scowled at the prospect, he seemed to be pleased to be given the task, the Mercian thought.

On the horizon, lightning flickered. A low boom rumbled across the waves, and the wind picked up. As Hereward looked towards the approaching storm, he glimpsed tiny dots of colour in the distance. Sails.

Kraki had seen them too. 'Sea wolves?'

'We should not tarry here,' Hereward replied. 'Push us free of this ship of ghosts, and let us be away before we join them.'

CHAPTER TWO

The spitting fire-pot trailed showers of sparks with each wild swing on its creaking chain. Shadows flickered across the rain-lashed faces of the men hunched over the oars. Like statues, they seemed, as they looked out across the heaving waves to the black horizon. The light of the pot's flames carved deep furrows into their drawn features. All eyes watched the distant ship. The roiling clouds had near turned day to night and they would have missed it if not for the blaze of lightning sheeting across the horizon.

'What do you say?' Kraki bellowed.

'A fisherman. Or a merchant. Lost in the storm.' Hereward shielded his eyes against the elements and waited for the vessel to reappear on the roll of grey swell. He could sense all his men waiting for his judgement. He braced himself against the bucking deck, holding still with a warrior's strength and grace. The rain pasted his long fair hair to his head and stung his eyes, but still he watched.

The ship came and went, came and went. Scarlet sails billowed, but whoever manned that vessel was lost to the gloom.

Kraki heaved himself to his feet. Dragging his axe from

under his bench, he used its weight to balance himself. 'Or a sea wolf, blown off course?' he growled. The howling wind almost snatched the words from his lips.

'Perhaps.'

Hereward looked across the bowed heads of his men and saw many quaking with the terror of the waves. Who could blame them? The sea was a monster that could not be tamed, only respected. Few of these men were sailors, and they had learned their new skills the hard way, with stomachs filled with sea water.

A figure clawed its way across the benches. As it neared the fire-pot, Hereward saw it was Alric. The flames lit the terror that contorted his face.

'We must put to shore,' he yelled above the gale. 'This storm will send us to the bottom.'

The monk's fear seemed to ease Kraki's own worries. The Viking raised one eyebrow and said, 'Are you not praying to your God? Surely at your plea his great hands will scoop us up and carry us all to calm waters.'

Alric glared. 'He tests me, I know. I have been all but drowned every time I have dared to cross the whale road. Enough, I say!'

'We should have been warned of this before we agreed to sail with you,' Kraki said. He jabbed a finger into the monk's chest so that the younger man almost tumbled backwards. The men around laughed, the humour easing their concern.

'These waters are known for their terrible storms, so we have been told,' Hereward said, 'and putting in to shore is a good plan. But first we have another worry.'

Kraki's eyes flicked out across the waves once more. The red-sailed ship was nearer still. In that gale, there was now no question it had set a course for them. 'Fight, or run like dogs?' he asked. Both options had their risks.

'How do you fight at sea?' Alric asked.

'The same as on land,' Kraki replied. 'For your life.'

Hereward's hand fell to the golden hilt of his sword, Brainbiter. He sensed his friends' fear. If fight they must, they would have to rely on their instincts and God's judgement.

'No doubt now,' Kraki said, peering into the storm. 'Those curs are bearing down on us.'

Hereward nodded. 'Ready yourselves,' he bellowed, his voice cutting through the gale. Heads ducked down to search for spears and axes secreted beneath benches. He gave an approving nod. Though his men were afraid, they showed none of it. They all knew death had many guises. It came as a winter storm. The thunderclap of a full-throated roar. The lightning strike of a keen axe blade in a churning field of mud and blood. Or a soft autumn wind when the leaves are turning gold and the fruits are heavy, or a whisper in the still of midnight. If they wanted to see their days continue, they had to be always vigilant, always ready.

As he clambered over the benches towards the prow, he felt the first flames of anger flicker to life. He was already sick of running.

'We will draw them on,' he shouted. 'If they decide a chase in these waters is a trouble too far, so be it. But if they come on, let them think us weak. They will let their guards down. And by the time they find the truth, it will be too late.'

More lightning flickered along the horizon. The pitching waves glimmered as a rumble of thunder rolled out. For one moment the world became black and white, and then the blood-red sails carved above the roll of dark water. Hereward felt the blood in his head begin to match the pounding of the elements. The part of him he loathed, the part of him that brought him bloody and brutal victory in battle, began its insidious whispering. So much had been torn from his grip, but now, by God, he would deny any man who would try to take all that he had left: the lives of his men, and the future they sought together.

'Keep your heads down,' he roared. 'Act as if you are bedraggled merchants lost at sea, little fish to be gutted and eaten.'

His crew obeyed in an instant. At the prow, Mad Hengist danced, his lank blond hair whipping in the gale. His feet whisked across the bucking, slick boards as if he were in an earl's hall. Since the Normans had slaughtered his kin his wits came and went, but he seemed to see things hidden to other men. He turned his rodent features towards Hereward, his eyes glittering. 'I smell gold,' he cackled, glancing ahead.

'And blood?' Hereward asked. 'Do you smell that on the wind this day, Hengist? Victory for the last of the English?'

The smaller man gave a wolfish grin.

Hereward nodded, grinning in return. 'Victory for the last of the English!' he called to his crew. 'Hengist has listened to the wind!' He watched the light begin to burn in the eyes of his men. They were wet and cold and their stomachs growled for the next meal. The terror of the sea tugged always at the back of their thoughts. But they trusted Hengist, for he spoke with God and gods. And if they were to go to the bottom this day, it would be with a fire in their hearts.

The storm loomed at their backs with towering cliffs of black thunderheads. Yet it did not advance. Perhaps God had smiled on them, Hereward thought. He watched Alric kneeling on the deck as salt water washed around his legs, hands clasped, eyes clamped shut, face contorted in desperate prayer.

The Mercian beckoned to Guthrinc at his place in the centre of the front bench. His old friend levered his huge frame up and cracked his knuckles.

'Put those hawk's eyes of yours to good use,' Hereward said.

Guthrinc wiped the spray from his face and peered towards the approaching vessel. 'I see shields along the side. I see the glint of axes, and helms, and bodies hunched over oars, speeding the ship towards us.'

Death, then. Death like a winter storm.

'Has the king recanted and sent his dogs to drive us to the deep?' the tall man added.

'The king is a butcher and a bastard, but he has honour. He said we could leave with our lives, and he would not go back on his word.'

'Sea wolves, then.'

Hereward nodded. 'They think us merchants, our ship laden with goods for the hot lands to the south.'

Balancing on the balls of his feet, he peered across the water as he made his way aft. The red sail glowed in the half-light. It had seen better days, he could now tell. The bottom edge was ragged, and it had been patched here and there. The paint on the shields was old and worn, the wood showing through. On one, a skull stared out with hollow eyes. Now the vessel was close enough for him not to need Guthrinc's sharp gaze to discern the outline of the dark figures crowded on deck. They heaved on the oars, adding to the force of the wind. Their ship sped towards their prey like an arrow.

'Wait,' Hereward growled to his men. 'Wait.' If the dogs did not fear resistance, any archers aboard would not waste shafts. 'Now. Ready yourselves,' he rumbled.

Hands ducked down for spears and axes. Guthrinc had his bow, though even his skill with an arrow would be tested on those heaving waves.

Hereward cast one furtive glance over his shoulder. The red-sailed ship was barely a spear's throw away. It had not slowed or deviated from its course. He saw the helms, and the leather armour the rowers wore, despite the heat. Ready for battle. He saw pale skin, too. These were not the swarthy, dark-haired people who lived along this coast. These warriors came from colder climes.

When he looked back towards the prow, a booming rose up above the sound of the ocean. At first, he thought it was more thunder. But it was too rhythmic, and soon it was accompanied

27

by a low, steady chant. The curs were hammering out the war-beat with their feet upon the deck, and they were singing open the gates of hell, as the Norman bastards always did before battle.

He cocked his head and listened. Words reached his ears above the moan of the wind. English, it was, he was sure. They sang of bones and blood and gold and glory.

In the prow, a warrior stood, his axe raised high. Hereward could see why this man had taken to a life on the whale road. Women and children would find it hard to rest their gaze upon him, so fearsome was his appearance. His nose was gone, sliced off in some fight or other. Two holes remained, so that at first glance his face had the look of a death's head. Both ears were missing too, and part of his hair had been torn out or burned away. His bottom lip was split in two. His eyes were sunken, one of them milky. What remained of his features seemed little more than a mass of ragged scars. Battle had not been kind to him; it looked as if he had been whittled down bit by bit. And yet he still had his life, and his stripped torso was powerfully built. If he could survive such deprivations and come back for more, he would never die easily. Hereward knew he should not underestimate such a warrior.

The ruined man pointed directly at the Mercian, and as his ship neared he tore his mouth wide and roared. As one, his men drew in their oars and roared in unison so that it seemed a wild beast was bearing down on them.

'Wait until you smell the reek of their sweat,' Hereward said, just loud enough for his own men to hear. 'And with luck we will take some more parts of their leader.'

The red-sailed ship's tillerman guided his charge with dexterity as it swept alongside. Still roaring, the crew rose from their benches and braced themselves. They were a motley group. Wild-haired and bearded, skin lashed red by the elements. Hereward wrinkled his nose. They stank of vinegar sweat, yes, but shit and piss too, as if they had not put ashore in many a day.

Iron hooks flew across the gulf and bit into the wood along the side of the English ship. Amid cheers and jeering laughter, the wild men of the sea braced themselves and hauled on the attached ropes to bring the two vessels together.

Wait, Hereward thought. *Wait*.

The churning black water between the ships shrank to a spear's width. The noise from the pirates grew so loud it drowned out the distant rumble of thunder. The English remained silent, heads bowed, as still as stones.

As the ships drew closer, the ruined man sensed something was wrong. Slowly his axe lowered. He looked across his quarry until his gaze settled on Hereward. The Mercian held that look, a warrior's stare, and though he could read nothing in those destroyed features he knew the other man must sense the deception.

'Now!' Hereward bellowed.

With a roar that dwarfed the enemy's battle-cry, the English wrenched up their weapons and leapt to their feet. Silence fell upon the other ship, but only for a moment. Fury erupted as the pirates recognized the trickery, driving them on to even wilder exhortations.

Guthrinc rested one foot upon the front bench, nocked an arrow and let the shaft fly. It rammed through the eye of a red-bearded man and burst out of the back of his skull, flipping his helm off his head. Stunned by the speed of the attack, the pirates were wrong-footed. A wave of English fighting men crashed upon them. Axes slammed down. Spears thrust. And for a while the spray turned red.

Once his fingers closed around the cool hilt of his sword, Hereward launched himself off the side of the ship. The heaving swell flew beneath his feet. As he came down with a furious yell, he swung Brainbiter in an arc. The blade tore through the neck of the man in front of him, almost severing the head in one stroke. Snarling his hands in the dead man's tunic, he yanked him forward into the brine between the ships, then stepped into the gap and hacked right and left. Two men howled as they buckled.

On the rolling swell, he felt as if he were fighting while standing on the back of a bucking stallion. But the reeking bodies were so closely packed in the confined space, he was locked in place. Unable to swing his sword, he gut-stabbed one man, then drove the blade up into the exposed jaw of another. Beside him, Kraki hooked with his axe. Guthrinc heaved a man above his head as if his victim were a sack of flour and hurled him into the sea. Others sliced groins or the backs of knees. Those with spears stayed by the gunwale, creating some room with their constant thrusting.

Under his feet, the deck was as slick with blood as the ghost ship they had discovered. The sea wolves fought on to the last. What else could they do? There was nowhere to flee, and any man who ended up in that turbulent sea was unlikely to survive long enough to swim to shore. And these were not true warriors, Hereward could see now. They handled their weapons like butchers' knives. No grace, no skill. They were only interested in plundering those who were weaker than they were. Now they would pay the price for a life without honour.

The Mercian drove Brainbiter through the stomach of the man in front of him. As the dead man toppled over the side, Hereward looked around and saw he had no more foes to fight.

A hubbub rose up from a crowd of his spear-brothers gathered at the prow. They had disarmed the last of the pirates and herded him towards the edge.

As the spears drew back to thrust, Hereward called out, 'Hold!'

At his command, his men held fast, looking back. The Mercian pushed his way among them. At the front, Sighard stood with the tip of his spear pressed against the neck of the pirates' leader. The fighting seemed to have cleared his despair, if only for a while.

The ruined man peered up at his captors with his one good eye. Hereward saw no fear in that look.

'Let him live,' the Mercian ordered.

'What value is his life?' Sighard snarled. 'He would have ended all our days if he had his way.'

'We will show mercy.'

Kraki stepped forward and snatched Sighard's spear away from the ruined man's neck. For a moment, the younger man resisted. Then, with a sullen expression, he unfurled his fingers from the shaft and let the Viking take his weapon.

'We will put him to shore and let him spread the word to any other wolves who sail these waters looking for lambs to prey upon,' the Mercian said, his voice brooking no resistance. 'The price for attacking Hereward and the last of the English will be more than any can stomach.'

'You are Hereward?' The ruined man's one good eye narrowed. His words came out muffled by his ragged bottom lip.

'You have heard of me?'

'Aye. There are few who do not know of the man who bloodied the nose of William the Bastard.'

Hereward weighed the man's accent and said, 'You are from the north?'

'Eoferwic. I owe the Norman dogs for this.' He raised one trembling finger to his face. 'One wrong word can cost a man everything.'

'Few escaped the hard hand of the enemy.' The Mercian eyed the sea wolf. He could tell a man's character from the briefest tremor on a cheek, or the curve of a lip, or the glimmer in an eye, but this man's disfigurement made him unreadable. 'What is your name?'

'Ragener.' His tongue flicked out to moisten his lips. 'Ragener the Hawk.'

31

Sighard laughed without mirth. 'You have the eye of a hawk? Only one.'

Recognizing who held the power here, the sea wolf ignored the younger man and kept his gaze fixed on Hereward. 'Put me ashore near a village and I will make sure you have gold to send you on your way.'

'Stolen gold, splashed with blood?' The Mercian shook his head slowly.

The Hawk flinched, his mouth jerking in what could have been a sneer. 'Too tainted for the likes of the great Hereward? Some of us have not been smiled upon by God and must make our own way in the world as best we can.'

Kraki growled and raised his axe. Hereward raised one hand to stay the Viking's arm. 'This world has not been kind to you, that is true. But a man shoulders his burden and makes his own way—'

'Words like that come easy. Walk in my shoes and see if you say the same. Women cannot look at me. Nor men. Even begging for alms is a trial.'

Kraki snorted. 'I have seen men who have suffered more than you. Aye, I have. Men without hands or feet. Eyes put out by hot iron. Even then they live their days with honour.'

Ragener's lips curled back from his teeth in rage. Before he could lunge, Sighard put one foot in his chest and drove him back on to the boards. The sea wolf's emotion was now so hot that the Mercian had no trouble reading it: the Hawk would kill them all if he could.

'Your life has no worth, then?' Hereward said. 'You would throw it away so easily?'

'You will end my days whatever I say,' the ruined man snapped. He caught himself. His good eye darted and he moistened his lips. 'I can offer you more than gold. Something with value beyond your dreams.'

Kraki laughed with contempt. 'Aye. You sail the whale road for joy alone.'

Ragener ignored the Viking, his eyes narrowing. 'Something that will set king against king, and see rivers of blood spilled to win it.'

Hereward looked around with a wry expression. 'And where is this great treasure? Not here. Only the blood of your men fills this boat.'

'You do not have the right eyes.'

The Mercian nodded. 'Speak, then.'

'Hereward!'

Spinning at the sound of his name, Hereward looked back along the ship. Alric had leapt aboard and was squatting next to a bench, pointing towards a mound of sailcloth aft. 'I saw it move. Someone hides there,' the monk called.

'Watch him,' the Mercian said with a nod to Ragener. 'I think he is more snake than hawk.' Drawing Brainbiter, he clambered over the benches to where Alric waited, a knot of men at his back. As the vessel heaved up on the swell, he watched the sailcloth. Nothing moved.

'I saw it!' Alric repeated in answer to the unspoken question.

As the beat of the Mercian's feet thudded along the deck, the mound shifted, barely perceptibly but enough for Hereward's keen eyes. A cowardly pirate hoping to escape the judgement of the rebel crew, he guessed. Catching the edge of the filthy cloth, he yanked it up. The figure beneath lunged so fast the Mercian barely saw it. A bloodstained blade lashed out. Wrong-footed, Hereward could only watch as the short sword whisked to open up his guts.

But Alric was quicker. The monk threw himself into his friend, propelling Hereward just beyond the reach of the cutting edge. Yet the figure rising from the mound of sailcloth was as fast as a viper. It struck again, this time catching Alric a glancing blow. Stunned, he flew over the edge of the ship and into the surging waters. Within an instant, he had been sucked beneath the surface.

For a moment, Hereward could not move. For the murderous

attacker who might well have claimed his friend's life was a naked woman. Slaked in blood, seemingly as feral as a wildcat, she hunched over, spitting and snarling, and ready to slay any man who came near her.

CHAPTER THREE

Waves boomed over Alric's head. The turbulent current's claws wrenched him into the maw of icy darkness. Brine surged into his nose, his mouth, and for a moment the shock of the cold slapped his senses away. As he flailed in the grip of the crushing swell, he felt the candle of his life gutter.

The last of his breath seeped away. Lights flashed in the dark deep in his head. Memories rushed up as if they had been freed from a sealed vault: times he missed, faces he half knew, days he hoped he would never recall again. His father, struggling to find the words to say goodbye as the old man delivered him to the door of the monastery at Jarrow. Fierce, cruel Father Leomas thrashing him with a willow cane for failing to recite the catechism. Dark, cold nights in his cell, listening to the scratching of the rats.

The blackness clawed at the edge of his vision and he thought his chest might burst.

More memories flooded his skull, some almost too painful to bear. His hands around the throat of Hereward's treacherous brother Redwald, throttling the life from him so that his friend could be free of that hated man's curse. And his desperate fear that, however selfless his actions, Hereward would only despise him if he discovered the truth of his crime.

Water surged into his mouth. *I am dying*, he thought. His arms drifted to the side. His panicked movements ebbed. Soon all would be gone. Perhaps it would be for the best.

But then his mind burned with one image: a sword, raised high, glinting in the sun. Hereward, a good man who carried a devil inside him. A soul to be saved, God's work that only he could do, for without him the devil would be free, and Hereward would kill wantonly, foe or friend, until he ultimately destroyed himself.

Once more he began to flail. He could not die, he would not. For if he did, Hereward, his friend, would be doomed. But the world was as black as pitch, he could not tell up from down, and he had no air left in his lungs.

An arm gripped him.

Instinctively, he tried to wrench himself free, but whoever was there held him fast. Strong kicks propelled him on. The water lightened. Dimly, Alric realized he was being dragged to safety. Bubbles streamed past his face. Though the swell tore at him, trying to suck him back down to the deep, his rescuer did not relent.

And then he broke the surface. With a cry, he filled his aching lungs. The waves heaved him up, tossed him around like a leaf in a winter gale. Alone, he would not have had the strength to resist.

'Go limp, monk! You will be the death of both of us!' It was Hereward's voice that bawled into his ear, his friend's arm pinning his chest.

The Mercian kicked out once more, fighting the furious force of the sea. And then, over the pounding of the water, Alric thought he could hear shouts of encouragement. In no time at all, hands were grasping his soaking tunic and he was hauled out of the waves and dumped on the sodden deck. Seawater sluiced around his face. For a long moment he lay there, gulping in deep draughts of air.

Once the darkness washed away from his thoughts, he felt a rush of passion and he all but cried in joy that he yet lived. Murmuring a prayer of thanks, he looked up, only to find he was alone.

His spear-brothers were clustered around the woman. Someone had draped a filthy cloak over her naked form. She crouched like a cornered dog, lips curled back from her teeth. A murderous look glowed in her eyes as she searched the faces of the men around her.

Alric could now see that she was not English, nor from the north countries, like the others who had sailed on that ship. Where the spray had streaked the blood on her face, dark skin showed through. Her eyes were almond-shaped and seemed to glint with gold at the core, her lips were full, and her matted hair had the lustrous sheen of raven wings. He guessed she had seen twenty-five summers. The monk had come across her kind before, on the quayside in Eoferwic and Lincylene. Strange men in loose-fitting tunics and trousers of bright amber and sapphire, thick layers of cloth wrapped around head and neck. They had journeyed from the hot lands in ships reeking of un-familiar spices.

Alric watched the woman give Hereward an ugly look. She seemed afraid behind her anger, but she would not allow her-self to show it. Yet for all the hatred that hardened her features she had a delicate beauty and a poise to the arch of her neck. Not peasant stock, this woman.

Hereward stood over her, his face like thunder. 'What is your name?' he growled.

The woman glared at him, uncomprehending.

'Like as much, she does not speak our tongue,' Kraki said, studying her. 'Stolen from her home, I would wager. These dogs no doubt thought they could make good coin selling her as slave or whore.'

Guthrinc towered over the woman. 'Only one? If these were slavers, they would have more on board.'

Alric watched Hereward soften as he crouched to look the prisoner in the face. Still defiant, she pressed herself back against a bench as if he might strike her. 'This blood is fresh.' He plucked up a length of rope, the ends frayed where they had been cut. 'They had her bound, lying here on the deck. She would have been soaked in the blood of those who had fallen. Her bonds were cut. Likely by herself, from a fallen weapon.'

Alric stumbled over the benches as the boat swung up and down on the back of the swell. 'Can you not see she is afrit?' he protested. 'She does not need fierce warriors poking and prodding her as if she were a side of meat.'

'Aye, I see that, and more.' Hereward ripped off a length of sailcloth and dipped it in the seawater running along the deck. He held it out to the woman and made a cleaning motion. For a moment, she held his gaze with those piercing eyes, and then she snatched the cloth from him and began to wipe the blood from her arms. As she did so, Hereward snatched her wrist and yanked it up. The woman cried out and made to strike him with a free hand, but the Mercian caught that wrist too.

'Hereward! Leave her!' Alric said, horrified.

'See here,' the warrior commanded.

Where the gore had washed from her skin, a patchwork of bruises showed, and long grooves cut into the flesh. Knife cuts.

The Mercian let go of the woman's wrists, his features softening once again. He reached out and she recoiled, spitting, but he held his arm steady, pointing at her left eye. Alric could now see it was black and swollen. Hereward's finger dropped to the woman's exposed thigh. A tapestry of bruises embroidered by rough hands. 'My words are strange to you,' he said in a gentle tone, 'but you may take some meaning from what I say.' Though she still eyed him with suspicion, Alric saw she seemed to respond to his calm voice. 'You will not be treated harshly by my men. You will be well cared for.'

He turned back to his men, his features darkening. 'These curs used her.' His words were almost lost beneath the pounding of the sea, but their power burned. Alric knew his friend was remembering his mother, beaten to death by his father's fists, and his wife, whose head was taken by the man he had called brother. 'They stole her days to come.' He looked along the ship to the prow where Ragener sprawled, the tip of Sighard's spear pressed against his neck. 'Bring the woman,' he snapped, 'and bring the fire-pot.'

Alric felt chilled by what he saw in his friend's face. Hereward's killing rage was a terrible thing to behold, but somehow this was much worse.

Guthrinc touched his leader's arm. 'Hereward. Those storm-clouds are drawing nearer again. We should not stay here. We will be caught in the storm and pay a terrible price.'

Hereward seemed not to hear.

As two men heaved down the fire-pot on its chain, the Mercian strode over the benches with such force, Alric thought he would gut the sea wolf where he lay. Yet Brainbiter never left its sheath. Hereward loomed over his captive in silence for a long moment. Trying to contain his emotion, the monk thought.

Guthrinc and Kraki brought the woman up, swathed in the cloak. She raised her head as she stepped over the benches, ignoring the stares of all the men there. But when she saw Ragener, her features contorted and she bared her teeth. Her eyes held such murderous hatred that the sea wolf flinched from her gaze. With a hiss, she tried to wrench herself free from Kraki and Guthrinc's grip upon her arms. Her fingers clawed and she lunged to rake out Ragener's eyes.

Hereward held out an arm to block her. 'You offered me gold,' he said to the pirate. 'There is no gold in the world to pay for what you took from this woman.'

Ragener knitted his brow, unable to understand the Mercian's anger.

'But you will pay with your life,' Hereward added.

'You do not know what you have there,' Ragener snapped,

refusing to meet the woman's accusing stare. 'If you take her with you, it will be the end of your days. A curse will hang over your head. You will be hunted wherever you go. Enemies will wait at every turn ready to take your head. There will be no safe place, no peace.'

'Because of this woman,' Hereward said with contempt.

'You have been warned.'

Alric watched shadows cross the faces of the men. They were a superstitious breed at the best of times. Talk of curses and portents troubled them. But here they could see the commitment in Ragener's face; he truly believed every word he was saying.

'Who is she?' the monk ventured. 'Why would she bring such wrath down upon our heads?'

Ragener stared ahead, saying nothing.

'He lies,' Hereward said. 'He tries to make his crimes against the woman seem just.' He sneered. 'What he did was punishment, not lust.'

The sea wolf raised his head. 'Slay me, then. I will die knowing you have doomed yourselves.'

Hereward was unmoved. 'Some would say justice would be to give this woman a knife and let her do what she will. That would be too easy.'

Alric grew cold. In his friend's words he could hear a hint of what lay within. That devil was capable of anything.

'Hold his left arm,' the Mercian commanded.

Ragener struggled, but Sighard kept the spear-tip hard against his throat as two men gripped his arm and pinned it against the side of the ship.

'Your body is ruined. Yet still it does not equal the ruin of your soul.' Hereward took Kraki's axe and swung it up high.

Ragener cried out, too late. The blade hammered through his wrist. His left hand flipped away, swallowed by the black waves. As the pirate howled in agony, Alric looked away. But it was the coldness in his friend's face that he could not bear to see.

The Mercian motioned for the fire-pot. Now that Ragener had fallen limp, Hereward wrenched the man's arm up and plunged the bloody stump into the coals. As the wound seared shut, the pirate roared in pain once more and then slipped into unconsciousness.

Hereward turned to the woman. She raised her head and peered into his eyes. Though she said nothing, Alric thought she seemed pleased.

'You will show him mercy?' the monk asked.

'Aye,' Hereward replied, but Alric felt troubled by the tight smile that followed.

With each moment, the swell swung to greater heights. The ropes holding the two ships together creaked as they strained. The monk turned and looked to the horizon. The sky was turning black and lightning danced across the water. Wind tore at his soaking tunic. Thunder cracked. They had run out of time.

At first Alric thought the Mercian had not heard, but then he nodded. 'Return to our ship and make ready,' he said.

'The woman?'

'Carry her. She will not struggle. She knows it is her only chance at life.'

As the men leapt across the gulf into their own ship, Hereward squatted on the front bench, his eyes never leaving the still form of the sea wolf. Unsettled, Alric hesitated, then decided to wait too, as did Kraki and Sighard.

The ship heaved, then fell. The thunder cracked closer. No one spoke. Finally Ragener's eyes flickered open.

'Have I not suffered enough?' he croaked.

'For what you did to that woman? Never.' Hereward stood, bracing himself against the rolling of the deck. 'I should carve you away, piece by piece. Finish the work the Normans began. And this world would be a better place without you in it. But my friend here, the monk, has pleaded for mercy and I cannot deny him.'

A mean smile of relief crept across the sea wolf's ragged lips.

'He speaks wisely, the churchman,' Hereward continued. 'He tells me of God above, and his will, and his plans for all men. I am but a poor warrior, with only a little learning to divide me from the beasts of the field. If there is a plan for me, I cannot see it, but my friend says there is, as there is for all men. Even you.' Hereward held out his hands. Ragener looked as puzzled as Alric felt. The Mercian prowled around the ruined man. 'What is God's plan for you, sea wolf?'

Ragener blinked, not knowing what to say.

'How can I kill you if God might have a plan for you?' Hereward crouched so he could look directly in the man's one good eye. 'Aye, I must listen to the monk. I cannot judge you. God will do that.'

Lunging, the Mercian snarled his hand in Ragener's belt and hauled him up as effortlessly as if he were lifting a child. The sea wolf gaped in shock. His opponent's calm words of reason had lulled him into believing he would escape his fate. But Alric had known the truth, as he always knew. The devil demanded his payment. The monk bowed his head in silent, despairing prayer as Hereward dragged Ragener to the side. The sea wolf's muttering turned to pleas of mercy, as the monk had demanded, as Hereward had promised.

'Aye, mercy, I said, and mercy you shall get.' When Alric looked up, Ragener was dangling over the turbulent sea, with only Hereward's grip on his belt keeping him up. 'By rights, a foul thing like you should be dead, but I will let you live,' the Mercian continued. 'The shore is not far away.'

Ragener cried out as he realized what was about to happen.

'You do not need your eye, or your nose, or your ears. You have one good hand, and two good feet. Swim, sea wolf. Swim hard, for a storm is coming and these waters are treacherous. God will decide your fate now.'

The Mercian unfurled his fingers. Ragener screamed out as he fell. Within a moment, he was gone.

Alric's heart sank with the sea wolf. He bowed his head once more, his prayers growing more urgent, but there were times when he thought his friend was beyond saving.

CHAPTER FOUR

A cliff of black water towered overhead. Darkness as deep as a moonless night engulfed the ship. The ocean roared and the sky cracked and no man could hear his own prayers, let alone the voice of another. Down into a gorge the vessel plunged, and down, and down, until every man there thought they were already on their way to hell. Faces the colour of bone loomed out of the gloom, eyes wide with terror, as the warriors gripped on to the ropes that lashed them to their benches.

Finally the descent into the underworld stopped. The world held its breath.

Standing at the mast so all his men could see him, Hereward looked up that obsidian wall. He could not see the top. Perhaps this was God's judgement on him for the fate he had inflicted upon Ragener. If he had not tarried so long to punish the sea wolf, they might have escaped the storm. Now they would all pay the price for his uncontrollable anger.

The cliff began to crumble.

With a roar louder than anything Hereward had heard in his life, the black wave rushed down towards them. Curses and oaths rang out all around. The torrent hit with the force of a thousand hammers. Water rammed into Hereward's nose and mouth, blinded him, dragged him. If he had not been tied to the mast he would have been ripped into the deep. The prow swung up near-vertical. An instant later the vessel slammed down, aft-up. Men spilled across each other. Faces smashed on benches. So strong was the torrent that none could tell which was ship and which was ocean.

Bracing himself, Hereward pressed his back against the mast. He had expected the ship to be smashed into pieces by now, but the deck still felt solid beneath his feet. He spat out a mouthful of brine. If the end was near, he would face it like a warrior, looking it clear in the eye. He thought again of his mother, and of his wife Turfrida, and felt a pang of regret that he had failed them both. He thought of his father, mean-faced old Asketil, his hatred and rage growing with the years that weighted him, and was glad his sire no longer cast a shadow over what remained of his life. A thin mercy.

Another sheet of lightning. In this one, Guthrinc was frozen in the prow. Desperation creased his face as he looked directly at Hereward, stabbing a finger towards the black waters behind him. He was shouting something. A futile gesture. All words were crushed beneath the booming of sea and sky.

Darkness flooded back. The ship whirled, heaved, crashed. Gasping for air in the deluge, Hereward clung on until his fingers burned.

The ship slammed to a hard halt. A terrible grinding reverberated through the hull. Hereward wrenched forward, his rope snapping taut. As the vessel lurched like a drunken man and the din of rending timber drowned out the storm, the Mercian realized what Guthrinc had seen beyond the bow. Rocks, protruding from the waves to catch them like a fish-hook.

Hereward loosened the rope from his wrist and bounded to the side. How far had the storm washed them that they were so close to land, he wondered? In a flare of lightning, he glimpsed ragged planks above the water-line. Rows of jagged brown teeth broke the surface of the surging torrent. All around the waves surged up higher than the mast. Soon they would be dashed to pieces, he could see that now. But if they abandoned ship, what chance did they have of surviving in the angry sea?

The Mercian spun round to command his men to prepare for the inevitable. Fierce eyes stared at him – the woman, the dried blood now washed from her, the wounds clear on her arms and face. She seemed to be accusing him, perhaps for the suffering that was to come, perhaps, because he was English, for the pain that had been inflicted upon her by Ragener.

His order died in his throat. A shadow darker than night loomed over him. For one moment, regrets flooded his mind, and then the wave smashed down.

His senses spun away.

Flashes reached him, like a light at the end of a dark cavern. Water engulfed him, waves hurled him, each one as hard as stone. Swirling, tumbling, turning, his breath burning. The thunder in his ears, deafening, then muffled. Madness, madness.

He had killed them all.

Chapter Five

The wind had dropped along the shoreline. Black storm-clouds scudded out to sea, lightning dancing in their midst. But there, on the beach, barbs of sunlight glinted off the rolling waves as the wheeling gulls shrieked their warning. A battered figure was clawing its way out of the surf. Spitting out gouts of brine, Ragener rolled on to his back and sucked in a juddering gasp of air. He shuddered, feeling his candle close to winking out. Had he overcome so much only to die on the brink of success?

Running feet slapped across the wet sand, drawing nearer. A face hove into view, framed against the azure sky. A young woman, dark-eyed and pretty, a yellow headscarf tied across her black hair. He watched her flinch when she saw his ruined features, could read those familiar thoughts of trepidation in her face. But to her credit, she did not flee.

'Wait here,' she said in the Almoravid dialect he had come to know. When she returned she had woollen blankets, which she wrapped him in, and then she lit a fire there on the beach, rolling him close so he could absorb the warmth. She bound the bloody stump of his wrist in clean white linen, all the while murmuring prayers to her god.

Ragener felt himself slipping in and out of a strange, dream-like existence. But after a while the fire worked its magic, and he felt the strength begin to return to his limbs.

'You must rest,' she whispered. 'The sea can end your days long after you have left it.'

Aye, death was close, as it had been from the moment that Mercian bastard tossed him into the waves like shit on to the midden. As it had been for much of his life. 'Though they have whittled down my body, they have not yet been able to end the fire in me,' he croaked.

She smiled at him, knowing that his defiance was a sign that he had the will to live.

For a while, she told him about her life to give warmth to his thoughts, how she lived with her father, and had cared for him since her mother died of the sickness the previous winter. The old man's heart had been broken – she thought he would never recover. And she told, in a quiet, hopeful voice, of how she had never travelled beyond her village but dreamed of the places the sailors described when they came searching for provisions. Ragener nodded along. He thought he understood her life.

When he was well enough to sit up, she brought him hot broth from her home nearby and the hard, seed-filled bread they ate in those parts. The stew was thin, little more than water, but he gulped it down and enjoyed the heat it brought to his arms and legs.

'Your ship . . . when you fell prey to the storm . . . you were bound for the Normans?' she asked, her face darkening.

He paused with the bowl at his lips and frowned.

'To see the knight . . . Vavasour . . . and his men?'

'Drogo Vavasour?'

'He has made camp to the west of here. Men in long mail-shirts, their hair cut short and shaved at the back.'

Ragener looked across the stark, brown landscape beyond the beach. 'What would a Norman knight and a war-band want in these parts?'

'They say his king is hungry for power and wants more lands to call his own.'

The ruined man shrugged. That was the Norman way. But Drogo Vavasour . . . he knew that name, knew the tales they told of him in the villages of England. 'There is no peace in this world anywhere,' he murmured. 'The drums of war beat in England, in Sicily, in Constantinople. And soon it will come here. That is the way of things. We cannot rest, ever. You fight or you are conquered. You fight or you die.' Thoughtful, he watched the gulls swirling overhead.

As she took the bowl, the woman bowed her head. 'God has not been kind to you,' she said in a soft voice, still unable to look him full in the face.

He felt a laugh rumble up from deep inside him. It rolled out, too high-pitched, and went on too long. The girl recoiled, thinking him mad. Perhaps he was. 'When I was thrown from my ship, I was told God would decide my fate,' he said when he was finally able to control his hooting. 'God has passed judgement on me. I live.'

'Then you have been chosen to do God's work.'

He nodded. 'God smiles upon me.' His fingers closed on a rock, as sharp as flint. A red line sliced across the ball of his thumb. He sucked the blood off, then weighed the rock in his remaining hand, remembering. 'When William the Bastard seized the crown, life became hard in England,' he said. 'In my village, many were close to starving. I stole a loaf of bread to fill an empty stomach. The Normans caught me and cut off my nose.' His face fell. 'The bread was not for me. It was for my mother,' he said in a quiet voice. 'She told the soldiers where I hid when they came looking for me.' He felt the stinging sense of betrayal rise up in him just as strongly as it had then, and the desperate loneliness that followed. 'The Normans took my ears because I spoke harshly to a knight, and they slit my lip . . .' he shrugged, 'because I was less to them than a rat.'

'How you must hate the Normans,' she said, her voice tremulous with compassion.

He examined the stains on the linen binding his stump. 'I have suffered greatly. Mine has been a life with no joy, and little love. I did not deserve this. No man does.'

'But now God smiles on you,' she reminded him, trying to raise his spirits with the sweetest smile he had seen upon a woman in many a year.

'But still you flinched when you looked upon me.' He peered into her eyes until she squirmed and looked away. Her smile faded.

After he had taken her face with the sharp rock, he wandered along the dusty coast path to the Norman camp. The white tents billowed in the hot breeze, the lines cracking. Over one, the pennant of Drogo Vavasour fluttered, a golden dragon against a red field. Ragener breathed in the sweet scent of woodsmoke from the fire. He thought he could smell meat cooking too and his stomach growled in response.

Two red-faced guards waited aside the track winding into the camp, their tunics stained with sweat. Their hauberks and shields were heaped to one side. When they saw him, they cried out a warning and snatched out their double-edged swords. They seemed surprised to see anyone approaching the camp, never mind one with such a ruined face.

Once he had made them understand what he wanted, they beat him around the face to show him his place, then all but hauled him through the camp to the commander's tent. As they dragged him through the flaps, they threw him to his knees and cuffed him again for good measure. He did not cry out.

Ragener breathed in sweet perfume. Such an odd scent for the tent of a military leader, he thought. As he looked up, he saw three women sprawled on embroidered cushions, local girls by the look of it, all of them seemingly naked under the thin covers draped over them. And when he looked higher, he saw a tall, muscular man looming over his playthings. This could only be Drogo Vavasour. Naked to the waist, his torso and arms were a map of his life, a mass of scar tissue from axe, sword and spear. From Drogo's reputation, Ragener expected a face as stern as granite cliffs, but the Norman was laughing silently to himself as he looked down on the sea wolf, his eyes playful. He swaggered across the tent to a trestle where a pitcher and goblet stood beside a cross, and bowed his head to the cross in a moment's silent contemplation. When he glanced back, all humour had drained from his face. Ragener thought he saw only disgust there. 'Remain silent until I am done,' the knight commanded.

He took a leather strap with iron nails hammered through it from a small casket and knelt before the cross, bowing his head in supplication. The first lash of the strap raised bloody weals across his back. Ragener winced, but this strange Norman did not stop there. Only when his back was running red did he stand up. Eyeing the women with contempt, he spat something in his native tongue and they fled from the tent in terror, not even pausing to hide their nakedness.

Once they had gone, the Norman turned back to his guest, or captive, Ragener was not sure which. 'We are all cauldrons of sin,' he intoned, 'and we must drive those devils out of us through suffering, as our Lord did upon the cross.' Reaching behind him, he trailed one finger across his back. When he examined the bloodstained tip he nodded, pleased, and poured himself a goblet of wine.

The sea wolf furrowed his brow as Vavasour's face lightened once more. It was almost as if he was two men sharing the same body.

By the time he had crossed the tent and was looking down upon his visitor, he was grinning. 'Half a man,' he said, cocking his head in mock-puzzlement, 'or perhaps not a man at all. What manner of creature are you?'

'My name is Ragener. The Hawk.'

'The Hawk, you say?' Drogo flashed a look at his guards. Ragener saw the faint mockery, and pushed aside his anger. 'And an English hawk too. Why have you dragged what remains of your body into my camp?'

Ragener clambered to his feet. 'In Hastinge, in Wincestre, aye, all over England I heard tell of the great Drogo Vavasour.'

The Norman raised his goblet in a silent cheer.

'Here is King William's most feared warrior, a man who killed more English than any other at Senlac Hill, who, they say, cut off the cock of the former king Harold and held it up high for all to see.'

Vavasour feigned a proud nod.

'Who herded the English rebels in Cestre into a village and roasted them alive, dining on a goose leg while he listened to the screams. Whenever King William spied a threat to his crown, he sent for Drogo Vavasour, it is said.'

'You are skilled in the art of flattery, Hawk.'

'For your service to the king you have been rewarded well, with land and gold. But there is one thing that has slipped through your fingers.'

The Norman's eyes narrowed.

'Hereward, the last of the English rebels. The man who murdered your brother.'

CHAPTER SIX

A suffocating blanket of heat was pressing down on him. Hereward stirred, wrinkling his nostrils at the reek of baking seaweed. He tasted brine upon his tongue, felt granules of sand grinding into his cheek. His head throbbed to the beat of the pounding waves. With weary strokes, his thoughts swam up from a world of darkness.

Coughing out seawater, he thrust himself up and looked around. He was lying in foaming surf amid the shattered bones of the ship. What remnants remained suggested the vessel had been torn to pieces. The coarse sand stretched up to a line of brown rocks. Above it was a sky burned silver. No trees, no vegetation of any kind. A bare and lifeless land.

His gaze flickered towards sudden movement. A figure silhouetted against the glare whirled across the beach in a wild dance of flailing arms and kicking legs. Lank wet hair flew and a high-pitched tuneless song rolled out. Squinting, Hereward realized it was Hengist finding his mad joys in the midst of disaster. The Mercian hauled himself up on shaking legs. Where there was one there could be more. His crew would fight to the last, even against turbulent seas, and they had been close to shore when the ship had been wrecked.

'Hengist,' he yelled, cupping his mouth. 'How many more yet live?'

Grinding to a halt, the other man beamed, then raised his head and his arms to the sun. Hereward cursed under his breath. Striding up the beach, he surveyed the shoreline. Sodden figures lay in the surf. Some did not move – dead or dazed, he did not know. Others clawed their way out of the foam or struggled to stand. His heart grew heavy. How few there were. He could not see Guthrinc, or Kraki, and perhaps fifteen more.

His gaze fell on a slight, still form and he felt a pang of fear. Racing along the beach, he dropped to his knees beside Alric. The monk lay face down, unmoving.

Hereward spun his friend on to his back and held his face between his huge hands. 'Monk,' he urged, shaking the other man. 'Monk.'

Alric jerked and vomited a mouthful of seawater. Feebly, he tried to bat away Hereward's grip as if he were swatting a fly. 'You have laid a curse upon me,' he croaked, 'to be thrown into the sea whenever I cross the whale road.'

With a grin, Hereward released his grip. His friend jolted back on to the sand. 'You live, monk,' the warrior called back as he strode to the next survivor. 'That is all that we can hope for on this journey.'

One of his men cried out, and he turned to see a figure clambering over the rock pools at the margin of the cove. It was the woman, still wrapped in the soaking cloak that had covered her nakedness aboard ship.

'Take her,' the Mercian commanded.

Two of the warriors raced down the beach and collected the woman.

Once they had gathered the men together at the top of the beach, Hereward saw that his first impression was correct. Near half the crew were missing, and five of their number there were dead. He bowed his head for a moment, feeling the weight of loss as if he had killed each one himself. And in truth he had, for he was their leader. He had made the choice that allowed the storm to claim them. Closing his eyes, he ran through the names, remembering the faces, the lives.

Eadlac. The best riddle-maker amongst them. Guthmaer. A gentle man who carved toys for children. Aliwin. A farmer from Wessex, dour but brave. Scirheah, who had sired ten children. His heart had broken to leave them all behind. And Yonwin, who took four cups of mead to find the courage to talk to the woman he secretly admired.

Every one felt like a knife in his heart.

Hereward forced aside his grief. It would not do for the others to dwell upon such matters. He eyed Sighard, who already seemed to have a cloud over him.

'No dark thoughts,' he commanded as he searched the faces of the ones who had survived. 'Look around you. This cove is small. Our spear-brothers could have washed up anywhere along this coast. They could be hunting for us now.' He cocked his head to listen for any calls, but only the wind moaned across the arid landscape. 'We will search until we find them.'

Alric, though, was peering away from the sea, across the brown rock and sand that stretched to the horizon. 'What then?' he asked. 'Where do we find water? What would you have us eat – the dirt beneath our feet?'

Hereward watched the brows of his men knit with worry. 'We will survive,' he snapped, annoyed by the effect the churchman's words were having, 'as we always do. No land is dead. If there are no birds, there will be lizards. And if not lizards, there will be rats. And if we find none of them, we will dig for worms and insects. You will eat what carries you to the next dawn. And by then, if God wills, we shall have found a village—'

His words drained along with the blood in Hengist's face. A rare spark of sanity gleamed in the man's eyes as he pointed past his leader's shoulder and out to sea. Hereward turned to see sails billowing, red, yellow, blue, on ships of varying shape and size. He counted at least thirty. Some were warships, others little more than merchants' vessels. But all of them had the shields of warriors hung along their sides. Spurs of light glinted in the molten sunlight, reflecting, he guessed, off helms, and axes, and perhaps mail-shirts. These were fighting men.

'A war-fleet,' Alric said, his brow knitting. 'Here?'

Hereward narrowed his eyes. 'We knew the sea wolves were hunting one of their own who had stolen something from them.' His gaze flickered towards the woman who sat alone, further along the beach.

'You think that woman is the prize?' Alric asked, his brow furrowing. 'What value could she have? And why would Ragener the Hawk have stolen her from his own, risking their wrath?'

'The ruined man said she was cursed,' Hengist reminded them.

'Then give her back,' Sighard called, flashing a sullen look. 'At least then we will not have to fear their anger.'

'We have offered this woman the hand of friendship. Now that she is in our care, we defend her with our lives,' Hereward said, his voice cold. He did not deign to look at the younger warrior. 'And you are mistaken if you think a pack of sea wolves will think twice about slaughtering us, if we give up this woman or not.' He half drew Brainbiter. 'They would kill me for this alone. And some of you still have your axes. No, they will take from us what they want and leave us as a feast for the gulls.'

His men shifted with unease. All knew there could be no gain in standing their ground.

'We will head inland,' Hereward said. 'They will find the wreckage on the beach and see our footprints, and follow. Our only hope is to keep going until they deem it too far to be worth their while.'

Alric gripped his forearm. 'What about the others? If any have survived—'

'We will return when we can,' Hereward snapped. It was an inadequate reply, and all there knew it, but there was nothing else he could say. His missing spear-brothers deserved more than to be abandoned while enemies roamed all around. But he had no doubt that Kraki, or Guthrinc, or any of them would have insisted that he follow the same course.

As he began to climb towards the rocks at the shore's edge, Hereward felt Alric tense beside him. The monk's gaze was turned to the approaching ships. From the bellows and jeers that echoed across the sea, there could be no doubt that the small band of men on the shore had been seen. On the lead vessel, a dragon-headed craft in the style of the Northmen, the oars plunged into the swell to guide it home. One of the pirates danced along the row of poles, pausing only to shake his axe at the English.

'A forest of spears at our backs, a sea of sand and rock ahead,' Hengist muttered. 'I do not like this choice.'

'It will keep your mind off your empty belly,' Hereward replied with dark humour.

When the woman stood before the Mercian, she looked into his face with the same fierce defiance he had seen when she had leapt out from beneath the bloody sailcloth. Here was someone as strong as the good wives who had stood firmly at Ely while the vast army of William the Bastard waited beyond the walls, threatening to end their days. He pointed towards the ships. 'Them,' he said. 'Or us.'

She looked back and seemed to understand his meaning. She nodded.

Hereward bowed his head. 'You need have no worry here,' he said. 'We shall protect you with our lives.'

Her brow knitted for a moment and she flashed him a curious look. But then she lowered her eyes, pulled the hood of the cloak over her black hair and strode over the ridge and into the baked landscape. With his eyes, Hereward urged Hengist and Sighard to accompany her. Dropping to his haunches, he snatched up three small slivers of driftwood that he had ordered his men to bring up from the tideline. He embedded them in the sand in an N shape and nodded. It was the sign they had used in the dense, intractable fenlands to mark the secret paths that wound among the treacherous bogs out of sight of the king's men. 'If Kraki or Herrig or any of the others yet live, they will see this and know we have gone on ahead,' he said, hoping against hope.

But when he looked up, he saw that Alric was frowning, distracted. He looked from the wall of colourful sails to the knot of men trudging into the arid land.

'What ails you, monk?'

'Ragener's words,' the churchman muttered. 'That the woman is cursed. The Hawk said she would bring a host of enemies upon our heads. What if this army will pursue us to the ends of the earth to get her?'

CHAPTER SEVEN

Constantinople boiled under the merciless sun. The narrow streets throbbed with life, too many people pressed into too small a space, red-faced, sweating, tempers fraying. Forges and abattoirs, steaming dyeworks and cesspits, all pumped their reek into the haze that hovered over the cluttered buildings. From every corner, the din boomed up to the heavens: the thunder of hammers, the rattle of looms, the voices roaring to be heard, whether slavers at the blocks, merchants and market traders, guildmasters and apprentices, or sailors unloading the ships at the quaysides. In Constantinople a man could find anything, so they said, except peace.

And yet, even then, Wulfrun could not help but think it was the greatest city on earth. He had been to Eoferwic, and to Wincestre, but they were like villages compared to this heaving, ceaseless mass. Here, on the high west wall above the Kharisios Gate, he could look down upon the grandeur, far removed from the grit of life.

Shielding his eyes against the glare, the captain of the Varangian Guard peered into the distance. Even then he could not see the far side of the sprawling city. Everywhere he looked, great stone buildings reached up towards the sun, the likes of which he had never seen in England. The monasteries and palaces, the great monuments to great men whose names were unknown to him, the hippodrome, the bath-houses, the zoo with its strange beasts that screeched and yowled and roared. And above it all, the magnificent dome of the Hagia Sophia floating against the blue sky. When he had first arrived from the west, he had knelt in that church to give thanks to God and had been almost blinded by the glittering of the gold which covered every surface like pebbles on a beach.

He felt his chest swell with pride. His father would have cried tears of joy to see his boy serving in the defence of such a place. 'All who are lost will find a place here in Constantinople,' he had been told when he sought a position in the Varangian Guard, and that surely was true.

'Use those things with points on the end!' The voice rang out along the top of the wall. The captain turned and saw his aide, Ricbert, leaning over the edge. He was shouting down to the guards who massed by the gate, watching the new arrivals streaming along the road that crossed the moat and the smaller walls into the city proper.

Ricbert came to meet him. 'These days they hire children, not men,' the smaller man sighed. 'Old women could beat them with sharpened sticks and rotting fruit.'

'There was a time when a toothless old hag could have laid you on your back with one blow.' A smile flickered on Wulfrun's lips. He remembered the callow youth fighting like a dog in the marketplace, more skin and bone than muscle. Ricbert didn't have much to commend him – no brawn, no skill with axe or sword, and a tongue that was too quick to mockery – but Wulfrun had seen something in him. He had dragged the smaller man along the streets by the scruff of his neck and thrown him at the feet of Hakon the Grim, who was recruiting to fill the Guard's depleted ranks. Hakon had turned up his nose, but he had bowed to Wulfrun's wishes. Many did not survive the ordeal of proving their worth. They now rested in the boneyard by the Petrion Gate, their graves unmarked, their names forgotten. But Ricbert surprised all except Wulfrun. He was flattened, beaten, broken, his wits kicked out of him, the lobe of his left ear and the tip of a finger lost to sharp teeth, but still he clawed his way back from the brink. And now he had found a role at which he excelled. The Varangian Guard had never seen a better master of spies. No whisper escaped his ears. His eyes were like a hawk's.

Ricbert sniffed. 'Some of those old hags would afrit even Hakon the Grim,' he said in an indignant tone. His face darkened as he glanced along the great Land Wall behind him. Four spear-lengths wide, it towered the height of seven men above the ground. From the Golden Horn to the Sea of Marmara it stretched, guarded by ninety-six towers with views across the rolling landscape to the west and north. No enemy could ever breach it.

'What is wrong?' Wulfrun asked.

'Not all enemies are beyond the Land Wall, as you well know,' Ricbert replied. 'And there are enemies and enemies. Enemies of the emperor, enemies of the empire. And we have our own enemies too. Watch your back, Wulfrun.'

'You speak in riddles.'

Along the wall, beyond the red banner of Constantinople with its white crescent of Diana, goddess of the hunt, and the white star of the virgin Mary, he glimpsed a throng approaching. The wall guards parted as if a sword carved through them. Ahead of a group of well-armed warriors strode a towering man, a good head or two above Wulfrun, who was himself taller than most of the local men. Long hair the colour of iron streamed out behind him. Despite his age – he had seen more than fifty summers – his chest was broad and his jaw was square. His lined face was tanned the colour of leather.

'Victor Verinus,' Wulfrun muttered.

'Aye. The Stallion. The man with a horse's cock, so they say.

At least, I think that is where his name comes from. Victor is a cock, one way or another.'

'He is the enemy of which you speak?'

An uneasy gaze flickered up towards Wulfrun. 'I hear he has designs upon Juliana.'

The captain could not hide his distaste. 'She is but a child to him.'

'Victor conquers women as he conquers land. He takes what he sees. All is about power to him. I say this as a friend. Keep your eyes upon her.'

'Has he not brought enough misery to the Nepotes?' Wulfrun watched the tall man approach. Victor's chin was raised, his stare supercilious as he surveyed the wall warriors, who would not meet his eye. His private guard kept close at his back. They were a pack of savage dogs, but they would die before they let an enemy reach their master.

'He plunged the knife into the skull of Juliana's father?' Ricbert asked.

'Aye. And that ended their struggle for power in one blow. Victor was victor, and he took the spoils, everything the Nepotes valued. All of Kalamdios' kin paid a high price.' *But Juliana will not be one of them*, he silently vowed.

Victor came to a halt in front of the two men. A sly smile danced on his lips. 'Wulfrun. The wolf of the Varangian Guard,' he said in a low, rich voice. 'In all the Guard, they say you have the coldest heart.'

'I have heard that.'

'And does that woman of yours not warm your icy depths?' His lips pulled back from his yellowing teeth. 'I hear you have not yet fucked her, Wulfrun. Surely that cannot be. Women need to be broken, and a woman that fine needs to have a man's mark put upon her.'

Wulfrun felt the heat grow, but he showed only a cold face. 'Juliana is chaste, and will remain so until we wed.'

Victor threw back his head and laughed. Overhead, the gulls

wheeled, shrieking. 'You English are a strange breed. All the women want your meat inside them, you and your Viking brothers. *So handsome! So brave!* I have seen them waiting in their multitudes outside the homes of the Varangian Guard in the Vlanga, begging for your tokens. Begging to be bedded.' He fluttered one hand, shaking his head incredulously. 'And yet you do not have your fill of their delights. Is killing all that weighs upon your minds?'

'Some say.'

'You are a man of few words. That is wise.' Victor's flat tone suggested a contempt that was not evident in the words. Wulfrun cared little. 'I am to pay a visit to the house of the Nepotes this even. I will pass your good wishes to the girl, if I should see her.' Folding his huge hands behind his back, the tall man strode away.

Wulfrun watched him go. 'You see and hear all, as always, Ricbert. I am in your debt.'

An outcry rose from the gate beneath them. The two men stepped to the edge and peered down the dizzying drop. The long column of refugees arriving from the conflicts in the west stretched into the hazy distance. Too many by far, and more arriving by the day, Wulfrun thought. The finances of Constantinople already creaked from having to accommodate them all.

'There,' Ricbert said, pointing.

His back to the Kharisios Gate, a warrior waved a sword in an arc to fend off an angry mob. A woman stood behind him, shouting. Wulfrun thought he heard the English tongue. 'Come,' he muttered. 'Before we have a war upon our own doorstep.'

Wulfrun and Ricbert dashed down the steep steps to the hubbub at the gate. Leaning on their spears, the guards stood back. Better to let the rabble fight it out amongst themselves than risk a knife in the ribs. Wulfrun shouldered his way through the throng till he reached the front of the semicircle facing the man and the woman. Once they saw his scarlet cape and gilded helm, the raucous crowd fell silent. Some stared in awe, at the riches shown by the golden hilt of his sword, or because word of the fearsome Varangian Guard had spread far beyond Constantinople's walls.

Though the cornered man lowered his sword in deference, Wulfrun could see no fear in those coal-black eyes. His hair was a mass of dark curls and he was taller than most, and slender, but strong, Wulfrun could see. His stance was that of a fighting man. A faint smile played on his lips. At ease, even when threatened by a mob.

Wulfrun hid his curiosity. 'What is the meaning of this outcry?' he demanded, one hand upon the haft of his axe.

'He is Norman,' someone spat.

The captain turned back to the stranger. 'Is this true?'

The man bowed his head. ''Tis true. I am Deda, a knight.' With a flamboyant swing of his hand, he indicated the woman at his back. 'This is my wife, Rowena.'

The woman was not unattractive, her eyes large and dark and filled with intelligence. Wulfrun saw a defiance there that warmed him. 'English?' he asked.

Her eyes lit up in delight at hearing her own tongue. 'And you,' she said, beaming.

The captain nodded, a greeting of familiars in a strange land. Glancing back at the knight, he said, 'You thought you could walk through the Kharisios Gate when your kind attack our lands in the west, and burn the villages, and drive the people out in their floods to us here?'

'I see how that could be a problem,' Deda said in a wry tone, 'if I were not being driven out by my own kind.'

'Listen to him,' Rowena pleaded. 'There is nothing William the Bastard would like more than to see my husband's head upon a spike.' She stepped closer to the knight, as ready to fight for his safety as to comfort him, Wulfrun could see.

'And why would Normans hunt a Norman?'

'Because I killed an ally of the king—'

'Who would have harmed me!' Rowena interjected, her eyes blazing. 'He is an honourable man who saved a woman in need.'

'I would expect no more from a knight,' Wulfrun said.

'And I aided the English rebels,' Deda continued. 'Not in battle against my own, never that, but when they were fleeing for their lives. The king could never forgive that, for they had wounded his pride, if not his body.'

Wulfrun stiffened, but he hid his emotions. 'The English rebels?'

'Aye, in Ely, in the east, where they made their stand.'

Choosing his words carefully, the captain enquired, 'And their leader . . .' He touched his forehead, pretending to have forgotten the name of the man he hated more than any other.

'Hereward. He is the reason we are here.'

Wulfrun furrowed his brow. 'How so?'

'Hereward offered the hand of friendship to my husband,' Rowena said. 'He deserved better than to be exiled by the bastard king.'

Deda sheathed his double-edged sword. 'Hereward and his men set sail for Constantinople. They are without a home, like us. We would join them here.'

'When I was a child, I knew Hereward,' Wulfrun said, forcing a smile. 'We ran together in Barholme in the fenlands. I would see my old friend again.'

'He is not yet arrived?' Rowena asked.

'If such a great war-leader had set foot in Constantinople, my eyes and ears would have told me,' Wulfrun said. 'But perhaps he follows a meandering path.' He paused, weighing his words, then grinned. 'You are friends of my friend. You must be treated well here in your new home.' He turned to Ricbert. 'Find them food, and wine. Their bellies shall not go empty. Somewhere . . .' He let the word hang.

Ricbert held up a finger. 'I know just the place.'

'Good.' Wulfrun turned back to the new arrivals. 'I will find you work. I ask only one thing in return. That when Hereward arrives, you do not speak of me. Instead, come to me first. I would surprise him with stories of days long gone.'

'You are kind,' Rowena replied. 'We are in your debt.'

Wulfrun turned to the crowd and bellowed, 'Any enemy of the Normans is a friend of Constantinople. These two are under my protection. Harm them not, or feel the edge of my axe.'

Muttering, the mob stepped back, cowed. Deda bowed and led his wife through the gate. They had few possessions, Wulfrun could see, but they held their heads high. He leaned in to Ricbert and whispered, 'Keep a close eye on him. I would not put it past the Norman bastards to send a spy into our midst.'

Ricbert nodded and hurried after his two charges.

For the rest of the day, Wulfrun went about his duties. With fifteen men, he quelled a dispute among masons repairing the soaring aqueduct of Valens after they shouted threats against the emperor. At the Boukoleon palace, he met the army's high command to discuss the threat from the east. He offered a gold coin in return for a blessing at the church of the Forty Martyrs. But the unease that had lain heavily upon him since his meeting with Victor Verinus never dissipated.

After he had eaten and washed at his home in the Vlanga, he wandered out into the warm night. The breeze had wafted away some of the city's stink, and all he could smell was the fragrance of roasting lamb, and the herbs in the pots of the gardens he passed.

The house of Nepos stood in the wealthy district not far from the forum of Constantine, where many of the city's richest merchants made their homes. From the outside, it looked a testament to the fortunes of Juliana's kin: towering, whitestone, surrounding a courtyard with a pool and trees that offered shade from the day's heat. But Wulfrun knew the truth. The slave admitted him without question and soon his footsteps were ringing as he walked through the empty, echoing halls. The house was a mausoleum, a *memento mori* to the once great Nepotes. Every piece of gold, every possession of any value, had been looted by the Verini, the day Victor had sealed the defeat of his rival.

For a moment, he thought the house deserted. But then he caught a glimpse of flickering candlelight. Turning a corner, he stiffened. Wreathed in shadow, a figure sat silently near to the wall to his left.

After a moment, Wulfrun realized it was Kalamdios. The head of the Nepotes sat upon his chair, alone. Not even the slaves who carried him everywhere were with him. Wulfrun felt a pang of pity. How terrible it must be to fall from such great heights to this.

The captain bowed his head in deference. 'Forgive me. I did not realize you were here. I have come to visit your daughter, but I cannot find . . .' He clamped down on his words, realizing he was babbling because he knew the other man was not able to fill the gaps in the conversation. 'Forgive me,' he repeated.

A long trail of drool glistened from Kalamdios' lower lip. Wulfrun wondered what thoughts flickered in that frozen body. Bitterness? Regret? Hatred? Surely there could be no joy or hope. Yet there must have been a great fire burning in his heart for him to survive such a grievous wound. The commander had seen men die from less upon the battlefield. As the notion crossed his mind, his gaze fell upon Kalamdios' hands, the one part of his body where there was some semblance of life. They twitched and turned, the fingers flexing as if he were distressed. As Wulfrun watched, puzzled, the ringing silence of the room was broken by a reedy mewling, whining higher by the moment. Kalamdios was trying to communicate with him.

'What is amiss?' he asked, concerned. When he took a step forward, he saw that the man's swivelling eyes were snapping towards a door to his right. *He wishes me gone*, Wulfrun thought. Bowing, he muttered a farewell and walked in the direction the crippled man had indicated. Barely had he passed into a small chamber when he heard the slam of the great door, and voices. The captain gritted his teeth. One of them rang with Victor's deep, mocking tones. The other, he guessed, was Juliana's mother, Simonis, who must have allowed their tormentor into the house. Wulfrun felt a slow-burning anger. How could the Nepotes live that way, with the man who had destroyed their lives coming and going as if he were king?

Now he understood. Kalamdios did not want his humiliation witnessed. And who could blame him?

Wulfrun eased across the marble floor, taking care that his boots did not even whisper. But before he reached the other side of the chamber, he paused. Victor was booming, 'Kalamdios! Your graven face fills my heart with joy. How is life within your prison? Do you yearn to feel the grass beneath your toes, or swim in the warm sea? Alas, that it will never be!'

The captain stiffened at Victor's cruelty. He took a step towards the door, then stopped, his breath catching in his throat.

'Where is your daughter?' Victor was asking.

'She walks in the forum with her brother, Leo, enjoying the night air,' Simonis replied. Her voice had a sing-song quality. Wulfrun knew she was trying to placate their visitor.

'A pity. I would have seen her fair face this even.' Victor's words rumbled with a sickening slyness.

His fingers closing around his sword hilt, Wulfrun fought to contain his anger. But he felt all his deepest fears stirred by the mention of Juliana. After a moment's hesitation, he crept back across the chamber. He decided it would be wise to spy on Victor. Here, where he felt in control, his tongue would be looser.

Standing in the shadows at the edge of the door, he peeked out into the candlelit hall. He could see Kalamdios, his face like stone, but his eyes filled with hate. Victor towered over him, caring little. His jewelled *dalmatica* sparkled in the flickering light. Wulfrun saw he had worn his finest clothes, the best to show off his power over the plainly dressed Nepotes. But Simonis still took pride in her appearance, he noted. Though she wore no headcloth, her hair had been combed and tied back with a blue bow. And she had on a dress the colour of a summer sky, sleeveless, with a belt designed to emphasize her heavy breasts. She held her face up with a defiance that Kalamdios could no longer muster. Wulfrun could still see the beauty that had drawn him to her daughter.

For a long moment, Victor peered into Kalamdios' eyes and then he smiled and nodded. 'I always take such joy from our talks,' he mocked, 'but time is short. Let us get down to it.'

Without looking back, he reached behind him and crooked a finger towards Simonis. After a moment's hesitation she strode forward and stood in front of the man who now ruled them all. Victor grinned. With a slow, deliberate movement, he cupped the woman's face in his hands and admired it, turning it this way and that so it caught the flickering light. Now Simonis' face was as fixed as her husband's. But she did not resist.

Wulfrun stifled a gasp at Victor's audacity. To touch another man's wife, and to do so in front of her husband! What power he felt he had over them. And that was not the end of it.

He tugged on the woman's belt and it fell away. Hooking his thumbs under the silk at her shoulders, he eased it down her arms. The dress slid over her curves and crumpled around her feet. Underneath, she was naked. Wulfrun wrenched away from the sight, appalled by what he was seeing. Instead, his gaze fell upon Victor's smile, and his twinkling eyes. Here was a man who believed he could do anything, anything, without redress. It was the smile of a man who thought himself a god.

In his prison-chair, Kalamdios' hands twitched and jerked. The captain could not bear to look at him either. He imagined the hatred building inside, the frustration, until the pressure seemed so great Kalamdios thought he would die. Pity welled up in Wulfrun. He wanted to step out there and cut Victor down with his axe, but he knew he could not. He had sworn an oath to his emperor and that prevented him from raising his weapon to a man who, for now, was in Michael's favour. He had to let this remain between the Nepotes and the Verini.

With his fingers at her bare shoulders, Victor spun Simonis round and then pressed her down until she was on all fours. Her breasts swung low, scraping the cold marble. She braced herself on her forearms as he hooked his fingers under her hips and raised them. Pulling aside his tunic, Victor exposed his erect cock. The Stallion. Ricbert had been correct. The tormentor spat upon his thumb and rubbed it between Simonis' legs, then eased his member inside her and began to thrust. He did not look at the woman before him. Instead, with a cruel smile, he stared deep into Kalamdios' eyes. And Kalamdios held that stare, for what else could he do?

Simonis made no sound. If she felt anything, Wulfrun could not tell. And yet somehow that was even worse. This was not a woman being taken by force, it was submission. It was about giving up the very last part of oneself. After this, there was nothing. Nothing.

Sickened, Wulfrun stepped away from the door and hurried across the room, no longer caring if his footsteps echoed. In any case, the noise would be lost beneath the sound of Victor's grunts. His thoughts rattled through his head as he imagined the private hell that existed in the house of Nepos, and finally only one notion burned bright: he would not . . . could not . . . let Juliana suffer so. If Victor laid one finger upon her, Wulfrun would slaughter him, even though it would cost him everything.

When he heard voices at the outer door, his heart thundered and he ran to intercept Juliana and her brother. Leo was a strange child, quiet and introspective, with dark eyes that seemed to look right through a man. When Juliana saw him, her face lit up. Afraid she would cry out and alert Victor, Wulfrun caught her arm and gently urged her, and Leo, out and across the courtyard to the deep shadows under the trees.

'You are hard to fathom, but you bring me such joy,' Juliana exclaimed. She sat, leaning back against a tree trunk. Her face was dappled by moon shadows. At that moment Wulfrun felt a yearning that shocked him.

'Is it true that if you unsheathe your sword, it must drink blood?' Leo asked. His sister tried to hush him. The boy looked up at the captain with wide eyes. Wulfrun remembered feeling that same sense of awe when he was a boy in England, watching the earl's men hunting in the wildwood.

'It does not hurt if our enemies believe that,' he replied with a smile. Glancing over his shoulder, he searched the doors to the house for any sign of movement. All was still. That was good, but he would not leave that night until Victor had gone.

'We went to the Hagia Sophia, to pray for the safe return of my brother,' Juliana said.

'Still no word?' Wulfrun asked.

Glancing down, she shook her head. But then she looked up at him, beaming. 'He yet lives, I know he does. As we knelt before the altar, Leo heard this truth. God spoke to him.'

'You hear God, lad?'

'Sometimes. He whispers to me. He guides me.'

'Then you are blessed.' Wulfrun did not want to dash any hopes – they had suffered enough as it was – but he knew that almost all those who had been with her brother when he disappeared had now returned to Constantinople. None could say for certain if he lived or died, but with each day that passed there was less chance of his ever coming home.

Victor's braying laughter echoed from the depths of the house and both Juliana and Leo flinched. Wulfrun glimpsed the shadows that crossed their faces, and he felt their hidden pain. He could stand by no longer. It was not in his nature.

Snatching up Juliana's hand, he knelt before her and said, 'I swear an oath to you this day. On my honour, I will protect you against all harm, though my own life is forfeit. I swear my axe to your service, so help me God.'

A dim part of him called out in protest, for a man of the Varangian Guard must only have one master, the emperor himself, but when he looked into her bright face he felt all his doubts fall away. If Victor Verinus dared take even one step towards this woman, this innocent and pure creature, there would be blood.

Chapter Eight

The hot wind licked across the dusty land. Whorls of sand whisked up over brown rock as the column of men trudged under the cruel sun. Their heads were bowed from the weight of that infernal heat, their throats as dry as the lifeless plain.

'Where are the foul-smelling bogs, and the willows and the insects and the rushing waters?' Mad Hengist whined. 'I would be home, in the fens, not in this hell.'

'I never thought I would be yearning for that damp, miserable place,' Alric agreed. 'This is hell indeed. Will the sun never set? And the dust . . . it tears at your eyes, and fills your nose and ears and mouth, even when the wind is not blowing.' He caught the arm of the one next to him. 'These men were raised with moss on their backs and rain in their faces. They were not prepared for this.'

'They are warriors,' Hereward growled. 'They fight. No matter where . . . in the snow of the north, or the heat, here. If they cannot survive a little sun, they will be no good when we get to Constantinople. What then for the glory and the gold?'

The Mercian watched the woman stride a few paces ahead of the shambling, sweating war-band. She seemed to float over that hard land, untouched by the heat or the dust. Her hood had been pulled up, her woollen cloak wrapped around her, while the men were all stripped to the waist, their skin reddening. Hereward hid his doubts from the others. Was he right to trust her? Once they had left the cooling breeze of the shore, she had indicated with gestures and mime that she should lead them, to water, to food, to safety. And before he could acknowledge her she had marched away with confidence. But what if Ragener was right and she was only leading them to their doom?

'She is used to this land,' Alric whispered as if he could read his friend's thoughts, 'while we sweat and burn. We need water, soon, or we will die.'

Hereward glanced behind him along the trail of footprints. He cocked his head against the wind and thought he could hear yells in the distance. 'We are still being hunted down like deer,' he replied. 'We cannot go back, we cannot stay here. We have no choice but to follow her.'

'How has it come to this?' the monk said with a despairing shake of his head. 'Constantinople! Glory! And now hell.'

The Mercian knew his friend was right. Despite the heat, the sweating had started to fade and his skin was growing dry. His mouth felt like the sand beneath his feet. How much longer before their bodies were drained of all water? And his worries for Kraki, Guthrinc and the others lay heavy on him. Even if the rest of his men had survived the shipwreck, how long could they last in this inhospitable place?

Sighard strode up, sullen, as he always seemed to be these days. 'I must speak my mind,' he said.

Hereward nodded.

'Take my tongue if you will, but this woman will be the death of us.' He wiped dust from his eyes. 'The sea wolves want her; they must. Why else would they follow a band of shipwrecked English curs with nothing but a few axes and swords into this oven? We have nothing worth their effort.'

Alric frowned. 'But what value can she have to that fleet of pirates? One woman!'

'It matters little,' Sighard snapped. 'It has to be her. And they will have bread and skins of water. While the sand covers our lifeless forms, they will keep coming. We should leave her to them. They will take what they want and we can—'

'What?' Hereward interjected. 'Call down water from the heavens? Monk, can you summon rain with your prayers? Will God save his poor lambs?'

'We could trade her for water,' Sighard said. How bitter he had become since the death of his brother, Hereward thought. Yet he had a good heart; he had shown that time and again. If only he could find that joy of living that had once brought a smile to his lips.

The Mercian slammed his fist into the man's jaw. Sighard flew back on the hard ground, dazed. Alric gasped. The other men stared, uneasy.

Snarling his fist in the long hair, Hereward jerked Sighard's head up. 'Your tongue is the least of your worries.'

'You would see us all die to save her?' the young warrior croaked.

'I would not throw an innocent to the wolves to save your miserable life. Or any of our lives.' The Mercian flung him back to the sand and turned away. 'All a man truly has is his honour. Never give that up, even in the face of death.' He glanced back. 'Your brother knew that. You did, once.'

Alric caught his friend's arm and pulled him to one side. 'Fists will not cure the black-heart,' he hissed.

'He needs to learn,' the Mercian muttered, pulling away. His thoughts flashed back to his own father laying fists upon him whenever he showed weakness, and he winced.

The woman was watching, her piercing eyes glinting in the depths of her hood. Did she understand the nature of the argument, or did she think them fools, fighting among each other while their enemies drew closer? He strode over to her. 'Water,' he said, miming putting a cup to his lips. 'We need water or we will die.'

The woman frowned, and then she turned and pointed in the direction in which they had been travelling. Across the distant horizon, purple mountains shimmered in the haze. Hereward followed the line of her arm and noticed a small mound rising an arm's length above the flat, rocky plain.

'*Khettara*,' she said. Her voice was musical. Hereward liked the sound of it.

He looked to Alric, then Hengist. They both shrugged. '*Khettara*,' he repeated. He glanced down at Sighard, then offered a hand. '*Khettara*.'

The red-haired warrior shook his head, grumbling to himself as he took the hand and clambered to his feet.

Setting a pace that was exhausting in the heat, the woman strode towards the mound. The English stumbled after her, coughing in the swirls of dust as they made futile attempts to cover their mouths and noses. Even as they neared it, Hereward sometimes lost sight of their goal. Whatever it meant to the woman, on his own he would not have given it a second look, even if he had seen it in the first place.

But when they reached it, he leapt up the side and looked down upon a fissure in the top, barely wider than a man's shoulders. Dropping to his knees, he peered inside. After the glare of the sun, the dark was impenetrable. His nostrils wrinkled at the scent of dank air. He dropped a stone into the hole and heard a splash.

Turning to the woman, he grinned. '*Khettara*.' She smiled back at him, the first softness he had seen in her face.

Hereward set Sighard to keep watch for their approaching enemies and eased himself into the hole. Feeling around, he found rough footholds. He lowered himself into the cool dark. As he passed the lip, he glimpsed tool marks. The hole had been cut through the very rock of the desert floor.

The makers had left numerous ledges in the well and he

descended with ease. When he reached the bottom, he splashed into gushing water glimmering in a circle of light illuminated from the hole above. Echoes rebounded off the rock around him and he found the dark refreshing after the constant glare. Dropping to his knees, he plunged his face into the icy water, sucking up huge mouthfuls to soothe his arid throat. How sweet it tasted.

Once he had drunk his fill, he flopped back into the stream and let the water flow over his burning limbs. After a moment, his eyes adjusted to the dark. When he sat up, he glimpsed a tunnel through which the stream cascaded. Hereward couldn't tell if the channel was man-made or natural, but he marvelled at how the well-makers had managed to find life-giving water in that inhospitable place. If this was created by the woman's people, they were great indeed.

When he looked up, he saw Alric's worried face framed against the brilliant blue sky. Hereward's laughter boomed up the well.

The monk gaped in shock. 'Have you gone mad?'

'We have found ourselves in a mad world, monk.' His words reverberated off the rock. 'Not too long ago we were fighting to keep the water out of our throats. Now we cannot swallow enough of it. Too much water, not enough water! A mad world!'

He pushed aside his relief. Their enemies were drawing closer by the moment and they could not afford to tarry. He scrambled back up the footholds, squinting when he pushed his head back out into the baking heat. The others stared in amazement when they saw his dripping clothes. Grabbing Alric's arm, he said, 'Our spear-brothers can climb down and drink their fill, one at a time. But make sure those in most need go first.'

When Alric went to round up the men, Hereward strode over to the woman, who was as still and unbowed as the rocks themselves. When he mimed if she wanted to drink, she shook her head. He tried to find some way to thank her, but she only smiled at his babbling.

Sighard stood to one side, glowering. 'Let this be a lesson,' Hereward said to him quietly. 'Without this woman, we would soon be dead, either from thirst or on the spears of our enemies. Let honour be your guide and good fortune will present itself.'

Sighard nodded, ashamed.

Once the men had all drunk their fill, the woman set off. The sun was slipping towards the horizon and the heat was easing. Hereward looked back in the direction of the coast. They had wasted too much time. He thought he could see movement now. His men had gone too long without sleep and they were all weary from the exertions of the shipwreck, but they would not be able to rest for even a moment.

'Stay strong,' he called. 'We will find a safe haven soon enough.' When he eyed the woman's decisive path, he decided that must be true.

The night came down hard.

'It is cold,' Alric grumbled, shivering. He wrapped his arms around himself and stamped his feet as he trudged.

'Too hot, too cold. Nothing is ever right for you, monk,' Hereward sighed.

'And some food for my belly would not go amiss,' the churchman muttered.

The Mercian looked up to the vault of the heavens where a milky river of stars flowed across the sable sky. The moon glowed bright enough to light their way across the vast, arid plain. Still featureless, he noted. No berries or roots to feed upon, not even the hope of a rabbit or a bird. Nor any place to hide.

'Are we to walk to those mountains?' Alric hissed. 'That is . . . two days' march?'

'More like three or four. In this flat land, all seems much closer than it is.' Hereward glanced back at his men. Their heads were bowed, their shoulders sagging. Their privations had taken a toll. They would be lucky to see out another day.

'How much longer will those sea wolves hunt us down? Can this woman be worth that much to them?' the churchman asked with a note of exasperation.

Hereward ignored the questions. He was watching Hengist, who had returned to the land of the sane after quenching his thirst. His wits came and went without any seeming pattern, but now he was bounding back and forth along the column of men, pausing every now and then to throw his head back and sniff the air.

'He thinks he is a dog,' Alric said, following his friend's gaze.

'Perhaps. Sometimes I think Hengist knows more than any of us. The mad are wise, they say. Touched by God, yes?'

'Some say, aye. And some say touched by the Devil.'

After racing around for a few moments longer, Hengist loped over. 'I smell death,' he blurted, his eyes rolling from side to side. When Hereward glanced in the direction of their pursuers, Mad Hengist shook his head furiously and pointed ahead. 'No, there. We walk towards death.'

The Mercian's eyes narrowed. Was the woman leading them into a trap? Had Hengist, with senses made keen by his madness, heard or smelled something that the rest of them had missed? He darted to the woman, holding up a hand. She frowned and tried to push by, but he stepped in front of her again. When she ground to a halt, he glanced over his shoulder across the moonlit landscape. Nothing moved.

'Keep her here,' he commanded. Alric and Hiroc flanked the woman. Her eyes glittered, seemingly hearing the suspicion in his voice.

Hereward turned and dropped low. The moon was too bright and he missed the shelter of the fens' woods and ditches. He squinted, scanning the rock-littered landscape. If anyone waited to attack them, they would have to be lying belly-down like snakes. His muscles tense, he crept forward.

The wind began to moan across the plain. Curls of dust whisked up, growing higher by the moment as the breeze strengthened. Hereward cursed under his breath. Even the elements conspired against him.

As he loped across the rocks, his hand never far from the hilt of Brainbiter, he looked up and saw that the mountains had faded from view. A haze now hung across the horizon. The breeze had become a gale, tearing at his hair and driving needles of sand into his face. Lowering his head, he threw his left arm across his nose and mouth. Tears blurred his eyes. He would not see any attacker until the last.

Soon the wind was howling so loud he could not hear his own voice. A bank of dust swirled, as dense as any of the fogs that blanketed the fens. Glancing back, he realized he could no longer see the others. The sand had swallowed his tracks. He had been too confident, he could see that now. Buffeted, he stood his ground, trying to get his bearings.

As he turned, he thought he glimpsed movement in the corner of his eye. Whipping out his sword, he whirled, but if anyone had been there, they were lost to the dust-storm. For a moment, he waited, doing his best to pierce the haze.

After a while, the wind dropped a little. Hereward realized he could see shapes at least two spear-lengths away. A jagged rock loomed up with an edge like a shark's fin, one he had spied before. Deciding to wait beside it until the gale passed, he prowled towards it, but as he neared it his nose wrinkled at the reek of rot.

Beyond the rock, he glimpsed what looked like a large cross lying on the desert floor. His face twisted with distaste as he smelled the foul odour again. The remains of a man were staked out in front of him, the arms and legs stretched, the wrists and ankles lashed to what seemed to be the shattered remnants of a spear-haft hammered into the ground. Hereward stiffened, shocked to see such a sight in that lonely place. Covering his mouth against the stench, he crouched down to inspect the body. Birds had feasted upon the face and stolen the eyes. What skin remained on the legs had blackened. The Mercian could see little to distinguish the fallen man's origin. Rats or some such had devoured the flesh upon the arms down to the bone. On one finger, a gold signet ring gleamed. The victim had not been slain by thieves. The corpse's tunic was patterned with black squares at the hem, and stained on the left side where a blade had stabbed. The wound would not have been lethal, and Hereward guessed the victim had then been tied up and left to die in the hot sun. An act of cruelty.

'A man wandering in the desert alone finds only death.'

Hereward whirled at the rich, musical voice that rolled out at his back. At first he could not see who had spoken those deeply accented words. But then the swirling dust seemed to part and a figure revealed itself, a man, tall and slender, black bristles framing the slash of his mouth. He was dressed in black robes and had a black scarf wrapped around his head. Only the lower part of his face was visible. He carried a gnarled staff, taller even than himself, and hanging on a sash at his waist was a long, curved knife in a silver scabbard. When he tilted his head back, Hereward saw eyes that burned with a fierce intelligence. Though the stranger smiled in greeting, those eyes were like knives, peeling Hereward open.

Undeterred, the Mercian swung his sword up to the man's chest. The stranger did not flinch. 'Who are you?' Hereward growled.

'My name is Salih ibn Ziyad,' he replied with a deep bow. 'And you will do as I say or you will join that poor soul in death.'

CHAPTER NINE

Out of the clouds of dust, the sea wolves stormed. Hoods pulled low to shield their eyes, they swung their axes high and prodded the air with their spears, as if bared throats were only a moment away. But it was only anger at play. Though the wind howled, their frustrated calls and responses rang out across the desert plain as they roamed back and forth.

A knot of pirates came together. Their cloaks lashed around them. They were big men, faces like the rocks of that place, features carved from lives of hardship.

'This godforsaken storm has hidden their tracks,' one bellowed, gesticulating.

Another leaned in, shouting into the depths of the other man's hood. 'Siward will have our balls if we go back empty-handed.'

A third jabbed a finger to one side. 'They cannot be far ahead. Let us keep on—'

'And what?' The fourth shook his axe in the other man's face. 'Stumble across them by chance? Has the pox rotted your brain? If we are turned around out here, we will be dead before we know it.'

You will *be dead before you know it*, Hereward thought.

Squinting through the crack in the rocks heaped upon him by Salih ibn Ziyad, he studied his prey. The sun had started to rise, its thin light reaching through the storm to draw grey shapes out of the gloom. The warrior estimated the enemy numbered around thirty. They were better armed than his men, but no more fresh. Salih's information had been correct, he could see that now, and he felt pleased that he had decided to trust the stranger.

For the first time in that inhospitable place, the English were on familiar ground, even if their cloak was no longer dense, shadowy woods but a wall of swirling sand, and instead of water-filled ditches to hide their attack they had shallow graves in the dust and rock. In the fens they were the *silvanti*, the wild men of the woods. Here they were the ghosts of the sand.

The group of sea wolves broke up. Three disappeared into the whirling brown cloud. The other bowed his head into the gale, searching the ground for any signs of their prey. Closer he came, and closer still.

Hereward's fingers tightened around the hilt of his sword beneath the folds of sand. Without a sound, he rose up from his hiding place. The rocks tumbled away. Dust cascaded from him; more crusted his sweat-slick face, his torso, his arms. And when he opened his eyes wide and grinned he must have looked a frightful sight, a vision of death itself, for the sea wolf reeled back. His free hand swung up to his mouth in shock. His axe hung limply at his side.

Hereward's blade hacked straight through his neck. Rubies glistened in the air. Still bearing a startled expression, the head bounced away into the cloud of sand and was gone. Before the rest of the body had fallen, the Mercian was already loping away, low to the ground. The muffled shouts of his enemies throbbed through the howling wind, guiding him.

Ahead of him, the grey shape of a sea wolf coalesced. He was hunched over, examining something on the ground. As Hereward prowled nearer, he saw that the other man was peering down at a strange pale plant, five stalks protruding from the desert floor. The shoots wavered, once, twice, and then began to grow. A hand pushed up out of the sand. Fingers reached up. Reeling, the sea wolf stumbled over his heels and crashed down on his back. Sighard surged out of his hiding place. In one fluid movement, his axe swung up and then down, splitting the fallen foe's face in two.

The Englishman wrenched out his weapon. His eyes flickered towards Hereward. A nod, a silent communication, and then they swept away, a growing storm of iron within the storm of sand.

Apparitions rose from their burial places on every side. Eyes as black as coals, skin dusted the colour of bone. They were there only to kill, to earn their survival as they had fought to earn it for so long under the brutal rule of William the Bastard. The sea wolves, though greater in number, were unprepared for such a terrible sight. They faltered, too slow to raise their weapons, too shocked that the whipped dogs they thought they were hunting had turned upon them.

Hereward's men were well trained, waiting until their enemies were close enough for them to smell the reek of their sweat. Spears stabbed, axes hacked. Heads were stove in with rocks. Snapping and snarling, Mad Hengist raked flesh with jagged, dirty nails. His teeth sank into the cheek of a howling sea wolf. When he ripped his head back, blood sprayed across his contorted face.

Bodies littered the desert floor. As Hereward raced through the whipping clouds of dust, he came across one after another, their blood draining into the sand.

Finally the cries of the dying ebbed away. The howling of the wind was all. For a while, the Mercian and his men roamed around, searching. They would not be surprised by any survivors.

Only one sea wolf remained. Kneeling beside the jagged rock, he whimpered like a babe. His face was scarred, his axe notched from where it had bitten through bone, his broad torso marked with the black and blue spirals of the warrior, but still he mewled before the might of the last of the English. Hereward nodded. He was pleased.

As his men gathered in a circle around the pirate, the gale began to move away. The bank of swirling brown dust drifted past them and into the distance. The wind dropped and the oven heat enveloped them. The blue sky was cloudless, the sun boiling just above the horizon. All was still.

Across the desert towards the knot of men came three figures, Salih, Alric and the woman emerging from wherever the stranger had taken them to hide before the battle began.

Hereward raised Brainbiter and rested its tip against the chest of the kneeling sea wolf. 'You are the last,' the Mercian said, his voice low but resonant. 'You thought we were less than rats. That we could be run down and picked off one by one until you had what you needed. Now you know better.'

'Show mercy,' the prisoner begged.

'I have already shown mercy to one of your kind. I threw him into storm-tossed waves on the whale road. If he lived, it would be because God willed it. That was mercy. Should I do the same to you? Send you off under this hot sun? Would you wager you can reach your ships before dust fills your throat and your bones are picked clean by the birds?' Hereward felt Salih ibn Ziyad, the woman and Alric step beside him, but he kept his gaze upon the bowed head of his captive. 'There is a third way,' he said.

With a shudder, the kneeling man looked up. 'Gold?' he began. 'My freedom . . . I will buy it with my share of our plunder . . .'

The Mercian shook his head. 'Why do you hunt us? Of what value is this woman to you?'

The sea wolf's eyes darted towards the woman and he grinned. 'You have a gale of axes breaking around you, and you do not know why you will be hounded to the ends of the earth?' He laughed in amazement.

'Speak.'

With a sly look, the captive nodded. 'I will tell you what was told to me. And then you will show me mercy.'

Hereward lowered his blade. The sea wolf looked up at the woman and showed a gap-toothed grin. 'You have no idea what you hold. She is worth more than gold—'

The woman lunged with such speed that Hereward barely saw it. Snatching the cruel, curved knife from the silver scabbard hanging at Salih's waist, she slashed across the sea wolf's throat. A gush of crimson glittered in the hot sun. The prisoner gurgled, clutching at his neck, then pitched forward into the sand.

With a snarl, the woman spat upon the lifeless form. 'Justice is done,' she snarled.

Hereward stepped back, stunned. All around, his men were gaping, as much at the woman's command of the English tongue as at her savagery.

Salih leaned forward and gently took the dripping blade from the woman's hand. Crouching down, he wiped the knife clean on the sea wolf's breeches and returned it to its scabbard. When he stood, he turned to Hereward and said in a calm voice, 'Judgement has been passed. This is as it should be, and it is just.'

The Mercian looked to the woman, but she would not meet his gaze. She raised her chin, aloof. With a deep bow, Salih swept his arm and the woman strode away without a glance at any of the men staring after her.

'She is no slave?' Sighard asked. 'No good wife?'

Salih smiled, but his eyes glittered darkly. 'She is Meghigda, known as al-Kahina. Priestess, soothsayer, leader of her people. The spirit of Dihya has entered into her. Now men bow their heads at al-Kahina's command, and her enemies flee as their blood drains into the sand.' He bowed. 'You have done a great thing, Hereward of the English, and God will smile upon you. You have returned Meghigda to the bosom of her people. War is coming, brutal and bloody, and now, with al-Kahina at our head once again, we will see victory rising like the dawn.'

With a swirl of his robes, he turned and joined his queen. Hereward frowned. 'There is much here that remains to be seen,' he said.

'That is true,' Alric said, his brow knitted as he watched them. 'Did she slay our captive in vengeance for her treatment at the hands of those sea wolves? Or to silence him?'

CHAPTER TEN

The man sprawled across the baked mud. Along the narrow street, a few people glanced over at his plight, but none came to his aid. Constantinople was too hot for that. Or perhaps, Deda thought, it was not wise to interfere in the business of strangers in that part of the city. Standing in the doorway of the hovel, the knight looked along the row of ramshackle houses, taking in the faces peering out from the shadowy interiors. A multitude of races congregated in that overcrowded, dust-choked quarter. They seemed to come from all four corners of the world, seeking out fresh beginnings in the city of gold, as he and Rowena had. There was no gold here, though. The hot air reeked from the cesspits and middens and the competing aromas of strange spices. The babble of unfamiliar tongues was swallowed up by angry shouts and the barking of dogs and the incessant bawling of babes. But still there was the promise of gold, and in hard times that was enough.

The rogue who had tried to rob their home pushed himself up from the filth of the street and shook his ringing head. Glancing back with murderous eyes, he sneered, 'You have a fine sword. Are you afraid to use it?'

'And what good would killing you do? Should I end your days for having an empty belly?'

The thief narrowed his eyes, unsure what this creature was. 'There are plenty here who would.'

'Then God has smiled upon you this day. Enjoy your good fortune as you go about your business,' Deda replied in a wry tone.

The man scrutinized this black-haired, dark-eyed knight for a moment longer, then, still puzzled, he stood up and lurched away along the street. Deda turned back into the shadowy room.

'Four thieves you have sent on your way now, in as many days,' Rowena said. She had combed her hair and tied it back with a new blue ribbon. 'Is this how it is to be now? A daily battle for . . . what?' She swept out one hand to indicate two stools, a straw bed and the hearth, the only comforts in their cramped home. He smiled. There was no bitterness in his wife's voice, and for that he had only admiration.

'But we have riches beyond measure,' he said, gesturing to the basket containing bread and olives that Ricbert the guardsman had sent them at first light.

Rowena smiled. 'And friends too. That is more than we ever hoped for when we set off upon our journey. In England we thought keeping our heads upon our shoulders would be reward aplenty.'

'If Wulfrun makes good on his promise of work, then truly we shall be blessed.'

Placing her arms around his neck, she rested her head on his shoulder. 'I have had enough of killing,' she murmured. He could feel the stiffness in her back, the strain of this new life that they had been forced to adopt.

'England is far behind us,' he soothed. 'The days of war and fighting are done.'

His thoughts drifted back, over the dusty land and across the sea, to those last days in the fenlands when he realized that

King William would never leave him in peace. The monarch was a man who held his grudges tight to his chest, and though he could forgive an English rebel, he could never forgive a fellow Norman who had broken with his own people. Bands of the king's men had scoured those wet eastern lands searching for him. They would never have rested until his head was taken back to William's fine new palace in Wincestre.

'I do not regret anything,' Rowena whispered as if she could read his thoughts. She hugged him tighter still, for she knew his doubts.

He still felt guilt; he doubted that would ever leave him. Out of love, Rowena had chosen to leave behind everything she had ever known and had readily accepted a new existence where death was always only a whisper away. He would never forget that. Easing her back, he rested his hands on her shoulders and peered deep into her eyes. 'The days to come will be hard, but no harder than the ones behind us. We will stand together unto the last, and if God is willing we will win ourselves a new life, free from the suffering we have known before.'

Though she smiled, her eyes blazed. 'We are exiles. We have no land to call our own, no folk, no kin. We have nothing left to lose. And that is our strength, husband. Let Constantinople be warned – we will fight as never before to find a place we can call home.'

CHAPTER ELEVEN

The red sun blazed on the western horizon. Tongues of shadow licked across the rolling dunes and ridges of blackened rock towards the cluster of whispering trees around the still pool. As the heat of the day ebbed away, a group of black tents billowed, the lines cracking in the cooling dusk breeze.

Hereward stood in the entrance to the largest tent, watching the gleaming river of stars wash across the darkening sky. The sweat and grime of the long trek had been sluiced from his body in the lake. He had assuaged his thirst with fresh, clean water and soon he would fill his grumbling belly. As he breathed in the sweet scent of roasting lamb and unfamiliar spices drifting across the camp, he felt the knots in his shoulders begin to unwind.

Through the camp, the men and women of Meghigda's tribe wandered with languid steps. They were a strange breed. Quick to smile, the babble of their voices was filled with music. They dressed in swathes of cloth that he thought would only have made them sweat more under the desert sun. Sapphire, amber, rose, their robes glowed against the old bones of the dusty landscape. Only warmth had they shown to the bloodstained English warriors trailing into their camp, even though the strangers had eyes that gleamed with the fierce look of cornered dogs and bristled with weapons plundered from the slain sea wolves. He felt comforted by that show of hospitality amid the harshness of this new world in which they found themselves.

Sighard strode up, his hair still dripping from his dunking in the lake. Many of the spear-brothers still lingered on the fringes of the pool, no doubt trying to wash away the terrors of the midday sun.

'I am a poor excuse for a warrior,' Sighard began, his head bowed. 'My head spins, and I say things I do not mean—'

Hereward silenced him with a hand upon his shoulder. 'I was wrong to strike you,' he said. 'We have all lost so much. We cannot see what lies ahead. This can turn any man's heart black. But we beat these things by standing together, not fighting among ourselves.'

Sighard nodded, but added, 'And yet I feel I will never know peace again, or kindness, or warmth.' Glancing around the verdant lake, his gaze fell on Alric who sat at the foot of a tree, the shadows of the fronded leaves swaying across him. Children danced around him laughing. The monk beamed, playing along with their jokes. 'I could not see myself ever sitting there.'

'Good things lie ahead. We must have faith.'

The younger warrior nodded. 'In Constantinople. Only that keeps me putting one foot in front of another. Once we are there, we can carve out a new life for ourselves. Forget days long gone. The world will be brighter. That is my only hope.'

'And I will lead you to that new world,' Hereward said, silently vowing that he would not fail his men again. He would die first.

From deep in the trees came the clash of steel. Hereward squinted, picking out whirling grey shapes in the half-light. Even at that late hour, the desert people's warriors still honed their skills with mock-battles. Over their heads they swept the long, straight, double-edged sword that they called the *akouba*, similar in style to the deadly blades of the Normans. They knew how to fight, he would give them that. They danced across the sand as if they were floating, striking high and then low with fluid sweeps. On their left arms were long shields covered in white hide and strapped to their forearms were daggers for those moments in battle when a swift thrust with a knife was the difference between life and death.

Sighard shrugged. 'I have seen better warriors.'

'Not many. They would make us sweat, that is certain.'

The younger warrior's attention drifted to men leaping over a fallen tree. Each one had a heavy stone fastened to his right arm. 'Are they mad? Why would they do such a thing?'

'You would do well to talk to our hosts,' Hereward replied. 'There is much we could learn here.' He pointed to the stones. 'They carry those weights to build up the strength in their arms. These warriors, the noblemen, ride into battle carrying an iron lance . . . a heavy lance . . . which they call the *allarh*. Their servants ride with javelins and daggers. The slaves fight with bow and arrow. They can hit a bird at five spear-throws, but the nobles think the bow is not a weapon for a man. Only the weak would kill without seeing their foe's eyes.' He grinned. 'We will tell Guthrinc that when next we meet.'

Hearing movement at his back, Hereward turned. Salih ibn Ziyad was emerging from behind a wall of cloth that hung across the centre of the tent. He beckoned.

The Mercian moved slowly into the cool interior. He was still not sure if he could trust Salih. A smile was always playing on the dark-skinned man's lips, but the look in his eyes tempered its warmth. Hereward sensed a fierce intelligence in his host, and as with all clever men there were dark depths hidden beneath the surface.

'Come,' Salih said, wagging a finger. 'You are an honoured guest. You saved al-Kahina when all here feared her lost for ever.'

'I would have done the same for any woman who suffered so.'

'Still, we will always be in your debt.'

Easing aside the wall of cloth, Salih swept one arm to guide Hereward into the hidden quarters. The scent of honey and cardamom wafted out from the shadowy recess. The Mercian was surprised to see how opulent it was. Intricately embroidered tapestries hung on the walls, and sumptuous cushions were scattered across another tapestry that had been laid upon the ground. On a small chest, silver pendants and earrings gleamed in the half-light.

Meghigda sat upon a large cushion. She was now dressed in robes of the brightest blue, a golden headdress covering her sleek black hair. The wounds upon her face had been cleaned and were now barely visible against her dark skin.

'I am pleased to see you well,' he said.

She nodded, her face giving nothing away. Holding out a slender hand, she urged him to sit. Hereward could not hide his resentment that she had tricked him. 'You speak my tongue,' he said. 'Why did you hide it?'

'I speak some,' she said in heavily accented English. 'Words I have learned . . .' She frowned, struggling with the unfamiliar sounds.

'Words she learned from the men who captured her and tormented her,' Salih said, finishing Meghigda's sentence. 'From those who came here, offering trade, but thinking we were barbarians who could be tricked. Men who offered an open hand while hiding a knife behind their backs. We have all learned that our trust must be earned.'

Hereward nodded, understanding. 'You are wise. But there is more here than meets the eye. It seems there are many who are prepared to go to great lengths to take you prisoner,' he added, directing the implicit question to the queen.

Meghigda looked past him. Now he could not tell if she was feigning her lack of understanding. Salih held out both hands. 'We have many enemies. We will not bow our heads to the great powers who lay claim to the world. Beyond the sea, battles rage. Games are played for the thrones of emperors. Plots are made, blood is spilled. And there are some who feel we have a part in that.'

Hereward narrowed his eyes. Once again a smile danced on the man's lips, and the words tumbled from him as if he were speaking openly. But the Mercian felt he was in the presence of one of the tricksters who performed wordplay in the halls of kings and earls on a winter's night.

Salih ibn Ziyad must have seen the suspicion flicker in the warrior's eyes for he said, 'Let me tell you of my people, Hereward of the English, and of Meghigda, al-Kahina, that you may more easily understand.'

Pressing his palms together as if in prayer, he leaned forward and said, 'We are the Imazighen. The Free. Some of my people are farmers in the valleys and the mountains. But the ones you see here . . .' Smiling, he held out his hands once more. 'No city will hold us. No warlord will press us to his service. We go where our hearts take us. Here one day . . .' he raised his left hand and snapped his fingers, 'gone the next, like shadows at dusk.'

Hereward nodded. 'Earth-walkers. I have been called that too.'

'We are traders. We know the secret paths across the hot desert that has claimed the lives of so many pale-skinned men. And the wares we take to the souks across this land are much in demand. But we are warriors too. We will fight unto death for our freedom. And there are many who would take that, and everything, from us. We are at war, even as we speak, a war with many players.' A shadow crossed his face. 'In Kemet, the Fatimids have decided we must be destroyed, and they have set our brothers, the Banu Hilal, against us. And in Constantinople too . . .' He caught himself, and smiled. 'We have many enemies. We can trust no one. And if we are to see out our days we must be prepared to fight with every weapon we can find.'

Hereward still could not see what part the sea wolves played, but he kept his mouth closed, waiting for his moment.

'But we are blessed by God,' Salih continued, raising one hand towards Meghigda, 'for we have been sent al-Kahina.'

A faint smile ghosted the queen's lips as if she knew this was all a game at the Englishman's expense. 'And you are more than you seem?' he asked.

'The spirit of Dihya burns in her breast,' Salih said, standing. From a silver pot, he poured a hot brown liquid into three goblets and handed them round. Small leaves floated on the surface. Hereward sniffed the contents. It was perfumed, and when he touched it to his lips he tasted the sweetness of honey. 'Drink,' Salih urged. 'The nights here grow cold. This will put a fire into your bones.'

Once Meghigda had sipped her own drink, she said in faltering English, 'Here there is the sun and the sand and the rocks and the Imazighen, all eternal. And one other. Blood.'

'Blood has drenched the dust of this place since God first made the world.' Salih retook his seat, cupping his hands around his goblet. 'The history of the world is blood and war, my friend, and that will never change.'

'My mother told me of Dihya, as her mother told her, and all the mothers before her,' Meghigda said. 'It is said that there came a man whose hands were stained in blood. His name was Hasan ibn-al Nu'man.' Her eyes flashed as she recollected the story she had been told. Hereward thought how well she spoke the English tongue when her thoughts were elsewhere. Games everywhere, and nothing as it seemed. 'With his vast army, he marched from Kemet, to crush all before him. All the peoples of the world. Cities burned.' She clenched her fists in passion, and then seemed to sense that she had let her mask slip, for she added, 'The words . . . so hard . . .' She looked to Salih. Hereward thought he saw tears in her eyes, but he could not tell if this too was a trick.

'Hasan ibn-al Nu'man was the devil,' Salih said, picking

up the tale. His voice rustled out through the tent, dark and low. 'He could not rest until he had made every man and woman his slave. In Carthage, he asked the fallen, "Who is the greatest monarch? Who are the proudest people? Who would dare defy me?" And every man and woman there told him, the Imazighen. And their queen – *malikat al-barbar* – was the bravest, the strongest, the most loved, the most feared. Her name was Dihya. Hasan ibn-al Nu'man could not let this stand. He marched his army to Numidia. But Dihya had her spies, and she was ready for him. In Meskiana, they met.' Salih smiled and sipped his warm liquor. Over the rim of his goblet, his eyes connected with Meghigda's and she smiled too.

'Dihya, filled with God's fire,' the queen breathed. 'How those invaders must have felt when they saw her army bearing down upon them with *malikat al-barbar* at their head.'

'The desert turned red as far as the eye could see,' Salih continued, 'and the army of Hasan ibn-al Nu'man was torn asunder. He fled like a whipped cur, back to Cyrenaica, and Dihya followed, slaying any of his men who fell behind, until the invaders had been driven off the land of the Imazighen.'

'And God's fire is in you now,' Hereward said to Meghigda.

The queen raised her chin. 'We will not be defeated by the Banu Hilal. That is my vow.'

'And they are the rival tribe who are in the pay of your enemies?' Hereward said, probing the twists and turns of the power struggles in this strange corner of the world. Meghigda nodded, and he understood the passions that raged inside her. Whatever deception she played, the two of them were alike, he knew. Was her war against the rival tribe and their foreign lords any different from the one he had waged in the fens against the Norman dogs? Was this Hasan ibn-al Nu'man any different from William the Bastard who had stolen the English crown?

'Then I am proud I have brought you back to your home to defend your people,' he said.

'God will smile on you for your good works,' Salih replied, pressing his palms together once more.

'And yet there are still some things that make little sense to me,' the Mercian mused, draining his goblet. He could feel the eyes of the other two upon him. He did not meet them. 'In the desert, the body of a man, staked out to die under the cruel sun . . .'

'The desert is filled with those who would prey upon a lone traveller,' Salih said quickly, 'who would take a life in exchange for little more than a ring, or a knife. This is not your home, Hereward of the English. The rules you know do not apply here, and there is danger everywhere, in a glance, in an un-guarded word, in a step off a familiar path. It would be wise to remember that.'

'You have been to England?'

'I have been to England.' Salih's face gave nothing away. Hereward set his goblet aside. Though the other man's words were measured, he sensed a deeper warning in them. He eyed Meghigda, who was watching him like a hawk.

'I see a queen, whether or not that is the title you give her. A leader of men. But who are you, Salih ibn Ziyad? What part do you play in these matters?'

'I am a humble servant of al-Kahina,' he said with a faint bow of his head.

'A priest?'

'I am a guide. A calm voice in the storm.'

'You have had some learning.'

The adviser pursed his lips, nodding slowly.

'Salih ibn Ziyad knows the patterns the stars make and how they guide the ways of men,' Meghigda said. 'He knows the secrets of the trees and the water and the shifting of the sands. He can see days yet to come in a still pool, and hear the whispers in the wind.'

'In the wild woods of England, there are women who do the same,' Hereward replied. 'We call them witches.'

'To know these hidden things is to see the hand of God at work. I am blessed,' Salih replied. Moistening his lips, he eyed his guest. 'You English, from your cold, wet land. You are not traders, any man can see that. What pulls you from the comfort of your home?'

'England is not what it was, not now the Norman bastard wears the crown. We seek a new home, and peace. Gold. Glory.'

'Gold and glory,' Salih repeated. 'And where will you find these riches?'

'In Constantinople.'

'Ah. The city of gold.' Salih nodded. 'It is also known as the city of shadows. Like all things, it has two faces. The one it shows to the world, and the one it keeps to itself. And there you will . . . ?' He raised his hands in a questioning manner.

'Join the Varangian Guard.'

'The emperor's feared war-band.'

'You know of them?' Hereward asked.

Salih nodded.

'Strong arms and sharp blades, that is what we have to offer. And that, so we are told, is what they need. Good fighting men can always earn coin.'

'You are wise, but you would do well to take care. Constantinople is not England. There are worse weapons than axe and spear, and a shield may not be able to protect you from them.'

Hereward's eyes narrowed. 'What say you?'

Salih shrugged. 'No matter. You speak truly. The emperor needs warriors and he will pay well to get them. War is coming to Constantinople, as it comes to all places in these times. But you are no stranger to killing, I can see that.' He fluttered a hand in the air as if dismissing his words, and continued, 'But now we have found common ground among us, and we are all friends here. Come – it is time to fill your belly. The feast in honour of your men is about to begin.' He rose, gesturing towards the wall of cloth and the tent entrance beyond. 'You will find the Imazighen are warm hosts. We will not soon forget this great thing you have done in bringing al-Kahina back to us.'

Salih pulled aside the curtain to let the guest out. Meghigda remained sitting on her cushion. Hereward could feel her eyes upon him as he stepped out of the private quarter. She remained a mystery to him.

Outside the night had grown as cool as late autumn in the fens. Constellations glittered in the sable sky and the full moon had turned the desert landscape into a sweep of silver and shadow. Through the trees, a great fire blazed. The succulent aromas of the roasting lamb were even stronger now and his stomach growled in response. Voices rose up in jubilation, cheers and laughter. And music too. Someone was plucking out a tune on a stringed instrument, the notes swirling fast. Others pounded upon drums. He puzzled over the curious noises of unfamiliar instruments, one that sounded like the lowing of cattle, and another that groaned, deep and resonant, like a whale heaving itself out of deep water. Though he and his men were a world away from all they knew, and the wind was filled with the reek of strange spices, and though his throat was as dry as the desert sand, he felt comforted. This could have been the feast at Ely, on the day when they thought victory over King William was assured.

Hereward felt a shadow fall over him. That day had proved that they must always be on their guard. Even when all seemed well, their enemies never rested. Plans were laid away in the dark and doom could strike in an instant.

CHAPTER TWELVE

The night was filled with music and laughter. Soon the feast would begin. But Hereward could not settle. Restless, he prowled around the camp, watching the featureless landscape in case more sea wolves had picked up their trail. As he completed yet another circuit, he heard a woman's voice in the trees. Though she spoke in the lilting Imazighen tongue, he thought it might be the queen.

He found Meghigda sitting in the middle of a circle of young girls. Their faces were rapt as they hung on her every word. He furrowed his brow. Here was a side of the Imazighen leader that he had not seen before. There was a softness in her face as she looked with fondness around the group, and she was quick to laugh. The girls would laugh too, at ease in the presence of this woman who could kill a man in an instant and was prepared to lead an army to war.

Once the circle had broken up and the girls had drifted away to the feast, Hereward caught the queen's eye. 'What did you tell them?' he asked.

'That they should laugh and play and love every moment.' She narrowed her eyes as if she expected this warrior to mock her.

But Hereward understood. Like him, she had had her child-hood stolen from her and that only made her value it more.

'And that they have as much fire in their breast as any man,' she added. 'No Imazighen woman will ever walk with her head bowed while I lead.'

'You are a good teacher.'

Nodding, she lowered her eyes. 'These girls are strong and clever and spirited. I would have them grow up into a world where blood is never spilled. I would have them be happy.'

Hereward thought of his own son, so far away across the whale road. He wished he had had the strength to be a good father for the lad. But he was afraid he would turn out no bet-ter than old Asketil, his own father. The boy deserved better. 'These are the burdens of a leader,' he replied.

'You understand. That is good.' She seemed relieved, he thought. Looking up to the stars, she continued in a reflective voice, 'I know there can never be any peace for me. My life will be one of fighting, always. And then death will come and I will be snatched away before my work is complete.'

'You do not know this.'

'I do. I have seen it,' she said, fixing an eye on him. 'And I am not afraid. As long as I have changed the course of one life, my own life will be complete. Change one heart, and they can go on to change another, and another, and another, and all the days to come. That is good work. Small things, English. Victory does not always come in winning the war.'

Before he could answer, a cry rang out, then another, and a shout in the Imazighen tongue. On the edge of the trees, Hereward and Meghigda found Salih ibn Ziyad huddled with the guards. He turned at their approach. 'Strangers are coming.'

Hereward peered out into the stark waste. In the distance, he could just make out a trail of shadows moving across the silvery landscape.

As they neared, he felt his heart leap. Afraid to believe the evidence of his eyes, he raced out across the sand. But it was true. Against all the odds, the missing spear-brothers had made their way through the wilderness to find him. Guthrinc led the way, with Kraki a step behind. Some of the men staggered on shaking legs, but Hereward thought they looked in better health than they had any right to.

Guthrinc laughed and flung his great arms around his friend.

'Is this a miracle?' Hereward demanded.

'I could say the same,' the tall man replied, 'for you did not have Herrig the Rat to save your neck.'

The scout was the best the Mercian had ever known. A disturbed leaf, a hint of a footprint in wet grass, no sign had ever escaped his eyes when he had scouted for the rebels in England. He could live for weeks at a time upon the berries and roots of the forest. 'Even here, in the desert?'

'Aye. God or the Devil has touched him, that I know.'

Herrig bounded up. He was more beast than man, lithe and lean and fierce, hair lank and greasy, tunic stained with mud and mould. His front teeth had been knocked out by the hilt of a sword, so that when he grinned he seemed to have fangs at the sides of his mouth. And on a thong round his neck rattled the finger bones of the Normans he had slain, too many to count.

'Sand and stone, or water and tree, it is all the same if you have eyes to see,' he snickered.

'He found us rats to eat and led us to water,' Guthrinc said. 'And somehow he found your trail. Without Herrig, we would have been dead in no time.'

Relief flooded Hereward. But as he looked along the line of weary men, his heart fell. They were fewer than he had hoped. 'How many?' he whispered.

Guthrinc lowered his eyes. 'Three, dead in the sea. Higbald, Cerdic and Waegmund. Good men.'

The Mercian nodded. 'Good men.' He remembered them all, the jokes they had shared, the battles they had fought, the lives they had lived, and he mourned them. 'Eight gone since we left England. Too many.' Each life lost was his burden.

As they walked across the sand towards the trees, the dark mood ebbed and Hereward felt the joy of their reunion rush back in. Salih ibn Ziyad welcomed the new arrivals like long-lost brothers and ushered them towards the feast. With whoops and cries, the exhausted warriors raced to their brothers, drawing on the last of their reserves.

Hereward watched them go, relieved that he had not been responsible for even more deaths. But as he stepped towards the fire, he sensed someone approaching under the swaying palms. A low voice hissed his name.

Sighard waited in the shadows, glancing around.

'You are not at the feast?' the Mercian asked.

'Trust comes hard to me these days,' the young warrior whispered, 'and that grates on all who travel with me, I know that. But sometimes I am right.'

Hereward stepped closer so they could not be overheard. 'What have you found?'

'When we parted, I saw a guard carrying a water-skin out into the desert. This seemed strange to me. I followed him.' He paused, one hand falling to the hilt of the axe hanging at his hip. 'You must come with me. There are lies here that may mean all our lives are in danger.'

CHAPTER THIRTEEN

Beyond the circle of palms, the wild dogs fought over bones. Their snapping and snarling echoed across the lonely desert. The night was bright and the wind was chill as Hereward and Sighard crept to the tree-line. The Mercian glanced back. The feast was in full flow. The women lashed their hair as they danced around the fire to the swirl of the wild music. Men tore at chunks of meat, the grease dripping from their chins, and swilled back bowls of the thick, spicy stew. Though there was no beer or wine to dull the wits and fire the heart, Hereward saw his men grinning with relief after the hardships they had endured.

'We will not be seen,' Sighard hissed.

The two men crept out of the trees. 'You are sure this is the way?' the Mercian asked. 'We cannot risk getting lost in the desert at night.'

The younger warrior pointed to a low, rocky ridge silhouetted against the starry sky. 'Just beyond there,' he whispered.

As they set off across the rough ground, the music faded away, and the voices and the laughter. The drumming became a distant heartbeat. They kept low until they reached the ridge, knowing that they could easily be seen in the bright of the moon on that flat landscape. Scrambling up the rocks, they lay on their bellies and looked out into the desert.

'I see nothing,' Hereward said, his brow knitting.

'No. They are cunning, these sand people.' Pointing to a narrow track winding round the ridge, Sighard traced the almost invisible path it cut across the landscape. It came to a halt at a low mound. Hereward squinted. Though it blended into the grey background, now the other man had indicated it, he could see it was man-made.

'Come,' Sighard whispered. He crawled over the top of the ridge and slithered down the other side. Scanning once again for guards, the Mercian followed. The ridge hid all signs of the fire, the trees and the Imazighen camp. Hereward felt pleased, for that meant it hid them too. He loped across the open space with Sighard at his side, heading for a dark square on the side of the mound, a layer of branches and palm fronds.

'It is a frame of wood and leaves on which they have laid sand and rock to hide it,' the young warrior said as they came to a halt.

Hereward knelt and reached out to pull aside the square of fronds.

Sighard grabbed his wrist. 'Take care,' he whispered.

Drawing his sword, the Mercian let his hand hover over the fronds for a moment and then he snatched them aside. Beyond the roughly made door lay darkness.

A voice boomed out, babbling in an unfamiliar tongue.

Exchanging a look with Sighard, Hereward tightened his grip on Brainbiter. Though the words made no sense to him, the Mercian decided the voice had a swaggering tone. Arrogant. Unafraid, certainly.

'Do not waste your breath,' he called back into the dark. 'Your speech has all the meaning of a yapping dog.'

For a moment there was silence. Whoever hid in that shelter was evaluating this strange tongue. Then the voice boomed back, still brash, but this time in accented English. 'Come.

I see you there against a starry sky. Do not cower outside my home like a frightened girl. Enter. Bring all the torments your feeble mind can muster. You are no more to me than a horsefly.'

Stepping into that dark space seemed foolhardy. Hereward snorted. 'Who are you?'

'Who are *you*?'

'Hereward of the English.'

This time the pause was longer. 'English? Here?' For the first time the Mercian heard a note of uncertainty. 'And you stand with the Imazighen?'

'I am my own man.'

'If that is true, come closer, where I can see you.'

'And have my throat slit in the dark?' Hereward grinned without humour.

'I can no more slit a throat than scratch my nose. My wrists are bound. Come.'

For a moment, the Mercian weighed his response. Then, holding his blade before him, he eased through the hole and dropped into a chill, dry chamber dug out of the desert floor. Sighard fell beside him. Once his eyes had adjusted to the gloom, he saw the dark outline of a man lying on the ground, his back resting against the far wall. While Sighard stayed by the door to keep watch, Hereward stepped to one side so that the shaft of moonlight fell upon the captive.

At first, the Mercian saw only the grin. Here was a man who looked around his prison and saw only a king's hall, he thought. Although his hands were bound behind his back, the captive was lounging, seemingly at ease, his feet crossed and his head to one side as he surveyed his guest. His black hair curled down to his shoulders. A beard, once well clipped, now starting to straggle, framed a square jaw. His eyes were dark, but where the moonlight glinted in them Hereward saw a sardonic look. His shoulders were broad, his arm muscles hard. A fighting man, by the look of it. But no scars marred his skin. He could well have been one of the earls who fawned around the king in Wincestre. His tunic, once no doubt fine, was now stained with the dirt and sweat of his imprisonment. When Hereward glimpsed the border design of black squares, he was reminded of the clothes worn by the body staked out in the desert. On a finger of his right hand glittered an ornate gold signet ring with a ruby inlay. Hereward saw a fortune there, but the Imazighen had not seen fit to rob their prisoner.

'Hereward of the English,' the captive repeated, shaping each word.

'You have a name?'

'I do. Yes, I do. I am Maximos Nepos. My home is . . .' He looked around him and shrugged. 'Here. For now. But once it was the great city of Constantinople. Have you heard of that, English?'

'The home of eunuchs.'

Maximos pursed his lips. 'Do not take offence that I thought you ignorant. There are some who say the English are nothing but drunks, and lazy ones at that. They rolled over and bared their throats when the Normans danced to their door. I, of course, would never think such a thing.'

'Aye, we like our drink. And we like to be left alone. But prod us and you wake a sleeping bear.'

'In truth, I have not been known to turn down a goblet of wine myself.' He rolled on to his side and waggled his hands. 'A good deed would not go amiss.'

When Hereward did not move, Maximos sighed and rolled back. 'Brother, you wound me.'

'I would know that you are a brother before I set you free.' Hereward prowled around the captive, sizing him up. 'What crime has seen you shut away here in the dark?'

The other man gave a hollow laugh. 'My crime is being too trusting. I have wronged no man. But these desert people took me under their wing, with promises of food and shelter from the hot sun, and when my guard was down they brought me here.' He took a deep breath. 'At least I have been fed and wa-tered. A pig in a pen, but not yet ham.'

The Mercian crouched. He tapped the tip of his sword upon the captive's chest. 'And why were you allowed to keep your life?'

'I am worth more to the Imazighen alive. They think they can ransom me to my kin for gold to use in their war.'

'And your kin would pay for your neck?'

He shrugged, making light. 'They have some standing in Constantinople.'

'Wealth? Power?'

Maximos rolled his head, giving little away. 'If it would help, I am certain that they would dig deep into their coffers for any-one who brought home their favoured son.'

Hereward thought on this a moment. 'To find a place in the Varangian Guard for my men, that might sway me.'

'You drive a hard bargain.' He nodded. 'My mother has the ear of the emperor. And he does like his English sword-arms.'

'Aye, why spill the blood of good Constantinople men, when you have English to fight for you?'

Maximos laughed. 'We care little whether you are English, Norman, or Roman. Constantinople is not one of your English towns. Men and women from the four corners of the world gather there. Strange tongues babble in every street, in every inn. In time, you see that men are men and all that sets any apart is—'

'Honour.'

The captive nodded. 'Or lack of it. And in truth, though it pains me to say it, the English, and the Vikings too, are thought to have some skill in fighting. Fire in their hearts, more than any others.'

'Not only drunks, then.'

Maximos grinned. 'No. But I have your measure now.' He raised his eyebrow in silent questioning.

'One more thing.' With his foot, Hereward rolled the man

on to his side. He tapped the tip of his blade against the signet ring. 'In the desert, I came across another man who wore a ring like this.'

The captive jerked his head around, all humour gone from his features. 'Arcadius? What do you know of him?'

'I know he is dead. Staked out under the hot sun, a wound in his side. What was he to you?'

Maximos slumped back, bowing his head to the dusty ground. After a long moment of silence, he replied in a low voice, 'My friend. Since childhood we were rarely apart. He was like a brother.'

'It may not be him. I could not be certain the ring was the same . . .'

Maximos nodded at the kindness. He eased himself back up against the wall. 'We travelled here in search of adventure. Yes, gold and glory. Little did we know what awaited us.' Bitterness laced his final words and he looked up at the Mercian, his eyes burning in the moonlight. 'Know that the Imazighen cannot be trusted. Only lies issue from their smiling mouths.'

'Their queen, Meghigda, she has more enemies than friends, it would seem. I rescued her from a ship of sea wolves. What they wanted with her, I do not know and she will not say.'

The captive snorted. 'You freed her? A good deed that will only result in misery. But how could you have known her true face?' He paused, thinking. 'When the Imazighen attacked us while our guard was down, some of my men escaped the slaughter and carried a message from me to Constantinople. Meghigda does not realize what a storm she has unleashed. My kin . . . Arcadius' kin . . . they will not rest. They will pay any price to have their sons returned to them, or to see the queen and her people destroyed for the terrible crime they have committed.' Rolling on to his side once more, Maximos bared his bonds. 'Now. Free me. We can be away from here before—'

'I hear something,' Sighard hissed from the entrance.

Bounding to his spear-brother's side, Hereward cocked his head and listened.

'Hurry,' Maximos urged.

The Mercian silenced him with a raised hand. He could hear nothing. After a moment, Sighard gripped the edge of the entrance and hauled himself up. Barely had his head poked through the gap before hands grabbed him and wrenched him up into the desert night. His cry of surprise was cut short.

Stepping back, Hereward pointed the tip of his blade at the square of starry sky, but he knew it was already too late.

The stars disappeared as a head hove into view. Salih ibn Ziyad grinned at him, but his eyes glittered icily. 'You should have left well alone, Hereward of the English,' he said. 'But now you have doomed not only yourself, but all your men.'

CHAPTER FOURTEEN

The flames roared up towards the stars. Around the bonfire, the women danced to the pounding of the drums in a swirl of robes. Grinning men plucked at their stringed instruments or blew into the long, lowing tubes. The night breeze whisked up the billowing smoke and swept the fragrant scent of crisped lamb and spices across the camp.

Alric leaned back against a palm tree, his belly full for the first time since they had left England. The children had long since left him at peace, lured away by the food and the music. From under eyelids growing heavy, he watched the dancers. In and out of the whirling women Mad Hengist capered, laughing like a fool. As at ease as all the other men, the monk thought, his gaze turning to the hardened warriors lounging among the shadows of the swaying fronds. They had survived a shipwreck. They had overcome the brutal desert sun. Many of them were now starting to feel like their old selves, the ones who had challenged the might of the king with little more than a rag-tag army of earth-walkers at their backs. Drifting, he wondered if Hereward knew how much faith his spear-brothers placed in him. Perhaps it was best if he did not know. That burden would be too much for many men.

A strange noise rose up behind the music. Still dreaming, he cocked his head and half listened. It was those humped beasts that the desert people rode, blaring their irritation and stamping their two-toed feet.

His thoughts drifted. And they had been reunited, when he had started to feel all hope had been lost for their missing companions. He smiled to himself, surprised that he now looked fondly on men who had terrified and disgusted him when they had first met. God's world was filled with many mysteries.

The whisper of feet nearby. He opened one eye, but there were only the shivering moon shadows.

For some reason he could not explain, he felt unease creep up on him. His heart began to patter. In that floating state, he found himself back in the filthy hut in Ely, his blood leaking from the wound in his side. How he had survived, he did not know. And since that day, it seemed death had never been more than a few paces behind him.

A piercing whistle rang out across the camp. The drumming stopped, the music snapped off, the dancers ground to a halt.

Alric jerked alert as a silence fell across the lake, broken only by the crackle of the fire. For a moment, the world seemed to hold its breath. Nothing moved in the flickering orange light of the dancing flames. He glimpsed the frozen faces of the Imazighen, and the English warriors craning their necks, puzzled.

And then furious battle-cries echoed from all sides. As the women plucked up their robes and raced towards their tents, the fighting men of the desert people swept out of the shadows and fell upon the startled English. Jumping to his feet in horror, Alric felt his breath catch in his throat.

Amid high-pitched shrieking, the Imazighen warriors attacked from all sides. Their robes swirled around them. Curved swords glimmered as they whisked through the air. Hereward's men could do nothing but stare. Thinking they were among friends, they had abandoned their weapons in their tents. Most were dull from too much food, or, like Alric, half asleep.

The monk cried out. Where was Hereward? How could he have let his guard down sufficiently for such a thing to happen?

But before he could reach his friends, a blow struck the back of his head and he crashed to the dusty ground. Running feet thundered all about him. Dazed, he twisted his head around. An Imazighen warrior loomed over him, sword swung high over his head for the killing blow. Yet he did not strike. Instead, he babbled what sounded like a furious epithet in his strange tongue and thundered his foot into Alric's face.

The monk knew no more.

CHAPTER FIFTEEN

The red sun shimmered in the haze on the eastern horizon. The dawn breeze whipped the sand across the desert pan to the circle of warriors in their azure and ebony robes. At their centre knelt the English, hunched and rigid. Sweat dripped in the fast-rising heat. Beyond the whisper of the wind, all was silent.

From under hooded brow, Hereward looked up at his captors. Robes wavering in the breeze, they had pulled scarves across their mouths against the choking dust so that only their fierce eyes glowed beneath their *ghutrah* headcloths. In their burning stares, the Mercian could only see loathing for a hated enemy.

On the back of his neck, the blade bit deeper and he winced. A tall, powerfully built Imazighen warrior stood behind each spear-brother, pressing one of the cruel curved swords into his captive's flesh. Each executioner was stripped to the waist so that their fine robes would not be stained with the gushing of the blood. The Mercian could sense the swordsmen waiting for the order. Their bodies were tense, their gaze turned to where the queen, Meghigda, stood beside her trusted counsel. Her chin raised, she cast a cold eye over the humbled men.

Hereward held her gaze for a long moment, showing his contempt for this betrayal. She did not flinch.

'We will take your heads,' Salih ibn Ziyad said, one hand resting upon the silver knife hanging at his waist. His voice, though calm, cut through the moan of the wind. 'Your blood will drain into the sand, where it will mix with the blood of all our enemies.'

'How can you commit this crime? Hereward saved your life!' Alric exclaimed. As he glared at the queen, tears of frustration flecked his eyes.

Afraid that the monk's outburst would make him the first victim, Hereward raised his head against the sword and called, 'The churchman speaks true. Where would you be now if we had not rescued you from the clutches of your captors? Dead, most likely. Or standing on a slaver's block, on your way to becoming a whore for filthy sailors in some rat-filled port.' He felt his blood trickle down his back. Meghigda glowered at him. 'You brought us into your home, treated us like guests to bring our guard down,' he spat. 'You have no honour.'

'*You* have no honour,' Salih snapped, darting forward. He whipped out his knife and pressed the tip just beneath the Mercian's eye. 'While you filled your bellies, you bided your time. Would you have slit our throats while we slept?'

'This is madness,' Alric choked, his chin slumping to his chest. 'We have done no wrong.'

Salih dug his knife deeper. A bubble of blood formed. One twist and his eye would be gone, Hereward knew.

'Every word you say is a lie,' the wise man snarled. 'You are snakes, all of you.' For a moment he hesitated, and then he removed his knife and slotted it back into its scabbard. Pushing aside his anger, he looked down on the Mercian with cold contempt. 'You are here to save the worthless life of that Roman dog—'

Hereward frowned, realizing the wise man was talking

about the prisoner, Maximos Nepos. 'No man here knew that you kept him captive—'

'Lies!'

'He speaks the truth,' the voice of Maximos boomed out. The circle of warriors parted as he pushed his way to the front, hands still bound behind his back. No one would ever guess he had been a prisoner in a hole in the ground, so straight was his back and clear his eyes. 'Do you think my kin would have sent this English rabble to save my neck?' He grinned at the glowering spear-brothers. 'Take no offence, friends!'

Salih narrowed his eyes. 'The Varangian Guard—'

'Fights for the emperor,' Maximos retorted. 'However much my mother wishes she could command them to do her bidding, they would never obey the word of any of the Nepotes. These . . .' he prowled along the row of kneeling men, 'these are who they say they are. Outlaws, thrown out of their homeland, adrift on the seas of fate. Desperate to find gold or glory to fill the hollow in their hearts.'

Meghigda thrust her way forward, her eyes blazing. Hereward thought how strong she looked, an oak that would not be broken however powerful the gale. 'We can trust no one. No one!' she stormed. 'Our enemies are everywhere.' She glanced towards the lake where the women, children and old men were breaking up the tents, ready to move on. A line of the strange hump-backed animals, horses and mules waited on the edge of the trees, chewing lazily. 'We have been punished too many times for trusting. I . . . I have been . . .' The words choked in her throat and for a moment she trembled. 'And you . . .' she said to Maximos, her voice thick with contempt, 'you are the worst liar of them all.' Hereward glimpsed something in the glint in her eye, or the way she held the captive's gaze too long. There was a history there, he was sure; and a deep hurt.

The queen looked Maximos up and down and then spat at his feet. Striding away, she commanded, 'Kill them all.'

Along the line, the lengths of steel whisked up.

'Wait,' Hereward called. 'If some wrong has been done here, take my life only. These men obey my commands. They should not face your wrath—'

'No.' When Hereward jerked his head around, he saw that it was Sighard who had called out. 'I am at fault here.' He did his best not to show any fear, and Hereward felt proud of his spear-brother. 'I discovered your captive. I took Hereward there. You say you trust too much. I trusted too little. That is my crime. Take my head, if you will, and free the others.'

Meghigda looked along the line, frowning as she struggled to comprehend this sacrifice. For a moment her face softened. But then she caught Salih's eye and nodded. 'If we do not take our stand, we will be the Free no more. We will be slaves. Or worse. The time has passed for open hands and open arms. We have no friends anywhere, we see that now, and we must fight if we want to live to see another dawn.' She turned her back and began to walk away. 'Let us be done with this. Take their heads.'

As Salih strode forward to give the order, Hereward could see that any chance of escaping their fate had gone. Now there was only the ending, and that would be with honour. 'Hold fast, brothers,' he called. 'If we are to die, it will be as warriors, not mewling like babes.' He showed a defiant face to the wise man. 'Come. Be done with it.'

Salih bowed. Hereward saw no anger there, no hatred, no contempt. This was war. An act of survival from a people afraid that their days were passing. He could understand that.

The desolate wind moaned. The Imazighen watched, impassive. The glinting swords hung at the top of their arc.

Before Salih could utter the command, a drumbeat rolled across the arid wastes. In the distance, a cloud of dust billowed up, lit ruddy by the rising sun. Meghigda stopped and looked back, her brow furrowing. Hereward saw a shadow cross her features. Salih turned and peered towards the approaching rider, and all his men followed his gaze.

From the cloud of dust, the newcomer emerged. He was slumped across the neck of one of the hump-backed beasts, clinging on with what seemed to be only the weakest of grips. As it neared, it slowed its rolling gait until the rider tugged at the rope tied around its snout and brought it to a halt. He tried to clamber down, but could only manage to slide off into a heap upon the ground. His face was gashed, and dark patches stained his ragged robes. Reaching out one trembling arm, he croaked a few words in the Imazighen tongue.

Whatever he said, it had an instant effect upon the gathered warriors, and upon the queen too. Meghigda's jaw dropped and her face cracked with shock, and she ran back to join the men racing towards the fallen rider. Babbling, they circled him, no doubt demanding more information. His voice was too weak to be heard and Salih yelled for silence.

While the throng listened to the rustling words of the wounded man, Hereward glanced back. The blade above his neck wavered, the executioner distracted by the activity, as were all the other swordsmen. The Mercian's gaze flickered towards Sighard. His face was strained and Hereward knew he was thinking the same thing: when should they make their move.

Before any of them could act, another cloud of dust swirled up along the horizon, much larger than the one they had first seen. Though the English glimpsed it first, the Imazighen were soon pointing and jabbering. Salih tried to calm them, but Meghigda's anxious voice cut through the chaos. A moment later the desert people were running towards what remained of their camp. Unsure what to do, the executioners looked down at their captives. Their swords wavered again. But no order had been given, so finally they sheathed them and ran after their brothers.

Hereward pulled himself to his feet. Relief burst in the faces of his men. Exuberant laughter rolled out and they clapped each other on the shoulder, scarcely able to believe they had escaped their fate.

Alric stumbled up, beaming. 'God has smiled upon us once more,' he said.

'Save your cheers,' Maximos called. Growing silent, the English warriors eyed him with suspicion.

'You know their tongue?' Hereward demanded.

The Roman nodded. 'Some, at least.' He glanced back at the plume of dust. 'Their enemy attacks. The Banu Hilal, the tribe who take the coin of the great power to the east.'

Hereward watched the dust-cloud. In that flat landscape, there was no element of surprise. It would take long moments for the enemy force to reach the oasis. 'What scares the Imazighen so much? They knew this battle was coming.'

'Not so soon. They are not ready. Meghigda has been hiding here while she tries to forge alliances with other tribes. She strains every sinew to build a great force that will crush her enemies so completely that no one will dare attack again.'

'The rest of her men . . . ?'

'Her generals have ridden to the four corners to sway the minds of the other tribes.' Maximos flexed against his bonds like a dog straining to free itself. 'What you see here is all she has.'

The Mercian looked to the rising wall of dust and tried to guess what numbers could raise that cloud.

Mad Hengist pointed to the camp, his eyes dull with sanity at that moment. 'We cannot steal their beasts to ride away from here. Are we to try to escape on foot? We will not survive, you know that.'

'You always see more than any man here,' Hereward said as the other men gathered round. 'And will these Banu Hilal let us walk away? I wager they are here for a slaughter, and Imazighen or English will mean little to them. Blood is blood and it spills just the same.'

He eyed the Roman. Maximos grinned back. 'It seems our path has been mapped for us.'

CHAPTER SIXTEEN

Under the ruddy glare of the rising sun, the cloud of brown dust was sweeping across the desert waste. The earth drummed and blood-curdling battle-cries rang out as the Banu Hilal bore down upon the oasis.

Hereward and the English raced towards the cool shade under the swaying palms. Only confusion was waiting for them. The Imazighen warriors crashed among the trees and the scrubby bushes, scrambling to retrieve their weapons from what remained of the camp. The Mercian could see that they were unprepared, and fear had its grip upon them.

Frightened by the fearful expressions on the faces of the fighting men, the women ushered the children across the circle of vegetation to the column of heavily laden mules, horses and hump-backed beasts. It was too late for them, too late for all the Imazighen, Hereward knew. The attackers would carve through the fragmented defences in no time.

Salih ibn Ziyad ordered his men to their positions along the tree-line. Meghigda stood beside him, her shield already on her arm and her sword in her hand. As the English ran up, the wise man whipped out his curved knife. 'Fate has granted you mercy,' he snarled. 'Do not throw it away.'

Ten Imazighen warriors darted in front of the queen and her counsel, their swords levelled. Staring down that length of steel, Hereward said, 'We will fight alongside you.'

Salih snorted. 'Do you think us fools? We should hand you weapons so you can slay us while our backs are turned? Away now, or my men will cut you down where you stand.' His gaze flickered towards the approaching plume of dust. He could not afford to be distracted. Nor could he afford a battle that would further deplete his forces, the Mercian could see that.

'Time is short, Salih ibn Ziyad,' he pressed. 'Your numbers are few, and here you have the fiercest warriors in all England ready to stand by your side. Arm us. You have my word that we will not betray you.'

As he watched the enemy drawing near, desperation contorted the wise man's face. The Mercian stepped into Meghigda's line of vision. 'We have a common enemy here. The Banu Hilal will never let us walk away from this place.' When he saw her hesitation, he added, 'We are your only hope.'

Meghigda glared past him at Maximos. For a moment, hurt stung her features. 'You are dogs, all of you. You cannot be trusted. You . . . *you* cannot be trusted.' Overcome with passion, she thrust her way through the line of men and swung her sword up to the Roman's chest.

Maximos pressed against the tip of the blade. Looking her full in the eye, he said, 'I know you think I have wronged you. Perhaps I have. But the words that passed between us remain. Punish me if you will, but do so later.' He flashed a grin. 'But first let us make sure we have days yet to come in which to continue our argument.'

Meghigda held his gaze for a moment longer and then whirled. Striding towards her warriors, she called back, 'We stand together and die together. But if I see any sign of betrayal I will command my men to turn on you, even if it means showing their backs to the Banu Hilal.'

Salih scowled, unhappy with his queen's decision. But he

pointed to where her tent had been and said, 'There is a pit hidden there. A store of weapons for when we might need them. Take what you need. Do not betray us, Hereward of the English.' His eyes glittered as he looked at the Mercian, his words heavy with implied threat.

Once the English warriors had thrown off the covering of branches, palm fronds and sand, they dragged out the spears and axes that had been taken from them, and the long shields covered in white hide. Racing back to the edge of the trees, they pushed their way through the milling Imazighen warriors. At the front, the slaves knelt with their bows. On the flanks waited the meagre cavalry, a handful of riders on ponies, each one armed with an iron lance.

'Is this all they have?' Kraki grunted, turning up his nose at the small force.

'They have their wits,' Maximos replied. He rubbed his wrists where his bonds had been cut. 'You may be surprised.'

Hereward shielded his eyes against the sun's glare. The air was filled with thunder now, but he could see in the dust-cloud that the force was not as overwhelming as he had imagined.

Sweeping his silver dagger in the air, Salih bellowed in the tongue of the desert people. The riders kicked their heels into the ponies' flanks and the cavalry pounded away.

Racing back to his queen, the wise man began to jabber, waving his arms in an imploring manner. 'He wants Meghigda to leave with the women and children and old men,' Maximos said, listening.

Hereward watched fury contort the woman's face. Though he caught nothing of what she shouted, he understood her meaning: she was a leader – she would stand or fall with her army. He was surprised to see Maximos dart over. 'You must do as Salih ibn Ziyad advises,' the Roman said.

'I am al-Kahina,' she snapped. 'I will not let my men think I have abandoned them.'

'They will never doubt you, you know that. They will die to

see you safe. Whatever happens this day, your people will need a leader who can carry on the fight against your enemies.'

Gritting her teeth, Meghigda bowed and marched away. She glanced back once at Maximos before the Imazighen warriors surrounded her.

A roar went up from the fighting men. Hereward spun round to see the cavalry bearing down upon the enemy. They were too few – they would be cut down in an instant. But at the last, the Imazighen lancers brought their steeds around along the enemy line and urged them back towards the oasis.

A furious roar from the Banu Hilal rang out above the drumming of hooves as they saw they had put fear into their foes. They had them now. Hereward glanced at Salih. The wise man watched intently, unconcerned that his men had turned tail. As the cavalry thundered back to their lines, he shouted an order and the riders dug in their heels, urging the ponies to leap as one. Landing with grace, they continued on their way. The Banu Hilal were hard at their backs.

Rigid, the Imazighen warriors held their breath as they faced the approaching army. And then a resounding cheer rose up when chaos descended upon the enemy horsemen. As if they had been struck by an unseen weapon, the first row crashed down in a confusion of flailing limbs and frightened neighing. Riders were thrown across the rocky desert floor. Necks snapped, arms twisted. The earth itself seemed to be consuming the horses.

Hereward nodded with approval. Salih and his generals had been clever. The oasis was protected by a system of hidden ditches.

Salih grinned, his teeth white against his black bristles. He bellowed another command. The row of kneeling archers stood, nocked their shafts and snapped their bowstrings. A volley of arrows soared up against the blue sky and rained down hard on the milling enemy ranks. The screams of the wounded and the dying echoed across the wasteland.

The wise man nodded, pleased with his handiwork. With a high-pitched scream, he swept his arm over his head. His warriors roared a full-throated battle-cry and raced forwards.

Whirling, Hereward snatched Alric's arm. 'This battle will be brutal. It is no place for a churchman,' the Mercian shouted. 'Go with the queen. Watch out for her – and the children.' He knew the final exhortation would leave the cleric's protests stillborn. 'We will find you once this battle is done.'

Once he was sure his friend was safe, Hereward spun back to his men and yelled, 'Let us show these desert people how we fight in England!'

The Imazighen were skilled with their weapons, but there was no shape to their attack. They swarmed at their enemy from all sides. Swords hacked, shields splintered. But often as not they blocked the lines of their brothers in the confusion. Brutal they were for certain, and effective to a degree, but they lost more men than they needed. And soon, he knew, the Banu Hilal's greater numbers would begin to tell.

Now the Imazighen cavalry struck like daggers to the heart of the roiling mass of foes. Iron lances plunged through chests. Dark-skinned fighters screamed as they twitched and died on the skewers. But they were too few. As the remaining riders of the Banu Hilal got their mounts under control, the Imazighen's horsemen were driven back.

'This will be a slaughter in no time,' Sighard shouted as the English reached the edge of the battle. 'And we will be in the centre of it.'

'Then let us not forget all we learned in our long fight against William the Bastard,' Hereward replied. 'Shield wall!'

His men surged into place with Hereward at the centre. Shields slotted into place, spears bristling out. Over the wooden rim, the Mercian watched their enemies as the wall advanced. The Banu Hilal had seen nothing like this. Their flowing robes were black, as were the headdresses and the scarfs tied across their mouths to keep out the whipping sand. In their framed eyes, wide and white, the Mercian saw incredulousness at first, then mockery for this strange breed who advanced behind a wall of wood and hide.

One warrior let out a gleeful battle-cry. Leaping towards the English, he swung his *akouba* above his head. Guthrinc braced himself as the blade thundered into his shield. The sword bit deep. As the scowling desert warrior struggled to wrench it free, a spear burst through a gap in the wall and rammed through his gut. His eyes widened in disbelief. By the time the spear tore free, he was dead.

Across his range of vision, Hereward saw the Banu Hilal pause as they tried to comprehend this strange attack.

'Forward!' he yelled. 'Let us take this fight into the heart of these dogs!'

Keeping their heads low, the English drove their shield wall into the thick of the battle. Spears lanced out, slashing tendons, punching through ribcages. Without mail-shirts or armour of any kind, these desert warriors were vulnerable in any fight.

But as he looked around Hereward could see that his spear-brothers were at just as great a disadvantage. The enclosing shields had formed an oven and the English sweltered in the suffocating heat. Stinging sweat blinded them. Dust choked their noses and mouths. He sensed some of his men beginning to falter.

'Fight on,' he urged. 'There will be enough water to slake any thirst once we have won.'

But near the edge of the shield wall, Bedric stumbled and fell. In an instant, an iron lance rammed through his chest. The Mercian winced as if the killing blow had taken his own life. Bedric had once been a scop, entertaining earls and kings with his recitations. A gentle man who had picked up the spear to help defend Ely. He would be mourned.

'Close the wall!' Hereward roared as their enemies bore down upon the gap. The shields locked together just in time. Blade after blade crashed against them.

On the English pressed, carving a path through the startled Banu Hilal. Bodies fell on all sides. With a heavy heart, the Mercian watched two more of his men die: Ceolbald, a dour warrior from the cold north; and Hardwin, who trapped fowl better than any man there.

Squinting through the wind-whipped sand, Hereward glimpsed one foe who seemed braver than most. He was tall, perhaps two heads on Hereward himself. A broad scar cut across the bridge of his nose. He had torn away the scarf that covered his mouth, and when his eyes locked on the Mercian's he gave a gap-toothed grin that showed he was unafraid of this strange breed of warriors.

With a whooping battle-cry, he charged. His *akouba* flew around his head in a shimmer of dazzling sunlight. When he brought it down, Hereward was all but crushed to his knees by the jarring impact. His shield cracked, splinters of wood flying out, but it held. Sighard jabbed his spear through the wall but the tribesman danced out of reach, jabbering in a tone that could only have been mockery.

When the warrior attacked again, Hereward set his shoulder hard against his shield. The sword boomed against wood and hide like a wave crashing on the beach. More shards spewed up. The shield would not last much longer under such blows, Hereward knew. Quickly, he uttered a command to the men around him.

The desert warrior flexed his muscles ready for his third strike. The Mercian held his gaze, silently taunting. The tribesman's eyes narrowed, his laughter draining away. With another high-pitched whoop, he whirled the sword around his head and threw himself forward.

At the last, Hereward yelled. The men behind him eased back, and he pulled away from the wall. As his enemy's sword whisked down, the point skimmed down the surface of the shield and bit into the desert floor.

Hereward lunged. Hooking his axe into the man's side, he

yanked it forward, tearing the flesh. Howling, the tribesman staggered. Seizing his moment, the Mercian hacked at his neck. So strong were the towering warrior's sinews that it took two more strikes to cut deep and even then Hereward could not free the head from the body.

His eyes rolling back, the tribesman crashed down into the sand.

'Cunning,' Sighard said from behind his shield.

'A strong arm is not enough,' Hereward replied. 'Sharp wits win battles.'

The death of their formidable brother seemed to drive the Banu Hilal into an even wilder frenzy. With blood-curdling shrieks, wave after wave crashed down upon the English. A storm of swords thundered upon the shields, the bodies pressing tighter on all sides.

Hereward's ears were dulled by the clash of swords, the shriek of the strange, high-pitched battle-cries, the screams of the dying, the constant drumming of hooves as the battling cavalry circled the field of war. Underfoot, the sand churned into thick mud with the blood and piss of the wounded. So many bodies littered the desert around them that they could not move without tripping over the remains. And so they stood their ground as the waves crashed against them, unable to advance, unable to retreat.

Blinking the filthy sweat from his eyes, Hereward glanced at the hardened faces of his men on either side. Heads bowed in the shade of their shields, they thrust their spears between the gaps in the wall. If he were to die this day, he felt proud to be alongside his brothers.

After what seemed an age, he looked up and saw a broad space among the chaos of the fighting. He could barely believe how few of the Banu Hilal remained. The Imazighen knew victory was within their grasp. Somehow they found new energy, striking harder, faster.

Hereward glimpsed Salih ibn Ziyad, confident and controlled

in the heat of the fighting. He swung a sword with his right arm, and with his left he slashed his silver dagger across the throats of his staggering victims. And beyond the wise man, a hellish apparition loomed. For a long moment, Hereward could not comprehend what he was seeing. But then he realized it was Maximos Nepos, slicked from head to toe in the blood of his victims, laughing like a madman as he swung his double-edged sword. So strong was his arm, it looked as though he was scything corn in the fields of England. Ceaselessly, untiring, he reaped his crop of bodies.

A cry spiralled up into the cloudless sky, undulating for a moment before dying away. Waving their swords in front of them, the Banu Hilal backed away from the men they faced, and then spun on their heels and raced away. On the edge of the battlefield, the circling riders, too, brought up their steeds and sent them galloping back towards the eastern horizon.

A cacophony of whoops and shrieks rang out from the Imazighen. The men waved their swords in the air, and held high their shields.

Exhausted, the English warriors slumped to the ground. To a man, they looked up at Hereward, scarcely able to believe they had survived that day.

'Life is good, brothers,' the Mercian roared. 'Drink deep.' He glanced around the corpse-littered land and nodded with pride. 'We turned the tide of this battle. We . . . the English. The Imazighen will be in our debt now. Good fortune comes our way and we will seize it with both hands.'

CHAPTER SEVENTEEN

The distant shrieks of the dying ebbed away. The clash of steel ended, and the rumble of hooves faded into the distance. On his mule, Alric turned and shielded his eyes against the glare of the sun. The oasis was a dark smudge on the horizon at the end of the long, straight trail the caravan had carved across the rolling dunes. Was the battle over? And who had won?

He muttered a prayer and promised himself he would think of it no more. Hereward had faced greater odds before and he had survived. It was in God's hands now, and if the Lord thought fondly of his good works here upon the earth, he would be reunited with his friend soon enough.

Turning back, the monk looked along the column of laden beasts, and the white-bearded old men on their horses, as upright as young warriors. The women and children walked alongside, seemingly oblivious of the merciless heat. The undulating line snaked on, moving at a steady pace beneath the azure sky. The only sound was the smacking of the men's lips as they chewed their mash of foul brown leaves, pausing every now and then to spit a clot upon the earth.

The desert out here was not so flat. Fewer rocks and more of the sweeping waves of sand that sucked at a man's feet. Alric grimaced. Oh to be back in Ely, with the rain drumming on the church roof and the north wind swirling leaves across the reeking marshlands. He felt a brief ache for simpler times. This hellish place would be the death of him.

Ahead of him rode the queen. Her back was straight, her chin raised. She had never looked back, even when the screams and the sounds of the fighting were at their loudest.

Alric dug his heels into the mule's flank, urging it alongside Meghigda's pony. She did not look down at him. Her gaze was fixed upon the distant horizon.

'What Hereward said was true,' he ventured. 'He will fight alongside your people unto the end.' When she still did not acknowledge his presence, he added, 'He is a good man.'

'So you say,' she replied in a dismissive voice.

'So I swear, as God is my witness.'

This time she eyed him, looking him up and down as if measuring his very worth. 'I have trusted men from beyond the sea before. They are all *good men*. But then they shed their skins, as all snakes do, and the truth is revealed.'

Alric felt surprised by her command of English and wondered how much else she kept from her guests, but he passed no judgement. 'Not all men from beyond the sea are the same.'

She sniffed, looked away.

'The betrayal you feel . . . You speak of Maximos Nepos.'

Meghigda glared at him. 'Enough. I will not hear his name spoken in front of me.'

The monk wondered what the Roman could have done to create the depth of hurt he saw in the queen's eyes. 'Hereward speaks highly of you,' he said, changing the subject.

She narrowed her eyes. 'He does?'

'You are a good leader of men, he says. Strong. Just. You are not like our own King William, who would see all England burned to the ground to achieve his heart's desire. Your people have placed their faith in you, and you have accepted it.' He paused. 'You would die for them?'

'Of course.'

The monk nodded, pleased. 'That is rare. But good.'

With a slender hand, Meghigda unfastened the scarf from her mouth and let it fall away. For an instant, Alric thought how sad she looked. 'I was but a girl when I took up the sword of the Imazighen. It has been my life, and I was prepared for it from the moment I came into this world. In our tent, the one my father and my father's father and my father's father's father had carried across the hot lands, I would sit upon my mother's knee and hear the stories of my people. Stories of pain and blood and suffering. Since the time when we first walked the sands, we have looked to the east and the invaders who want to bring us to our knees and make us slaves. We have never been beaten. Never!' Her eyes sparked with passion.

'And now you must fight yet another war.'

She snorted. 'This is no hardship. Battle . . . that is the soul of the Imazighen. When I had seen eight years pass, raiders came to our camp. They killed my father. And my young sister. And they cut off my mother's head and set it on the floor of our tent, and made me stare into her eyes all night. Oh, how they laughed!'

Alric winced.

'And when six more years had passed,' she continued in a quiet voice, 'I led my men across the sands until I found them. And with my own knife I cut them open and left them under the sun for the birds to eat. Left them alive, so they could think on the crimes they had committed before they stood before God.' She looked at him, her face drained of all emotion. 'I am al-Kahina.'

The monk felt chilled by what he saw there.

From up ahead, shouts and cries echoed through the still air. The disturbance rippled along the column.

Meghigda frowned. 'What now? We must reach the rest of my men before dusk to warn them of the Banu Hilal.' Before she could investigate, warriors swarmed over the rolling dunes on both sides. Alric gasped. He had seen no sign that anyone had waited there. His shock burned even brighter when he saw that these were not the desert people. Their skin was pale.

Before the Imazighen could react, arrows showered down. Crossbow bolts thumped into faces and chests of men, women and children too. Horses and mules and the hump-backed beasts cried and fell and thrashed as the shafts lashed into them. Screams filled the hot air.

Old men plunged backwards down the brown drifts, trailing glittering arcs of blood. The survivors ran aimlessly, but the attackers seemed to be everywhere. A spear rammed through the back of a fleeing woman. An axe slashed the chest of an old man as he thrust a short-bladed knife. Everywhere the Imazighen fell. The caravan broke up, the surviving beasts thundering away into the wastes.

Aghast at the slaughter, Alric called upon God to help these poor souls, to no avail. He watched as Meghigda drove her pony into the fray. Snarling and spitting like a wildcat, she drew her sword. But she was one and her foes were many, and all the fighting men had been left behind. The monk's heart fell as warriors surged around her, forcing her mount to a halt. Once, twice, she hacked down into skulls and shoulders, but then hands caught her wrist and she was dragged from her pony. A cheer rang out from the warriors as she disappeared from view.

Alric felt rough hands yank on his arm and hurl him to the ground. Dust filled his mouth and stung his eyes. As he flailed, feet thundered into his ribs, his stomach, his head. For a moment, the world spun into darkness.

When he came round, he was being dragged across the sand. Craning his neck, he saw the bodies of the old men littering the dunes, their blood already turning brown in the heat. Only a

handful of the women and their children had survived. Wailing, they knelt in a circle under the cold gaze of their captors.

'Who are you?' the monk gasped.

A hard boot in his gut ended his questions.

Relief flooded him when he saw that Meghigda had survived. Small surprise if she was as valuable as he had been told.
Head bowed, she knelt, the tip of a sword pressed into the back
of her neck. But Alric could see that her face was contorted
with loathing.

'Be strong,' he called to her.

Glancing at him, she spat a clot of blood into the sand. 'Let
the monk live,' she called. 'He is a man of God.'

'I know full well who the monk is. We are old friends.'

Alric flinched at the strangely familiar voice. Squinting
against the glare of the boiling sun, he searched for the speaker,
but only silhouettes hovered before his eyes. 'Who is there?' he
asked.

Laughter rolled out. A figure swaggered forward and set its
fists upon its hips. As the man moved to block the sun, his
features fell into relief. He was tall and strong, his hair shaven
at the back in the Norman manner. Playful eyes surveyed the
churchman, a grin falling easily upon the lips. 'My name is
Drogo Vavasour, monk.'

Alric frowned. 'You are not the one who spoke.'

Another figure wriggled forward, and the churchman all
but recoiled at the sight of the ravaged features of Ragener the
Hawk. 'You live,' he gasped.

'God chose to raise me up from the jaws of death, monk, and
he watches over me now. You cannot harm Ragener.'

Before he could begin to understand how the sea wolf had
survived those turbulent seas, Drogo wagged a finger at him. 'I
had heard that Hereward, the last of the English, travelled with
a monk.'

Alric showed a defiant face. 'You know of us.'

'Aye. Tales of the rebels and their dark deeds in the English fenlands have spread far and wide. Your names are known by many. Even yours, monk. Murderers and thieves to a man.'

The churchman glared. Drogo laughed silently.

'See,' Ragener gushed. 'I told you Hereward was here.'

''Twas hard to believe, so far from his home,' the Norman said with a slow nod. 'But if the monk is here, the English dog cannot be far behind.'

'What care you about Hereward?' Alric said. 'The rebellion is long over. England is lost. The king himself spared our lives and sent us out across the whale road.'

For an instant, Drogo's eyes hardened, but he hid his thoughts before Alric could read them. 'England is lost, that is true, and I would not give that dark, wet land another thought. What lies between Hereward and me is . . .' he looked out across the wastes, choosing his words, 'a matter of blood. One that can only be ended with your friend's death.'

'You waste your breath,' Meghigda snarled. When she looked up at her captors, Alric was impressed to see there was no fear in her face, though she must have known what hardships lay ahead for her. 'Even now he fights with my army, even now as more warriors arrive to swell our force.' She cast a contemptuous look across the war-band. 'This . . . You would challenge us with this few. You will be torn apart before you can even cry for mercy.'

Ragener's eyes flickered towards the Norman commander, sensing the doubt. 'Do not listen to her! You are Normans, the greatest warriors known to man. A few barbarians like her . . .' He spat at the queen. 'They will be no match for you.'

'But if she is right . . .' Drogo mused.

'She is right.' Alric set his jaw. 'The army of the Imazighen is great indeed. You risk everything if you try to attack them.'

Ragener lashed out with his one hand, cuffing the monk across his cheek. Alric saw stars.

'Hold,' the Norman said in a light tone. 'I have waited long to look in Hereward's eyes. A little longer will make no difference. We have our prize.' He eyed Meghigda. 'If what you say is true, she will earn a fine reward.' He looked down at Alric, smiling. 'And if what I have heard of that English dog is true, he will not abandon even one of his men. It seems God has smiled on you too, monk, for your days will not end here. What say you, Ragener?'

The sea wolf seemed to read the intent in the other man's words for his eyes sparked with glee. 'Aye. Here is judgement indeed. His master took my hand. Now I will take a part of him, and another, and another, until there is nothing left, and I will leave a trail for Hereward to find. The rebel leader will come to us soon enough, Drogo, that I can tell you. And then you can have your revenge.'

CHAPTER EIGHTEEN

The figure staggered across the blasted waste. The moaning wind whipped at his ochre robes and snagged in his white beard. Swirls of sand whirled around him, but he kept his head high, his eyes clear, as he focused on his destination.

'Another enemy?' Sighard asked, shielding his eyes against the gritty sand caught in the breeze. He was caked in blood, some of it even his own. His long hair was matted with the filth and the sweat, and his legs trembled with exhaustion. For too long after the battle they had laboured, helping the wounded back to the oasis where Salih ibn Ziyad oversaw their treatment. The bodies of the fallen were dragged to a pyre where they could at least be sent into the arms of God. All any of them wanted was to wash away the gore and rest.

'Too old,' Hereward replied as he studied the lurching figure. 'And the Banu Hilal will be licking their wounds. They would not dare attack so soon after we sent them fleeing.'

Cracking his knuckles, Maximos Nepos strode up. Somehow he had found the time to wash himself in the lake, and he looked as fresh as if he had woken from a long sleep. 'That is one of the Imazighen elders,' he said, frowning. 'He rode with Meghigda.'

'He is wounded,' the Mercian exclaimed. Before the others could respond, he was racing out from the shade of the palm trees towards the approaching figure. By the time he reached the old man, Maximos had caught up with him. Hereward could see that his first impression had been right. Blood from numerous wounds blackened the elder's robes, though none seemed life-threatening. However, he was weak from his trek under the midday sun and he all but collapsed into the arms of the two men.

'Ask him what has happened,' Hereward commanded after they had lowered him to the ground, but before Maximos could speak Salih darted up and knelt beside the old man. Anxious, he reached out pleading hands and whispered in the tongue of the desert people.

The elder moistened his cracked lips and croaked his response. Salih listened, his face growing grimmer by the moment. When he looked up at the other two men, his voice was almost lost beneath the whine of the wind. 'The caravan was attacked by warriors with skin as pale as yours. They took al-Kahina . . .'

'The bounty upon her head,' Maximos said, nodding. 'The self-same sea wolves who stole her before. We should have guessed they would return. That much gold . . .' He swallowed his words when he saw Salih bow his head and cover his eyes in despair. Turning to Hereward, the Roman added in a whisper, 'They must have waited until the Banu Hilal attacked, knowing that our eyes would be averted.'

Hereward could barely hear the other man's words. Only one thought burned in his mind. 'The others,' he demanded. 'What of the others?'

'Slaughtered, all of them. May God go with their souls,' Salih murmured. He looked up, adding, 'Except your friend. They took him too.'

Hereward felt a rush of relief, but it passed quickly. Why would the sea wolves kill all but Alric? That he could not understand.

The old man croaked more strange words to Salih, then held out his right hand and unfurled his fingers. In his palm nestled a small pouch made of hide. As the elder continued to speak, Salih's eyes widened and he could not seem to tear his gaze away from that pouch.

'What is amiss?' the Mercian asked.

'The man who took your friend, and al-Kahina, is known to you. He has a ruined face.'

The blood thundered in Hereward's ears. Ragener?

Plucking up the pouch between thumb and forefinger, Salih held it out. 'Mundir says this ruined man bade him seek you out in return for his life. He sent you this, as a message. It belonged to your friend.'

In his head, Hereward felt the blood hammer harder still, drowning out the sound of the wind. Taking the pouch, he weighed it for a moment. Too light to contain much of import. He tipped it up and emptied the contents on to the sand.

A finger lay there, Alric's finger, the end ragged and bloody where the knife had sawn through the flesh and bone.

The blood surged through him in a torrent, pushing out the desert and the other men, closing in upon his vision. In that red world he could hear his devil whispering to him, demanding vengeance.

For the next few moments, he had no idea what he did. When his vision cleared and the pulsing subsided, he found Maximos and Sighard gripping his arms and wrestling to hold him back. Brainbiter lay on the ground beside the severed finger. The old man was sprawled on his back, his face contorted in terror.

Salih pressed his fingertips against the Mercian's chest. 'Calm yourself, my friend,' he was urging. 'There will be time enough for vengeance. Your enemy taunts you, but think, think . . . he could have sent your friend's head.'

As Hereward calmed, his wits sharpened. 'Ragener lures us on, but where? North, south, east or west? There must be more. Ask Mundir. Press him. That dog will want us on his trail.'

With a nod, Salih squatted beside the old man and once again questioned him. As the elder dredged up what fragments he could find in his aged memory, the wise man's face fell.

'The ruined man was aided by Normans,' Salih said when he was done. 'A seasoned war-band, so Mundir says, and well armed too.'

'Normans? Here?'

'In time, all who seek riches and power pass through the land of the Imazighen,' the wise man replied with a cold smile.

Hereward cursed under his breath. Would he never be done with the bastard king's bastard men?

'They have taken the queen and your friend with them, to Sabta. Do you know this place?'

'Aye,' the Mercian replied, his brow wrinkling as he remembered, 'I have heard tell of it, in Flanders, when I sold my right arm and axe for coin. But . . . what . . .' He shook his head. 'Tell me why it troubles you so.'

'Sabta is a city of thieves and murderers. When the caliph fell in the year of my birth, God, too, abandoned that place, so it is said. There are no laws there except the law of the sword. No honour, only greed. No beauty, only decay. The traitorous dogs have gone to Sabta because they know they cannot be touched there. Walk through the city gates and you will never walk out.'

CHAPTER NINETEEN

The candles on the altar guttered. Shadows flew across the body slumped on the marble steps leading to God's table. In the dark pool around the corpse, stars glimmered. Though Constantinople slumbered under the blanket of a hot night, in that vast, dark church the sound of running feet rang out. Fearful whispers echoed and the wailing of the monks soared up to the vaulted roof.

Wulfrun strode along the nave to the edge of the wavering circle of candlelight. Surveying the twisted remains, he muttered, 'A wild beast attacked him?'

'You would think,' Ricbert murmured at his side. He rubbed a hand across his mouth, as much to hide his uneasiness as to wipe the sweat from his upper lip. 'Look closer. You will see he has been stabbed. Not once, but a hundred times. A thousand times. A frenzy . . .' He choked back on the word. 'Yes. A wild beast.'

Wrinkling his nose at the reek of the blood in the heat, Wulfrun prowled around the body. From the tunic, he could see it was a man, though it lay face down. But so much blood had matted the hair and stained the clothes, and the skin was so ragged from the fury of the attack, he could not guess at

141

the age. He glanced around the dark belly of the church to ensure they could not be overheard. Gold gleamed everywhere, crosses and chalices and leaf. In the shadows of the far wall, the cowering monks knelt in supplication, their hands thrown up to the heavens. Turning slowly, Wulfrun surveyed the stone columns, the worn mosaics, the dark alcoves. As far as he could tell, no one observed them. But in that city he knew one was never far from spying eyes.

The monastery of St George of Mangana kept its secrets close among its whispered prayers. It was no accident that this gleaming seat of worship stood so near to the imperial palace. Power lay here. Those who claimed to speak for God could move the minds of men, great and small, Wulfrun knew.

'He is the one you were supposed to meet?' the commander asked.

Ricbert nodded. 'John. He was my eyes and ears here among the godly. And the not so godly. He sent word that he wished to meet this even, as a matter of great urgency.'

'He had heard some news of a plot? Against the emperor?'

Ricbert shrugged.

Crouching beside the body, Wulfrun watched the blood seep along the joints of the steps. 'This was a desperate act, so soon before you were to meet. The murderer risked discovery.'

'Aye, desperate. If his name was to be spoken here, he had no choice.'

'One stab would have done the task. Silence. Stealth. The body could have been hidden, and none the wiser. Why this . . . this butchery?' Pushing himself up, Wulfrun felt the weight of his office upon his shoulders. These days there was no rest. Plots were everywhere, always. Sometimes he yearned for the heat of battle, the blood pumping through his head, the juice of the toadstools singing in his veins.

His gaze fell upon spatters of blood leading away from the altar to a large door of dark wood. In the gloom, it was almost invisible.

'Come,' he said.

The two guardsmen followed the trail. Through the door, a corridor led past a maze of silent rooms to the cloister and a fragrant garden, where two spectral figures walked among the trees. Wulfrun felt a prickle of suspicion when he recognized them. Nathaniel was one of the senior monks, a tall, ascetic man with thin lips, sallow skin and a frame like a newly exhumed corpse. He was also Victor Verinus' younger brother, and he commanded as much influence within the church as his sibling did in the profane world. But where Victor spoke loudly, Nathaniel whispered of sins and salvation and bent men to his will in this life with the seduction and threats of the next.

The one who walked beside him had seen perhaps fifteen summers. A thatch of russet hair topped a face as pale as the moon, and as still as a mill-pond. His eyes were dark and unnaturally large. Justin was Victor's son, the product of a roll with a Frankish whore, so tongues whispered. Victor kept the lad away from public scrutiny as much as he could, and never took him near the court. But since news had surfaced of the death of his favoured son, Arcadius, Justin was all he had left to see his legacy grow down the years.

'That boy unsettles me,' Ricbert muttered. 'I feel I should cross myself, or spit to ward off the evil eye.'

'He is a boy, no more,' the commander replied. He raised one arm and called out, 'Hold.'

'The Varangian Guard? Here, in our monastery?' Nathaniel said, turning. The monk pressed the palms of his hands together as if in prayer. 'To what do we owe this great honour?'

'There has been murder, in the church. You have not heard?'

'I heard someone had fallen and bashed out his brains upon the steps. But murder? No!' A faint sibilance licked around his words. He pressed the tips of his fingers to his lips. 'Who would kill in a house of God?'

'In Constantinople?' Ricbert laughed without humour.

When the commander eyed him, he flashed an apologetic look, feigned though it was.

'You have seen no one passing through here with a weapon? The killer would have been soaked in blood, so frenzied was the attack,' Wulfrun said.

'No one. There has been only peace in this garden as we discussed God's plan for us all.' Nathaniel looked around. 'And I see no blood here. The murderer must have left by another path.'

'You, boy. Did you hear cries? Running feet?'

Justin cast a blank look among the trees as if deep in thought. When he spoke, his voice was dreamy. 'I heard an owl hoot. Perhaps this was the work of a witch.'

Nathaniel laughed and tousled the lad's hair. Wulfrun thought the churchman let his fingers linger there for a moment too long. 'When we speak of God, we are lost to his wonders. The ground could shake, and this monastery fall, and we would not know.'

A pale figure appeared among the shadows at the end of the garden; a girl, a year or two older than Justin. Her greasy hair hung limply around a gaunt face, and she wore a plain dress that was threadbare and smudged with ashes. She beckoned.

'Ariadne,' the boy exclaimed.

Nathaniel's face darkened. 'You should not be here,' he snapped. 'If the abbot sees you—'

'My father wishes to speak to you.'

'This is your sister?' Wulfrun asked.

Justin nodded.

As she stepped out into a pool of silvery moonlight, Wulfrun saw that bruises dappled her face and her bottom lip was split. He had heard tell that, even more than Justin, Victor had kept the girl hidden away. She had little value to him. The Stallion valued no woman, perhaps no man either, only the power that could be earned through their devices.

'I must go,' Nathaniel said. 'May God guide your hand and

your heart, Wulfrun.' He hurried away with Justin trailing at his heels. When he reached the girl, he clipped her cheek with the back of his hand and snarled some words under his breath.

Wulfrun watched them disappear into the dark. The Verini spun their web wide, and the strands seemed to reach into all parts of Constantinople.

'The lad's hair was wet. He has bathed,' he mused.

'To wash the blood off him?'

Wulfrun shrugged. He could not imagine a boy committing so frenzied a murder, but there were stranger things abroad. With plots circling like ravens over a battlefield, he could afford to rule out nothing.

'You think the Verini have designs upon the crown?'

'I would put nothing beyond Victor Verinus.'

'Then we should speak to him.' Ricbert smiled without humour. 'Quietly, but backed with the sharpness of a blade.'

Wulfrun bowed his head, reflecting for a moment. He wished he was wiser, like his father. 'No,' he said eventually. 'Not yet. Victor is a clever man. If we speak too soon, he will cover his path and we will never find where it leads.'

'But if we leave it too late . . .' the smaller man began. He let the words hang.

'And Victor is a powerful man. He has chosen his allies well and placed them in positions where they can aid him. If we move too soon, it could be our heads that roll.'

Wulfrun tried to clear his head of all emotion. That was the way of the Varangian Guard. The only heat to be felt was in battle. And yet he could not push Juliana's face out of his mind, not with the shadow of Victor Verinus looming over her. A pang of disgust rushed through him when he thought of Victor taking Juliana's mother, Simonis, in front of her own husband. Was his loathing of the Stallion, and his fear of what that venomous man might do to the woman he loved, colouring his thoughts? His axe could fall with justice if he could hold Victor to blame for a plot against the emperor.

Reaching a decision, he commanded, 'Come with me.'
They strode back across the cloister and made their way to
the refectory. At the head of one of the long wooden tables,
a mound of a man hunched over a sumptuous feast: a pile
of *apaki*, the pork salted and smoked, a partridge, eggs, flat
bread, olives, a dish of *taricha* reeking sharply of fish, and a jug
of wine. His pale blue eyes shone in a face of such pendulous
jowls that his hairless head resembled melted candle wax. A
cream tunic as big as a soldier's tent barely covered his rolls
of fat. Stubby fingers plucked at the food, pushing it into his
mouth. He chewed slowly, relentlessly.

The monk glanced up when the two men entered. Embar-
rassment coloured his face, and he wiped the grease from his
mouth with the back of his hand. 'You see before you a glut-
ton,' he said in a high-pitched voice. 'But you will forgive me, I
hope. It is the only pleasure I have left in this life.'

'Eat your fill, Neophytos. You have earned your pleasure.'
Wulfrun sat on the bench beyond the array of dishes, and
motioned to Ricbert to join him.

'How is Juliana?' The monk's words sighed with a mournful
tone. 'How long it has been since I heard her sweet voice.'

'Your cousin is well.' The captain paused, choosing his
words carefully. 'As well as can be with Victor Verinus' shadow
falling across her.'

Neophytos bowed his head for a moment. 'I fear for her,'
he said in a quiet, tremulous voice. 'She escaped the Stallion's
vengeance. I would not wish her to suffer as we all have suffered.'

'It is true that Victor gelded you himself?'

'Yes,' Neophytos said dispassionately. 'He took my balls with
his own knife. And he made me watch as he sawed them off.'

Ricbert winced.

The monk shrugged. 'A brief moment of pain. These things
pass.'

'You are not bitter?' the younger man asked, incredulous.

'God teaches us to accept these things.'

When Neophytos reached out for a slice of *apaki*, Wulfrun pressed his fingers on the back of his hand to halt him. With his other hand, the commander plucked an egg from the bowl and held it up; a reminder of what had been lost. 'I cannot believe you feel nothing, Neophytos. If not for yourself, then for all the Nepotes who have suffered.'

For a moment the monk stared at the egg, and then his gaze flickered away. Answer enough, Wulfrun thought.

'Even here, in this great monastery, you have not been able to escape the watchful eye of the Verini,' he continued. 'A slave to their whims, is that it?'

The monk coloured. 'I chose to enter this brotherhood. I . . .' He choked back his words.

Wulfrun dropped the egg back in the bowl. 'There has been murder committed in this monastery. Blood spilled on God's table. I would know what part the Verini played in this crime. And what crimes are yet to come.'

Neophytos lowered his head as if a great weight had been placed on his neck. 'How can I help?' he squeaked.

'You see all here. I would think you see Nathaniel the most. The brother of the man who cut off your balls would not go unseen, yes?'

The monk trembled as he struggled with himself, and then he heaved his huge bulk up from the bench. 'Follow me,' he said, glancing around with unease.

'Nathaniel is not here,' Ricbert said. 'He has been summoned, by Victor. That does not bode well, I would think. The Verini are in conclave.'

Wheezing, Neophytos pushed his way through door after door until they came out into the warm night. He pointed to a filthy alley that ran behind the hall where the meat was prepared. The reek of rot hung in the air.

'Since Victor learned of his son's death, his plans have changed,' the monk whispered. 'Arcadius was being groomed for great things. I know not what—'

'To steal the crown?' Ricbert asked.

Neophytos held out his hands. 'All I can say is that Arcadius lay at the heart of Victor's plans, that was always clear. Arcadius wanted none of it. That was why he fled with Maximos. You know as well as I that here in Constantinople Victor would not brook any challenge. Escape was the only choice that poor fool had. And so he is dead.' He glanced back towards the alley. 'Now Justin spends all his days here being tutored by Nathaniel.'

Wulfrun frowned. 'You believe Victor has decided to groom Justin for the greatest power in all Christendom?'

'I know not. But I suspect. What other choice does he have to achieve his ambitions?'

'That moon-faced boy?' Ricbert said with incredulity. 'Let a pig in a cap rule the empire, that would make more sense.'

The monk beckoned with two of his fat fingers. Wulfrun and Ricbert strode to the edge of the alley. The smaller man choked, clutching his hand to his mouth. In the shadows lay a fly-blown dog. The stomach had been torn open, the entrails scattered all around. The throat gaped ragged too. And as Wulfrun cast his eye over the carcass, he saw that the fur had been burned here and there. He glanced back at Neophytos.

'Justin is not what he seems,' the monk murmured. 'He is not one of God's children, that one.'

The commander looked back at the dead dog, trying to make sense of the eunuch's words. He saw savagery, torment, cruelty. And he thought back to the tattered corpse upon the altar steps and began to understand.

'This,' Neophytos said in his high-pitched voice, 'is the least of what that foul creature is capable of. Soon, Wulfrun, you may be swearing your axe, swearing to give up your very life, to one of the Devil's own. One who will lead us all to the gates of hell.'

CHAPTER TWENTY

A thin band of red edged the western sky. The wind had fallen across the desert and a stillness had settled under the sweep of glittering stars. In the last of the ruddy light, two men stood in silent contemplation. Daggers of shadow plunged into the body in front of them. The skull stared eyelessly into the heavens. Ropes hung loosely around the wrists and ankles, and the folds of the filthy tunic showed that little was left of what had once been a man. Fingers of wind-blown sand reached over the torso. Soon the desert would have consumed all that remained.

Hereward wrinkled his nose but he could now smell no rot on the dry, cooling air. Death worked differently out here under the hot sun. Beside him, his head bowed, Maximos Nepos' dark hair fell across his face, but the Mercian could sense the grief etched into every part of him. 'Your friend?'

The Roman nodded slowly. 'As you said . . . the ring . . . the tunic . . .' The words were little more than a croak.

Hereward understood the man's feelings. The blade Maximos was feeling deep in his heart was only the start of long weeks of suffering. And though the initial pain would diminish it would continue to cut his thoughts until one day it did not.

It could not be hurried. This was the burden of the fighting man. For every mead-cup raised in celebration of victory, there would be days like this. Two sides locked together in the dance until some axe or spear or sword brought it to a juddering halt. Warriors were filled with the joys of a life lived deeply. And they were the saddest men in the world.

When the other man had had time to sift through his memories, Hereward murmured, 'Who did this thing?' When Maximos did not answer immediately, he continued, 'Did Meghigda end your friend's days?'

The Roman shrugged. 'I cannot say.'

'She has it within her.'

'Aye, she does. A fire burns in her heart. Sometimes it threatens to consume her. If she thought Arcadius a threat to her or her people—'

'Was he a threat?' Hereward hid his irritation at his companion's secrecy. Since Maximos had been freed, every question had been met with a grin and a glib tongue. This time, however, whether from grief or some other cause, the other man's guard was down.

'Arcadius was a threat to no one. He had a pure heart, unlike many of his kin.' Maximos gritted his teeth. 'His father had plans for him in Constantinople. Riches . . . power . . . all of it waited for Arcadius, but he wanted none of it. And so, with a few good men, we fled the plots and the whispering and the lies and the guarded tongues, and went in search of our own destiny. We drank, we wenched, we fought any who stood in our way, and then we came here, to this cursed land . . .' He choked back the words.

'And here Arcadius was killed—'

'Murdered!' Maximos' eyes flashed.

'The men you brought with you . . . ?'

'Fled, back to Constantinople when Arcadius and I were taken, so I am told. For all I know, they are dead too, but . . .' His chest swelled as he sucked in a deep breath and looked up to the sweep of stars. 'There is a price upon Meghigda's head, you told me, and it seems it is known far and wide. That tells me our men returned to Constantinople and Arcadius' father demanded retribution for his son's death.'

Hereward prowled around the body. A single stroke from a blade had laid this man low. It would not have been beyond the queen. Or Salih ibn Ziyad. He chose his words carefully, knowing that anything he said would sting. 'Would Meghigda have killed your friend to punish you?'

The other man fell silent for a long moment. 'God knows, I have wronged her. But I never wished her harm . . . would never wish it. Yet if she did this . . .' His voice drained away.

Hereward did not know what had passed between Maximos and Meghigda, but he could guess. He had met the Roman's kind before, men of standing who saw women as another victory to be earned on the great battlefield of life. It never ended well.

'I will help you bury your friend,' he said. 'He should not be left here like this.'

Maximos nodded, seemingly touched by this show of fellowship. 'Let us do this thing, and then I can say farewell,' he replied.

As they collected stones to pile over the body, Maximos drifted into a reverie of remembrance. 'We bury the bodies, but the past lives on. However much we run, and hide, we can never escape it. In Constantinople, your days yet to come are mapped out for you.' He was almost talking to himself as he loaded the rocks on his friend's remains. 'Blood cries out to blood. We owe allegiance to family above all. Plans are made, paths are mapped, and whether we like it or not we do what we must for the greater good. It is a burden we shoulder for the sake of our kin, but sometimes . . . sometimes . . . I would give all of it up for a clear road ahead of me, one of my own choosing.'

Hereward's thoughts flew away to his own father, bitter

old Asketil, who had killed his mother and tried to end the Mercian's own life. 'Choose your own path,' he growled. 'You will be better for it.'

Maximos jerked round, his eyes gleaming in the moonlight. 'And you think you can walk away from all that shaped you?'

Hereward could not answer.

'By rights, I should be dead,' the Roman continued, his gaze drifting across the grave of his friend. 'Our families were at war. Mine . . . the Nepotes. Arcadius' . . . the Verini.' He laughed without humour. 'The Verini. Arcadius' father, Victor, the Stallion, a man who would choke the life from a child without a second thought. And Nathaniel, a man of God, who sits in his monastery and dreams only of earthly power.' He paused. 'There was a third. Victor's brother, Karas, but he left Constantinople to tend to his lands in the east.' Hereward watched a shadow cross Maximos' face at the mention of Karas. 'Thank God,' the Roman added.

'How did this feud begin?'

'No one even knows. Some slight . . . some word spoken out of turn . . . in the days of my father's father, or my father's father's father. And so we struggled for ascendancy. Fortunes came and went. Power slipped through fingers like sand. The miseries piled high, small and great. Through little victories, and sour retreats, no one ever gained the upper hand. Until three years gone. My father made a monstrous error, in arrogance, or desperation, or weariness of a battle that seemed never-ending, with everyone's hopes crushed under its wheels. Thinking he could win all with one wild gamble, and thereby bring the suffering to an end, he moved too soon. The Nepotes were crushed, once and for all. And the price exacted from my kin was . . .' the word choked in his throat, 'terrible indeed. As the first-born, and my family's hope for the future, I was to be sacrificed.'

Maximos slumped on to his haunches, staring at the pile of rocks, limned silver by the moon. After a long moment, he continued. 'Arcadius pleaded for my life. His father is a hard man, not afraid of using his fists. But Arcadius risked his ire. For me. I do not know what price Arcadius paid . . . he would never say . . . but I was spared. I owe him my life. I owe him everything.'

'And so you both fled, thinking you could escape.'

'If only for a while. To enjoy days free of the demands placed upon us. We were in a jail no less harsh than the one in which Meghigda held me, only the walls were not of stone, but of words. Rules. Commands. And we thought we had escaped. Our days and nights were filled with a joy we had not known since we were children. But then fate made a mockery of our hopes.'

Maximos pushed himself up on trembling legs. 'Arcadius could have been emperor. That was his father's wish. To steal the crown and replace the weak man who rules the greatest empire the world has known. But, as I said, Arcadius wanted none of it.' He bowed his head. 'Rest peacefully, my friend,' he murmured. 'You, at least, are free now.'

After long moments of silent reflection, the Roman led the way back to where the rest of the English and Salih had made camp. The men huddled around the fire against the desert cold, their shadows dancing across the waste. Someone was singing a plaintive song of a lost home, and a wife and a child he would never see again, and Hereward decided it was a night for reflection.

He feared for Alric. He feared it was himself that God was punishing for his crimes, whittling down the good men who had accompanied him from England, whittling down the monk's body as he, in his lust for retribution, had whittled down Ragener's.

As they approached the golden glow, Maximos leaned in and whispered, 'Do not speak to Salih of Arcadius' murder. I would not have him think we doubt him, or his mistress. A smile comes easily to his lips, but his eyes are always cold. He sees everything, but says little, and he is not someone you would wish for an enemy.'

'Agreed,' Hereward replied. 'There will be time enough for that kind of talk when we have reclaimed what is ours and taken our vengeance. You are certain you still wish to walk this road? It will not be easy.'

'I would see Meghigda safe.' Maximos seemed on the brink of saying more, but then the song snapped off and an angry cry rang out. Sighard loomed over Salih, who sat cross-legged on the edge of the circle of firelight. An amused smile played on the wise man's lips.

Hereward darted forward and pushed the English warrior back. 'Angering Salih ibn Ziyad is a quick way to get a silver knife in your guts,' he said.

'Not if I take his head first,' Sighard snapped.

The wise man held out his hands. 'If I have caused offence, it was not my wish.'

'He taunts Hengist!' Sighard protested. He pointed into the dark where a grey shape whirled in a wild dance in the moonlight.

'No,' Salih insisted. 'I offer only praise to one who has been touched by God.'

'Do not mock him.' Rage twisted Sighard's face and he pushed against his leader's hand.

With a gentle shove, Hereward urged his companion back a few paces. He turned to Salih and said, 'Sometimes Hengist is in this world and sometimes he is in another. When he wanders away from the vales we know, he is ill prepared to keep himself safe. In those times, we have all learned to look after him. He is our spear-brother.' He glanced over his shoulder at the glowering warrior. 'More than others, Sighard here has taken it upon himself to be Hengist's guardian. It is not wise to provoke him.'

'I do not look down upon your friend. I bow my head before him,' Salih said. 'This is a truth.' He watched Hengist whirl, arms outstretched, a reedy cry swirling up towards the stars.

'The dead are always with us,' he continued, his voice rustling out into the night. 'They walk one pace behind our shoulder, our fathers and our fathers' fathers, our mothers and our wives. They watch and they guide, and if we stray from the path God has set for us they punish. This too is a truth.'

Hereward squatted, soothed by the rich voice, as were all his warriors. He could sense their eyes locked upon the wise man. He felt as if he were being lulled into a dream, and for a moment he was convinced he could feel his wife Turfrida just behind him. Her fingertips reaching out to brush his neck. The bloom of her breath upon his ear. How much he missed her. Since his mother's murder, only Turfrida and Alric had brought him peace. And now both were gone.

'Those who go before us ascend to the gods. They become gods,' Salih ibn Ziyad continued. 'From the day when the sun first rose upon the sands, the Imazighen prepared the dead for the journey that was to come, and offered our thanks for when they would return to walk behind us. We painted the bodies with red ochre and buried them in caves and in tombs under rocks so their remains would be safe from animals.' With a ghost of a smile, he looked around the rapt faces. 'We left them their weapons, if they were warriors, and the treasures of their lives, and ostrich eggs and food. And if we wished to know which road to take into days yet to come, we would utter our question aloud, then sleep in the tomb. For in their new home, the dead can speak back to us. They enter into us, and we meet them again in dreams.'

Like a wolf, Hengist bounded across the dunes and landed on his haunches next to the fire. In his wide, staring eyes, the golden flames flickered.

'And sometimes when the dead have entered into us in those dreams, they do not leave,' Salih murmured, peering deep into Hengist's stare.

Hereward saw the admiration in the wise man's face and knew that he spoke the truth.

'Your brother here is wiser than me,' Salih added, 'for he has all the knowledge of the dead, and their all-seeing gaze, locked inside him. He has God inside him.'

Sighard rested a comforting hand on Hengist's shoulder and the madman looked up and smiled. 'We are blessed, then.'

Hereward watched the other warriors nod. Anywhere else, Hengist would be mocked and beaten and thrown out of every village into which he wandered. But here he had been accepted for all his faults, a brother among brothers. Perhaps they were all madmen. Hengist only showed it more than most.

'With the gods on our side, how can we not find victory?' Salih said, his eyes gleaming.

'We have a long road to walk before we can raise a cup in cheer,' Maximos replied, warming his hands by the fire. 'We are but few, and we must storm the walls of a city of cut-throats. Before I fling myself on to those rocks of despair, I would at least know that we had a plan.' He glanced at Hereward, questioning.

The Mercian showed a confident face, but that thought had troubled him from the moment he had heard of their destination. Even creeping into Sabta in disguise would probably fail. Their pale skin would shine out like a beacon, and a band of them would raise suspicions the moment they entered the gates. 'What say you, Hengist? Do the gods whisper a plan we can use?'

Flicking back his lank hair, the madman grinned through lips gritty with sand. 'Stealth is no good. An army, that is what we need. An army like the one we had in Ely when we bloodied William the Bastard's nose. Then the streets of Sabta will run red with blood.' For a moment, he watched the billowing smoke from the fire and seemed to see something in the streams of sparks caught in the grey cloud. 'We do not have an army. And so we must find a ship, and sail on the grey waves to Sabta, and then we may arrive afore our prey.'

Chapter Twenty-One

Waves pounded the shore. Across the grey waters, ships strained at their anchors, a creaking forest of masts swaying against the darkening skies. The wind moaned and the last of the gulls shrieked. Both were all but drowned out by the hubbub of voices rising from the sprawling camp on the edge of the beach. Flapping tents and crackling fires reached into the gloom almost as far as the eye could see. The scent of woodsmoke and cooking fish drifted on the breeze, and the reek of shit and piss too. Sea wolves wandered among their makeshift homes. Some sang full-throated bawdy songs. Some fought, rolling around the dusty ground. And others cleaned their mail-shirts in sacks of sand, or sharpened their blades on whetstones. To the handful of men lying on their bellies on the ridge overlooking the bay, it seemed almost a city in itself.

'How many there are,' Salih murmured, his gaze skittering across the camp.

Hereward watched that rats' nest, imagining if it were disturbed. 'I see no guards. These dogs find comfort in their numbers. They do not fear attack.'

'Why would they?' Sighard said. 'Surely there are few in these parts who could challenge that force.'

'Then it is good that we do not seek to fight them. The night and silence will be our friends here.'

'Some would call it madness to venture into the very heart of the enemies who seek to kill you,' Salih said with a smile.

'Aye. I have been called mad before,' Hereward replied. 'But caution is not for us. Time is no longer on our side. We must set sail tonight if we are to reach Sabta afore Ragener.'

'Fortune favours the bold, so they say.' Salih slithered forward to get a better look at the enemy encampment. 'But never have I heard the like. A handful of men trying to steal a ship from under the noses of an army.'

As the Mercian tried to estimate the number sheltering in the camp, his thoughts flew back over the last few days. When they neared the coast, their journey became harder by far. Raiding parties criss-crossed the rolling dunes, no doubt the sea wolves searching for any sign of Meghigda to claim what must be a truly handsome bounty upon her head. In that open landscape, even a lone figure stood out like a beacon in the night. Twenty Englishmen used to the shelters of deep woods should have stood little chance of escaping the eyes of those enemies. But they had Salih ibn Ziyad as an ally. He taught them how to disappear into the sand, how to cover their tracks as they wandered. He showed them the best hiding places among the rocky outcroppings. He listened to the wind, and he watched the stars, and he guided them on the fastest, safest route to the coast. And in all the long journey they never once wanted for water.

Sighard's voice jerked him from his reverie. 'You take too much of a risk,' he said, his face sullen. His brooding gaze flickered along the short distance between the noisy camp and the ships. 'Sound carries far in these hot lands. One noise, one error, and every man there will be upon us. We will have no chance to flee.'

'There is little choice,' Hereward began, biting down on his irritation that the younger man was questioning him.

'There are always choices!' Sighard's eyes glowed in the growing gloom. 'Madulf chose to put his faith in you and it cost him his life . . .'

'Hold your tongue,' Salih cautioned, 'or you will be the one to bring the wrath of our enemies upon us.'

But Hereward could see Sighard could barely contain his seething emotions. 'We will talk of this later.'

'When we are all dead? Every choice you make leads us on to further disaster. Only Alric could contain your worst instincts, and he is no longer here—'

'Do not breathe his name,' the Mercian snapped. He could feel his blood start to burn.

'I should. We all should. Because you caused his fate. If you had not let your wrath get the better of you, if you had not tarried to torment the Hawk for the sake of that . . . that woman, we would not have been caught in the storm. We would not have been shipwrecked. And then we would not have almost died in the hellish cauldron of that desert. We would not have near lost our heads to the axes of the Imazighen. And Alric would not have been captured.' Spittle spraying from his mouth, he stabbed a finger. 'You led us to this place. And if the monk is suffering, it is on your head.'

Hereward felt his rage surge. The young warrior's stinging words only echoed what he believed himself. Lunging, he snagged his fist in Sighard's tunic and dragged him across the stones. It was foolish, he knew, but he could no longer control himself, even if it brought disaster down upon them. The other man snarled, as adrift from his wits as Hereward. He bunched his fists and prepared to swing.

Breathing a curse, Salih threw himself between the two warriors. 'Stay your hands, you wild wolves,' he spat, his eyes blazing. 'I will cut both your throats before I let you doom my queen.' With a thrust of a hand, he spun Sighard across the rocks. Then as quick as a snake, he curled his fingers around the hilt of his silver dagger and snatched it out, turning his back on Sighard and levelling his blade at Hereward. Salih knew the real threat here, the Mercian saw. 'You fear for your friend and so your temper runs high. But take another step down this road and you may as well plunge your sword into his chest yourself.'

Hereward could barely hear the words through the thunder of blood in his head. But Alric's face floated behind his eyes, and he remembered what the monk had said to him in times past. Somehow he managed to push aside his anger. 'Your words are true,' he growled to Salih before jabbing a finger towards Sighard. 'We will speak of this again.' Before the younger warrior could respond, he crept away into the lengthening shadows. As the dusk closed around him, he could hear his devil still whispering in his head. The thing that had been with him since he was a boy had awakened, and it would not readily sleep again.

Beyond the ridge, the rest of his men crouched in the dark. No one spoke. Kraki sat with his axe in his lap, his fingers tight around the haft. Guthrinc balanced himself against his spear, watching the spray of stars. Even Mad Hengist was quiet. No longer filled with their faraway look, his eyes were sharp. They were ready.

As they settled in for a tense wait, Salih crawled over. Smelling of strange spices, he leaned in to Hereward and whispered, 'In the small things, there are matters of great import.' The wise man nodded across the circle of men. Separated from his brothers, Sighard sat on the ridge. Moonlight limned him against the backdrop of stars. At first the Mercian could not guess what Salih meant. But as he studied the young warrior he saw the bowed head, the hunched shoulders, and glimpsed the fingers plucking at each other in worry or doubt or fear.

'You have let your own feelings for your lost friend consume you,' the wise man murmured, 'and you have not seen how the monk's capture lies upon others.' He held up the palm of his right hand as if he were weighing his words. 'It eats into him,' he continued, jerking his head towards Sighard. 'Eats his heart.

He has already lost a brother. He sees the world as his enemy, and only the churchman gave him hope of a better day. Now that hope has been snatched away.'

As Hereward watched Sighard, he felt another pang of guilt. It was true. He was a poor leader. He had thought only of his own pain.

'You must watch him closely now,' Salih continued, in his low, steady voice. 'Watch every move with the eyes of a hawk. Sighard can no longer be trusted, for he cannot trust himself. His torment now rides him like a mare, and he must go wherever it takes him.' Leaning back, he folded his hands upon his chest. 'Watch him,' he whispered. 'Watch him.'

Chapter Twenty-Two

And Hereward did watch Sighard. The moon crept across the arc of the sky and the raucous voices of the sea wolves ebbed away. Soon there was only the crashing of the waves and the whine of the wind across the wastes. But the young warrior barely moved, a hunched figure silhouetted against the stars.

When Herrig the Rat crawled over the ridge to say that their enemies slumbered, Hereward pushed himself up. Pressing one finger to his lips, he lifted the other hand and his men rose like ghosts ascending from their graves. Only Sighard continued to sit. After a moment, he stirred himself and stumbled up to the war-band. The Mercian looked around the faces of his spear-brothers, silently communicating his confidence in them. After so long fighting shoulder to shoulder, they no longer needed words. They were of one mind, one heart.

Hereward led the way, as he always did. Creeping over the ridge, he picked a path among the ragged brown rocks. His men followed, staying low, like wolves. The line wound down against the steep wall of the cove, keeping to the deepest shadow so they would not be seen against the lighter sky.

Time and again, the Mercian's eyes darted towards the pirate camp. The fires were burning low. A few torches sizzled here and there in the gulf of night. He cocked his head, but could hear nothing.

As they clambered over rock pools to the edge of the beach, the wind dropped. A path of shimmering moonlight stretched out across the still sea. The low, steady beat of the waves throbbed in their ears. Crouching on the sand, Hereward balanced on the fingertips of his right hand and studied the forest of masts. Many ships had been dragged up on to the strand, the bungs knocked out with mallets to drain the bilge. Further out, other vessels rolled on the swell, straining at creaking hemp ropes fastened to stone anchors.

Creeping beside him, Kraki levelled his axe towards a ship on the edge of the fleet. The prow had been carved into the shape of a horse. The vessel lay in water shallow enough for them to reach and its course out of the cove was not blocked by any of the others. Hereward nodded. A good choice.

Raising his right hand, he gestured towards the ship. The silent message was passed along the line, and the warriors loped forward into the surf.

As the cool waters surged around the Mercian's calves, a hand grabbed his arm. Guthrinc flashed a concerned look and pointed back up the beach.

On the edge of the sand, a dark figure waited, silent and un-moving.

Hereward squinted through the gloom and saw it was Sighard.

'Why does he wait?' Guthrinc hissed above the wash of the breakers.

Kraki cursed under his breath. 'That jolt-head will be the death of us.'

'We should have let him take his own life when he had the chance,' someone growled.

Eyes blazing, Hereward whirled and saw that the speaker was Hiroc the Three-fingered, so-called because he had lost two digits on his left hand. He was a sour man, prone to complaining. 'He is one of us,' the Mercian snapped, 'a spear-brother. Would you have us send you out into the wilderness when you have served your purpose?'

Hiroc looked down into the swirl of foam.

Hereward turned and looked back up the beach. Sighard had thrown his head back and was staring into the vault of the heavens. The Mercian could almost sense the cloud of desolation enveloping the young warrior. Once again he was thinking about giving up his life, Hereward was certain. Walking into the waves and then swimming out until the black water sucked him down to the deep. A step into the enemy camp and a sword raised in anger until spears rammed through his chest. He had seen this despair before, in men who had fought too much, too long, until only blood and death filled their thoughts.

'Fetch him,' he commanded.

Kraki and Guthrinc bounded out of the surf and crunched up the sand. Barely had they travelled a few paces when they skidded to a halt.

Hereward stared past them. Along the crest where the rising beach flattened out into the featureless desert, torches bobbed in the dark like fireflies in England's summer fields. The lights trailed towards the camp.

The Mercian stiffened. It could only be one of the raiding parties returning from another day's futile search for Meghigda. 'Fetch Sighard,' he hissed. Dropping low, Kraki and Guthrinc began to creep forward. Their progress was too slow, Hereward could see, but they could not risk drawing attention to themselves.

The torches danced. The sea wolves would be weary, thirsty, yearning for sleep. Surely they would be so keen to reach their camp their eyes would barely stray from the path ahead.

Fingers scraping the sand, Kraki and Guthrinc inched forward. The rest of the English stood like statues in the swirling surf. All heads were turned towards the unmoving figure of

Sighard. Breath burned in tight chests. Hereward heard a muttered prayer. Another man crossed himself.

And then Sighard threw his arms wide and his head back. 'Let God decide!' he cried out.

In the still of the desert night, the words rang out as clear as a church bell. For a moment, Kraki and Guthrinc froze. Then, realizing the moment for stealth had passed, they bounded forward. The beach was a gulf of darkness. Amid the crashing of the waves, the sea wolves might think the voice had echoed from the camp, Hereward hoped.

But Sighard was not done. 'That is what you said to Ragener, Hereward! Let God decide!' he yelled. 'And he did, and he let the cur live. That judgement has been passed on us too. So, I say now, let God decide *my* fate! If he wills that I live . . .'

The words died in his throat. Kraki and Guthrinc slammed into the young warrior and flattened him to the sand. Too late. Though the sea wolves surely could not see the bundle of bodies on the beach, Sighard's passion-filled cry had resounded far and wide.

A querying call chimed from the top of the slope, then another. A whistle cut through the rising babble of shouts. An instant later a response echoed from the depths of the camp. More shouts boomed out as the sea wolves threw off their sleep.

'Now what?' Maximos called. But he knew as well as Hereward that there was no chance of retreating. All the English warriors could hear the sound of feet thundering over the rocks towards the shore.

'The ship,' Hereward ordered.

As Kraki and Guthrinc dragged Sighard down to the water's edge, the war-band plunged into the swell. Hereward thought how dazed the young warrior looked. His eyes were flecked with tears.

'You have doomed us,' Hiroc the Three-fingered spat.

Sighard's face crumpled. 'I meant you no harm,' he sobbed.

Over his shoulder, the Mercian could see torch after torch flaring into life in the camp. A river of fire began to flow down the beach towards them.

'There is still time,' he called to his men. 'Board the vessel. We'll cut the anchor and row like devils until we are in deep water.'

Maximos forged ahead of him, his huge frame ploughing a furrow through the swell. As the cold brine washed up to his chest, Hereward could hear the sea wolves' angry shouts drawing nearer. Some of the wading English warriors tried to swim, but their shields and their weapons pulled them down. Hereward saw them flounder and felt his desperation grow.

Maximos' strong strokes swept him to the edge of the vessel they had selected. But as he reached up to grasp one of the hooks that supported the shields at sea, a dark shape loomed over him.

'Beware!' Hereward roared above the din of the ocean.

An axe swung down. The Roman must have glimpsed the sudden movement for he threw himself back into the waves. The blade whistled past him by a hair's breadth.

Wiping the brine from his eyes, the Mercian could see three figures prowling along the deck of the ship, their weapons poised to hack down anyone who tried to climb aboard. Dark shapes moved around the other vessels bobbing out on the swell. He had been too complacent, he could see that now. The sea wolves were cunning. They had left men sleeping aboard all the anchored ships to counter just such an attack.

'Too late! We must fight!' Kraki bellowed. 'They will cut us down with our backs turned if we try to get aboard that ship.' The Viking whirled, seawater streaming from his axe.

As Hereward forced himself round, he could see that his spear-brother was right. A wall of men lined the water's edge, their jeering faces lit orange by the dancing light of the torches. Axes waved. Spears jabbed towards the sky. And the chorus of mocking threats drowned out even the pounding of the waves.

More sea wolves flooded down the beach by the moment. An army, ranged there, five deep or more.

'Hold!' the Mercian called as Kraki began to wade towards the fierce band.

When he looked around, Hereward saw how futile was their resistance. The force of the currents dragged the English warriors this way and that. Waves crashed against their backs, threatening to drag their legs from under them. The sea wolves had all the advantage, and they knew it. Within moments, the waters would run red with English blood.

The waves flickered with orange fire. Maximos shook his fist, his raging words lost to the turbulent elements. Salih's eyes glittered as he watched the curs who had hunted his queen. And Sighard bowed his head, tears and salt water streaming down a face ragged with despair.

Hereward stiffened. All sound ebbed away until there was only a frozen moment. Here was his choice, his destiny. He could heed the voice of his devil and see his men slaughtered. Or he could be the leader the others imagined him to be.

'Lay down your arms,' he bellowed, choosing thin hope. 'Our fight is done.'

Chapter Twenty-Three

The horizon shimmered like glass. Through the heat haze, the creamy walls of an ancient city wavered in a baking landscape of brown rock and ochre sand. Trails of smoke drifted upwards from the flat roofs into a sky the colour of old skulls. Though it seemed close enough to touch, Sabta was still a day or two away. The men breaking camp in the lee of a low hill knew that, took their time. Too much exertion was not wise in the oven of the day.

Alric leaned back against a rock at the top of the rise, taking advantage of what little shade remained. His face was the colour of the sky, his cheeks hollow. Through eyes haunted by pain, he glanced down at the bloody cloth bound around his left hand. The stump of his finger whined, and needles of agony stabbed into his knuckle.

Hearing a noise behind him, he glanced back to see Meghigda hurrying towards him across the sand. Her expression was fierce, and in that moment he understood how she instilled fear in her enemies. There was a power to her.

At first he wondered how he had wronged her, but then she swooped down and plucked up one of the poisonous scurrying creatures that infested that land. Within a moment, it could have stung him with its lashing, spiked tail and he knew from past warnings that he could have been dead by nightfall. He expected Meghigda to crush it underfoot as he had seen their captors do. Instead, she carried it far off and let it loose in the dunes, smiling as it crawled away.

Alric frowned. There was much about this woman that he did not understand. She was as fierce as any English warrior, and yet, as now, there was a gentle side to her. At the Imazighen camp he had watched her care for the children, the elderly and the sick. She claimed to be possessed by the spirit of that ancient warrior Dihya, but he knew that was only her way to manipulate her followers. So she was skilled in the art of deception too. So many contradictions. Of all those he had met on the long road of life, she was the only one he could not fathom.

As she sat beside him, he welcomed the chance to distract himself from the debilitating pain. He offered his thanks for her swift aid, then asked her about the Imazighen.

Her eyes took on a wistful look as she peered into the distance. 'We are a wandering people. Our homeland is wherever we are. You know where England is. You know your shores, your frontiers. We roam across the desert from the Almoravid empire to the edges of the Fatimid caliphate, from Alodia and Makuria and Bornu to the land of the Banu Hilal. We face attacks from all sides. Others covet our trade routes, our water. Even the sand beneath our feet – they want it because they do not have it. It is all our home, all this vast northern desert, and we will allow no others to take it from us.'

'And all your life, even when you were a child, this has been your destiny – to be queen of the Imazighen?'

Since she had been taken from her people her unguarded moments had been more frequent, and this time Alric glimpsed a hint of sadness in her face. 'If my mother and father had not been slain, many years would have passed before I had to bear that burden. But God did not choose that road for me.

169

My training began before the blood of my family had soaked into the sand. The elders guided me, advised me. I learned all I would need to be a queen who would keep her people safe.' She bowed her head, remembering.

Alric thought how sad that life must have been. The simple times of childhood had been stolen from her. To shoulder the burdens of a ruler at such a young age must have taken a great toll upon her.

Meghigda smiled as if she could read his thoughts. 'I do not regret one day. This life I have is a gift, an honour. All I have I give freely for my people. If I die tomorrow, it will have been a life well spent. It is good to live this way. It means I know no fear.'

Alric feigned an annoyed expression. 'You speak English well. That was not how it seemed when we met.'

She laughed. 'A queen must wear many masks, man of God. I have met English before, warriors like your friends, knights. Men from all four corners of this world. And I have tried to learn from all of them. And then Salih ibn Ziyad arrived at our camp one day. His wisdom was greater even than our elders', and I listened as he told me of many wonders, and of secret knowledge. A great man. Why he stayed I do not know, but I gave thanks every day that he was by my side to guide me.'

Alric felt surprised to see a deep joy in her that she had kept hidden until then. It pleased him. But then he winced as a lance of pain spiked up his arm.

Meghigda leaned forward, concerned. Reaching out, she let her slender fingers hover over his bandage. 'Put your hand to your nose,' she said. When he only stared at her, puzzled, she snatched his wrist and thrust his fingers under his nostrils. 'Does it smell of ripe fruit?'

Alric shook his head.

'Good. You must do this every day. Every day,' she stressed, 'without fail. And if one day you do smell fruit, we must take your hand at the wrist and put the stump to the fire.'

The monk recoiled, horrified. 'Are you mad?'

'If not, you will die. The black rot will eat up your arm and into your heart. You must trust me on this.'

For a moment he hesitated, and then he gave a slow, reluctant nod. He could not think about that course. Fear of what lay ahead would consume him. When his finger had been removed, the pain had almost torn him apart. He remembered the sawing, and the blood, and his screams, and his terror that the unbearable suffering would drive him mad.

Meghigda seemed to sense his thoughts, for he saw her face soften. 'You have suffered,' she murmured, 'but you have endured.'

'To face more suffering ahead?' He caught himself, dismayed by the bitterness he heard in his own words.

'We are at war, all of us. Day by day, we fight, and we fight. We see peace . . .' she glanced towards Sabta, shimmering in the haze, 'like some distant palace, but we never reach it. But what choice do we have? Lie down in the dust and die? And so we fight.'

Alric glimpsed a hint of deep pain in her eyes, and felt a pang of guilt at his own complaints. 'You speak true,' he said in a quiet voice. 'Death holds dominion over God's earth. It is his way of teaching us to be humble, for the grave waits for king and slave, and judgement will come in the next world, not this one.' He tried to show a defiant face, but the agony in his hand contorted it. 'There is something for us amid all this suffering, if only we can find it,' he added, almost to himself.

On the slope, the Norman warriors folded the tent-cloth and packed away the poles with the discipline of men who fought and died together. Two figures broke away from the pack and began to climb the hill. Ragener the Hawk had a rolling gait as if his missing parts had thrown him off balance. His good eye roved around, watching for any threat, but his milky orb carried with it the look of the dead.

Beside him, Drogo Vavasour threw back his head and

laughed at some humorous word or other. His back was straight, his shoulders were square, and he strode as if he had not a care in the world.

When the two men stood in front of them, Alric looked up. He had prepared himself for what was to come.

'You still live. That is good,' the noble said with a faint smile. 'I feared the Hawk had been too rough with you.'

'I thought the Normans were a godly folk,' the monk said, 'and yet you allowed a man of the church to be harmed. And for what?'

Drogo rolled his head as if puzzling over his answer. 'You complain about a little scratch?'

'A scratch?' Alric exclaimed.

'You have your life, monk, and that is more than my brother.' Though the commander grinned, there was thunder in his eyes. 'I am a godly man. My prayers are offered five times a day. But the Lord has given us power over our own affairs, and to seek out justice—'

'Justice! Your brother and his men slaughtered Hereward's own brother! A boy! This circle never ends. There is hypocrisy here.'

'Nevertheless, Hereward must be punished.' He folded his hands behind his back. 'My brother no doubt had his reasons. The boy was a thief, or he raped girls . . .'

'Or he would not bow his head to Norman dogs.'

Drogo held his taut smile for a long moment. Alric braced himself, expecting a blow, but none came. 'Let us talk about heads,' the Norman said through a clenched jaw. 'Hereward cut off my brother's head and set it upon a spike. That is not justice. That is not a clean and honourable death. It is the work of a wild beast. A devil. One that must be cut down for the sake of all that is good and holy. God is on *my* side, monk. Not yours – you stood with that devil. Do not forget that.'

The monk hesitated. He could not deny much of what Drogo had said. ''Tis true. Hereward has slaughtered. He has robbed and beaten and killed for little more than a wrong word. But that man no longer exists.'

The Norman laughed without humour. 'You believe that?'

'How long must a man keep paying for his sins?'

'Is that not a question for God? Here is my answer. If a man's sins are great enough, he pays, and he pays, and he pays, and then he dies.'

'There is no escape?'

'From the things you have wrought? Never. There is always a price to pay.'

The monk felt hollowed out. He could see no end to it now, for any of them.

The Norman turned to Meghigda and bowed. 'Would that I did not have to turn you over to those Roman dogs. But I have reached agreement with my good friend here, and the gold heaped upon your head would dazzle any man.'

'Do what you will. You must live with your choice. There is always a price to pay.'

Drogo frowned to hear his words spoken back to him, and at the defiance he saw in the woman's face. The Normans liked their women pliant. Alric allowed himself a smile. Clearly the nobleman was not used to one who had fire in her heart and a tongue in her head.

But then Ragener stooped to snarl his hand in Alric's dusty tunic, hauling him to his feet. 'I have no qualms about seeing you suffer, monk,' he mumbled through his ragged lips. 'Any man who can stand by and witness the agony inflicted upon me is not worthy of my care. God watches over me now and I do his work, not you.'

Alric was aghast that the Hawk seemed oblivious of the crimes that had led Hereward to punish him. Yet as he looked into the sea wolf's ruined face, he felt his cheeks flush with passion. 'So you both think you act for God? Your pride will doom you both.'

Ragener snickered, shaking the monk back and forth. 'He

bares his fangs! See, Drogo!' The sea wolf pushed his face forward so he was barely a finger's width from Alric's nose. He smelled of rotten meat and sweat. 'Let us see how much fight there is in you when I take the next piece.'

'Wait until Sabta, Hawk,' the Norman commander said, walking away. 'I would wash the filth of the desert off me, and have a bed to sleep in.'

'Aye, then I can take my time,' Ragener breathed. He bared his broken teeth in a monstrous grin. 'What next for my knife? A toe? An ear? An eye? You have two. Look at this face, monk, and think upon it. Soon it will be yours.'

CHAPTER TWENTY-FOUR

Blood dripped from a broken nose. Eyes swelled shut. Bruises bloomed. But no complaints issued from the battered English warriors squatting on the floor of the billowing tent. Only the crack of the lines and the whistle of the wind broke the silence that lay over them.

Hereward looked across the bowed heads and hunched shoulders. Their wrists were bound, their weapons taken. Scowling guards watched over them, spears levelled to ram through chests at the slightest provocation. The air was sharp with the reek of sweat and brine and blood. But not defeat. They all yet lived. But for how much longer? After the sea wolves had dragged them from the surf, the Mercian remembered the deafening chorus of jeers as fists and boots, the hafts of spears and the flats of blades rained down on them until their wits fled. The numbers had been too uneven to fight back.

But they all yet lived.

Through the open tent flaps, Hereward could see the brightness of a new day. Gulls shrieked, and waves crashed. Smoke from fresh campfires drifted by. Voices still raw with sleep chimed as the camp woke. The hour of reckoning was drawing near.

'I have doomed you all.' Sighard's voice was barely more than a croak. His cheeks, filthy with the dust of the desert, were streaked.

After such a long period of silent reflection, heads jerked up at the sound. Kraki hawked up a mouthful of phlegm and spat into the sand.

'I will die first,' Sighard insisted, his voice breaking.

Guthrinc sniffed. 'I have seen worse.'

'Worse?' The young warrior gaped.

'Aye.' Guthrinc shrugged. 'What say you, Kraki?'

The Viking nodded. 'Worse.' He sucked on his teeth. 'I once drank the tavern out of mead.'

Sighard stared, his brow creased.

'No mead,' Kraki said with a sad shake of his head.

'A harsh blow. You took it like a warrior?' Guthrinc asked.

The Viking nodded slowly. 'I know not how.'

'There was this time in Grentabridge,' Guthrinc began, his voice heavy with regret. 'My stomach growled, and the air was heavy with the most wondrous scent. Goose, I think it was. And I had no coin.'

'You went hungry?'

'I went hungry.'

Maximos nodded. 'I have only been bound in a hole in the ground for day upon day and night upon night. But still . . .' He frowned, reflecting. 'But no wine or women. So . . . yes . . . worse.'

Sighard looked around the war-band. 'Have you lost your wits? These sea wolves will drag us out and slaughter us one by one.'

'Aye. Likely,' Guthrinc nodded. 'Still . . . I have seen worse.'

Hereward felt proud of his men for distracting Sighard from his despair in such a way. Strength was not only shown in the thick of battle.

Eight men appeared at the opening. The English warriors fell silent. The time had come. Like Hereward, the leader of the

new arrivals had arms dappled with the tattooed circles and
spirals of a warrior. His broad chest was bare, the tanned skin
criss-crossed with a mass of scars. Another scar ran from the
edge of his mouth to his left ear so that it seemed he had a
permanent sneer. 'Bring them,' he barked. A Northumbrian
man from the sound of it, the Mercian thought.

The sea wolves stabbed their spears, not caring if the tips bit
too deeply. Even then the English would not be cowed.

As the captives trailed out, Hereward caught Salih's eye.
The wise man, too, had not given himself up to despair, the
Mercian could see that. He observed calmly, his gaze always
searching for an advantage. For the sake of his queen, he could
not allow this day to end in disaster. And for the sake of Alric,
Hereward knew he had to do the same.

Salih sidled next to him. 'We cannot fight our way out,' he
whispered. 'We must bargain with them. Wits are needed more
than axes here.'

'When we meet their leader, we will see if he has ears that
will listen. But that is not our only hope.'

The Imazighen wise man eyed him askance. 'What say you?'

'Count the heads. There is one of us missing.'

'What can one man do?'

Hereward smiled.

Through the furnace heat of the day they trailed past tents
of red and gold and emerald. Banners fluttered in the light
breeze, the flags of an old England slowly slipping into shade:
Mercia, Northumbria, Wessex. As the sea wolves jeered and
threw rocks at the prisoners, Hereward saw them in a new
light. Deep in their eyes, he glimpsed glimmers of desperation.
They might have been farmers or merchants, soldiers too, but
now they were all exiles as he was. Their country stolen from
them by William the Bastard. The old ways of doing things,
the certainties, snatched away. Perhaps their land and their
livelihood too. They needed a new place in the world, a new
home, and here was their one chance of reaching it.

l12 4ane

Gepohs.

Shaking their spears, the roaring sea wolves crowded in on every side. So deafening was the din, so furious their captors' faces, Hereward wondered if his men were being herded like swine to the slaughter. Would their enemies merely fall upon them and tear them apart?

Stones clattered against skulls. Blood spattered. But the English would never go meekly, Hereward knew that. Kraki rounded on one tormentor and rammed his forehead into the man's face. Cartilage and bone shattered. The sea wolf reeled back with a bloody pulp where his nose had been, an arc of crimson droplets following him down. Grinning, the Viking reared up to the cheers of his spear-brothers, but only for a moment. The hafts of axes rained down on him. Hereward flinched as Kraki disappeared among the bodies. But when he was hauled to his feet he was still grinning, though his legs could barely support him.

Jabbing spears herded them into a natural amphitheatre. Stumbling down over steep rocks, they came to a halt on the dusty floor of the bowl. Waves of oven heat stifled them. Walls rose up high on three sides, lower on the fourth. Over it, Hereward could see white-crested waves reaching to the blue horizon.

The English shuffled together, scowling as they watched the sea wolves trail in and perch on the rocks, like gulls waiting for a twilight feast. Hereward showed a defiant face. His men followed his lead, even Sighard, who looked more like a boy than ever with his tear-streaked face.

'A trial,' Guthrinc mused. 'Either that or they would have us dance for them. I am light on my feet for a big man, but I do not think they would pay good coin to watch me, never mind set us free.'

'I will dance,' Kraki growled, spitting a mouthful of blood into the sand. 'On their heads.'

'You are mad,' Sighard gasped. 'You speak of fighting . . .

challenge . . . when we are bound and defeated. There is no
hope.'

'We still live,' Hereward said, his eyes fixed ahead.

Sighard glanced at him and fell silent.

Murmurs rustled through the crowd. The Mercian glanced
up to the opening into the amphitheatre, where bodies were
parting. A knot of men pushed through. There were six of
them, bare-chested, showing warrior tattoos, clutching axes,
and a seventh at their centre. The leader, Hereward guessed.
He steadied himself, holding his devil in check as best he could.
Salih was right. Now it was time for words and hard bargains.

The new arrivals barged through the sea wolves until they
reached a spot on the low fourth wall where they could look
over their captives. The six guards spread out, eyes darting all
around as if they expected an attack from their own side as
well as the battered men in front of them.

But as the leader swaggered out, Hereward stiffened, and he
saw his captor do the same. For a long moment, they held each
other's gaze.

'Siward?' Hereward said.

'Cousin?'

The other man flashed a broad grin. Though young, his long
hair was as white as snow and all but glowing in the sun. He
was tall and rangy, with the poise of a warrior. A fair swordsman, Hereward recalled from when they were boys. The last
time he had seen Siward was at old King Edward's court when
he had ridden off to fight one of the monarch's battles. With
shame, Hereward remembered being so drunk at the time he
could barely stand, and bloodied from a fight with one of the
kitchen lads in the filthy area where they threw the scraps for
the dogs. But unlike his own father, Siward had always shown
him respect. There had been much laughter between them.

Hereward could tell his cousin was pleased to see a familiar
face. But after a moment the sea wolf leader became aware of

his surroundings. His eyes flickered, his grin faded. One of the guards whispered something in his ear and he nodded.

Stepping forward, Siward threw his arms wide. 'Brothers,' he called. The jeers and yells subsided. 'You thought you had brought me rats who wanted to feast from our table. Yes, they would steal from us, and yes, these are the curs who took our prize, the woman worth riches beyond measure.'

Hereward watched his cousin at work. Siward had always spun silvered words, but here he was draining the well of his skills to turn these men to his ends. The Mercian looked around at the ranks of glowering faces, then at the strained lines of his cousin's own features, which even his forced grin could not hide.

'But look, brothers,' Siward continued. 'Here is no rat, but Hereward, the last of the English, who fought so bravely at Ely against the Bastard's forces.'

'And he lost,' someone bellowed. Braying laughter rang out all around.

Hereward watched his cousin's face grow taut, but still he smiled. 'These are great warriors, brothers. Their axes have spilled an ocean of Norman blood. Should we not let them fight alongside us—'

'We already have too many mouths to feed,' another sea wolf shouted. Ayes rang out.

When Siward hesitated, Hereward's moment of hope was extinguished. Even his cousin could not save them.

'But we have even greater prizes ahead of us,' Siward said, adding steel to his voice. His men fell silent once more. 'We are strong already, this is true, but if we were stronger still we could plunder Majorca . . . even Sicily. I say we need these good English warriors alongside us.'

For a long moment, only the wind whined among the rocks. Hereward could see no welcome among the sea wolves for their leader's words. They wanted blood, and they would not be satisfied until they had it.

'Let them prove themselves,' one man called out.

'Aye,' another said, sneering. 'If these warriors are so great, let their leader fight Bedhelm the Giant.'

Laughter turned to cheers, ones that ran on and on. Hereward could see that Siward had lost control of his pack. There was no way out of this.

'If he is so great, let him fight as he is,' someone else roared. 'With his hands tied behind his back. Surely it would not be a fair fight if Hereward the Giant-killer had his magic sword!'

The cheers drowned out the crashing of the waves and the shrieking of the gulls.

'Very well,' Siward announced when the din had ebbed. 'Bedhelm! Prepare yourself!'

A towering figure loomed up from the crowd. A giant he was, Hereward could see, almost half as tall again as any warrior the Mercian had ever encountered. His chest was broad, his arms like tree-trunks, and as he stepped forward he dragged an axe that must have been made for him alone, so big was it.

'I should take this challenge,' Guthrinc sighed. 'At least he will not think me a dwarf.'

Hereward shook his head. 'No, old friend. This is my burden and mine alone.' He stepped forward before any of his men could volunteer, as he knew they would. The Mercian tested his bonds once more, but the rope was still taut and cut into his wrists.

The giant was prowling along the ranks of his sea wolf brothers, enjoying the cheers. Hereward studied him. There were weaknesses. For all his size, he had no grace. He lumbered like a bear, and his axe, though huge enough to bring down an oak, was heavy and clumsy to wield. More thin hope, but he would take whatever he could.

Stepping down from the rocks, Siward came over, seemingly to jeer. But at the last he leaned in and whispered, 'My sorrow is great, cousin. I did what I could. But this rabble will not be contained, once they have the smell of blood in their noses.

When we fled William's wrath, I fought hard to seize control of this fleet. But it is a poisoned chalice.' He looked down as a shadow crossed his face. 'My hands are tied.'

'As are mine.'

Siward smiled. 'Good. Keep your spirits high, cousin. And stay on Bedhelm's left side. He is half blind in that eye. May God watch over you.'

When he was alone in the centre of the arena, Hereward bowed his head. The chanting of the crowd faded into the background. Now he urged his devil to rise. He welcomed it. Only the rage could help him match his opponent's advantage, even though all there saw him for the dog he truly was. The beast his father had always called him, when old Asketil had shut him in the space under the boards of his hall with only rats for company. He pushed aside his shame and raised his head to peer at his foe. Bedhelm the Giant grinned back. He swung up his axe and whirled it around his head. The crowd roared.

'Come to me,' Hereward murmured to his dark companion. But as the words left his lips, he glanced past the towering warrior and saw a familiar face among the pirates on the edge of the battlefield. The head was bowed, the figure still so as not to draw eyes, but still it was Herrig the Rat. He recalled watching the scout swim away into the night like his namesake as the English stood in the surf offering up their surrender. If any man could have survived and crept back into the heart of their enemy, it was Herrig, a ghost, who left no trace in his passing, no footprint, not even a sigh.

'Come, you little bastard,' Bedhelm said, grinning. 'Let my axe sup your blood.'

Something the giant saw in his opponent's eyes gave him pause for a moment. But then he strode forward, scowling. The axe whisked up.

Balancing on the balls of his feet, the Mercian danced out of the way of the first strike. A cloud of dust plumed where the blade bit into the ground. But his bound hands threw him off balance, and when his foe tried to lop off his head Hereward stumbled. The axe whisked by only a hair's breadth away from opening his skull. Skidding along the stones and sand, he ripped open his cheek. The blood throbbed in his head at the pain.

The blade slammed down again. He rolled out of the way at the last, staggering back to his feet. Remembering Siward's words, he kept to the left, bounding this way and that. Whirling, the giant flailed. The crowd's jeers whipped up into an even greater frenzy, now tinged with frustration. They had expected a head on the ground by this time.

Hereward gritted his teeth and thought of Alric and his suffering. Finally, his devil answered his call.

His vision closed in. The booming in his head drowned out the crowd. There was only Bedhelm. The giant spun round, hacking wildly. Blinking away sweat and grit, Hereward stepped back from the axe. The moment it raised a shower of sparks on the stones, he hurled himself forward. Placing one foot on his foe's thigh, he launched himself up.

Bedhelm jerked his head back, too late. The Mercian clamped his teeth on to the other man's cheek and bit deep. Blood bubbled around his teeth. With a yank of his head, he ripped the meat away from the bone. The giant howled in agony.

Hereward spat out the torn cheek as he fell. When he crashed into the ground on the edge of the arena, he heard Bedhelm's roars dully through the pulsing of his own blood. He had bought himself a moment. Jerking into a kneeling position, he felt the sea wolves try to press him back into the battle. But his fall had not been by chance.

As filthy hands clawed at his back, he felt a lighter pressure on his bonds. In an instant, they broke, and an instant later something cold pressed into his palm. He wrenched forward. Glancing back, he saw that Herrig the Rat had wriggled back into the mass of bodies and was gone. But he had done enough.

Hereward's fingers closed around the hilt of the knife. Distantly, he was aware of the crowd yelling in fury that his hands were free and that he was now armed. But somewhere Siward was smiling. He would not allow his men to interfere in this battle, the Mercian knew that.

Fury engulfed him. Anger at the betrayal that had cost him victory against William the Bastard. Anger at his cold dismissal from his homeland. Anger at all the miseries fate had dealt him in his life.

Through the crimson haze, he glimpsed Bedhelm, eyes wide in shock at the apparition bearing down upon him. The sea wolf swung his axe half-heartedly in his confusion. Hereward slid under the blade and ripped the edge of the knife across his foe's wrist.

Bedhelm barely had time to cry out in pain. The Mercian clawed his way up the towering frame and rammed the knife into the giant's right eye. Hooking his left arm around Bedhelm's neck, Hereward swung his body around and used his weight to drag his foe back. The giant clawed at the air. Releasing his grip, Hereward plunged the blade into his defeated foe's neck and wrenched it across the throat.

The world turned red.

Silence fell across the arena. Slowly Hereward turned, staring back at the army of sea wolves, who could scarcely believe what they had seen. As the thunder in his head faded away, he realized how he must look, slicked in blood from head to toe. More beast than man. As he once had been; as, it seemed, he was fated always to be.

CHAPTER TWENTY-FIVE

The sea wolves swept across the aquamarine swell. Sails billowed in the ocean breeze. At the oars the men chanted a song of blood and gold to keep the rhythm of their rowing. Sunlight shimmered off helms and hauberks, spear-tips and axe-heads so that it seemed a brittle, unearthly illumination shone out of the sea itself. From the walls of Sabta, perched on a finger of land reaching out from the northern coast of Afrique, the guards must have been struck by fear when they saw such a force bearing down on them.

Standing in the prow of the lead vessel, Hereward watched the town approaching across the white-crested waves. Even from that distance he could tell that Sabta had seen better days. Sections of the walls had crumbled and no effort had been made to repair them. Towers were broken teeth and roofs sagged. Black smoke plumed and white clouds of screeching gulls fed upon the refuse dumped in the lapping waters. No flag flew.

'If your grand plan works, you will earn yourself many new friends,' Siward said, his white-blond hair flying in the wind.

'Salih ibn Ziyad knows this town well. There is gold aplenty here.' That was no lie, and it was only fair that Siward would get some reward for unknowingly aiding his cousin's plans, Hereward thought.

The sea wolf leader gave a wry smile. 'Lying in the streets for us to pluck up as we pass.'

'Sabta is a city of thieves. They plunder the length of this coast and the lands beyond the whale road and bring it all here. But there is no rule of law. No wergilds. No army, no *fyrd*. No king or earls or thegns to see justice done. In Sabta there is only the rule of the axe. Once the Umayyad caliph abandoned the place, every rogue with ten men to command thought himself king.' The Mercian shielded his eyes against the sun. 'There will be no true defence. When we strike we will carve through the town like hot pork and take everything we wish.'

Siward nodded. 'It is good to have you at my side again, cousin.'

Hereward looked across the fleet of ships. 'You have done well for yourself.'

His cousin laughed without humour. 'William the Bastard left me . . . left all of us . . . with little choice. Our land was stolen. Our kin were hunted. The England we remembered was razed to the ground. You know that as well as any man. These . . .' He swept his arm out to indicate the vessels. 'These are not sea wolves. They are farmers, millers, woodworkers, huscarls, warriors who fought for their earls. Good men who have had all they knew ripped from their hands. Who have seen their wives and children murdered.'

The Mercian heard the crack of emotion in his cousin's voice. Siward peered towards their goal, his face drawn. 'We do what we must to survive, as all men do.'

'Survival—'

'Is not the filling of an empty belly, or a drink when the throat is dry, or a hearth-fire in the cold of winter. It is home, cousin. It is a place where we can be the men we were meant to be.'

Hereward felt a surprising pang. These words he understood.

It was as if he had been searching for such a place all his life. Glancing back at the benches, he saw Guthrinc and Kraki and Sighard and all the others, just as lost, just as hopeful.

Siward pointed to the town's defences. 'We will break through where the walls have collapsed. Sweep into the heart of Sabta from all sides. They have no army, no generals. They will not know where to defend first.'

Hereward nodded. 'We will run them ragged.'

The leader of the sea wolves looked across his fleet, frowning. 'How many have fled England?' he mused, his voice wistful. 'There was a time when it seemed every ship was used to escape those shores. All those who could leave have done so. None of us here could face another winter with William's boot upon our throat.'

'I heard tell that many ran to join the Danes, and others went in search of a great land to the west. The Vikings told tales of a place far beyond the whale road that could only be reached by their secret routes, even though they were never out of sight of land.' Hereward shook his head in amazement.

'Once we have all the gold we need, we will sail to a new land and there we will build a new England,' Siward said. 'A safe place where we can have our comforts as we knew them. Our hearth-fires, our kin, our earls and thegns, our fine art, our laws. A place where women can speak freely and hold their head high as they once did, before William insisted they bow their heads to their husbands.' His wistful voice hardened. 'The Normans live in a cold world of castles, and vast, empty churches, and tax ledgers, as cold as William the Bastard's heart. Our new home will be . . .' For a moment he let the words hang as he looked towards the sunlit horizon, and then he clapped the Mercian on the shoulder and smiled. 'When our attack begins, watch yourself, Hereward. Bedhelm had friends. They will not forgive you easily. In the thick of battle in a narrow street, it is as easy to get a blade in the back as in the front.'

Once Siward had returned to the tiller-man, Hereward studied the town. His plan was unfolding as he had hoped. The lure of great riches had been enough to convince the sea wolves that an attack on Sabta was a worthy goal, especially when Salih had told them that only chaos existed behind the town's crumbling walls. No one guessed that by now Meghigda would be a captive there. And with the bounty that Arcadius' father had placed upon her head making her a prize worth more than all else that could be looted from the town, he intended that they never should.

Hereward watched the ships race across the swell to surround the promontory. Siward had planned well. Whatever ragged defence Sabta could muster would be stretched thin along three sides of the town. Resting one foot on the side of the ship, he let his gaze run along the broken walls, seeing the guards scurrying along the ancient stones, their cries of warning ringing deep into the heart of the town.

Another yell echoed, this time from behind him. A hubbub of alarm followed. The Mercian whirled to see Maximos held against the mast by Salih, the silver dagger pressed against the Roman's neck. The wise man's eyes bulged with fury, his lips curling back from his teeth.

Hereward bounded across the deck and dragged him back. 'Have you lost your wits?' he hissed. 'This will not help us rescue your queen.' He kept his voice low so that the sea wolves could not overhear.

For a moment Salih remained rigid, staring coldly into the other man's eyes. Finally he threw off the Mercian's grip and walked away without a word. Hereward turned to the Roman.

'What did you say to him to drive him to such anger?'

Maximos brushed himself down, grinning. 'He is a sour man. He does not laugh enough.'

The Mercian pressed his hand in the other man's chest to prevent him from leaving. The Roman's eyes narrowed. 'This is not the time to be fighting among ourselves. I will cut you down before you place Alric at risk, know that.'

'I have fought in Phrygia and Duklja, aye, and at Manzikert too,' Maximos snapped, pushing the English warrior's hand to one side. 'I know the battlefield, and I know what it is like to have sword-brothers beside me, men whose lives are in the palm of my hand. Do not insult me.'

Hereward nodded. 'Very well. But understand, we need Salih if we are to reach Alric and Meghigda. Only he can guide us through that maze.'

'He loves her,' the Roman said abruptly.

'The queen?'

Maximos snorted. 'Could you not see it? It is present in every look he ever cast at her, every gesture, every word. Salih ibn Ziyad once had the ear of the caliph himself, so they say, and riches and power were set before him. But he gave it all up to stand beside a warrior queen fighting for a patch of sand. He loves her, Hereward, and he has always resented that Meghigda only had eyes for me.'

Hereward eyed the wise man, who was brooding astern with Siward. 'Do not vex him, then,' he commanded. 'Our enemies are waiting for us. And there will be no victory if we do not stand together.' He felt the familiar throb of blood in his temples. He needed the din of battle to still the voices that had been whispering in his head since he had slain the giant. Only then would he find peace. 'Keep your spears and axes and shields to hand,' he called to his warriors. 'When the ship nears the shore, there will be little time to prepare yourselves.'

The faces of the English lit with an inner light. Here was purpose. Honour. No more running and hiding.

Maximos joined him in the prow to watch the town walls racing towards them. 'The Carthaginians were here first. It was Abyla then.' With a note of pride, he added, 'But it was not until the Romans took the city that it became a force to be reckoned with. They named it Septa, and from here the army controlled vast swathes of the dry land in these parts.'

'You know your days long gone,' Hereward grunted.

'I know the long and illustrious history of our empire. We are taught it as children, for our days yet to come are seeded in the pride we feel for the power we have wielded since ancient times.'

Hereward heard an odd note in the other man's voice, and when he glanced at him it seemed that tears glistened in his eyes. But there was no time to puzzle over that. Spray whisked over the prow as the ship ploughed into the shallows. He heard Siward give the order for his sea wolves to stop rowing. On every side the ships swept in. Raucous voices rang out across the swell, everyone there fired up for the coming battle.

Along the walls, men swathed in robes and headcloths swarmed, their swords glinting in the sunlight. But as he squinted, Hereward glimpsed other movement. Whirling, he roared, 'Shields!'

His warriors responded without a second thought, their shields whisking up above their heads. Behind them, Siward's men only gaped. An instant later, arrows rained down from the sky.

Hereward braced himself, his head bowed behind his white Imazighen shield. Shafts whistled by his head. Two rattled off the hide covering, but a third and a fourth punched through the wood. Splinters spun at him.

At his back, screams rang out. He glanced over his shoulder and saw a sea wolf clawing at his face as he staggered across the deck. An arrow was embedded in his right eye. The man was dead; he had not yet realized it. Three other men slumped on the benches, shafts bristling from their torsos.

His face contorted with fury, Siward was bellowing at his slow-moving sea wolves. Finally they dragged their shields from the sides of the ship and raised them high.

More shafts whisked down. Most splashed harmlessly into the waves. Sabta had sent its slaves to the walls to try to cut down as many of the attackers as they could before land was reached. But they were not trained bowmen. Only the numbers were a threat.

In the shade of his own shield, Maximos was grinning. The tip of an arrow had burst through the wood a hand's width from his face. Reaching around the edge, he snapped off the shaft and tossed it away.

'This is what we live for,' he said, his voice filled with exuberance.

'Battle is a serious business.'

The Roman laughed. 'You are too grim, Mercian. You must drink deep of every moment. Our days are short.' And with that, he put one hand on the side of the ship and vaulted into the shallows.

Hereward thrust one arm into the air and snapped it forward. Instantly, his warriors leapt from their benches. Over the lips of their shields, he could see eyes afire with passion. He felt proud.

'For England,' he yelled, and his men picked up the cry.

Leaping over the side, he splashed into the sea. His spear-brothers streamed after him. The din of full-throated battle-cries drowned out even the sound of the ocean as hundreds of sea wolves leapt from their ships at every point where the walls could be breached. Arrows whined through the air. The shafts thumped against shields, rattled off helms. Sabta's defenders had not been expecting an attack. Soon their store of shafts would be exhausted, Hereward knew. Then it would be man against man.

Maximos had his back pressed against the town wall, looking this way and that for the best path. He was laughing as if he were drunk. While wave upon wave of sea wolves broke upon the narrow, rocky shore near where the walls had crumbled most, the Roman pointed with his sword away from the fiercest activity. Hereward followed the line of his blade. By a small jetty, the maw of a narrow archway gaped. Deep shadow engulfed the passage. There would undoubtedly be men waiting on the other side to pick off any invader who dared venture through the small space.

The Mercian nodded to Maximos and waved his men to follow him. 'Come, brothers,' he yelled as he splashed through the surf. 'Today we must fight like never before.'

Chapter Twenty-Six

The sun glared off the creamy walls of Sabta. But in the narrow archway, the deep shadow seemed endless and impenetrable. Hereward crept to one side of the opening. Maximos darted to the other. Both men pressed their backs against the stone, listening. The deafening roar of the attacking sea wolves drowned out any sound that might have emanated from within.

The Mercian glanced back to the line of warriors sheltering behind their shields along the foot of the wall. When he spied Salih, he beckoned. Arrows whistling by his head, the wise man scrambled over the rocks to the head of the war-band. Cupping his hand against Salih's ear, Hereward whispered his command. The other man nodded. He edged into the dark under the archway. When he heard Salih begin to speak in his throaty native tongue, the Mercian crept in behind him. Sliding Brainbiter out of its sheath, he kept low.

The cramped passage reeked of piss. As his eyes adjusted to the gloom, he eased close behind the wise man. Salih was babbling loudly now, the intonation sounding like prayers. Beyond him, framed in the arch at the end of the short alley, was a long, thin street, thrown into shade by the houses on either side.

After a moment, a questioning voice answered Salih in the same musical tongue. The wise man responded with a stream of impassioned pleas. He stepped through the arch, then darted ahead as Hereward leapt out of the shadows and slashed right and left. He half glimpsed men waiting on either side, two of them, armed with swords. But their guard was down, and both fell. One gurgled his last, but the other twitched on the edge of death.

Kneeling, Salih pressed his lips close to the fallen man's ear. Whatever he said, it made the dying warrior's eyes widen with terror. He jabbered a stream of words and tried to point along the street until the light in his eyes faded. Salih glanced up at the Mercian and nodded.

Satisfied, Hereward poked his head back into the stinking passage and whistled. Maximos and his men eased through the arch at the other end and hurried towards him. Emerging into the street, the warriors gathered by the wall and looked along the deserted way ahead.

Some of the houses were tall and made of stone, heavy with age, perhaps from when the Romans ruled the town. Others were constructed from clay bricks, so roughly made it seemed children had thrown them together. In places the residences had become little more than piles of rubble, and there bands of sunlight punched through the gloom of the street. Most of the din echoed from further along the walls where the fighting was heaviest, but here it was eerily still. Dogs barked, but no voices could be heard. Hiding in their houses, the Mercian thought as he scanned the dark doorways. Smoke drifted along the street from bonfires burning on the areas of rubble. He wrinkled his nose. The place stank of shit and rotting rubbish and age.

'Take care,' he murmured. 'Death could wait anywhere. Not all the defenders will be on the walls.'

Kraki shook his axe. 'If they are wise, they will let us pass.'

'Are we to search the whole town?' Sighard said, looking around. 'How will we ever find Alric in this maze?'

'You think a band of pale-skinned Normans with axes and mail-shirts and helms would not be noticed here?' Salih ibn Ziyad replied with a sly grin. 'There is not a man or woman in all Sabta who does not know where they are.' He glanced down at the dead man he had questioned. 'All will be revealed.'

He whispered the directions to Herrig the Rat. With a gap-toothed grin, the scout crept away, little more than a shadow winding along the foot of the buildings. He glanced into doorways, down alleys. When he was sure the path was safe, he crooked his fingers and beckoned the others to follow.

Hereward nodded, pleased, as he watched the men creep along the edge of the houses. They were as stealthy as if they hunted deer. Let the sea wolves draw all the attention with their noisy plundering. To find their prize, the English needed to be like ghosts, as they had been in the fens.

As they prowled past a low clay shack, a bump echoed from within. Kraki stepped up to the door and waited, listening. Raising his axe, he swung the door open. The smoke of an oven drifted out. Like a wolf ready to leap, the Viking poised on the balls of his feet.

Looking past him, Hereward saw a women squatting in the centre of the bare, smoky room with an infant in her arms. Her eyes glistened with tears of fear and she pulled the child closer to her breast. Rigid, Kraki stared at her for a long moment. The Mercian did not know what the other man was thinking – perhaps remembering Acha, the woman he had left behind in England, and the future that had been lost to him – but then he swung the door shut and hurried back into the line of warriors.

'You should have searched the room,' Sighard said. 'She might not have been alone.'

'If she was not, it would be her husband and she needs him to protect her,' the Viking growled. He looked away, refusing to meet the other man's eyes.

Raucous cheering erupted from several streets away, followed by throat-rending screams. The sea wolves had broken through the meagre defences and were slaughtering anyone who stood between them and their plunder. Hereward imagined the savage fighters flooding into the town. They would be smashing their way into homes and merchants' stores, carrying off anything of value. Anyone who dared try to stop them would be ruthlessly cut down. Sabta might be a town of rogues, but they did not know what had been unleashed upon them that day.

'Let us hurry,' he urged. 'We must reach our prize before Siward's men come. If they realize Meghigda is here, they will not think twice about cutting us down to carry her away.'

Salih wrenched his dagger from its sheath. His eyes flickered along the buildings as the sound of Siward's army ransacking the town thundered along the streets.

Hereward snapped his arm forward, and his men broke into a lope. Soon they had outpaced the noise of the invaders.

Ahead, a bank of smoke drifted across the street. The English warriors slowed. Hereward felt the stink of burning refuse catch in the back of his throat.

'We are close now,' Salih murmured as he sidled up. He jabbed his dagger towards the smoke. 'The ruined man and his Norman allies have found their fortress beyond there, past the forum. The basilica. An old Roman building, made of stone.'

'They will be able to defend it well,' Maximos said.

'Only if they are expecting us,' Hereward replied. 'Surprise is still on our side.' He waved his men on.

The choking smoke closed around them. Through the haze, Hereward glimpsed the ruddy glow of the bonfire in a space between two houses. Nearby, two dogs fought over a bone, snapping as they tore at each other.

When he prowled forward, the Mercian sensed movement on the edge of his vision. A warning cry rang out. He levelled his blade as two men raced from the dense cloud, whirling swords above their heads. Their robes were black and smudged with ashes. Above the cloths tied across their mouths their eyes shone with a cold light.

As they ran, the defenders shrieked a battle-cry. It was answered away in the smoke, and again, and again. Eight times Hereward heard that cry. Running feet thundered across the baked mud of the street at his back.

The first attacker brought his blade down. Bracing himself, the Mercian swung Brainbiter up to parry the strike. Sparks flew as iron met iron. Furious fighting erupted around him.

For a moment, Hereward and his foe held each other tight, their blades locked together. Then the Mercian heaved. When his enemy stumbled on to his back foot, the English warrior carved the edge of his sword across his opponent's stomach. The defender reeled back into the smoke, screaming.

Hereward glanced round to see Guthrinc lifting the other attacker high off the ground upon his spear. The man thrashed like a fish on a spike and then grew still.

The clash of weapons ebbed, even as the Mercian turned. His spear-brothers had made short shrift of the attackers. Robed bodies littered the street.

'Too much noise,' he muttered, trying to peer ahead through the drifting smoke.

'There are screams and battle-cries all over Sabta,' Guthrinc said with a shrug. 'A few more will make no difference.'

Hengist had stopped cleaning his blade upon one of the fallen men's headcloths and was frowning as he peered towards the bonfire.

'What do you see?' Hereward asked.

The madman crept towards a pile of dust among the rubble as if he were approaching a sleeping dog. A round, dark lump was just visible in the sand. Turning his head this way and that, Hengist stood before it, before stretching out an index finger and slowly reaching towards the spot. As he pressed it, the lump seemed to give. The dust fell away on either side to reveal a nose. An instant later, more sand streamed away and two eyes appeared. They blinked.

Hengist jumped back as a young boy pushed himself up from the fine covering of dust. He looked around the group and grinned. 'English,' he said in a heavily accented voice. Before anyone could react, he had leapt to his feet and was racing in the direction where Salih had said the basilica lay.

'Stop him!' Hereward commanded.

The madman sprinted away, but the Mercian could already see the boy was too fast for him. Hengist loped back a moment later, shaking his head.

Salih uttered a cackling epithet in his own tongue. 'A spy for our enemies. He will warn them.'

'What is done is done,' Hereward replied. 'Come.' He bounded off along the street. He would not, could not, think what would happen to Alric if Ragener knew his hated enemy was coming for him.

Breaking through the smoke, the English warriors found themselves on the edge of a wide, deserted forum. The ancient flagstones lay shattered, buckling up in parts, missing in others. Trails of coarse sand streamed across the square. In the centre stood a plinth and the remnants of a statue of some great person or other, broken away at the calves.

And beyond the forum, the basilica loomed up against the blue sky. Though it had seen better days, Hereward thought it still looked formidable compared to the wood and thatch halls of his homeland. Columns on plinths marched across the front of the towering stone building, reaching up for two storeys. On the upper level, a white marble frieze glowed in the sun. Shadows flooded three doorways.

The Mercian imagined the interior would be a warren of chambers, corridors and stairs. In their fortress, the Normans would be almost impregnable. He looked around at his men and saw they thought the same.

'Alric is a spear-brother. We leave no man to die alone,' he reminded them.

Guthrinc looked at Sighard and gave a wry smile. 'I have seen worse.'

'Come, then,' Kraki growled, shaking his axe in the air. 'Let us spill a little Norman blood and put paid to the memory of our loss in Ely. For the monk! For England!'

CHAPTER TWENTY-SEVEN

Thunder rumbled in the distance. Sunlight flashed through a canopy of leaves. England was turning to autumn, the land growing golden and ochre, the sweet scent of fallen fruit on the breeze. Alric drifted, at peace. Here was his favourite time of the year, as the heat faded and the cool nights drew in. What better place to be than England in autumn! With the hearth-fire lit, and friends gathered by. Comfort.

Thunder cracked.

Through the trees, voices murmured. Ghosts. The monk threw an arm across his face. He did not want to hear them. He did not want them to intrude upon this peace.

But the voices hissed on, growing louder, and the distant booms drew nearer, no longer thunder. His body was afire. He yearned to be back in the woods once more, but he could feel them slipping away.

A foot thundered into his ribs and he yelped and jerked up. Misery descended upon him. The air was hot and dry. His head rang, and his body was a web of pain. No autumnal woods, no peace. His torment had not ended, would not end.

'Leave him be!' Meghigda's fingers crooked into claws. Alric knew she would tear away whatever remained of Ragener's face if she could. Without looking, the Hawk waved a finger at her. As always, the Norman guards were close by. They would be upon her before she moved.

Alric shuffled up and rested his back against the stone wall. He could not bring himself to look down at the filthy, bloody cloth tied around what remained of his left hand. But the ringing agony told its own story. Two fingers gone now. Ragener was making good his threat to whittle him down bit by bit. How much more of this he could bear he did not know.

'Your friend has come for you,' the Hawk lisped, pushing his face close. He forced a grin through ragged lips. 'But he will find only his death.'

'Hereward?' the monk croaked. He looked past the ruined man and saw a boy waiting on the far side of the deserted chamber.

Ragener stood up, and turned to the guard near the door. The Norman had not been unkind during his captivity, Alric thought. Even he seemed sickened by the horrors that the sea wolf was inflicting. 'Fetch Drogo,' the Hawk said. 'He would know that his enemy is here.'

'He will not be disturbed. He is with his women,' the guard replied in faltering English.

'If the English attack and he is not prepared, you will be the first to fall to his blade.'

The guard hesitated for only a moment and then strode out.

Alric felt cool fingers on his burning wrist. Meghigda had reached out to comfort him, but he felt sickened by the pity he saw on her face. Had he fallen so low? Was his life truly ebbing away?

'All will be well,' she murmured.

He forced a smile. They had grown close during his suffering. Though she never spoke of her thoughts, he glimpsed a kindly nature behind the hardness he had first witnessed.

Ragener wandered across the room and suddenly lashed out at the boy with the back of his hand. The lad seemed prepared for this assault, for he danced away, cowering in one corner. The Hawk only ever attacked those he thought weaker than himself, Alric reflected. To the pirate, kindness was a weakness. Care. Love. Beauty. All of them, weaknesses. How he hated him. Though he was a gentle man in all things, he knew that if he had the chance he would kill Ragener to be free of him; to free the world of him. The monk felt cold anger burn inside him, and loathing.

As Ragener prowled the room, casting hungry glances towards his victim, Alric realized that what he had thought was thunder was the sound of a tremendous battle raging across the town. Before he could work out what this meant, Drogo Vavasour whirled in. He was stripped to the waist, his torso still slick with the sweat of his lovemaking. Three naked women hovered outside the door.

'Is this true?' the nobleman snapped.

Ragener nodded, his eyes gleaming with eagerness. 'We will both get our revenge.'

Drogo snorted. He seemed to have little love for the sea wolf. He barked an order to his guards and they hurried out. Alric heard the rest of the force emerge from their resting place. He felt his heart sink. Ragener was right – Hereward and all of the English had been lured to their deaths, and he was responsible. If only he had been quicker to react when the war-band first attacked.

The nobleman crossed the chamber and knelt before his crucifix, which he had hung on one wall. Alric had watched him pray ten times a day. Never had he seen a profane man so devout. After muttering a prayer, the knight strode to the window and peered out into the blazing sun. He seemed unperturbed by the sound of fighting, but as he peered down into the forum he gritted his teeth.

'You are right, Hawk. The English are there,' Drogo growled. 'But they are waiting. Too scared to come to us. They hope we will venture out into the forum where the battlefield is level.'

'Then we must make sure they come to us,' Ragener said with a grin. Alric's eyes widened as he glimpsed the knife that had tortured him so much. Meghigda screamed in fury, but the Hawk only laughed as he strode towards his prey.

CHAPTER TWENTY-EIGHT

The throat-rending scream rang out across the forum. So loud was it that for an instant it cut through the rumble of the approaching battle. The English warriors stiffened as they sheltered in the shade of the smoky street. Hereward felt ice-water rush through him. Though anyone could have been responsible for that harrowing cry, his instincts told him the truth.

A figure appeared at one of the dark windows on the upper level. At that distance, Hereward found it impossible to identify the shape, but the lisping voice of Ragener was unmistakable. 'Come, you dogs. Come! Or there will be nothing left of him!' He leaned out and tossed something into the forum.

Herrig the Rat bounded forward. Fearing a trap, he scurried along one edge of the square and then raced into the centre, stooping to snatch up whatever had been thrown before darting back. Hereward knew what it was before the scout offered up the bloody index finger, severed just below the knuckle.

Kraki gripped his leader's arm. 'Do not let your anger consume you. They want to lure us into a trap.'

'We have no choice,' the Mercian replied, his voice cold and dead. But in his head the blood began to pound its familiar beat of rage and destruction and doom.

Sighard stepped in front of him. 'We will follow you to the death, if need be. You know that.'

The Mercian shook his head. Now he had seen this fortress, he had weighed all possible outcomes and made his decision. 'It is me they want. I go alone,' he heard himself say, the words echoing as if from the bottom of a well. 'Leave here. Go to Constantinople. Find your fortune.'

'No!' Salih insisted. 'We cannot abandon al-Kahina.' He looked to Maximos. 'What say you?'

The Roman nodded. 'Aye. You do not go alone, Mercian. You have two more at least.'

But Hereward did not hear his words. Throwing his head back, he roared his fury, a terrible sound that rang off the stone walls. And then he was racing across the forum, axe in hand.

As he drew nearer to the basilica, he glimpsed movement in the windows. Crossbow bolts whisked by, smashing against the flagstones. Dimly, he heard Sighard cry out, no doubt remembering how one of those bolts had taken the life of his brother. Hereward swung his shield up just in time. A bolt rammed through the wood. As he ran, he wrenched it out and tossed it away.

For a brief moment, the air seemed black with shafts, but then the volley ended. There would be no second volley, he knew. It would take them too long to reload their weapons.

He reached the shadow of the portico and slowed his step. When the drumbeat of running feet echoed behind him, he realized all his men had followed him into the jaws of death. Through the haze of his rage, he felt a pang of pride.

The central doorway loomed ahead, thick with shadow. Darting to one side of the opening, Sighard knelt and listened. Hiroc the Three-fingered ghosted to the other side. Hereward had no time for their caution.

Gritting his teeth, he sprinted to the entrance. At the last, he dived and rolled, swinging his axe to the right. He had been right. One of his enemies waited on the inside of the doorway, his double-edged sword ready to sweep down the moment Hereward marched into the basilica. The Mercian's blade hacked through the man's ankle. Screaming, the Norman toppled backwards.

Another warrior waited on the other side. Hereward's rolling entrance had taken him by surprise. But he was a seasoned fighting man, and he had steadied himself quickly. His sword was already hacking down. Continuing his roll into a sitting position, the Mercian thrust up. With all his weight behind his weapon, the axe smashed through the man's chin and tore his face in two. His helm flew off, rattling across the chill stone.

The guard had not even fallen to the ground before Hereward had whirled, ready to face the other Normans sweeping across the hall. A low growl rumbled from his throat. He had the taste for blood now, and the devil in his heart. This was how it had been when he was a youth, tearing through the east recognizing no law that could bind him. This was how he had been on that first night when he had met Alric in the frozen Northumbrian forest, before the monk had helped to tame him.

He felt no shame now. He felt nothing at all.

Roaring, he ran at the first warrior, with scant regard for his own safety. His fearless approach seemed to stun the Norman, for he failed to raise his guard in time. Hereward hacked his axe into the man's forearm, almost severing his hand. The sword clattered to the floor.

The next man was upon him in an instant. This one brought his long shield up in good time, so that the Mercian's weapon slammed into the centre of the wood. Splinters flew as he wrenched the axe back and hacked again.

His men surged in on every side, forming a shield wall, protecting his back. As if through a fog, Hereward heard the clash of steel, the crack of breaking wood, the cries of the wounded.

His vision closed in on the man in front of him. The Norman warrior was a skilled swordsman, the Mercian could see. His blade danced high, then low, round the edge of his shield. But he was not prepared for Hereward's ferocity. The axe rained down, the sheer force of the blows driving the man back. When Hereward glimpsed the flicker of unease in his foe's eyes, he knew he had him. As the warrior raised his shield in anticipation of another direct assault, the Mercian switched his attack. His axe swung around the back of the swordsman at waist height, and then he yanked it towards him. Hooked by the weapon, the Norman could do nothing as it tore through his side. Within a moment, he lay dead.

Spinning round, Hereward threw himself at the remaining Normans, who were trapped between his whirling axe and the spears stabbing from behind the shield wall. Soon, they too fell.

'How many more are there?' Sighard gasped.

'Ten. Twenty. An army.' Kraki shrugged. 'The worst lies ahead.'

'You speak truth,' Maximos said, wiping his sword clean on a dead man's tunic. 'They have chosen well where to make their stand. Above us is a rabbit's warren. Small chambers, large chambers, a narrow path between them. Easy to defend. Easy to die.'

'We cannot wait,' Salih said, glancing towards the stairs. 'They will harm their captives to try to draw us in too fast . . . make mistakes . . .'

Hereward let the words ebb away. Beckoning his men to follow him, he loped through the pool of blood. Red footprints trailed him across the marble floor.

At the foot of the stone steps, he glanced up. A shaft of sunlight streamed through a window. All was still, and he put his foot on the first step. Immediately, a dark figure stepped into the glare. Hereward ducked back, and not a moment too soon. A crossbow bolt whistled down the stairs and slammed into the wall, raising a cloud of dust.

Maximos cursed. 'They will pick us off one by one if we try to climb.'

Hereward smothered his fury. He needed a clear head now. 'When the Normans invaded England, King Harold had the high ground at Senlac Ridge,' he snarled. 'It did him no good. If we use our wits and our skills as warriors we will overcome.' He glanced back up the stairs. 'The way turns at the top. There is little space. They will not be able to send out more than a few men at a time—'

Another cry rang out from the upper levels. This time it was a woman. The blood drained from Maximos' face and he would have bounded up the steps had not Hereward caught his arm. 'Save your rage. Use it wisely,' the Mercian hissed.

The Roman's face simmered with angry frustration, but he caught himself.

'Shield wall,' Hereward commanded. 'Don't think that you are in a great hall in a strange land. We are climbing a hill in the fens to defeat our enemies. We have done it before. We can do it again.' Even as he spoke, the Mercian knew this would be far harder. The steps allowed space for only three men abreast, and they were steep. One turned ankle would split open their defences.

Hereward called Guthrinc and Hiroc the Three-fingered to join him in the first rank. Their spears were necessary for what he had planned. The shields locked into place across the front and above their heads.

'In step,' he bellowed, 'and watch your feet.'

Behind the shields, the heat swelled. Sweat dripped from their brows, stinging their eyes. Feeling for each step, they began to climb.

A volley of crossbow bolts thundered off the wood. Silence followed for a long moment, then more bolts rattled down. Wood cracked. The Normans were sending their men in waves, giving each spent one time to reload.

'Keep the fire in your hearts, brothers,' Hereward hissed.

'They will not have an endless supply of shafts. Soon they will have wasted them all.'

The wall edged up the steps. When they neared the top, a command rang out in the Norman tongue. 'Brace yourselves!' Hereward shouted, knowing what was coming.

Axes rained down, each clash jolting deep into English bones. The boots of their enemies slammed against the shields as the Normans tried to press the English back down the steps. The line buckled under the weight.

'Now!' Hereward shouted.

The front shields slid apart. With a roar, Guthrinc and Hiroc stabbed their spears through the gaps. Agonized cries echoed as the tips ripped through groins and thighs. The tumbling wounded were enough to cause confusion in the Norman ranks. The English swept up the final steps like a battering ram, crushing their enemies against the wall at the top. An instant later the wounded Normans had been put out of their misery, and the survivors had retreated.

Hereward lifted his shield. 'Catch your breath,' he said to his warriors as he wiped the sweat from his eyes. Edging across the space at the top of the stairs, he looked out. A passage ran along the length of the building with chambers leading off it.

But from here the basilica looked very different. As Hereward glanced around the upper level, he could see only ruin. He looked up into clear blue sky. A large section of the roof had collapsed, the tiles lying shattered across the floor. Much of the structure seemed to have slid into the area at the rear of the building. Interior walls had crumbled, with gaping holes leading from chamber to chamber. The parts that were open to the elements baked in the heat of the midday sun.

Whirling, he pressed his finger to his lips. He pointed at Herrig the Rat, Sighard and three others, the smallest men in his war-band, and whisked his hand, directing them across the passage into the gaping chamber on the other side. No questions were asked; they were well trained.

As they darted across the gap, crossbow bolts whined down the passage and thudded into the far wall. When the echoes had faded, an accented voice called out, 'Hereward.'

The Mercian hesitated for a moment, then replied, 'Who is there?'

From the opposite chamber, Herrig was flashing a grin. The Rat seemed to know no fear. Hereward jabbed a finger towards the heavens, and the other man nodded.

'My name is Drogo Vavasour,' the voice called back. 'Have you heard of me?'

'I have not.' He watched as his five men crossed the chamber and used the shattered window sill as a ledge to lever themselves up to a point where they could reach the broken roof timbers. In the window, Sighard swayed dangerously, flailing his arms to try to regain his balance. Without looking, Herrig snaked out a hand and snarled it in the younger man's tunic to steady him. Sighard looked queasy, but to his credit he pushed aside his fears and followed Herrig up through the gaping timbers and on to the roof.

'No doubt you did not know my brother's name, when you cut off his head and stuck it on a spike outside your father's hall.' The Norman voice wavered, as if the owner were fighting to control his simmering emotion.

Hereward grimaced. Even here, a world away from his home, he could not escape his days gone by. Sometimes he thought he would be paying for his actions for the rest of his life. 'That was war, Norman.'

'That was slaughter!' This time the voice cracked. 'There was no honour in what you did. My brother did not die as a warrior on the battlefield. He was stuck like a pig at a feast.'

The Mercian would never forget his fury that night. The Normans had driven his father out of his fine hall and had made it their home while they brought terror to the folk of his village. And worse. He gritted his teeth. 'Your brother had no honour. He killed my own brother, and cut off *his* head, and placed it above my father's gate, for nothing more than a word out of turn. I showed him a kindness, Norman. He deserved far worse than a head for a head.'

The timbers creaked. A tile slid off and shattered in the forum far below.

'Lies!' Drogo roared, too inflamed to pay attention to what was happening over his head. 'Step out where I can see your face. You have my word my men will not send their bolts into you.'

Though Guthrinc reached out to stop him, Hereward strode into the passage. At the far end, six men trained their crossbow bolts upon his heart. In the doorways, the Mercian glimpsed other warriors. The number of Normans remaining was about the same as that of his own men, he estimated. That was good. A tall, muscular warrior studied him. Hereward guessed this was Drogo Vavasour.

'Over the years I have dreamed of this moment,' the knight said. 'Your face is not how I imagined. I thought you a wild beast . . . but you are just a man.'

'Aye,' Hereward replied. 'As are we all.'

His grip trembling, the Norman levelled his sword. 'I want your head. Then my brother can know peace.'

'Your brother is dead and gone. As is mine.' His anger began to simmer once more and he tried to stifle it. 'All this, all the suffering you have inflicted on my friend, because of something that happened so long ago.'

'There is no escaping judgement, you English dog. I *will* take your head. And your men will be put to the sword. And you will all be forgotten here, as you have been forgotten in England. And then, only then, will there be an ending.'

While Vavasour spoke, Hereward listened for any sounds from above. 'Then we waste our breath. Let us be done with this.' He stepped back into the space at the top of the steps. Along the passage, he heard the knight bark orders in the guttural Norman tongue. Footsteps rang out as the warriors repositioned themselves.

Turning, Hereward gave his command. In twos and threes, half his men dashed into the opposite chamber and crept through the broken wall into the adjoining room. Before the Normans could understand what was happening, the Mercian led the rest of his men out into the passage, crouching behind their shields. Bolts thumped into the wood. The order of the shield wall had always worked well for the English on the battlefield, but here it was little use. Only their own strength and courage would see them through this fight.

Hereward exchanged looks with Kraki and Guthrinc. They were ready. His fingers tightened around the haft of his axe, and, with a roar, he threw himself into battle.

CHAPTER TWENTY-NINE

Alric jerked awake. The screams of the dying rang through the sweltering heat. For a moment he thought he had descended into the very depths of hell. But then his wits began their march back from the edge of that great black ocean where they had fled when Ragener had started to take his third finger. Through the haze, he could smell burned flesh and he glanced down. To stem the bleeding, the stump above his knuckle had been seared by the blade the Hawk kept in the smouldering coals in one of the other rooms. He looked away, tears stinging his eyes.

Through the blur, his gaze fell upon Meghigda and he was surprised to see she was smiling. She tugged at his sleeve and whispered, 'Our moment has come.'

'What is this madness?' he croaked.

'Listen,' she murmured, her eyes twinkling.

The monk forced his way through the swathes of pain until he could focus upon the crash of iron upon wood, the battle-cries, the moans, the rattle of mail-shirts, the shrieks. A battle was raging nearby. In that very hall?

'Your friends are here,' the queen said. 'They have come to save you.'

Alric could scarcely believe her words. He had consigned himself to days of agony before a slow, lingering death. All hope had gone.

Trembling, he glanced towards the door. Ragener crouched there, craning his neck to see what was happening. Too much of a coward to join the battle, the churchman thought with contempt.

Whatever the sea wolf could see outside left him shaking with fear. When a loud crash reverberated as if something had fallen through the roof itself, he jumped to his feet and raced back across the chamber to kneel beside Alric, relief flooding his face. 'You yet live – I did not think you would survive this time,' he lisped. 'Then you still have some value. Come with me. We will use your life to bargain for our own.' He crooked the fingers of his good hand in the monk's tunic and began to haul him upright.

But before he could stand, Meghigda leapt. Wrapping her headcloth around his neck, she yanked it tight. Fury twisted her face, and when Alric looked into it he felt afraid. 'I am al-Kahina,' she snarled, 'priestess, soothsayer, slayer of devils, and I have seen your future, sea wolf. Only death awaits you.'

Eyes bulging, the Hawk bucked and thrashed as he tried to throw her off. But she was stronger than she looked, stronger than any of them realized. The muscles in her forearms were knotted like cords as she hauled the cloth tight and tighter still. Her lips pulled back from her teeth, and her eyes burned with a cold fire.

Hard as the sea wolf tried to push backwards against her, she kept her grip, stepping back every time he thrust so his feet could gain no traction. Spittle flew from his mouth and his face turned red. Desperately, he clawed at the cloth, but he had only one hand and it was not enough.

Finally, his eyelids fluttered, his hand fell away and he became as limp as the weeds in a fenland lake. Once Meghigda was satisfied there was no fight left in him, she opened her

HEREWARD – WOLVES OF NEW ROME

fingers and let him crash to the floor. Alric could see that his tormentor's chest still rose and anger flared in him. He had already choked one man to death, for the sake of Hereward. He could do it again.

'Leave him,' the queen said as if she could read his mind. 'We must help the others.' She felt inside Ragener's tunic until her fingers closed around his knife, still stained with Alric's blood. Turning, she bounded to the door.

Alric pushed himself up on shaking legs. His head spun and he felt too weak to stand. But Meghigda was filled with a righteous anger and he could not see her face danger alone. He felt a surge of admiration as he watched her. She was more fierce than many a seasoned warrior, and braver too. She had more courage than he had, he was sure. Now he could understand how men would follow her to the jaws of hell itself.

His vision blurred. His hand and arm sang with a pain so excruciating he had never felt the like before. Staggering across the chamber, he slumped against the wall next to the queen. 'Tell me,' he croaked, 'how goes it?'

'The battle is hard,' she whispered, 'but Hereward is clever. His men come from two sides, and from the roof itself. They fight like devils.' She leapt back as a bloody sword flew past the doorway and crashed on to the floor.

The queen did not hesitate. As the battle raged near, she darted out into the melee.

Lurching out into the passage after her, Alric found himself looking across a hellish scene. The fighting raged from chamber to chamber. Blood puddled on the marble and bodies and shields and fallen weapons littered the floor. Through the curtain of pain, he found it hard to get his bearings. But then he glimpsed Kraki hacking with his axe and Guthrinc running his spear through a Norman warrior and he realized that Meghigda had been right. Hope surged within him.

Though the fighting had seemed to be evenly matched, the odds turned when al-Kahina flung herself into the fray.

Crimson gushed as she rammed her knife into the neck of one Norman and then slashed it across the throat of another. Her eyes blazed and her hair flew wildly around her head as she waded into the battle without a care for her own safety.

When yet another warrior fell under her blade, Drogo Vavasour wrenched round and saw what havoc she was wreaking. Throwing himself back, the knight swung his shield up and clattered it against the side of her head. The knife flew from her grasp. Stunned, she slammed against the wall and went down hard.

Alric cried out; he could not help himself. But it was clear even then that the Normans had lost; Meghigda's interference had been decisive. Furious, Drogo looked around as man after man fell.

Hearing the monk's cry, Maximos saw the fallen queen and raced to her aid. But the floor was so slick with blood that he slipped and careered into Hereward. The two warriors crashed to the ground.

Vavasour seized his chance. Darting forward, he swung his sword up and cried, 'Now, English dog, I will take that head.'

CHAPTER THIRTY

Hereward felt no fear as he looked up at the man about to take his life. A part of him almost welcomed death. No more whispers from the devil inside him. No more fleeing a past he could never escape. Peace, at last.

The sounds of fighting had ebbed away. Only the moans of the dying rolled out through the basilica. *We have won*, he thought with a note of irony. Though he could feel the eyes of all his men upon him, no one was close enough to save his worthless life, not even Maximos who lay in a heap of tangled limbs and half stunned by the fall.

Drogo uttered some prayer or other in his own tongue and swung the blade down.

But the blow never came. The Norman knight crashed against the wall, a slender figure flailing against him.

Only when he pushed himself back out of harm's way did Hereward see it was Alric. The Mercian felt a pang of horror. The monk looked half dead. His face was bloodless, his eyes fluttered and he could barely stand on his buckling legs. And yet for all that, still he had saved his friend's life.

Acid rose in Hereward's mouth. Drogo Vavasour would not be thwarted. Jerking round, the knight hooked one arm across the churchman's throat and brought his sword up. The monk hung there like a child, too weak to move. 'Your life for his,' the Norman growled.

The Mercian could see his men waiting for his order. Drogo was the only Norman left standing. Getting to his feet, Hereward half raised his axe, then let it fall to his side as Vavasour pressed his blade against Alric's side. His friend would be gutted before he could move.

The tableau was broken when a figure clawed its way out of a chamber further along the passage. Ragener the Hawk lurched towards them on trembling legs, a headcloth trailing from his fingers. 'Wait,' he croaked. 'Before you claim your vengeance—'

'Take her,' Drogo snapped. 'And never let me set eyes upon your cursed face again.'

The sea wolf stumbled up to Meghigda's prone form. For a moment, he looked down upon her with loathing, and then he grabbed a handful of her hair and dragged her towards the door.

'Leave her be!' Salih cried from the end of the passage. He thrust his way forward as Maximos too cried out.

'Stay back,' Drogo spat, digging his sword into Alric's side. 'I gave my word that that snake would go free.' He stared at Hereward and added in a cold voice, 'And we are men of honour, are we not?'

As Maximos jumped to his feet, Kraki and Guthrinc grabbed his arms to hold him back. The Roman raged and tried to throw them off, but they were too strong for him. With their spears, Sighard and Hiroc barred Salih's way. He spat an epithet in his guttural tongue, but he could only watch as Ragener dragged his queen, his love, through the door and out of that blood-soaked place.

Vavasour tightened his arm around the monk's neck, jerking the younger man like a child's corn doll. 'One more time,' he said, backing towards the door. 'Your life for his. Do not doubt me. I have waited too long for this. It is all I have thought of. Come with us . . . just you . . . down these steps and out. I will take your head and leave it – and your friend, alive – for your men.'

Before Hereward could respond, Alric's lips began to move. At first no sound issued from his mouth. But then a rustle of a prayer floated out, his voice rising steadily in devotion, as if the words had released a last reserve of strength within him.

The Mercian could not understand why his friend had chosen this moment to make his supplication, but then he saw a strange shadow cross the Norman knight's face. His eyes darted uneasily towards the monk.

Ending his prayer, Alric said in a husky voice, 'I am God's servant upon this earth. Would you defy his word by taking my life?'

Drogo's sword hand wavered. 'Still your tongue.'

'Your cross hangs in that chamber there,' the monk croaked. 'You know our Lord listens to you. You know he watches. Are you not afraid of his wrath?'

For an instant, the Norman's eyes widened in fear. His lips pulled back from his teeth in frustration and he dragged the monk towards the door. Glowering at Hereward, he said, 'This is not an ending. It is a beginning. Now that I have found you, I will not lose you again. One day, when your eyes are fixed on a distant horizon, I will be at your back. You will not hear me. You will not hear death coming for you. There will be light, and then only darkness, and silence. Think on this as you go about your days. Think on it, and know you will never know peace again.'

Vavasour hurled the churchman away from him. Lunging, Hereward caught Alric and slowly lowered him to the filthy stone. He heard the Norman thunder down the steps, and his own men cry out as they gave pursuit, but now his only care was for his friend.

'Stay with us, monk,' he urged. 'Your days are not yet done.'

He cradled his friend in his arms, sickened by how frail he felt, just a sack of bones. The churchman's breathing was shallow, barely there at all. His eyelids fluttered intermittently, the space between each movement growing longer.

'Stay with us,' Hereward pressed.

His gaze drifted to the monk's ruined hand and he felt his rage grow. Better that than the desperation that clutched at him, or the guilt of the responsibility for all this suffering. Since they had met, Alric had faced death too many times, and all of it, all of it, was his fault.

As he held his friend to his heart, he heard footsteps pounding back up the steps. Sighard burst in, breathless. 'The Norman is gone. He has run towards the battle. Kraki and Guthrinc are searching for him. Maximos and Salih are gone too, after the woman . . .' His voice drifted away when he realized Hereward was paying no heed.

Alric had stirred. His lips were moving as if he wished to make confession. Hereward pressed his ear close to the churchman's mouth. Even then the words were so faint he could barely hear them.

'You must forgive me,' the monk croaked. 'I murdered your brother.'

CHAPTER THIRTY-ONE

A blade of shadow carved a line across the sun-bleached heart of the forum. A man raced across it, his face contorted with terror. Behind him boots thundered upon stone and crimson capes flapped. On every side, the crowd surged as cries of panic swelled across Constantinople. But no sound issued from those running men. Death always waits in silence. The Varangian Guard were hunting down their prey.

Like a frightened rabbit, the fleeing man ran hither and thither, searching for a way to lose himself among the churning bodies. But the citizens scattered too fast ahead of the approaching warriors, and he was left with nowhere to hide. On the edge of the forum, he glanced back in fear at the wave of steel about to break upon him, and he stumbled. As he sprawled on the flagstones, the Varangian Guard swallowed him up.

Standing in the line of shadow bisecting the forum, Deda the knight watched the warriors drag the fugitive to his feet and haul him back the way he had come. The captive's face was bloodless, his knees so weak he could barely stand. From what he had heard of the Guard's fearsome reputation, Deda had expected their victim to be hacked to pieces there and then. Perhaps they wanted answers first.

As the milling crowd calmed, Deda kept his head bowed, his black hair falling in ringlets around his face. Yet his eyes flickered all around, watching for any sign of danger. He felt the weight upon his shoulders, the weariness deep in his bones. Normans were not well liked here; he could not afford to lower his guard for a moment, as he had never rested since he had left England with his wife. Threat was a regular companion these days.

Sensing no enemies, he turned and looked along the shadow to the base of the stone column, then up its dizzying height. Framed against the azure sky, the marble statue of Constantine blazed in the sunlight. In this forum where Nova Roma had been founded, the forgotten sculptor had fashioned the ancient emperor as Apollo, the sun god of the Rome of old, even though Constantine had been the man who had brought forth the word of the Christ. It was fitting, Deda mused. Constantinople was a strange place, caught between pagan and Christian, east and west. Not as openly savage as his Norman homeland, nor as placid as England, where he had, for a while, hoped to find a new home. Even after so many days, he found much of this place a mystery. People said one thing, but meant another. Hands offered in seeming friendship were often turned at the last to their own advantage. Trust was as thin as the autumn mist.

'Men do not run unless they have something to hide.' Wulfrun had ghosted up to his side and was looking up to the top of the column. His face was as graven as the statue atop it. Deda allowed himself a secret smile. So grim, these guards. Did they not see that life was good?

'Men run for many reasons,' he replied. 'Some of them are even good.'

The commander shrugged. 'We shall see, once he has answered all our questions, and given up those who aid him.'

'Plots?'

'Everyone plots.' Wulfrun looked around. 'Where is your wife?'

Deda searched the crowd until he saw Rowena's head bobbing as she laughed with two other women. He was pleased. She had made friends quickly, as was her way. For a while he had feared that wrenching her away from all she had known would be like a blade to the heart. But she was wise, wiser than him. The old ways were gone and they would not be coming back, Rowena knew that. A fresh dawn, in a new home, where they could live their lives as they hoped, was all she wanted.

Leaving her friends, she hurried over. Her eyes narrowed when she saw Wulfrun. 'I have never known a man of the fens to be so mirthless. Did you lie to us when you said you came from Barholme?'

'Barholme lies behind me,' Wulfrun replied without emotion.

'You cannot escape your days gone by. They are always with you.' Rowena's words were playful, but Deda thought he glimpsed a shadow flashing across the commander's face.

'Come.' The guardsman turned and walked towards the east.

When Rowena glanced at Deda with one eyebrow raised, he pressed a finger to his lips to caution her not to tease Wulfrun any more. Sighing a little too loudly, she brushed her shoulder against his in a silent promise that she would comply with his wishes.

When they left the forum, they strode to that part of the city where the wealthy merchants and senators lived. The dome of the Hagia Sophia rose up against the blue sky ahead.

Rowena marvelled at the fine, large houses on either side. The white walls were pristine. Pots of sweet-smelling herbs stood outside each door so that visitors might break a sprig and perfume their fingers as they entered. Here the streets were brighter, cleaner, not like the ones surrounding the shack where they had found lodging on their arrival. No beggars, no roaming dogs, no drunken men fighting in the filth. And yet Deda saw that Wulfrun's fingers never strayed far from the hilt of his sword, and his eyes continually searched the alleys between the houses.

'Never have I seen a place filled with so many wonders,' she whispered. 'And so many folk here! This must be the greatest city in all the world.'

Deda could not disagree. In their short time in Constantinople, he had met not only Englishmen and Danes, but Franks and Arabs and Jews, Syrians, Armenians, Lombards and Hungarians, and others he could not identify, with hair like raven-wings and narrow, slanting eyes. All the peoples of the world were in the process of making their way to this place, it seemed.

Wulfrun brought them to a halt outside an oddly shabby house with, Deda thought, an unsettling air hanging over it. 'The house of Nepos,' the commander said, waving a hand towards the door. 'I promised to find you work. Here is your new home.' He narrowed his eyes at Deda. 'The Nepotes will not pay you. Do not shame them by asking. Come to me for your coin. Understood?'

The Norman nodded. This was an odd arrangement, he thought. But he would not question the kindness, if that was truly what it was.

A slave admitted them to a cool, quiet house. Deda looked around, puzzled by the stark surroundings. In England, a hall like this would be filled with gold chalices and plate, with sumptuous tapestries covering the walls. Hard times must have fallen upon his new employers.

'Wait here,' Wulfrun commanded. He stepped through an archway into an adjoining chamber where he was met by a young woman with hair that gleamed golden in the sunlight streaming through from the courtyard at the rear. After a brief exchange, she glanced over and flashed a sweet smile.

'She is pretty,' Rowena breathed. 'It seems our fierce Varangian is in love.'

Deda gave a wry smile. 'Sadly, it afflicts the best of us.'

The young woman disappeared and returned a moment later with a boy and an older woman, her auburn hair streaked with silver. Though still attractive, the Norman thought how sad she looked. But when she came over to them, a smile lit her face. 'I am Simonis, mistress of this house, and this is my daughter, Juliana. We welcome you to the house of the Nepotes.'

'And we thank you for providing us with shelter,' Rowena said with a bow.

'You will earn your keep,' Wulfrun interjected.

Juliana laughed. 'So gruff!'

The commander's eyes darted towards her, but he remained solemn. Deda was pleased to see that the other man took no offence at the teasing. Perhaps there was more to him than there seemed. 'Your mistress will find you work aplenty,' he said to Rowena. Turning to Deda, he continued, 'The boy's name is Leo. His father is ailing so he is the man of this house and there is much that he must learn to do his duty. Teach him your skills.'

The Norman bowed to Leo. 'I am honoured. I have no doubt you will be a good student.'

'Will you show me how to use a sword to kill?' the boy asked. His look seemed too old for his age. Remembering the harsh days of his own childhood in Normandy, Deda felt a pang of pity for whatever had advanced the lad's years so fast.

'Knights use a sword to fight for honour,' he replied with a smile. 'I will teach you about honour, if you so wish.'

As he turned away, Rowena caught his eye and a look flashed between them: a brief flare of hope that finally the days of struggle and threat could be put behind them.

When Simonis and Juliana led Rowena away to show her her duties, Wulfrun pulled the Norman to one side. 'You are satisfied with this?'

'Of course,' Deda said. 'I am in your debt that you have found work for a man and a woman from beyond this city's walls.'

225

'In Constantinople it matters not where a man comes from, nor a woman either, only what they can do. Men from all countries are running the emperor's offices, and owning land, and making good coin as merchants.' He held out his hands. 'And here am I, an English mud-crawler, well paid for my services to the emperor himself. A good man will thrive here. A weak man, a poor man, will not survive. Make sure you are one of the former.'

'I will.'

The commander leaned in so he would not be overheard. 'I have more work for you than teaching the boy. I cannot always be around so I would have you guard this family too, as part of your duties.'

'They need my protection?'

'You will soon encounter a visitor to this house. Victor Verinus. He is vermin, feeding upon all the good things in life, and he is the source of much of the Nepotes' misfortune. I would not have him cause more.'

'And what would you have me do when I meet this man?'

Wulfrun sighed. Deda could see that this question had troubled him for a while. 'Do not confront him. He is too powerful.' He pointed two fingers to his eyes. 'Watch. Whenever he is under this roof, watch, and hear all. And watch . . .' the word hovered on his lips, 'watch him around Juliana. See that she comes to no harm.'

The Norman nodded. He understood what the other man was saying.

'And protect yourself. Victor Verinus will not like it that there is a spy in the house. Keep out of his way at all times.'

'I have spent many a day around powerful men with tempers as taut as a bowstring,' Deda said in a wry tone, 'not knowing if I am to be given wine or the edge of a blade. That is a good way to learn how to keep your head attached to your neck.'

'Good. Report back to me alone.' Looking around one more

time as if Victor might be there listening, Wulfrun nodded and took his leave.

As the day wound on, Deda sat with Leo and listened to him read. The boy was too serious, rarely smiling at any of his teacher's humour. But he was driven, and determined to learn all that he could to help his kin. The knight understood that. His own father had been a hard man, but he had instilled a sense of duty above all else. Later Deda let the boy take him to meet his father, Kalamdios. The older man's troubles were great indeed, the Norman saw. He was locked inside a useless body, with hands that could only twitch and grasp. And yet his eyes were keen with a fierce intelligence, passion even. The knight felt unsettled that he could not read what he saw there. Was it hatred for the world, despair at his lot in life, or something else?

At dusk, Deda was gnawing on a thin meal of bread and salted fish in the courtyard when he heard a booming voice. Setting aside his food, he strode into the entrance hall where a tall man with a leathery face and long grey hair looked around as if he could smell something unpleasant. He fixed a cold eye upon the new arrival.

'Who are you?'

'My name is Deda. I am a knight.' He offered a friendly smile and a slight bow.

The other man cocked his head, listening to the accent. 'A Norman?'

'Yes.'

'It is not enough that you nibble at our western borders, now you see what you can loot from the city itself?' Contemptuous, he fluttered his fingers at the surroundings. 'You will find little in this place.'

'I am only here to serve the Nepotes.'

At that the man laughed. 'What gain is there in that?'

'A roof, and food.'

The visitor's eyes narrowed. 'Who brought you here?'

Deda did not answer.

'A knight, you say?' The tall man prowled around him. Deda sensed eyes sizing him up. 'What use do the Nepotes have for a knight?'

'I could not say. I would wager there could be some, or I would not be here.'

'And they have coin to waste upon another mouth to feed?' The visitor was musing, but the Norman could hear an edge of suspicion growing in his voice. 'How low you must have fallen to accept this work.' A jab, to provoke a reaction.

'There is no dishonour in serving.'

The man's laughter rumbled out. 'Honour? Let that fill your belly!'

Deda heard the clatter of feet on flagstones as Simonis swept in with Rowena at her heels. The mistress flushed when she saw her guest. 'Oh . . . Victor.'

The knight nodded. The identity of the visitor was no surprise to him. Men like Victor Verinus thrived in Normandy, where even the duke had to fight for his power. Perhaps this land was not as strange as he had first thought.

'Leave us,' Simonis snapped, and when Rowena hesitated for only a moment, the mistress's voice cracked louder: 'Go!'

As the English woman hurried out, she flashed a puzzled glance at Deda. With a shake of his head, he silenced her, pretending to follow her out into the courtyard. But once in the twilight, he pressed a finger to his lips and turned back.

Creeping through the hall, he followed the sound of voices. 'The time for your games has passed, Simonis,' Victor was saying.

'What games?'

'Do not test me. I speak of Juliana.'

In the dark by a doorway, Deda came to a halt. Candlelight cast dancing shadows on the wall of the chamber. Simonis seemed to be pouring her guest a goblet of wine.

After a long period of silence, she said in a quiet voice, 'If you want her, why do you not take her?'

The shadow lifted the goblet high. 'Where is the joy in that? She must come to me . . . perhaps creeping on all fours. Give herself to me, freely. I want her to prostrate herself before me and beg for my cock in her cunt.'

Deda grew cold at the other man's cruelty. Now he understood well why Wulfrun had set him on watch.

Simonis must have taken too long to respond for Victor snapped, 'Would you resist me?'

'I do your bidding, you know that. That is the pact we agreed.'

Victor grunted. 'You would be wise to heed me,' he continued, calmer now. 'Everything is changing here in Constantinople, and soon. If you fear my power now, that will be as nothing to what is to come.'

Simonis tried to speak, but the words were muffled, incomprehensible. Deda could not understand why.

Victor seemed to understand her, though. 'That is right, wife of my hated enemy. Soon, perhaps only a few nights hence. All has been leading to this. The loss of Arcadius dealt a blow to my plans, but there is always another way. Be patient, wait for an opportunity, and one will surely come. And then all will change.'

Simonis said nothing.

'I will seize my opportunity with both hands,' Victor growled. 'A river of blood will be spilled. Doom will come to all who stand in my way. But great power always demands a high price. Strength is required to see it through, and there are so many who are weak, eh, Simonis?' He laughed quietly. 'Bring Juliana to me, or all that you have suffered so far will pale before what is to come when I have achieved all the power I could ever imagine.'

As Deda slipped away, he felt dread licking at his spine. The threat against that innocent girl was as real as Wulfrun had feared. But there was more, much more. *Blood. Doom.* What horrors were unfolding, here in the city of light?

CHAPTER THIRTY-TWO

The gulls shrieked above the mast. Land could not be far away, Hereward thought as he rode the deck of the stolen ship. Beside him, Kraki brooded as he mended the net that had brought them sustenance on the long journey across the whale road.

'What is on your mind?' the Mercian asked.

'England,' the Viking replied, but Hereward knew he was really thinking of Acha.

'You are free to return. William the Bastard will have too much on his mind to care about one lone warrior returning from the east.'

Grunting, Kraki shook his head. 'You would be lost without me.'

As he searched the blue horizon for the first signs of land, or sight of Ragener's ship, the Mercian felt pride that his men had stood by him. He was on a cold quest for vengeance now. The gold and glory of Constantinople would come later. Once they had left the massacre in the basilica, it had been easy to find a ship to steal. Siward's men were busy looting Sabta under a pall of black smoke, and the seamen of the old town were too distracted to watch their vessels in the harbour. And Maximos and Salih ibn Ziyad had been eager to accompany them on the voyage.

Hereward could remember little of that time. After he had seen Alric so close to death, his rage had consumed his wits. Ragener would pay for the misery he had inflicted upon the monk. They had set the churchman between the benches astern, and Salih ibn Ziyad had tended to him as best he could. But they had lost too much time finding a Muslim leech to provide them with herbs and balm, and locating supplies to see them through the journey. Night was already falling when they had set sail north-east from Afrique with the fire-pot ablaze on its hook to give them enough light to row by. Once they had reached open water, though, the wind filled their sail as if God himself was speeding them on their way.

Hereward prowled to the mast where Maximos watched the horizon. His gaze had barely left the ocean since their departure. 'No sign of that dog,' the Mercian said. 'If he sailed to Rome instead, or—'

Maximos shook his head. 'He is driven by lust for gold. Constantinople can be his only port.' Worry etched lines into the Roman's face, and when his guard was down flickers of fear lit his eyes. How deeply he must care for Meghigda, Hereward thought. Lowering his eyes, Maximos added in a quiet voice, 'If Ragener reaches Victor before us, all is lost.'

'At least you know the sea wolf will not end her days. That bounty is keeping her alive.'

'There is a world of pain between life and death . . .' He caught himself. 'But once she has been delivered . . .'

'We may still have time to save her.'

'You do not know Victor. He wants vengeance for the loss of his son. Meghigda will suffer until she speaks the truth, and Victor is skilled in the art of suffering. There is no resisting him. He stabbed my father in the head and left him for dead. He ordered my cousin's balls to be sliced off. My mother . . . my sister . . .' He shook his head, looked away. 'I know not . . . I pray not . . . And he would have ended my days too if Arcadius, his son, had not pleaded for mercy.' He swallowed, pressing down upon the well of emotion. 'I owe Arcadius everything.'

Hereward frowned, struggling to comprehend this degree of agony. 'And all this in Constantinople, city of gold, with its men of learning, and books, and philosophy, and laws, and churches?'

Maximos laughed with contempt. 'Aye, Constantinople, where cut-throats wear fine silk. The greater the gold, the greater the power, the worse the crimes. Do not mistake it for England. That will be your undoing.'

'We will do everything in our power to save Meghigda, you have my word on that. And Ragener will pay . . .'

Hereward's words died in his throat when he glanced along the deck and saw Salih beckoning to him. The wise man's face was drawn. Pushing aside his fears, the Mercian clambered over the benches and crouched down beside his friend.

The monk's face was bloodless. Though his chest still rose and fell, he had not stirred since they had left the basilica in Sabta. Hereward bowed his head for a moment as guilt clutched at his heart.

'You have my thanks for all you have done to help Alric,' he murmured.

'God is within him. I could do no other.' Salih rested a friendly hand upon Hereward's shoulder and added, 'You have offered your axe to help save my queen. I . . . and all the Imazighen . . . will never forget that.'

Hereward felt troubled by the weight of that hand, and the strength of the compassion behind it. 'What is wrong?' he asked.

'Your friend ails. I have done all I can for him, but it has not been enough.'

'He still breathes.'

Salih nodded, allowing the words, and the understanding, to settle gently. 'Wounds fester. You have seen this after a battle.'

Every warrior had seen it. Men who received only a scratch had died days later. He could never forget the fruity stink of the rotting flesh. Reaching down, he unfastened the cloth tied around the stumps of Alric's severed fingers. That same sickly-sweet reek wafted up. The skin had started to blacken.

Hereward felt a wave of anger rush through him. Here was another reason to make Ragener suffer. Would there be no end to the miseries he had inflicted? He would not lose his friend, not this way. 'Is there nothing you can do?'

The Mercian sensed the other men gathering around. Shadows fell across Alric. A stillness descended upon the ship. Only the sounds of the world rolled on, the wind in the sails, the lapping of the waves against the hull, the shriek of the gulls.

'If you would save his life, we must stop the black rot eating its way into his body.' As Salih held his gaze, Hereward knew the words that would come next. 'You must cut off his hand.'

'No!' The Mercian leapt to his feet, bunching his fist as if he were about to strike the wise man for his audacity.

'You must. It is the only way.' Salih held out both arms, imploring.

'And leave him with only one hand? No! There must be another way.'

The wise man grabbed Hereward's arm. 'He will still have his wits . . . his eyes . . . his tongue. He will still speak to God—'

'No!'

'Then you condemn him to death.'

Hereward felt the words like a knife. He looked down at the monk, so pale, so close to death. *He* had made his friend this way. *He* had brought this misery down upon him.

Guthrinc rested his huge hand on Hereward's shoulder. 'You know this must be done,' he murmured. 'We have done it time and again upon the battlefield.'

But not like this, the Mercian thought.

'The monk will forgive you,' Guthrinc continued, his voice growing quieter still. 'He will forgive you anything.'

233

Hereward felt a blade in his heart.

Kraki strode forward. 'I will do it.'

'No,' the Mercian said, holding up one finger to the Viking. 'It is my burden. Fetch me my axe.'

Sensing the weight of feeling upon their leader, the other men shuffled away. Hereward could feel their eyes flickering towards him, each gaze filled with pity.

'Losing the hand might kill him,' the warrior whispered.

Salih nodded. 'But if we do not act, he will certainly die. This is the right course.'

Hereward nodded. He knew; he had always known. He thought back to the basilica and the last time the monk had spoken. Had the sickness already reached his brain that he thought he had killed Hereward's brother? Why would he say such a thing? He crouched down, pressing his lips close to Alric's ear. 'You *will* live, monk. You have answers to give me.' It sounded too harsh so he added in a gentler tone, 'Live, monk. Live.'

Salih jabbed a knife into the glowing embers of the fire-pot. The hot blade would stem the blood and, Hereward hoped, stop the black rot reaching its fingers into his friend's arm, and thence into his heart.

'When you are done, I will pray over him. His fate will be in God's hands.'

Kraki strode up and handed over the axe. Hereward weighed it in his palms as Salih lifted the monk's frail form and stretched his arm out across a bench. As he looked down at his friend, all the Mercian could think was how he had taken this same axe and lopped off Ragener's own hand, and thereby set this entire chain of events in motion.

Raising the weapon above his head, he whispered, 'Forgive me.'

The axe swept down.

CHAPTER THIRTY-THREE

The blade shimmered on the purple velvet cloth. It was a warrior's knife, steel polished so brightly it reflected the faces of all who peered down at it. The handle was an angel, intricately carved from ivory, inlaid with sable and capped with gold. A knife fit for a hero, perhaps the best in all Constantinople.

Rowena sighed as she admired the craftsmanship. Around her the market throbbed with life. Merchants jabbered at customers. Bodies jostled for space among the wooden tables and the sellers sitting cross-legged with their wares laid out on cloths. The rich scent of rare spices and cooking food wafted in the air. But Rowena was lost to all of it. She stared at the gleaming knife, but her thoughts were only of Deda and how much she yearned to buy this blade for him. He asked for nothing. When their bellies had growled as they trudged through dark forests on their way out of England, he had always given her the biggest share of what little food they could scrape together. While she had slept, he kept watch. When she was too tired to walk, he carried her. And when their lives had been threatened by rogues and murderers, he risked his own neck to save her without a second thought. Words could never begin to express her gratitude for all that he had given her, or the love she felt for a man with a heart as big as an oak.

'A fine gift for your husband,' Simonis breathed in her ear. 'He would be proud to have such a blade in his hand.'

Rowena felt surprised at the other woman's seemingly uncanny ability to know what was on her mind. 'I could not afford this,' she whispered, feeling her disappointment swell. 'Not now, not—'

'Do not say another word,' her mistress cautioned. 'We all know hardship here. But this is not an ending.' She glanced at Juliana, who gave a rueful smile. 'Our stories are not yet written. Each new day brings new hope. We can rise up. We can reach a better place. Everyone in Constantinople knows that if there is a fire in your heart, you can earn your rightful place in the sun.' Simonis rested a comforting hand on Rowena's arm. 'One day, perhaps soon, you will return here and buy this blade. I know it.'

'This knife would make you happy?' Juliana asked, her forehead furrowed.

Rowena could hear the compassion in the girl's voice and felt touched. 'To show my love for Deda, and my thanks for all that he has done for me. His sacrifices have been great. And I . . . I can give him so little in return.'

'You give him your love and support,' Simonis encouraged her. 'He is a good man. For him, that is more than enough.'

Smothering her disenchantment, Rowena looked down at the merchant. He had a wild beard and a milky eye, and oiled skin despite the heat. A Viking by the looks of him. She shook her head and moved away.

As they passed a large display of dyed silk, Rowena realized that Juliana was not with them. When she glanced back, she glimpsed the girl pushing her way through the heaving bodies. She was holding the knife.

'For you,' Juliana said, proffering the blade. 'I had some coin saved in my purse, and . . .' She smiled awkwardly.

'I cannot accept this,' Rowena replied, her eyes bright. 'It is too much.'

Simonis cupped Rowena's hand in hers. 'Take it,' she urged in a gentle voice. Her smile eased the sadness that always seemed to haunt her features.

Rowena blinked away a stray tear. After the long weeks of doubt and fear and worry since they had fled England's shores, weeks when it had seemed they might never know joy again, this simple act of kindness burned into her. The speed at which she had become friends with the Roman women had taken her by surprise. Though she worked in their house, they never treated her as a servant. They shared with her what food they had. They chatted brightly and openly about their deepest thoughts, and offered warm words and support when she had revealed the suffering she had endured in William the Bastard's England. Their shared hardships had seemed to create a bond from the very beginning, and it felt good to know that she was not alone in that strange city.

But as they moved away, Rowena glimpsed an unguarded glance between Simonis and Juliana and began to suspect the truth. The Nepotes barely had enough coin to buy food. Juliana could not have afforded that knife. Realizing that the blade must have been stolen, she slipped away as the others watched a falconer at play. When she eased through the crowd to the Viking merchant's pitch, she found him angrily berating a group of men nearby. She had been correct. In passing, she dropped the knife back on the cloth, and was lost in the churn of bodies when she heard the merchant's startled cry of discovery. She could never have kept something she knew to be stolen. But it did not diminish the other women's kindness. They wanted only the best for her, and she knew that it was only her desperate life that had driven Juliana to such extremes.

As she made her way back to her friends, she heard shouts ring out from the heart of the market. 'Enough!' someone was crying. 'The emperor must pay!' another voice exclaimed. The bellows roared into a tumult. Within moments, men and women were fleeing past her, eyes wide in terror. As the crashing of overturned stalls thundered out, Rowena threw herself into the flow. Protests against the emperor's rule seemed to be rising up on a daily basis. Frustrations had turned to simmering anger – she had heard the loud protestations in the fora time and again – and that in turn had become violence. Four dead in as many days, or so she had been told.

Retracing her steps to where she had last seen Simonis and Juliana, she did her best to search all around. But she was like a leaf caught in an autumn flood, thrown this way and that by the surge of bodies. Slammed into a wall, she staggered, dazed, until a hand caught her arm. It was Simonis.

'This way,' she urged, dragging Rowena into an alley where Juliana was hiding. 'It is not safe here.'

In the shadowy refuge, Rowena rested one hand against her head and caught her breath. The crowd thundered past the entrance to the alley.

'This emperor will destroy us all,' Simonis fumed as she listened to the din of angry protests.

Juliana crept forward to peer into the narrow street. 'We should not tarry here,' she said. 'This kind of trouble always draws thieves . . .'

The words died in her throat. When Rowena looked up, she saw the girl backing away from a man who had lurched into the entrance to the alley. He was tall and thin, dressed in threadbare clothes, and streaks of dirt marred his face.

As his gaze fell upon the three women, a hungry grin spread across his features. Rowena felt disgust. She had seen that look too many times before.

'Leave here,' she demanded, holding her chin up in defiance.

The rogue glanced over his shoulder at the racing crowd. Rowena could read the thoughts passing through his mind. Folk were too frightened to pay any heed to what was happening in the alley. He licked his lips as he examined each woman in turn.

'I said, leave here!' Rowena stormed. She took a step forward, but the man was not threatened. He drew a knife, waving it in the air.

'Move back,' he growled.

Juliana whirled. 'Quickly! Your blade,' she whispered.

'I . . . I have lost it,' Rowena murmured. 'In the crowd.' She watched Juliana's eyes grow dull with a faraway look as she weighed her response.

The rogue edged forward, and Rowena could see from his grim face that he would not be deterred. He wanted one of them, all of them, and he was prepared to do anything to quench his desire.

'Take me,' Juliana said suddenly, spinning back to their would-be attacker.

'No!' Rowena exclaimed, but as she tried to restrain the girl Simonis caught her arm. With one pointed glance, the mistress silenced her.

With a coquettish smile, Juliana swayed up to the rogue. 'I would have a man like you,' she breathed, pushing out her breasts. 'Strong. You would make me cry out in delight, I would wager.' She pressed her hip into the man's groin, as brazen a display as Rowena had ever seen.

The rogue was flattered by the advance. He moistened his lips, trying to mouth a response that never came.

Juliana played her part to the full. As she eased her body against him, the man's knife hand wavered, fell. In that instant, Juliana lashed out like a striking snake. Swinging both hands against his head, she slammed it against the wall. Rowena gasped at the ferocity she saw in the girl's face.

The attacker cried out, cursing. Stunned, his legs half buckled, but he kept his grip on the knife. One hand flew to his head, and when it came away it was sticky with blood. Fury blazed in his eyes. Snarling, he rounded on Juliana. The blade swung up.

Without a thought for her own safety, Rowena threw herself forward. Grabbing hold of the rogue, she hurled him back against the wall. Before he could recover, her hands snarled into his hair and she crashed his head against the stone again and again. The sound of shattering bone echoed out.

Staggering back, Rowena let the man slip to the ground. She gaped, filled with self-loathing at the crime she had committed. Her hands were shaking as they fluttered to her mouth.

Simonis and Juliana were around her in a moment, hugging her. 'You saved my life,' Juliana murmured, pressing her face into Rowena's shoulder.

'Do not blame yourself,' Simonis added. 'You saved us all.'

Rowena swallowed, unable to take her eyes off the fallen man. But then he stirred and she sucked in a juddering breath of relief. 'We must fetch help for him,' she said.

'And we will.' Taking her by the shoulders, Simonis spun her round and looked deep into her eyes. 'We all do what we must to survive. Now come. You are with friends, and we stand together.'

CHAPTER THIRTY-FOUR

The jeering crowds lined the street. Boys scooped up handfuls of filth and hurled it with all their strength. The men threw stones. But the women were the worst. Calling to each other, they pointed and laughed until tears streamed down their faces.

As he hurried through the streets of Constantinople, Ragener the Hawk felt his face burn with humiliation. Here were riches beyond imagination. Towering public buildings in gleaming white marble, churches stuffed with gold, reflecting pools and statues in the fora, cool gardens where citizens could shelter from the shade. But though the folk wore the finest embroidered Syrian silk and jewels beyond counting, Ragener decided they were little more than pigs, snorting and snuffling as they wallowed in mud.

His ruined face would never be accepted anywhere. Some even called him eunuch – the life that was half death! Only when he had a pile of gold to sit upon could he lift himself above their cruel gaze. Only then could he find peace.

Behind him, the woman stumbled along on trembling legs. Despite the sweltering heat, he had swathed her in a thick cloak with the hood pulled low so none could guess at her

241

true identity. He would not risk losing her to some other gold-hungry cur, not now he was so close to his dream. He had gagged her with a filthy rag to prevent her calling out. And he gripped tight to the length of rope between them, the other end lashed around her wrists.

On the long journey across the whale road from Afrique, he had starved her and beaten her so she would not show any resistance. Now it was all she could do to stagger in a straight line. He would never forget how she had taken him to the edge of death in Sabta. A woman! And he, with his one hand, had not been able to resist her feeble attack. If she had not been worth more in gold than he could imagine in his wildest dreams, he would have taken her eyes, then her face, before throwing her over the side for the fish to feed upon.

Ragener shouldered his way through the thronging streets. He could endure this mockery, as he had endured so much in his life.

And God, once again, had smiled upon him during the crossing. The weather had been fine, the wind had been at his back and the sea had been as still as a mill-pond. And when he had sailed into the harbour that morning, he had leapt from his stolen boat and kissed the very ground itself, for his ordeal was almost at an end.

The search for whoever had placed the bounty upon Meghigda's head had been harder than he anticipated, but after questioning countless folk in the marketplace he finally had a name.

The home of the Verini was as opulent as he had hoped. Vast and white and pristine, with columns standing each side of the door to support a portico which would shelter visitors from the hot sun or the rain. Ragener felt awed. Never had he seen the like in England; not even the great halls of earls were so wondrous. Those in the marketplace had been quick to spin their tales of Victor Verinus, though there was little agreement: a courageous general who had led his army to victory after victory, a cruel despot who would crush any man or woman to achieve his heart's desire, a wealthy merchant, a cunning speaker who had the young emperor's ear. The Hawk cared little. Victor was a great man, a powerful man, and that was all that mattered.

Disgusted by his ravaged features, the slave refused him entry. Like a dog, he was forced to wait on the front step while the slave went in search of his master. He kept his head down. He did not want more jeers ringing out when he was introduced to the Stallion, as one of the men in the marketplace had called Victor with a sly smile.

But when the door swung open once again, only a boy of perhaps fifteen summers stood there. The pirate sensed something odd about the lad. Under his russet hair, his moon face was unnaturally still, as if carved from marble. He stared at Ragener's face until the Hawk squirmed.

Expecting only disgust, Ragener felt shocked when the boy murmured, 'You have been touched by God.' The sea wolf could only gape as the lad reached out a hand towards his face. 'May I?' he asked. Almost tenderly, his fingers traced the edges of the holes where the nose had been, across the scar tissue and around the milky eyes, and then down to the ragged lips. Finally he took the ruined man's arm and felt the stump where his hand had been. 'Suffering has shaped you,' the boy whispered, entranced. 'This flesh means nothing. It is of the earth. And you have risen above it. You have become a thing of beauty, a god set free from the clay that contained him.'

Ragener stared into the boy's face. Tears stung the corners of his eyes. 'Who are you?' he croaked.

'I am Justin. And one day I will be emperor.'

Dazed, the Hawk let the boy take him by the arm and lead him across the threshold. As they entered, Meghigda tried to pull away, but Ragener yanked on the rope so hard that she almost fell.

In the cool hall, the sea wolf glanced around, dazzled by the gold that gleamed from every surface. The air was scented with sweet perfume, and he could hear the sound of tinkling water. Surely this was heaven.

'I will bring my father to you,' Justin said.

The boy slipped out, and soon after a tall, powerful man with a leathery face and hair the colour of iron swept in. He surveyed Ragener down the length of his nose. The Hawk saw none of the wonder the man's son had displayed, but nor was there any of the revulsion he usually encountered. Victor Verinus treated him like any other man, as one who could be a dog or could be of some use. For that the Hawk was so grateful he all but cried.

'Speak,' Victor growled.

Ragener bowed his head, afraid to look in the other man's eyes. 'I have brought you the woman you seek. Meghigda, queen of the Imazighen, also known as al-Kahina, the torment of the desert.' He swept one hand behind him to indicate the hooded figure.

The Stallion grew rigid. His cold gaze licked over the sea wolf's captive and then he said, 'Show me her face.'

As Ragener turned, he glimpsed a young girl hiding in the shadow of a doorway. He guessed from her red hair that she was Justin's sister, but unlike the boy's her face was as hollow as a skull and dappled with bruises. She looked as if no good meal had passed her lips in days. She edged back into the shadows when she realized she had been seen, but the Hawk could sense her still there, watching.

With a flourish, he yanked off the queen's hood. Though she had suffered greatly, she drew back her shoulders and pushed her chin up with defiance. Her dark eyes flickered over Victor, and then she looked away as if he were beneath her notice.

'Did you murder my son?' he asked in a clear voice. When Meghigda did not respond, he strode across the hall and struck her with the back of his hand. A cry, quickly stifled, echoed from the hiding girl. The queen crumpled to the flagstones.

Blood spattered across the white marble. Eyes flashing, she craned her neck round to glare at her abuser. Ragener thought that if she could, she would have torn out Victor's throat with her teeth. The Roman should know that this was no normal woman.

'She is quick to claw,' he began in warning.

Victor held up a hand to silence him. Pulling aside his tunic, he unfurled his member and pissed upon his captive. Spitting epithets, Meghigda scrabbled backwards, but the Roman only stepped forward, directing the hard, hot stream at her face.

Like a wildcat, the queen hurled herself at his cock, determined to tear it off. Wrenching at the rope, Ragener dragged her back into the puddle.

When he had emptied his bladder, Victor rearranged his tunic and said, 'You will be well rewarded. The bounty I placed upon this whore's head was so great any man between here and Thule would have sought her out. But you, only you, brought her to me. You have the gratitude of the Verini now, and you will never want for anything again.'

Unable to hold back his tears, Ragener dropped to his knees. Never had he imagined that he could be treated so well by another. Once he had caught his breath, he looked up at his saviour and said, 'Beware, there are men hunting for her. English warriors . . . and a Roman.'

Victor's eyes narrowed. 'A Roman, you say? Maximos Nepos, it can be no other,' he said under his breath. 'He yet lives while my son lies dead.'

'They are savages.' As the words left his lips, the Hawk began to warm to his subject. He still craved vengeance for his humiliation. And after the injuries inflicted upon his friend, Hereward would never leave him alone. It would not be over until one of them lay dead. 'The Roman . . . Maximos . . . it is my belief that he loved this woman,' he continued, sweeping one hand towards the glowering Meghigda. 'He has sworn Hereward the English warrior, and his men, to his cause. They travel to this city to end the days of the man who put a price upon her head.'

Victor's stare was unblinking and for a moment Ragener feared the other man had seen through his lie. But then he said, 'Then I will be waiting for them. From the moment they set foot in this place they will be hunted, and when the time is right, they will be slaughtered.'

Ragener grinned. In truth, it felt as if he had been delivered to a heaven upon earth. In all his life, he had known no friends, and now he had the most powerful one of all.

'Worry not,' Victor continued, glancing at Meghigda. 'This sow's days of bloodshed are done. This is not Afrique. This is Constantinople. Here a sharp sword is not enough to thrive. It takes wits, and cunning, and gold, and of those she has none. She will rot in the dark, and think upon her crime, and when I am ready, I will take her head.'

CHAPTER THIRTY-FIVE

The City of Heaven hung between the earth and the blue, blue sky. Sunlight reflected off its white walls and soaring marble buildings, its towers and domes and columns and statues, so that it seemed to glow with an inner light.

After days with only the whale road beneath him, after weeks of hardship when the dream seemed to be slipping through their fingers like the desert sand, Kraki could only stare in awe. Was this how Valhalla looked, he wondered? Craning his neck, he let his gaze trail across the magnificence of the stone buildings. He had been told of the sheer scale of Constantinople, bigger than London and Wincestre and Eoferwic combined, but he had never imagined that to be true. Yet here it was. Surely this was the greatest city in all the earth.

Silence had descended upon the ship from the moment the wondrous sight had first hove into view. Heads were held rigid, eyes fixed on the prize that had always seemed just beyond their reach. No one had dared speak, as if to do so would break the spell.

As they neared, they heard the music of the place roll out across the waves: the voices of a multitude raised up in what could only be celebration. A forest of masts waited in the port of Boukoleon. So many vessels, so many shapes and sizes. Kraki could scarce believe it. Under swooping gulls shrieking with hunger, folk swarmed across the quayside, unloading bales and sacks and the day's catch. Merchants haggled over prices. Lads ran with messages from the guilds.

Once they had been given permission to moor in the harbour, the warriors sat on their benches for a moment longer, still staring. But then a dam seemed to break, and with cheers ringing out they scrambled on to the quayside. Eward, a lanky youth with a thatch of black hair, dropped to his knees and kissed the stones. The others wandered around, entranced by the buildings and the people and the ebb and flow of life.

'Even you will have to crack that stone face with a grin, eh?' Guthrinc said, nudging his friend as they stood at the waterside.

Kraki snorted. 'I never doubted for a moment that we would reach this place.' But he had, they all had. For too long it had seemed that fate was conspiring to drag them off course then dash them upon the rocks of the cold, hard world.

Guthrinc nodded, a smile playing on his lips. The strong man had always been able to see through him, Kraki thought. 'We needed this,' Guthrinc added, turning his attention to the great dome shimmering in the distant heat haze. 'A fresh start. A new dawn. A chance to forget what we have lost, all that we have left behind.' He eyed his friend. 'Even you.'

The Viking showed no emotion, but he wondered if he would ever forget Acha. She had changed him, and he was still not quite sure how. All his life, he had cared for nothing but gold and mead and battle. It mattered not where he called home, whose coin he took. But Acha had shown him something more, and now he felt as if he had misplaced his axe and would never find it again.

Guthrinc was right. They all needed Constantinople. They had to forget their losses, and learn once again how to look forward to days yet to come. If there was a chance for him, it would be here.

Of all of them there, only one man seemed untouched by joy that they had finally reached their heart's desire. Hereward stood over the monk's unmoving form while the harbour's dance whirled around him. Whether Alric would live or die, none could yet say. But that he needed good care, and healing, was certain.

Kraki strode over and stood before the Mercian. They had been enemies and they had been rivals and they had been friends, but respect had always lain between them. Awkward, the Viking struggled to find the words to express his gratitude. 'You said you would bring us here and you have,' he grunted. 'No warrior could ask for a better leader . . . in battle or in life.'

Hereward seemed touched by the words. 'We reached this place together, as brothers,' he replied. He looked around the harbour and then his gaze drifted down to his friend. 'We thought we had lost everything when we were forced to leave our home behind. But there has been a high price to pay to achieve this prize. Friends who set sail with us. Alric's hand. If all that had been for naught . . . if we had failed to reach Constantinople . . . that price would have been too terrible to bear. But know this: I will not lose any more. I will not give up on this new life we have earned.'

'Worry not,' Kraki replied. 'We are here now. Gold and glory. All will be well.'

Maximos marched up. The Viking thought how tense the Roman looked. Normally he was braying and bragging like a fool, even in the heat of battle. He seemed torn. His home held no attraction for him, he had said that often enough on the journey. But there was no mistaking his desire to find the woman.

'There is a monastery not far from here where your friend will be well cared for,' Maximos said. 'If anyone can save the monk's life, it is my cousin, Neophytos. He knows the herbs and potions and pastes as well as any leech.' The Roman pointed to a cart waiting by a row of stone urns. 'My name means something in Constantinople. The owner of that cart will deliver your friend to the monastery. I will pay him later once I have coin in my purse. But forgive me, I cannot tarry. If we are to find Meghigda, I must first find Victor Verinus.' His mouth jerked into a snarl as he hurried away into the throng.

When Hengist and Salih ibn Ziyad set off with Alric for the monastery, Kraki spied Sighard sitting alone on a bale. The shadow that had seemed to hang over his features since the death of his brother had been replaced by the ghost of a smile. The Viking sat beside him, searching once again for the right words. 'Death walks at our shoulders. That is the curse of the warrior,' he said after a moment. 'We know him like a friend. We learn to know his moods and his habits. You are young. You are still not on good terms with him. But trust me when I tell you his shadow will fade, with time.'

Sighard nodded. 'I believe you. Finally, we are here. Finally, we can find the peace that we all have sought. I will miss Madulf, but now I feel there is hope in my life, for the first time since we sent him into the arms of God.'

Kraki grunted, relieved by what he had heard. Loss was like a canker, he knew. Too much of it doomed a man. But now they could give thanks that they had escaped the dark days. They were safe. He clapped a hand on the young warrior's shoulder. 'You are a spear-brother. Never again do you have to fight alone. Do not forget that.'

He had reached his limit of this kind of talk, but he hoped his words had done some good. Heaving himself up, he wandered back to where the rest of the English gathered in a mood of barely contained excitement.

But as he neared, he glimpsed Maximos forcing his way back through the crowd, his face like thunder. 'I have found that dog,' the Roman spat. 'Come . . . there may still be time before he passes his judgement upon Meghigda.'

CHAPTER THIRTY-SIX

The crowd roared to the heavens. Feet thundered on stone and fists punched the air, thousand upon thousand of them, a multitude. As Hereward burst out of the dark stairwell high up on the eastern rank of the towering stone circus, he reeled from the spectacle that confronted him.

The sun blasted down into the baked centre of the hippo-drome where soon the horses would race. All around him, tiers of benches were filled to the brim by more people than he had ever seen in one place. His head rang from the din, so loud that a man would have to bellow to make himself heard. Nothing he had ever encountered in England had prepared him for this sight. His home seemed so small in comparison, a place of winds whistling through the trees in the desolate fens, and knots of folk huddled around hearth-fires against the encroaching dark.

Kraki, Guthrinc and Sighard lurched to a halt beside him. All three gaped. In awe, the Viking surveyed the mass of bodies and yelled, 'What is this place?' It was yet another wonder on top of the many they had witnessed as they ran through the streets from the harbour. After an England built of wood and thatch, they could only marvel at the vast stone bulk of the

Great Palace and the soaring dome of the Hagia Sophia, the towers of the churches and the great walls of the basilica and government halls.

Jerked from his stupor, Hereward searched the teeming benches. Maximos had only been a few paces ahead of him as they raced up the steps above the Black Gate. Yet he had seemed so consumed by terror that Meghigda might be harmed that he had lost all thought for the men who had accompanied him.

This man who had set such a high bounty on Meghigda's head, this Victor Verinus, was a great man, it seemed, for almost everyone in the harbour seemed to know his whereabouts. Aye, and a man who wielded his power with a hard hand. The Mercian had recognized the uneasy looks in the eyes of those who spoke his name.

The crowd's roar grew louder still as the riders led their steeds out into the circus. Amid the ocean of waving arms he glimpsed Maximos, the only one facing away from the day's event. One fist was raised, his face contorted with fury. He was shouting at a glowering man with skin like leather and hair the colour of a sword blade. Though Maximos was tall, the man he was confronting loomed over him.

'We want no fight here,' the Mercian shouted to his men as he pushed his way into the throng. 'If this crowd turns on us we shall be torn limb from limb.'

The two men were arguing in their own tongue, but when Victor saw Hereward approaching he called out, 'I see English dogs.' Aloof, he turned back to Maximos. 'And once again I will tell you, I know of no woman, nor of any sea wolf.'

The Roman could barely contain his rage. 'They are here, I know it.'

'If you have been told that is true, then it must be so. But they have not darkened my door. Why would they? I no longer wish to pay good coin for the woman who killed my son. My grief lies heavy on me, but I do not need vengeance to assuage it.' Victor looked down his long nose, his cold eyes daring the other man to challenge him.

Maximos held that gaze for a long moment, and Hereward thought much more than Meghigda's disappearance raced between them. Unable to control himself any longer, the younger man lunged, snarling. As he whipped back his right fist to throw a punch, Victor lashed out like a snake. With one huge hand, the older man caught the wrist, while the other snapped round Maximos' throat. He began to squeeze.

'Why have you survived, while Arcadius lies dead in some foreign land?' the general shouted above the thunder of the crowd. 'There is no justice in this world.'

All around, men and women scattered from their benches to avoid the fight. Victor seemed oblivious. Showing no emotion, he began to crush his fingers tighter. With time Maximos' youth might have given him the edge to break free. But long before then, Victor would have choked the life from him, Hereward could see.

The Mercian threw himself into the fray. He wrenched the two Romans apart, the heel of his hand thumping into Victor's breastbone to drive him back. The older man's face blazed at this audacity. But before he could speak, men leapt to their feet on every side, encircling the English warriors.

'Victor's guard,' Maximos called. 'Beware!'

Whirling, Kraki threw up his axe with a roar. As Hereward whipped Brainbiter up to Victor's throat, the other spear-brothers snatched out their own weapons and faced their enemies.

'Come on then, you dogs,' Kraki growled as he looked around the circle of cold faces. 'Though there are a thousand thousand of you here, I will take on every one of you.'

For a second, silence hung over that corner of the hippodrome, and then laughter rang out, growing louder by the moment. All around, the crowd stood on their benches and pointed, throwing their heads back and jeering. Kraki's cheeks coloured at the mockery. The English warriors' eyes darted around, uncertain. Never before had they experienced such a reaction.

Victor stepped on to a bench and threw his arms wide, playing to the crowd. 'Barbarians!' he cried, to more ringing laughter.

Hereward watched his men's discomfort as their weapons wavered. They deserved better than this. Sheathing his blade, he ordered, 'Lay down your arms.'

Maximos pulled his way to the Mercian's side, seemingly embarrassed by the display. 'This is Constantinople,' he hissed. 'Not some mud-spattered village in Thule.'

Hereward silenced the other man with a stare. 'No, we are not in England,' he said. 'Would that we were. But it seems we have new rules to learn.'

The crowd's mockery died down as their attention swung back to the circus, where the riders were bringing their mounts to the starting line.

'We must be away,' Maximos urged, his voice low. 'I lost my temper. I was a fool. But Victor will not take kindly to this insult. He has had men killed for less.'

The leather-faced general was still making a play of humour, laughing silently at the *barbarians*. But his eyes were like nail-heads. He leaned in to the Mercian and whispered, 'My guard will hunt you down like the dogs you are, you and all your men. Your days are done.' Pulling back, he announced in a loud voice, 'Now, leave my sight. The race will soon begin.'

A lull settled on the hippodrome as the horses lined up. But with the starting cry and the first rumble of hooves, the full-throated roar soared up to even greater heights. Back on his bench, Victor watched the race. But Hereward could sense the general's eyes upon his back as he walked away and he knew he had made an enemy that day.

Outside in the shade of the street, where the crowd's exultations had become a distant drone, Maximos hung his head.

HEREWARD − WOLVES OF NEW ROME

'Do you believe him?' Hereward asked.

'Victor Verinus keeps his plans and his plots to himself,' Maximos said, 'and if he believes there is an advantage for him, his tongue will lie easily.'

The Mercian felt puzzled. For all his words, the Roman's fear for the queen had ebbed, and if anything he seemed to be filled with relief.

'You must forgive me,' Maximos continued. 'In my passion to find Meghigda, I acted too rashly. I have led you all into danger.'

Kraki turned up his nose. 'Let him come. My axe will be ready.'

Maximos held his hands out in weary despair. 'Your axe will only lead you to a cell. There are laws. And you do not know Victor Verinus. He always finds a way to destroy anything that offends him.'

Guthrinc looked up at the towering walls of the hippodrome. 'I would think in a city this big there are plenty of places for rats like us to hide, until we decide on a plan.'

'It might be better to leave this place,' Maximos began.

Hereward silenced him with a cold stare.

'Then hide well,' the Roman went on, 'because if Victor takes against you, he will leave no stone unturned. For myself, I must find Meghigda before . . .' He let the words die in his throat, his cheeks flushing as if he had caught himself on the brink of speaking too boldly. Hereward tried to read his face. Did he fear the queen was already dead? Or was it something more that was preying on his mind?

'Find the woman. Stay alive,' Kraki snorted. 'Good. Now I know what I am doing.'

Hereward felt fire burn in his breast. He would not let the promise of Constantinople be snatched away from them. They could not bear any more loss. He would fight even a man as powerful and dangerous as Victor Verinus to win the new life they so desperately needed. He would fight as never before.

CHAPTER THIRTY-SEVEN

Raven wings thrashed the air. Beady black eyes and rending beaks, a sound like thunder. Amid that storm of sable feathers, a watcher. A man, with bone-white face and eyes dark from lid to lid shining in the holes of his helm. He wore a mailshirt rusted and crusted with blood, and furs, and the bones of small creatures swinging on leather thongs. An axe hung in his hand, the blade notched from too many battles. Grim was its name, Alric remembered. Grim.

'It is not yet your time.' His lips never moved, but the words rolled out, somehow cutting through the roar of the wings. Unblinking, the man watched, and waited.

From the darkness of his dream, if dream it were, the monk surfaced. Light hurt his eyes, and he screwed up his face until he was used to the glare.

He must have jerked in the tremor of waking, for he felt the weight of a hand on his arm and a soothing voice saying, 'All is well.' A man, it was, though the voice was somehow too reedy.

Opening his eyes, Alric looked into the plump, smiling face of a fellow monk, by the look of his tunic. He was huge, layers of fat straining at the cloth that covered it, and he was hairless. Letting his gaze flicker around, the Englishman realized he was lying on a cold slab looking up at a vaulted stone roof. 'Where am I?' he croaked.

'You are in the monastery of St George,' the bald monk said. 'At the behest of my cousin, Maximos, your friends, the desert man and the one who has been touched by God . . . Hengist . . . brought you here so I can care for your wounds and help you recover.'

'Then I am free of the sea wolf? Hereward saved me.' Alric allowed himself a smile of relief until he realized the pain in his arm was burning hotter than it ever had before. Could Ragener have taken yet another finger? Raising his arm, he stared at the cloth wrapped around it. But his wits were failing him, even as he tried to make sense of this thing before them. After a moment, realization, and horror, raced up to him.

'Look!' Alric cried, holding his stump high. 'Look!'

'Oh,' the Roman monk said, 'you have lost your hand.' His light tone sounded to Alric's ears like mockery.

'Have you no pity?' the Englishman demanded, incredulous. His head was spinning and he thought he might faint.

'Pity?' The fat man lifted his tunic. He was naked beneath it. Alric gaped at the ragged mass of scar tissue where his balls should have been. 'Ah, if only I had lost a hand.' Dropping his tunic, he added, ''Twas not my choice, but there it is. It is God's way, and we shoulder our burden as we walk his road.'

Alric felt no comfort at the words. He blinked away hot tears. But gradually he felt the rush ebb away and a desperate calmness settle on him. 'Who did this?' he whispered.

'Your friend.'

'Friend?' he snapped. He wanted to cry out that no friend would wound him in such a way. 'Hereward?'

'Yes. He is a good friend. He took your hand to save your life. The black rot was creeping into your arm. When it reached your heart, and your brain, your days would have ended.' The monk leaned in until his smiling moon face filled Alric's whole vision. 'Now you will feel grief for your loss, and then anger.

But you must trust me: what is gone is gone, and you will learn to live without it. Be grateful you still have your life, English.'

Alric wondered if he would ever learn to live with this loss. But Neophytos brought him salted fish and wine infused with some aromatic herbs that made his head sing and doused the fire in his wrist. In no time his thoughts were already drifting elsewhere.

When the door to the leech-chamber creaked open, he was pleased to see Salih ibn Ziyad and Hengist there. Neophytos was long since gone.

'See,' the madman cried as he gambolled around the slab on which the monk lay, 'I said he would return to us from the shores of the great black ocean! What tales do you have to tell us of the Land of the Dead, monk?'

Alric thought back to the figure standing amid the swirling flock of ravens and shivered. 'I will say this, my friend. For all its hardships, I prefer this world.'

Salih pressed his fingertips against the throb of blood in his neck and after a while he nodded, pleased. 'It will take time until you feel whole again, but you will, even without this.' He pointed at the stump. 'You are strong. You have already survived the worst. And you are doing better than any man who has lost a hand should be. Are you sure you are a monk and not a warrior?' he added with a smile.

Alric felt warmed by the kindness. 'When Kraki next shows off his wounds as he boasts of his prowess, he will be forced to bow before a meek man of God,' he said, trying to make light, though he felt the world was shifting beneath him. 'There is much I need to know,' he added through the dreamy haze. 'Of Sabta, and how we survived . . . and Drogo Vavasour and Ragener . . . of the journey across the whale road . . .'

A cry rang out from somewhere deep in the monastery. Hengist jerked to a halt, cocking his head to one side as if he were listening to someone no one else could hear. 'Death,' he muttered. 'Death.'

When the sound of running feet echoed, Alric waved aside Salih's protests that he should rest and insisted that they investigate. With the wise man supporting him, they followed the sound of the tumult along ringing stone corridors.

A small crowd of monks had gathered in that part of the monastery that held the monks' cells. The doors to the tiny rooms hung open. Alric glimpsed low, rough beds, straw-covered floors and small, rickety tables and stools. As they neared the hubbub, he caught sight of Neophytos standing in the shadows at the end of the corridor. The eunuch's face was drawn with worry.

When a tall, bony monk with sallow skin and thin lips pushed his way through the churchmen, Alric urged Salih to follow in his footsteps. A strange reek hung in the air, vinegar-sour. The tall man entered another small chamber and halted abruptly. Bowing his head, he muttered a prayer.

By the far wall, a monk with lank grey hair and a bald pate was slumped across his table. His dead eyes were wide with horror and his lips were black and foaming. Alric crossed himself.

'Nathaniel,' one of the others called, and then asked some question in the Roman tongue. The tall man replied in a grave tone, but the English monk did not need to understand the words to know the meaning. 'Poison!' he murmured. 'What den of devils have we entered?'

CHAPTER THIRTY-EIGHT

The Bull and the Lion stared out across the white-tipped waves of the Marmara Sea. As Hereward led his men along the shore and through the harbour towards the great palace of Boukoleon, he glanced up at the stone sentinels. He could not help but be impressed by the majesty of this city, but a part of him still yearned for the peace of the fenlands where often the only voice was that of the wind in the trees.

Once they had passed the guardian statues, a quiet fell upon the men. The palace rose up before them, larger even than King William's new home in Wincestre. White stone reflected the sun as if the place were afire. Every traveller crossing the whale road to Constantinople could not help but marvel as they saw this glory awaiting them. The vast bulk sprawled along the shoreline, with rows of arched windows along a covered walkway, and colonnades, and a tower with views far to the south. Its grandeur whispered of ancient days.

'Heads high, brothers,' Hereward called, prodding his men not to be awed by this sight. They had earned their right to be here. They must never forget that.

As they made their way past shady trees and reflecting pools along the sweeping approach to the palace, they saw groups of women waiting for something. Their cheeks were flushed, their eyes bright, and they clasped their hands in front of them, clutching coloured ribbons.

Sighard hailed them. 'Why do you wait?'

'For the Varangian Guard!' one of the women called back in perfect English, waving the ribbon she wanted to offer as a token. But as she looked along the line of warriors, her eyes widened and she gulped a mouthful of air. 'You are to join them? New recruits?'

'Aye, we are,' Sighard said with a grin. 'We will take your tokens.'

Picking up their skirts, the women flocked around the spear-brothers, gushing their praise for the English and Viking fighting men who made up the ranks of the feared guard. Kraki and the others gaped in amazement. Never had they received such a reception as this.

'Can this be?' Sighard gasped. 'They treat the Guard as heroes. No, as noblemen.'

'Hold tight to your spear,' Guthrinc urged with a wry smile, 'or you will be swept away into a marriage while your back is turned.'

'A good axe can lift skirts and open legs, it seems,' Kraki said with a shake of his weapon. 'This city was built for us.'

Hereward could see that his men were overwhelmed by the adulation. The women gushed accounts of the Varangian Guard's exploits as if they had been standing alongside them in battle. These warriors were braver than any Roman man, and stronger, and more handsome – aye, and wealthier than many too, so Hereward had heard. The fighting men of the Varangian Guard were well rewarded for their service to the emperor. Though their lives might be short, they would have riches beyond measure and, by the looks of it, any woman in the city that they desired. For all its glory, Constantinople was short of heroes of its own. Few Romans chose to join the army, preferring to earn their coin as merchants where they could grow fat while keeping their heads upon their shoulders, so Maximos had said.

'Keep your heads high, and keep your heads,' the Mercian growled once more as he urged his men on. 'When the Guard throws its doors open to us, we want their commanders to see the finest warriors in all the west, not lovesick children led by the nose.'

The spear-brothers eased their way through the crowd up to the palace gates. The palace was the Varangian Guard's home while they were on duty, Hereward had learned from the street-sellers outside the hippodrome. But all of them had been given fine houses in a part of the city called the Vlanga, so highly were they held in esteem.

At the gates, he called up to the guards who peered from the windows on either side. 'Open up. We are here to join the Varangian Guard.'

He heard the sound of muttering inside and then the echo of feet running down stone steps. The gates swung open. He was surprised to see a large group on the other side. Several were warriors – members of the Guard, he guessed – with shields upon their arms and axes in hand. One he took to be their commander stood at their head, a Viking with a long brown beard. His helm was tucked under his right arm and he wore a crimson cape. But around these were other men, Romans by the look of it, perhaps workers in the palace.

'You are here to join the Varangian Guard,' the commander repeated with a broad grin. Laughter rippled through the watching crowd.

Hereward felt his ears burn. He could see no humour in the situation. 'We are called the last of the English. We fought the Norman bastards at Ely . . .'

The commander nodded. 'And lost.'

The Mercian felt his men shift at his back. 'Betrayed at the last,' he snapped, angry that he was having to explain himself. 'But you will find no braver warriors than these.'

'Be that as it may,' the Viking said, looking around at the bedraggled English men, 'where is your gold?'

'Gold?'

The commander laughed, and those around him joined in with his mockery. 'Do you think we let any ceorl with a stick into the Varangian Guard? Not a day passes without some piss-leaking dog rolling up at these gates, boasting that he was the greatest warrior in whatever mud-soaked village spawned him. Most would cry like babes on the first day of proving them-selves here, or faint dead away. And if we let them all in, we would not be so feared, eh?'

Hereward showed a cold face. 'We will prove ourselves, gladly.'

More laughter rang out. 'Be scared, Haeming,' someone jeered. 'They have scars! And axes! And shields!'

'There are rules here,' the commander continued, still grin-ning. 'You buy your way into the Guard with gold, and lots of it. And then you prove yourselves. That way we see how serious you are, and how much you believe in your strong right arm. And if, as many are, you are broken within two days, we piss on your corpse and keep your gold.'

'How do we get gold?' Sighard's voice was edged with dismay.

And yet more laughter. Hereward flinched at the younger warrior's naivety. 'You work,' the Viking called. 'Or you steal. Or you find a patron. Come back when your purses are full. And waste no more of our time, or we will run you off with your spears shoved up your arses.'

The crowd disappeared into the palace grounds as the gates creaked shut.

For a long moment, Hereward glowered at the barred way. When he turned he saw that his spear-brothers' shoulders had sagged, the weariness that had eaten into them since they had fled England now carving lines into their faces. After all they had suffered, this had been a blow too far. They deserved better.

The rejection had struck Sighard the hardest. His eyes were hollow and he swayed as though he could barely stand.

'We are not done here.' Hereward's voice carried over the heads of his warriors. 'We will get our gold, and then we will return to show these bastards what we can do.'

Yet this time his words barely stirred a response. And as they trudged back the way they had come, more insult was heaped on their heads. The women no longer paid them any heed. Aloof now, they averted their gaze as if some filthy, reeking farmers strode by too near.

Hereward gritted his teeth. Though their dreams had been dashed, and they had nowhere to go, he would find a way to lead them to victory, he vowed.

Kraki and Guthrinc flanked him as they tramped back towards the fine houses in the shadow of the hippodrome. 'There is no greater city than this on earth,' Kraki grunted. 'It is filled with riches beyond my wildest dreams, and wise men and beautiful women, great buildings and statues and wonders. But the folk . . .' He spat. 'They look down on us as if we were dogs. Worse than dogs. Because we have no gold. Or no learning. Because we are nothing more than earth-walking axes-for-hire with no home. I have had a belly full of them. And if one more speaks to me as if I am the dirt under his shoe I will snap him over my knee like a rotten branch.'

'You will not be alone there,' Guthrinc put in. The Mercian rarely saw the strong man without a smile playing on his lips, but now he was as grim as his Viking friend.

'We have one friend here,' Hereward said. 'We risked our own necks when Maximos stood before Victor Verinus and now we have a price on our heads. Let us see if he will come to our aid in return.'

'Our last hope,' Sighard muttered from somewhere behind them.

Kraki whirled, shaking his axe at the young warrior. 'Have we taught you nothing, you jolt-headed rabbit? While there is a breath left in you, there is always hope.'

Chastened, Sighard looked down. But Guthrinc threw a huge arm across his shoulders and crushed him against his side. 'What do we say, eh?'

'We have seen worse,' the younger man murmured.

The street-sellers directed them to the house of the Nepotes. They found Maximos squatting against the wall outside. He had not yet found the strength to return to the responsibilities and demands placed upon him by his kin. Jumping to his feet, he flashed a grin to hide his troubled thoughts. 'Your lives are darker without me in them,' he boomed. 'You could not bear to live without the wit of Maximos Nepos.'

Hereward held up a hand to silence Kraki before the Viking's bubbling curses reached fever pitch. 'Our plans have changed,' he said. 'For now we need a place to rest, something to fill our bellies, and a way to earn coin.'

The Roman grinned. 'My family does not have much, but we will do what we can. And our army always needs good fighting men. But the work is hard, the pay is poor, and the risks are great. Constantinople is beset by enemies on all sides. The empire is close to crumbling, some say. You will be welcomed there, if that is what you want. But for now, come. Enjoy the kindness of House Nepotes.'

With a cry of surprise, the slave admitted Maximos, Hereward, Kraki and Guthrinc while the other English waited in the busy street. Soon Maximos was surrounded by people Hereward presumed were his mother, sister and young brother. The older woman held her head high and walked with the poise of a noble; the sister bounded around, barely able to contain her emotion as she smothered Maximos with hugs and shrieked with delight. And the boy showed a quiet strength that belied his years as he beamed at his brother, his eyes moist. So excited were they they paid no heed to their guests, and dragged the Roman away to see his father.

'Can this be?'

Hereward turned at the familiar voice. In an archway leading to a shady courtyard stood Deda, a wry smile playing on his lips. The Mercian could scarcely believe his eyes. The last time he had seen him was in a forest in England as the knight led Acha, Kraki's woman, to safety. Hereward was surprised at how pleased he was to see a friendly face. Deda was the only Norman Hereward had encountered who had acted with honour in his dealings with everyone, not just his fellow knights. He clapped the other man on the arm, roaring, 'Are you a ghost, here to haunt me with memories of my darkest days?'

'Not yet. Though I would have been if William had his way.'

'A Norman and an English rebel, still talking,' Guthrinc said drily. 'Fate confounds us with strange choices.'

Deda must have glimpsed something in Kraki's face, for he quickly turned to the Viking and said, 'Acha is well, or was when we parted company. I left her with the Cymri, who vowed to protect her from William's wrath.' He paused, then added, 'She said if I were ever to see you again, I should tell you that you remain in her heart.'

Nodding, Kraki looked away. Leaving him alone with his thoughts, Hereward and Guthrinc pulled Deda to one side. They listened as he told them of his adventures: how he had taken Rowena as his wife and the two of them had fled England; how Rowena had saved him from thieves upon the road; how they had almost died a hundred times, from hunger and thirst and wild beasts and rogues. The Mercian saw the deep affection in the other man's face when he spoke of his wife, and the resolve there. The world was a better place with men like Deda in it.

'And England?' Hereward asked finally, his face darkening.

'Is no better. Without you there to lead the fight, the English have no choice but to bow their heads to their king,' Deda replied. 'He is a hard man, but I think, given time, he will be a fair one, if there is no more rebellion. But for now he collects his taxes with a cold face and there is hardship in many places. And the women complain that he takes away their right to speak.'

Bowing his head, Hereward reflected on how different things might have been if he had not been betrayed before that final battle in the east.

From the street, a tumult of cries and angry shouts rang out. An instant later the door crashed open and Sighard burst in. Blood streaked his face and turned his tunic black.

'Come,' he cried. 'It is Germund.'

Outside, a crowd had gathered. Hereward shouldered his way through the onlookers and knelt beside a body. More blood soaked into the dust. Germund had been one of the last to join the rebel band in Ely, a quiet man who liked to catch eels, but had been a fierce fighter none the less. His throat had been slashed from ear to ear.

Sighard barged his way to the Mercian. 'I saw,' he began, gulping for air. 'Germund was just wandering along the street, exploring. A man stepped out . . . he was wearing a hood. And then he . . .' Sighard slashed his hand across his throat.

'Here?' Kraki roared. 'This is not the wildwood! In the clear light of the sun? And they called us barbarians!'

'It was one of Victor Verinus' men.'

Hereward looked up into the face of Maximos' sister, a sweet blonde woman who seemed untroubled by the sight of all the blood. She pointed at two slash marks forming a V on Germund's cheek. 'See – he has sent you a warning. This is a sign, from the Verini. They have marked you, English. This is the start of it, and they will not stop until you are all dead.'

The Mercian gaped at the bleeding mark. 'All because we stood up to him at the hippodrome?'

'Who knows the mind of Victor Verinus?' Maximos crouched beside the body. 'A wrong word there, perhaps. Or he has some larger plan that we cannot yet see. But for whatever reason, you have made a powerful enemy, and if he wishes you gone he will make his word good. Victor will not rest until you are all dead.'

His eyes narrowing, Kraki looked around. 'We are powerless here. Nowhere to hide. We do not know this city. He does. We are like rabbits to be hunted.'

'What, then?' Sighard demanded. 'We run? As we have been running ever since we left England?'

Hereward hunched over the dead man, feeling the guilt for this death weigh down on him as if he had thrust the blade himself. He thought of his father, who beat his mother to death. And he thought of King William who choked the life out of all England, slaughtering men, women and children to achieve his end. This Victor Verinus was no different. He felt his blood throb, his devil whisper. Maximos was right – one of them must die.

'We have been driven out of our home. We have had everything we value stolen from us. We will not be forced from here too. We are done with running.' Raising his head, he looked around his men and said, 'This is war.'

CHAPTER THIRTY-NINE

The dark was everything. The drip of water echoed through the gulf, accompanied every now and then by the frenzied scratching of rat claws. Pressed against the chill stone, Meghigda shivered. The dank scent of great age filled her nose. Under her heels, filthy straw crackled as she stretched out her aching legs. The space was too cramped, barely more than an arm's length from the rear wall to the cold iron bars.

How long had she been drifting there in the void? All sense of time had ebbed away. She recalled the moment Victor Verinus raised his fist, but little beyond that. Voices had come to her through the dull haze of pain as she had been dragged to this place, though speaking in a tongue she did not know. And then she had finally come to her senses in this cell, with nothing but the echoes and the gloom for companionship. Once a day a guard brought her a bowl of thin, foul-smelling gruel and a knob of dry bread. Not a word ever left his lips.

Sometimes faces seemed to float away in the dark, ghosts sent to haunt her. She had glimpsed her mother, as she lay dying, before they cut off her head. And Maximos, that night beneath the stars with the dunes rolling behind him, when he had professed his love and promised to stand beside her while she fought for her people. How quickly those words had turned to mist, she thought with bitterness. Perhaps the very moment she had opened her legs.

And she remembered Salih, loyal Salih, raising her up when she was at her lowest ebb and telling her the spirit of al-Kahina lived in her breast. Meghigda allowed herself a smile. She owed him everything. This hardship would not deter her from her path. She would find a way to escape, that she vowed. She would not let Salih ibn Ziyad down, nor her people.

Far off in the dark, a light was flickering. At first she thought it was in her head, another memory returning of the hardships that had forged her. But then the light danced closer, and she heard the shuffle of feet upon stone. Pushing her back up against the wall, she showed a defiant face.

The candle flame painted a shimmering glow on the wet walls of the passage. The footsteps echoed, closer. An odd gait. Not her guard, she decided.

And then the visitor came to a halt by the iron bars and raised his candle. Shadows flew across a face that seemed to belong to a devil. Only when the wavering illumination settled did she realize she was looking into the ravaged features of Ragener.

A chuckle crackled deep in his throat as he set the candle down on the floor. 'Have you been alone enough yet for even my face to bring a warmth to your heart?' he lisped through his ragged lips.

Meghigda spat, but that only seemed to drive the Hawk to greater laughter. He squatted on his haunches, gripping a bar with his remaining hand to balance himself. 'Do you find comfort in your new home? You have earned this place with your actions.'

'I should have throttled the life from you when I had the chance.'

'But you showed mercy, as did Hereward before you,' he replied with a sly grin, 'because you did not fear me enough. Now you have learned your lesson.'

'There will come another time when I have my hands round your throat, and then I will finish what I began,' she replied in a calm voice.

Ragener pretended to look around the cell. 'I could not leave you alone here without seeing how you fared, and bringing you news of the world you have left behind. You know you will never see the light again?'

'If I am to die, why has your new master not yet ended my days?' she sneered. 'There is no gain to him to leave me down here in the dark, wasting food to keep me alive.'

'Your time will come, be sure of that. Victor Verinus has plans for you, I am certain of it.' The Hawk pressed his face between the bars, the skin stretching so that he became even more of a grotesque in the dancing light. 'And I am proud to call him master. He holds great power in his grasp, and soon he will hold more still. And I will be there at his side.'

Meghigda laughed. 'Of what use are you to a man like that?'

Ragener scowled. 'Victor heeds my words. He sees value in me, whereas you and all your filthy kind saw me only as the dirt beneath your feet.'

'We saw you as you are. Look into your own heart, sea wolf.'

His one good eye bulging, the pirate roared his fury. Meghigda knew that if he could reach her at that moment he would have killed her. But then he sucked in a calming draught of cold air and said through gritted teeth, 'For bringing you to him, Victor has already made me rich beyond my dreams. I will not regret one moment of the agonies he is going to heap upon your head. But I am clever . . . more clever than you.' He bumped his head against the bars. 'That is why I am on this side. I see a chance here for great things. More than mere gold.'

'And you think this Victor Verinus will give you that? I know men like him. He will use you for what he can, and when he has drained you and left you a husk, he will toss you out to the rats.'

'No!' Ragener shouted. 'He heeds me! He heeds me! I told

him of your Roman love, and the English bastards . . . all of them . . . all of them who thought me nothing . . .'

The sea wolf was babbling now. Meghigda could see that his grip upon his wits was thin.

'And Victor will end all their days,' he continued. 'I will get my vengeance for the misery heaped upon me! Hear! And then he will raise me up with him, and all will see my true worth. I am wise . . . wise and clever . . . and he will heed my words . . . and you . . . and all of you will be forgotten—'

Meghigda rammed her heel against Ragener's fingers where they curled around the iron bar. With a howl of pain, he threw himself back. She thought she might have broken bones. She hoped so. Crawling forward, she looked down upon him writhing on the stone and said, 'Crawl back to your master, rat. Let him throw you a few crumbs. But know that when I am free from here, I will not rest until I have found you. And then I will take your other eye, and your hand, and your feet as well, and I will leave you in the filth of the street where you belong.'

Ragener hurled himself at the bars, but the queen was too quick for him. She slid back against the wall, letting the candle light her triumphant grin.

'I will see all of you killed,' the sea wolf yelled. 'Mark my words. Soon all of your days will be done. And you will be the first!'

Snatching up the candle, he stalked back along the passage, muttering to himself. Meghigda felt warmed by her defiance. It was a thin victory, but still a victory.

But as the light disappeared into the distance, she crawled back to the bars. Cocking her head, she listened. She was sure she had heard other footsteps following Ragener out of her prison. Someone else had been there, watching from the dark, someone even the pirate had not realized was present.

CHAPTER FORTY

Darkness engulfed the silent monastery. Holding his guttering candle in front of him, Alric brushed one shoulder along the cool stone wall to guide him in the gloom. Only the rasp of his breath and the whisper of his soles upon the flags rustled out in the stillness. He tried to smother his frustration. The other monks were in their cells, at prayer or asleep. But he was lost in the maze of corridors, and he was tired and his wrist felt as if it were on fire.

The day had been hard. At times a black despair settled upon his shoulders at the loss of his hand, until he felt he might never see the light again. And when it did finally pass, his thoughts were distracted by the murder of the sacrist. Even there, in a house of God, he could not escape the darkness in the human heart. He promised himself he would spend the night on his knees, offering his supplications to the Lord. Such reflection often eased his troubled soul. But here he was, still wandering, still anxious.

Somewhere nearby a door slammed. Loud laughter boomed out.

Alric slowed to a halt. No monk would make such unseemly noise in the hours of devotion, nor when all there were in mourning. Puzzled, he listened as a man's deep, rich voice drew nearer. An arrogant man, making no concessions to the monastery's inhabitants, Alric thought.

Some instinct tugged at his mind, and he found himself blowing out his candle-flame before he was seen. A wavering light glowed along a wall at the end of the passage, growing brighter. After a moment, a tall, powerful man with long grey hair emerged from a branching corridor. He was holding a lamp swinging on a hook. The dancing illumination transformed his features into a travesty of a human face. Beside him was a boy with a strangely blank expression. The lamp-flame danced in his staring eyes.

'Nathaniel!' the man roared, seemingly good-humoured.

A door swung open and light flooded out into the corridor. Alric pressed himself back into a doorway. The tall, bony monk he had seen earlier stepped out. As the two men grinned at each other, Alric saw the resemblance in their features.

'Brother,' the new arrival said in greeting, 'I have come to help you celebrate your new appointment. A sacrist now, eh? And while the dead man's seat is still warm.'

Alric heard a knowing tone in those words. He frowned. And Nathaniel had already been promoted to fill the dead monk's role? He knew from experience how slowly the wheels of monasteries usually turned.

Nathaniel glanced around, uneasy that they might be overheard. 'Come, come,' he urged, beckoning the new arrivals into his cell.

Once the door had closed, Alric crept forward from his hiding place. He wanted to hear more of what was being said in that chamber, but as he neared the door a hand fell upon his arm and he all but cried out in alarm. It was Neophytos. The eunuch pressed one finger to his chubby lips as he pulled Alric away.

When they reached the end of the corridor, Neophytos whispered, 'Some things should not be witnessed.'

'Who was that?' Alric hissed.

'Nathaniel is entertaining his brother, Victor Verinus, and Victor's son Justin.'

Laughter rang out from Nathaniel's chamber. The Verini seemed to be making merry.

'Let me take you back to your cell,' Neophytos said. 'Say nothing of what you have seen or heard this night.'

'I do not know what I have seen and heard, but it tugs at my thoughts still.'

'A wise man keeps his own counsel,' the eunuch said. 'Come.'

As they walked away, Alric narrowed his eyes, suddenly aware. 'Why are you here, at this hour?' he asked. 'Were you spying upon this meeting too?'

Neophytos smiled. 'And a wise man pays heed to everything. Who knows what useful morsels can be picked over?'

CHAPTER FORTY-ONE

A dog barked away in the night. A shout rang out. Another responded. A babe cried as its mother struggled to lull it to sleep with a lilting song. A whistle. The sound of running footsteps. A string instrument, gently plucked.

Hereward wandered along the narrow street, baked mud beneath his feet. The houses pressing close on either side were little more than shacks, a world away from the grand homes near the Great Palace and the hippodrome. Swarthy-skinned men sat by their doors, sipping wine. They watched him pass with sullen suspicion. From the shadows of doorways, women summoned him with coy eyes and flirtatious smiles. Rats scrabbled along the paths among the jumbled dwellings. Noise throbbed everywhere. And yet he could not complain, for the Nepotes had called in old favours to find him and his men a place to hide away, here in the quarter where the Syrians, Turks and Arabs gathered and Constantinople's rich rarely ventured.

His nose wrinkled at scents known and unknown. Odd spices, burning charcoal, sizzling meat, and earthier human reeks. And when he glanced up into the heavens, he saw that even the stars were different here. He had travelled from the land of his birth before, but never to so strange a place. Here, even the familiar was skewed.

One constant remained. Men acted as men always did, wherever they called home. They lusted for power, for money, for a woman's thighs. They loved, they hated, they envied.

They killed.

Behind him, a foot scraped across a rut during a rare lull in the rumble of life. Nothing out of the ordinary in that, but he had heard it three times now. It had followed him from the moment he had left the forum of Theodosios. Streams of folk drifted through that square, even when dusk had fallen. He had stood on the edge, hooded and, as he had thought, unobserved. And he had watched Victor Verinus press the palms of the powerful – senators, wealthy merchants, the emperor's advisers – as the Nepotes claimed he did each even.

Smoke drifted across the sweep of stars. The hearth-fires of Constantinople had been lit to ward off the night's chill. The Mercian peeled away from the street and plunged into an alley winding among the clustering houses. When the dark had closed around him, he paused and listened. The footsteps followed him, and not just one pair. Beneath his cloak, his hand slipped to the hilt of his sword. He tried to guess how many there were.

Dropping his shoulders, he strode on. The rats fled away from his boots. Now he thought he could hear voices, mutters and cursing as his pursuers stumbled over the obstacles on the narrow path. They could only be Victor's men. He had been seen in the forum and they had been dispatched to hunt him down like a deer. Another English corpse to be left in the street with the filth and soon forgotten, just like Germund.

He would never forget Germund.

At the end of the rat-run, he stepped out on to another narrow street. Here he could smell the dank waters of the Bosphorus on the breeze. Breaking into a run, he sped north-west towards the dismal shacks where his men had made their home.

At his back, someone barked an order. The sound of running feet echoed off the walls. Confident they had him, his pursuers were no longer trying to hide. And have him they did.

Hereward raced on past the last of the houses into an area filled with workshops. The sounds of the looms had long since stilled and the forges had grown cold. The stink of brimstone still lingered in the air.

In a small square of hard-packed mud and horse dung, he skidded to a halt, whirling. The street had come to an end. Only shadow-filled alleys crawled out between the workshops.

Cornered, like a rat. Cornered as he had been so many times before. Hereward felt his blood thrum in his temples. He backed against the cracked, sun-bleached wood of a workshop. Brainbiter sang as it slipped from its sheath.

His pursuers skidded to a halt as they entered the square. At first they were only silhouettes. But as they drew their swords and stepped forward the moon lit rough faces, slow eyes, lips quick to sneer. The faces of men who broke bones for a living.

Ten of them, the Mercian counted. Not even he, with his devil riding him, could defeat that number.

Victor's men fanned out around the square. Even though they were so many, they were wary, choosing their moment to strike. Someone had warned them of his prowess. Not Victor; he had seen none of it. Then who? He thought for a moment, and realized it could only have been Ragener. Hunching their shoulders, they raised their blades. The edges glimmered in the moonlight. One of them barked something in a tongue Hereward did not recognize. 'English!' someone else called, and they all laughed.

'Who speaks English?' the Mercian called back. Shifting his weight from foot to foot, he swung his blade along the line, ready for the first attack.

'I do.' The speaker was a tall, thin man with hollow cheeks and pox scars. He looked like a ceorl who worked the fields, with big fists, a mass of unruly hair and a mouth that hung open to reveal twisted teeth. Grinning, he glanced around at his brothers. He was enjoying the moment.

'You will be the last to die,' Hereward said.

The grin sagged. The man's eyes rolled, slow and stupid. He could not tell if that was some attempt at humour or if this cornered fool truly thought he could win.

As he raised Brainbiter, the Mercian flexed the fingers of his left hand, beckoning. 'But who dies first, that is the question.'

Victor's men eyed each other. They were unsettled by this show of confidence. But then, with a snarl, one of them lurched forward, swinging his sword up high.

Hereward only grinned.

An instant later, the clank of hauberks and axes rattled out across the square. Shadows separated from the gloom among the workshops. As the Romans whirled in surprise, the English flooded out and formed a line across the backs of the Mercian's pursuers.

'Cornered, yes,' Hereward said. 'But not me.'

Victor's men searched for a way out of this trap, but there was none. The English blocked the street and every alley, two of them for every Roman, all implacable faces and glinting eyes, their spears and axes and shields readied as if this were some distant battlefield and not the City of Gold, the city of learning, the city of gentle folk.

'Mercy,' the English-speaking man called.

'You would have killed me without thinking,' Hereward called back, 'and no doubt taken my head back to your master. And most likely one of you held the knife that ended Germund's days. The time for mercy has passed. Begone.'

The English fell upon their prey like wolves. Blades slashed, spears thrust, blood glittered like jewels in the moonlight. The screams of the dying men cleaved through the night, but no one came. The people who inhabited the meagre shacks of this reeking quarter knew that even in the city of gentle folk life could be hard.

The cries ceased. When ragged bodies littered the square, and the baked ruts had become a churned, ruddy marsh, the English gathered around the sole surviving figure. Whimpering, he crouched among the remains of his brothers. Hereward wondered what terrors flitted through his head as he looked up into the silent, judging faces silhouetted against the night sky.

He pushed his way through his spear-brothers and squatted beside the cowering man. It was the English-speaker. His jaw was still slack but his mocking grin had long since departed. Tears flecked his eyes as he wordlessly pleaded with his captor.

When he began to mewl at whatever he saw in that grim face, Hereward held up a finger to silence him. 'First, you will speak. You will tell me everything I need to know, or at least all that you know of these things. Do you hear me?'

Choking back a sob, the man nodded.

'You are in the employ of Victor Verinus?'

The man's eyes darted. Even here, he was afraid to speak, such was the power the Roman held over him. Hereward unsheathed his knife and tested the tip with the end of his finger. Swallowing, the prisoner nodded forcefully.

'Your task was to slay the English dogs, yes?'

'Yes.'

'Why does your master want us dead? We are . . . we were . . . no threat to him.'

'I do not know. Truly.'

Hereward balanced the knife upon his fingertip. 'Your master . . . he has a new friend? A man with a face that would haunt your nights?'

The rogue shuddered. 'I have seen such a man, but only once. He hides in the house of the Verini, never walking in the sun.'

Feet crunched along the dry street. Heads turned and then his men parted. Hereward saw Salih ibn Ziyad walking towards them. Black bristles framed a mouth that showed no emotion, but his eyes gleamed. 'Ask him,' he demanded.

'Now I would know of a woman,' Hereward said to the prisoner. 'Dark-skinned, from Afrique. Your master has her.'

'I have heard tell he keeps her captive. I know not why, or where.'

Hereward sensed Salih stiffen. 'She yet lives?'

'For now, I am told.'

'He plans to kill her?' the Mercian pressed. 'Soon?'

'I do not know his mind.'

Hereward looked up at the wise man. Salih nodded. They had the answer they needed. Now it was only the finding. The Mercian looked around the shadowed faces of his brothers. 'Victor Verinus killed one of us. We kill ten of his. From now on, that is how it will be. We will fight this like any other war, the way we fought William in the fens. We will not be driven out, crushed, made to run. We have found our acre of land, and it is ours, and it will remain ours, and no one will tell us otherwise. We have had our fill of powerful men choosing the roads we must walk. Never again.'

A whisper rustled around the English warriors. His final two words, repeated.

Hereward let the hilt of his knife fall into his palm. For a moment, he weighed it, and then he loomed over the cowering prisoner. 'Go, now,' he commanded his men without looking up. 'I have more questions, and I will have answers to them soon enough.'

CHAPTER FORTY-TWO

Waves licked at the body drifting in the Bosphorus. Nine more floated nearby, skin the colour of cave-fish, hair swirling like seaweed in the currents. The eyes had already been a feast for the gulls.

Along Constantinople's walls, folk gathered under the glaring morning sun to see the grisly spectacle. Hereward had already learned it took much to stir the hearts of these Romans. In their teeming city, filled with wonders from all corners of the earth, they thought they had seen everything under God. But bloody violence, that was another matter. For most it existed far beyond Constantinople's walls, a matter for the army, with victories proclaimed in the fora and defeats quietly forgotten. But now there was a war upon their doorstep, and, if the rumours were to be believed, only the first of many.

Death was coming to the city, and on this day he had brought it.

His hood pulled low, the Mercian edged away from the throng on the walls. He felt pleased that his men had lost none of their edge after their hardships.

Slipping through the streets, he made his way to the monastery of St George. The grand central dome was framed against the clear blue sky, the white stone incandescent. With its many windows and marching rows of columns, he thought how far removed it looked from the gloomy minsters of Ely and Eoferwic. Back in those grey places, the rain dripped through the thatch of the refectory and the wind howled under the boards. Here the majesty of God was burnished by the sun.

Within, he lost himself in the maze of corridors until he found a monk who could direct him to where the newly arrived English cleric toiled. Hereward found Alric kneeling at the shrine in the church, swathed in the sweet aroma of incense. His friend was laying down the offerings that had been delivered to the monastery gates that morning.

Alric seemed to sense his presence, for he looked round. For a long moment, they held each other's gaze.

'Have you come to take my other hand?' the monk enquired when the Mercian ventured over. But he caught himself, adding, 'That was unfair. You did what you had to do. You saved my life, and for that you have my eternal thanks.'

Hereward felt relief that his friend did not hate him. He had feared he would, and that they would never speak again. 'We have saved each other's life time and again across the years, and there will be more times to come, no doubt.' He glanced down at the stump, bound tightly with a clean cloth. 'If there was another way, I would have taken it.'

'Next time you need a hand removing, I will be the first to step forward,' the churchman said in a sardonic tone. Glancing around to make sure they could not be overheard, he added, 'The monks are abuzz with talk of ten bodies found in the water beyond the walls.'

'And you think I had something to do with that?'

'Did you?'

The Mercian showed a humourless smile. His friend knew him too well. 'Once again we are at war, monk. We came here in good faith, to earn our fortune through hard work and the battle-skills that are all we know. Instead, we have been mocked, and spat upon, and now we are being hunted down like dogs. Is this the way things are done in Constantinople?'

'Good men walk a hard road.'

'Good?' Hereward winced. 'No man would ever call me that . . . unless you were at my side to guide me along the right path.'

'And you shall have my aid again.' Alric clapped his remaining hand on his friend's arm. 'My wrist aches like the devil, but the wound is healing well. I will leave this sanctuary today and stand by you. And as we did in the fens, we will fight the one who hunts you down.'

'His name is Victor Verinus.'

The monk frowned. 'I have seen him, here, this last night. Speaking with his brother Nathaniel. A monk was poisoned. On the very day Nathaniel Verinus was made sacrist in his place, Victor came with his son, Justin, and they talked in the chamber long into the night. I heard their laughter myself.'

'Poisoned? Is that how you monks conduct your business? At least a warrior looks in his enemy's eyes before he kills him.'

The monk glanced down at his feet, uncomfortable. 'The church has great power here in Constantinople. Even the ear of the emperor himself, so it is said. This is not how we did things in Jarrow. But men who seek power will do terrible things, as you know as well as I.'

The door at the far end of the nave creaked open and a corpulent, bald man lumbered in.

'You think this Nathaniel poisoned the monk?' Hereward lowered his voice to a whisper.

'I could not say.'

'But it is at least possible?'

'From what I have seen of Nathaniel, anything is possible. He spends his time with boys in his chamber with the door closed. And Victor's boy too . . .' Alric bit his lip. 'No, I cannot say. Sometimes I think the worst, and that is not how God would have it. But Nathaniel has little kindness in him, that is certain.'

Hereward nodded, turning the news over in his head. 'A sacrist has no power. Overseeing the holy books and relics . . . why would any man kill for that?'

Alric shook his head.

'Though I would rather have you at my side, I think it best you stay here for a while,' the Mercian mused aloud. 'Be my eyes and ears in this monastery.'

The churchman shrugged. 'As you will. But you may be seeing plots where there are only shadows.'

The bald monk heaved his bulk towards them. A eunuch, by the looks of him, Hereward thought. He had met the kind before, in Wincestre when he was a boy.

'This is Neophytos,' Alric said, leaning in. 'He is the cousin of Maximos. He has cared for me well.'

Clasping Hereward's fingers in his chubby hands, the bald monk introduced himself. 'Maximos speaks well of you,' he gushed. 'A man of honour, and a brave one too. And now you work for the Nepotes—'

'Work for them?' Hereward's eyes narrowed. 'We are allies, of a kind.'

Neophytos bowed in apology. 'My English is poor. But your aid is still welcomed. My family have few friends, and they have suffered greatly.'

'There has been little justice in your world,' the Mercian agreed, 'but now Victor Verinus has chosen the wrong enemy.'

Neophytos smiled, and Hereward thought he saw tears spring to the monk's eyes. When the eunuch had promised to aid Alric in any way he could, he took his leave. But Hereward could see he had been deeply moved by the offer of support.

As Alric led the way back to the gate, the Mercian said, 'It is a strange war where you know not what your enemy wants, nor who all your enemies truly are.'

'We have much to learn if we are to survive in Constantinople,' the monk agreed.

'Aye, and learn quickly. Monks poisoned. Men's throats slit

in the street . . .' He shook his head, baffled. All he had worried about for a long time was that his friend might die, but now that fear had been assuaged, another trouble surfaced. 'Monk,' he began hesitantly, 'when we were in Sabta you said a strange thing. That you killed my brother.'

Alric's shoulders sagged. 'I thought . . . I hoped . . . that was a dream.' He sucked in a long, deep breath. 'Then I can hide it no longer. I must make my confession, for truly it has lain upon my heart like a rock until I thought I might die. Your brother Redwald is dead. I killed him.'

Hereward reeled. The brother he had loved and trusted all his life, but who had murdered his wife Turfrida and cut off her head, who had betrayed the English to their enemies. Who would have slit Hereward's throat in his sleep, if it would have benefited him. 'When was this done?' he demanded.

The monk was trembling. 'Redwald lay in wait to kill you after you had met King William at his palace in Wincestre.' He raised his remaining palm and stared at it in horror. 'I found him there, though he was already badly injured. And then I . . . I strangled him, Hereward. With my own hands. I took a life, God help my soul.'

Hereward could scarce believe what he was hearing. His belief that Redwald still lived had been the bitterest blow when England fell behind them, but now he was not sure how he felt. 'That vengeance should have been mine,' he said.

'No!' Alric grasped his friend's shoulder. 'If you had slain the man you once loved, the guilt would have eaten its way into your heart. You would never be able to escape that act. I know you well, Hereward. You speak of your devil, but you are not that thing. You are haunted by every savagery. I could not stand by and see you doom yourself, brother or not.' He wiped the snot from his nose with the back of his hand. 'Can you ever forgive me?'

As he let the news settle on him, Hereward realized a weight had lifted from his shoulders. His father was dead. His brother was dead. The ones who had done so much to ruin his life. Perhaps he was free of the lure of days gone by, for the first time. He smiled, not used to such freedom. 'If you forgive me for taking your hand, then I forgive you for taking the life of my brother. We have both punished each other, and saved each other. Mayhap that is our curse, eh, monk?' He crushed Alric to him until the churchman wriggled like an eel and gasped for breath.

Then, without another word, he turned and walked out into the busy streets. Perhaps there would be a fresh dawn for all of them in Constantinople after all.

CHAPTER FORTY-THREE

The shattered body sprawled across the heap of creamy stones waiting to be shaped by the masons. Spatters of blood had dried to rust-brown in the glare of the morning sun and fat flies were already buzzing lazily around the remains. The reek of death rose in the heat.

Kneeling beside the broken corpse, Wulfrun shielded his eyes and looked up the dizzying height of scaffolding to the top of the aqueduct of Valens. There was no doubt that the victim had fallen from that lofty perch. The guild of masons had been repairing the water course for long days now, toiling under the hot sun atop the rickety timber frame. But had this poor soul taken his own life, or had he been dragged up the ladders and hurled off the top during the night? 'Easier ways to end your days,' he mused.

Ricbert prowled around the bloody masonry. 'Perhaps he was admiring the view. Or trying to get closer to God. Too much wine . . .' he pressed a finger under his nose against the stink, 'thought he could fly with the birds . . .'

'Ten bodies in the Bosphorus this morn. This one here. Even for Constantinople, we are knee-deep in slaughter. Nothing from your spies?'

The smaller man shook his head. 'That is fine cloth,' he said, scrutinizing the clothes on the body. 'That pouch bulges with coin. He has not been robbed. Too rich to try flying from the top of the aqueduct.'

'Even the wealthy can have the weight of the world upon their shoulders, Ricbert.'

'Still, I would rather be rich and miserable than poor and the same.'

The skull had been smashed to pieces by the impact. Wulfrun glanced down at one hand, draped across a mason's mallet and chisel. A large gold signet ring gleamed. Frowning, he stood up, and took a step back. 'This is Apasios Basilacius, yes?'

Apasios was a fawning, acid-tongued man who oversaw the running of much of the young emperor's day-to-day business. He was rarely away from Michael's side and some said that, in his own waspish way, he carried as much influence as the finance minister Nikephoritzes himself.

'So much blood on his fine tunic,' Ricbert said with a shrug. 'He would be disgusted with himself.'

Wulfrun felt uneasy. He had a sense of a shadow forming in Constantinople, one that matched the growing dark beyond the city's walls. So many bloody events – a stabbing here, a poisoning there – and all seemingly unconnected. And yet he knew these Romans well enough by now. They were not as plain as the English, even those nobles who whispered and plotted at the king's court. They weaved their skeins with subtle hands, and oft-times the connecting threads were invisible until they were pulled taut.

Ricbert coughed and muttered, 'A bad day gets worse. Put steel in your spine.'

Glancing up, Wulfrun saw Victor Verinus approaching at the head of his band of cut-throats. The commander clenched his jaw. He was in no mood for more of the Stallion's hungry comments about Juliana. But for once the general's true feelings showed on his leathery face: a scowl. He was carrying a sack in one hand, and his strange, moon-faced son wandered at his heels like a lapdog.

'What use is the Varangian Guard if Constantinople falls into chaos around the emperor?' he boomed. 'How can you protect him when swords are drawn and lives are taken without a second thought?'

'The emperor is safe enough,' Wulfrun replied, unconsciously flinging his cloak over his shoulder so that his sword was visible. 'But you seem cut to the heart.'

'This was left upon my doorstep.' Gripping the bottom of the sack, Victor emptied the contents out into the masonry dust.

A head bounced, rolled and came to a stop near Wulfrun's boot. The white eyes stared up at him. The mouth was slack, the teeth jutting this way and that. The bloody skin hanging from the neck was ragged. No clean cut that, no axe or sword stroke. It looked as though it had been hacked at with a knife.

'One of the bodies we pulled from the waters was missing a head,' Ricbert said. 'All the parts are together now. I can rest easy.'

Wulfrun rested the tip of his boot on the forehead and rolled the head back to Victor. 'One of your men?'

The Stallion shifted with momentary discomfort. Wulfrun felt pleased. The general was hiding something, but this business had troubled him enough to bring his worries to the surface. 'He has done some work for me in the past,' the man grunted. 'But that is neither here nor there. We should not have to endure such slaughter. We are not barbarians. Those responsible must face justice.'

'All who threaten the emperor, and Constantinople, will be judged. Their crimes are punished, sooner or later.'

Victor's eyes narrowed. 'There are enemies abroad in Constantinople, I tell you. They come with the flow of miserable shit that streams in from our frontiers day and night. They hide among us, plotting . . . plotting against the emperor himself.'

'Give me names, then. Show me where they live. I will bring these plotters to justice.'

'My faith in the Varangian Guard wanes fast. You may have won the hearts of all the women in this city, but you failed us at Manzikert. I think you have grown weak. Too much gold, too much wine.' Victor smiled, turning the blade.

Wulfrun flinched. They both knew that Victor twisted the truth. But to show anger would be taken as weakness, so instead he swept a hand towards the body at their feet. 'And was Apasios Basilacius also murdered by these plotters?'

Victor Verinus did not even glance down at the tangled remains. 'Murder? Are you certain? I had heard that Apasios had lost so much gold at the hippodrome that soon he would be begging for scraps on the Mese. Despair drives a man to terrible things.'

'Debts,' Wulfrun said. 'I had not heard that.'

'So it is said.' The Stallion turned to leave. 'If any of those who have recently arrived in the city pose the smallest threat to the emperor, I cannot remain silent. I will make my voice heard, in the forum, on the steps of the senate, until all know what dangers we face. Constantinople needs a strong hand if it is to survive. Not the weakness we all see around us.'

When he had watched the general, his men and his son sweep away, Wulfrun turned to Ricbert. 'Find someone to move these remains, then meet me at the Great Palace.'

Marching east through the streets, Wulfrun knew that Victor Verinus was right about one thing: there was too much weakness in Constantinople. Everyone in the city knew that. But it was not the Varangian Guard who was to blame. Everywhere he went he heard the people lamenting the loss of the strength that had made the empire great. It was a gulf that many would have no qualms filling.

At the Great Palace, it was his intention to alert others to his increasing unease concerning the emperor's security, but although he spoke to general after general, minister after

291

minister, his words were wasted. Emperor Michael was like a leaf blown by the wind of whoever had his ear at the time. And most days it was that viper Nikephoritzes, who cared only that the coffers were full and nothing for the growing threats that assailed them from every side.

For a while Wulfrun wandered the corridors, gathering what information he could from the palace slaves. Once he had learned the emperor's plans for that morning, he loitered in the shadow of an arch in the long corridor running through the heart of the vast hall. After a while, he heard voices and care-free laughter, and saw the emperor approaching. Michael was surrounded by his friends, men with too much gold and too little desire to make any mark upon the empire. Behind him came a clutch of older men, led by the severe Nikephoritzes. The commander stepped out of his archway. A splash of colour in the grey corridor, his crimson cloak demanded attention.

'Loyal Wulfrun!' the emperor called when he saw him. 'I sleep easy in my bed knowing your sword is ever ready.'

The commander bowed. 'I would have words with you about matters of some import.'

'The emperor is too busy for the likes of you, Wulfrun,' Nikephoritzes said, stepping between the commander and the emperor. His voice was light and his lips curled in a pretence of humour, but his eyes were cold. The finance minister would only be happy if the emperor heeded his voice alone.

'Ah, Wulfrun, always so grim!' Michael said as he passed. 'I must hear the plans for our service to remember the dead of Manzikert. Why this should trouble my day, I do not know, but it shall be done. We will talk another time.'

The emperor moved on with his friends, but Nikephoritzes remained, no doubt to make sure Wulfrun did not pursue his request. Once Michael had disappeared, neither man felt the need to pretend warmth.

'Who speaks truth to the emperor? You?' the commander snapped.

'There are many truths. Not all need trouble him.'

'Our scouts in the east say the Turks are moving closer by the day. They eat the empire's land, yet we stand by and do naught. When should this matter trouble the emperor?'

'When the threat is clear.'

'It is clear now. We must build our army and strike before they are at our gates.'

Nikephoritzes forced a tight smile. 'Armies cost gold. We must be careful not to waste. You see only the stuff of swords and battles, Wulfrun, but the emperor and his government must weigh many matters, often ones that fight with each other.'

'Armies cost, yes. But what good full coffers if they are in the hands of the Turks?'

'Would you have us raise taxes further?' Nikephoritzes' smile grew wider.

Wulfrun set his jaw. The burden upon the people was already great. Many struggled to pay. The price of wheat was becoming too high for the common man, and in the markets angry voices could be heard on a daily basis.

'New coin will be minted. It will flow into the marketplace soon enough,' the finance minister said.

'Coin with less gold in it?'

Nikephoritzes pursed his lips. 'A little, perhaps.'

'Soon it will be as light as a feather.' Wulfrun wagged a finger at the other man. 'Mark my words, soon there will be trouble. More trouble than we can handle, both inside our walls and without.'

'Then you will deal with it,' the minister said. With a nod, he strode after the emperor.

Wulfrun swept from the palace, his feeling of powerlessness turning to anger. Ricbert waited on the steps, grinning at the women as they passed. He flinched when he heard the stream of curses at his back.

'A good morning, then,' the smaller man said.

Wulfrun gritted his teeth, forcing himself to be calm. 'War is coming to Constantinople, Ricbert, a greater war even than the horrors inflicted upon the English by William the Bastard and the Normans. But the emperor is blind to it. And its tendrils will reach out across the world as every power, great or small, jostles for influence and advantage. Michael is weak . . .' he glanced round to make sure he could not be overheard, 'and little more than a boy trying to grow his first beard. Weakness will lose this city, and the empire, to the Turks. And weakness will see us destroyed from within as all the vipers plot in the shadows, fighting for control. Their struggles, too, will ripple out across the world. In the face of that, what do men like you and I do, eh? Troop merrily towards doom?'

Ricbert shrugged. 'We serve the emperor, for good or ill. That is our oath. And if we are to die, we die at his command.'

Before Wulfrun could respond, he saw a figure break away from the throng streaming along the dusty street. As the man climbed the steps of the palace, he recognized Deda.

'I have good news. Your hopes have been fulfilled,' the Norman said with a bow. 'Your friend is here. Hereward has arrived in Constantinople.'

CHAPTER FORTY-FOUR

Slender fingers closed around the guard's throat. His howls of agony became rattling gasps, his clawing fingers fluttering in the air. As she straddled the man's chest, Meghigda felt his bucking subside to become twitches, then the faintest tremors, like raindrops on a pool. And finally he grew still. When she was sure he was dead, she let her hands go limp and her shoulders sag. Empty sockets stared up at her, the eyes lost somewhere among the filthy straw on the floor of the cell.

Pushing herself up, the queen flexed her sticky fingers. They ached from the exertion. But it had gone better than she had dared hope. The guards had been too confident, she had seen that from the outset. Thinking her weak, they did not treat her with the wariness they would have shown towards a male prisoner. They turned their backs to her when they came into her cell, squatting down to her level as they left her meagre meal in one corner. And they thought one of them at a time was enough. Once she had learned their routines, the rest was easy.

As she eased open the door, Meghigda felt a surge of defiance. She had been true to the spirit of al-Kahina. Her limbs ached and her belly growled with hunger, but the fire in her heart had never dimmed. She would not be caged, or broken, or contained. Freedom was all that mattered, to her, to her people, even unto death.

Creeping out of her cell, she plucked up the stubby candle the guard had left on the floor in its pewter holder. The light shimmered across crumbling walls slick with moisture.

Ragener would be first, she decided. Then Victor Verinus. Men without honour, both of them. They lived their lives in the dark, yet could not see what that cost them. And then she would return to her people and fight the war that she had been born to fight. Her own life meant nothing. Meghigda, the true Meghigda, had died the day her parents had been taken. Comfort, peace, aye, and love, all of that would be for ever denied her. For a while she had grown weak, thought there might be a chance of something else, but now she knew better.

She crept into the long, dank passage. The dark maws of other tunnels loomed up on either side. At each one, she paused, listening, but there was only silence. In some of them, she glimpsed spears, armour, axes; in others large stone urns. A store of secrets. Few knew of the existence of these catacombs, she guessed, and that made them perfect for Victor Verinus.

As she crept on, she began to hear strange, distorted echoes ahead. She sensed a vast space away in the dark, and water, lapping, booming, dripping. The air grew chill. The passage came to a ragged break in a wall. Rubble was strewn all around. Stepping through it, she found herself on the edge of an enormous vault filled with water. Stone columns rose up into a gulf of darkness. Her tiny candle barely penetrated a spear's length into the gloom.

Glancing around, she saw she stood on a stone step reaching to the water's edge. A flat-bottomed boat had been moored to a post – the guard's, she guessed – and that seemed to be the only way out.

But as she reached for the rope she glimpsed another light far off in the abyss, brighter than her candle. A lantern. It was sweeping towards her, no doubt on the prow of another boat. The water shimmered in front of it.

Her fingers hovered over the mooring post, but she knew she would not be able to escape without being seen. Silently cursing her misfortune, she wetted the tips of her fingers, extinguished the candle and crept back into the catacombs.

If only she had Salih's silver knife to defend herself. She could kill whoever was approaching while their back was turned, and then make her escape. Meghigda set her jaw. There was no point in complaining. Her blood-caked nails would have to suffice.

The dark swam around her. Feeling her way along the wall, she found one of the side passages and crawled along it. Her breath was tight in her chest. Her elbow clipped something – a spear? – and it clattered to the floor. The echoes rang out.

Meghigda's heart thundered. She stiffened, listening. In the distance, she heard a splash, a dull scraping. She imagined the boat bumping against the side, the passenger climbing out, tying it to a post. Could they have heard over the echoes of the water?

Pressing her hand over her mouth, she waited. Footsteps drew closer. Heavy ones. A big man. Her breath burning in her throat, the queen peered back along the way she had crawled. A soft glow lit the wall of the main passage, growing brighter. Meghigda pressed herself back against the stone, hoping the illumination would not reach into her hiding place. The lantern swung into view, the glare so bright in the gloom that she could not look at it.

Once the light had passed, she waited only a moment and then crawled back, taking care not to disturb any other obstacles. Her time was short, she knew. If she tried to get away on one of the boats, she would be caught. If she hid, she would be caught once the dead guard and the empty cell had been discovered. Her only hope was to attack from behind and pray that surprise would be enough of an advantage.

At the passage junction, she peeped around the edge. The light was not moving. The intruder had not ventured all the way to the cell. Perhaps he searched for something in one of the stores, she thought. Here was her chance. Like a wolf, she loped along the passage towards the lantern.

Her feet made not a sound on the stones. Keeping low, she crooked her fingers into claws, making ready. She strained to hear, but she could have been alone in all the world.

Meghigda focused all her attention on that light, waiting, perhaps, for a shadow to cross in front of it. And so she sensed movement beside her too late. A low growl, the pounding of feet, a looming silhouette hurtling from one of the side passages.

The fist smashed against her cheek before she even had time to turn. Her head slammed against the wall, and her wits spun away.

Through her daze, she heard only animal noises, of pleasure or anger she could not be sure. Her captor cuffed her again for good measure, snarled a rough hand in her dress and dragged her along the passage back towards the cell. Two more blows hammered into her. She felt hands lift her effortlessly and toss her back into the cell. When the door slammed shut, she felt a momentary pang of despair – to be so close and to have freedom snatched away.

Once he had retrieved the lantern, her captor pressed his face against the bars. In the grotesque shadows cast by the lantern, Victor Verinus looked more beast than man. Meghigda stared into that face and felt a depth of hatred she had never before experienced. Yet she kept calm. She would not give him the satisfaction of seeing how much she cared.

'You think yourself a warrior, woman,' he said, glancing down at the body of the guard. 'Very well. I shall treat you as one. Let us see how you like that.'

Meghigda held his gaze. She imagined tearing out his eyes, pressing her thumbs into his windpipe.

He seemed to sense her thoughts, for he nodded. 'Warriors

die by the sword. Sooner or later. I have seen enough battles to know that none slip off into an easy death.'

'You think I care?' She raised her chin in defiance.

'No. I think you do not. You have more fire than most men, I will give you that. But it will do you little good. Your time is almost done.'

Meghigda could not understand why this man had not yet killed her. He had wanted vengeance for the death of his son, but that now seemed the furthest thing from his mind. 'I have seen what happens to men like you,' she said, her voice calm. 'I would not wish it on a dog. Whichever god you worship, none of them can abide such cruelty. They will strike you down soon enough.'

'"Men like you",' he repeated with a humourless laugh.

'Men without honour. Men who lust for power above all else.'

'Perhaps,' he replied, caring nothing for her insult. 'Or they seize empires. And crush the weak before them. And make what was once strong and feared strong and feared again. Either way, you will not live to see it.' Victor stepped away from the bars. Meghigda thought how confident he seemed. Whatever he planned, he was sure it was in his grasp. 'You will do well to stand when the rats come feasting on your friend,' he added, nodding towards the dead guard. 'Once the frenzy is upon them, any meat is prey, warm or cold.'

Without another word, he turned and walked along the passage. In his eyes, she was not worthy of any farewell. She heard him rooting in one of the passages for whatever had brought him to that place, and then his footsteps, and the light, receded.

The dark closed around her once more.

For a while, Meghigda sat against the cool stone, letting the ringing in her head subside. When she felt strong once more, she said in a clear voice, 'Who are you?'

No response came back for a moment, and then a woman's voice said, 'How did you know I was here?'

'You have been before. Many times.'

The queen heard her visitor walk into the passage. The sound of a struck flint cracked out and a soft light shimmered. Meghigda furrowed her brow in surprise when she saw a girl of perhaps seventeen summers. Greasy red hair hung around a gaunt face dappled with bruises. Her dress was worn and filthy, the body beneath it little more than bones. She looked like a beggar-child. 'Why are you here?' the queen asked, baffled.

'Because my father deems you worth his attention.'

After a moment, Meghigda grasped the meaning of the words. She scowled. 'You are Victor's child?'

'By blood. By name.' The girl paused as though she were un-used to being questioned. 'I am Ariadne.'

'And you are here to gloat?'

Sitting cross-legged in the corner, the girl shook her head as if this was unthinkable. 'Why do you resist him? He will only hurt you more.'

The queen looked down her nose at her visitor, weighing her. 'I am al-Kahina, slayer of devils, ghost of the desert, priestess, soothsayer, warrior, and I will bow to no one.'

'Even though he hits you?'

'Even though he breaks my bones, cuts my flesh, rips out my heart, ends my days. At the final reckoning, all we have is that smallest part of us. That knowledge of who we truly are. We do not trade that away for any price, any gold, any suffering.'

Ariadne plucked at the hem of her dress, letting the words settle on her. Meghigda thought how sad the slight figure looked. There seemed little of Victor Verinus in her. 'What is it that you seek here?' she asked gently.

The girl looked up, her face determined. 'I saw you did not cry, even when the rats crawled around you. I saw that the dark and the hunger did not gnaw at you. I saw you hold your head high, even when there was little hope.'

'Even in the dark you see these things?' Meghigda said with a faint smile.

'I see better in the dark than all others because I have lived my life in it. I sleep in the dark. I eat my scraps off the floor in the dark. Whenever I have done wrong, and those times are many, I am punished by the dark. And sometimes . . . sometimes I choose the dark.' She blinked away hot tears. Meghigda was shocked by the passion she saw in the girl's face. Wiping the snot from her nose with the back of her hand, Ariadne steadied herself. 'I saw you kill the guard with your bare hands. I saw you defy my father. Now, I would know all that has shaped you. Tell me what it is to be the slayer of devils, the ghost of the desert. Tell me of the road that has brought you to this cold place, of your life, of your battles, of your pain, and most of all of your fears, so that I might know your heart. For in truth, I cannot understand you. Tell me all that, and I promise I will tell you what I seek here.'

And Meghigda did tell her, everything, from the slaughter of her mother and father to the hardship she endured to become the leader her people demanded. She told her because her heart went out to this fragile girl. And she told her because it reminded her of who she was, in that smallest part of her, that part that would never be extinguished.

When she was done, Meghigda took a deep breath. Her words rustled away into the gloom, and for a while there was only silence. Then Ariadne looked up from her deep reflection and said in a voice as hard and bare as a desert rock, 'Every third night, my father uses me like a wife.'

The queen did not know what to say.

'If I could only be you, I would,' the girl said, standing. 'I will help you. If you have friends here in Constantinople, I will tell them of your plight, and they will come and save you.'

Meghigda grimaced. 'I have no friends here.' Desperate, she racked her brain. 'Wait . . . I know of someone . . . of . . . a family. The Nepotes.'

Ariadne frowned. 'You know them?'

'I know of Maximos Nepos.'

The girl pursed her lips. 'Maximos has returned to Constantinople.'

Meghigda's heart leapt and she hated herself for it. He was the last person in the world she would choose to put her faith in, but she had no choice. 'Tell him of my plight. Tell him he owes me, and if he has any honour he will do all he can to save me.'

Picking up the lantern, the girl nodded. 'Very well. But I must be quick. My father has made up his mind to end your days, and he is always swift in his judgement. Your time is short, he told you that.' She stepped towards the passage.

'Wait. You promised you would tell me what you seek here.'

When Ariadne glanced back, her eyes were ablaze. She lifted the lantern to her lips, blew out the flame, and the dark swept in. 'Hope,' she said, the word ringing out clear.

And then she was gone.

CHAPTER FORTY-FIVE

'Hereward! Show yourself!' The voice boomed through the house of the Nepotes.

In the courtyard, the Mercian jumped to his feet from a shaded bench. His hand flew to his sword. The threat in that tone was undeniable.

Maximos was beside him in an instant, his eyes narrowing. 'That is not Victor Verinus.'

'One of his men, then. The Stallion will not have taken kindly to a head laid upon his doorstep. And he will know it was a gift from me.'

The Roman grinned. 'Was that not the point? Prod him until he rears up and shows his soft underbelly?'

As the two men swept into the cool of the entrance hall, a cry of fury rang out. Hereward had time only to glimpse the accoutrements of one of the Varangian Guard before the warrior drew his sword and rushed at him.

Brainbiter sang as it whisked from its sheath. As the guard's sword flashed down, Hereward met it. His ears rang from the clash of iron upon iron. Sparks glittered. With a heave of his blade, he threw the other man back.

But this warrior seemed to be caught up in a battle-rage.

Back he came in an instant, hacking high, then low, thrusting, slashing. Every move was fluid and powerful. The Mercian had no doubt that he was in the presence of a master swordsman, one who could match him in strength and resolve.

And yet for all his fury, the warrior was as silent as the grave. He remained as calm as deep water and just as dangerous.

Around the hall they danced, evenly matched. Their swords clanged, jarring bones. But the warrior had the advantage of his shield while Hereward had only his feet and his natural skill to evade the edge of his foe's weapon.

Finally the warrior put his shoulder behind his shield and charged. The Mercian slammed into the wall, his sword pinned between him and the hard wood. The guardsman rammed the tip of his blade against Hereward's neck.

'Now I will have your head,' he snarled.

'There will be no weapons raised in my house!' The voice cracked with anger. Simonis Nepa was standing in the doorway, her eyes blazing with the fire of the woman she no doubt once used to be.

The girl, Juliana, appeared at her back. Her eyes narrowed as she took in the scene and she pushed past her mother. 'Wulfrun,' she demanded. 'What is the meaning of this?'

Hereward could feel the other man trembling with passion. As he stared into those cold eyes, he sensed the warrior fighting against his instinct to drive his sword into flesh, as he had fought against his own urges so many times. But this Wulfrun was capable of winning that battle.

Juliana stepped into his line of vision. Her stare was unwavering and Hereward sensed a strength there that had, until now, been well hidden. 'No blood will be spilled in the house of the Nepotes,' she said in a clear voice. Though she smiled and the tone was pleasant there was an edge to it that brooked no dissent.

Wulfrun wavered. Then, with a flicker of regret, he took a

step back. 'I demand vengeance,' he said. 'My father would be alive this day if not for this dog.'

The Mercian's brow furrowed. If he had seen this man before, he could not recall it.

Anger flared in the warrior's eyes. 'You do not remember me?'

'Your voice crackles with the sound of the fens, but—'

'Aye,' Wulfrun snapped, almost driving his sword forward, 'we share a past, you dog. And that you cannot recall who suffered at your hand only adds to your crime.'

Juliana pushed her way between the two men, her eyes holding Wulfrun fast. The guardsman had no choice but to let his sword fall away. Her smile became flirtatious and she rested both hands on his chest. A lover's touch, Hereward thought, and yet, at the same time, both a barrier and a warning. She would not be defied. 'You are a man of honour, a strong man, who knows full well when to take a life and when to rise above killing,' she said, her voice honeyed. 'That man captured my heart. I know you would not disappoint me.'

Wulfrun winced, torn. He seemed incapable of seeing the subtle manipulations in his love's words, Hereward noted.

Juliana knew she had the advantage. Pressing her hands forward gently, she eased Wulfrun back another step. Her smile never wavered. 'This man is our friend, as you are the friend of the Nepotes, and more than friend to me,' she breathed. 'And he is an ally. My family needs his help. Would you see Victor Verinus truly triumphant? You know what he wants more than anything.'

'No more,' Wulfrun said, stung by whatever implication lay behind the words. His eyes flickered towards Hereward's face, still glinting with murderous intent.

Juliana's eyes flashed with a moment of pleasure at her victory and then she showed a concerned face. 'What is wrong?' she asked. Moving her hands to her love's cheeks, she forced him to look into her eyes. 'Why do you attack our guest? I have never seen you this way.'

'Yes, speak,' Hereward said. 'If I have wronged you in some way, tell me, so I can make amends.'

'Only your death will balance what you did,' Wulfrun spat.

At some point, Deda had slipped into the hall. He frowned with dismay and addressed the commander. 'You deceived me. You made me betray my friend. That is not honourable. It is you who should make amends. Speak. Tell us what has driven you to this.'

Wulfrun kept a cold eye on the Mercian. 'The days of my youth were spent in Barholme, in the east of England, as were this man's. But he was not my friend. He was no man's friend. Hereward was a blight on all who knew him. He robbed from anyone whose path he crossed. The rich and the poor. The strong and the weak. I saw him beat another lad with his fists until the boy's face was such a bloody mess his own mother would not have recognized him. And even then he kept beating until we felt sure the lad would be killed. Six of us dragged him off and paid for it with a whipping ourselves.' He swallowed. His voice had grown hoarse. 'There was not a man or woman in all Barholme who was not afraid of him. Others were wounded. Some died, so it was said. Bodies found in the waters. For too long, his father protected him – he was the son of a thegn, after all.'

Hereward felt his shame burning. All true.

Wulfrun's sword hand began to waver from the emotion coursing through him. He sheathed his blade, but still he did not break his accusing stare. 'One night after the harvests, he stole my father's horse. Our barn was set on fire – on purpose or by accident, I do not know – and we lost everything. Our plough. All that we had brought in from the fields to see us through the cold months. And when my father tried to stop him, this snake broke his arm. He could not work. We faced starvation and death – my mother, my three brothers and my sister. My father was a good man. He cared for us all, never raised a hand against us. He laughed, yet worked until his fingers bled to keep us fed.' He jabbed a finger at Hereward, barely able to contain all that seethed inside him. 'And in one night, this dog stole it all from him. My father became like one with the dead. I never saw him smile again. He walked from village to village, begging for aid. And when he had scraped together enough to see us through the winter, he ended his own days. A rope round his neck in the woods near our home, where I had hunted fowl as a boy. My mother died soon after. She wanted to be with him, I am certain.'

Silence had fallen across the hall. Hereward could sense the eyes of the others upon him. 'Now I remember,' he said. And he did, but still only snatches. So many crimes there had been, as he fled from his own father's cruelty, and they had become a blur. How terrible that was. He had cared for no one; had not given one thought to the people who fell before him.

'Should a price not be paid for such crimes?' Wulfrun implored as he looked around the hall. 'Should this man walk free, and live, and laugh, and love, while my father lies in his grave? Where is the justice in that? They called him hero when he fought against William the Bastard at Ely, but he is no hero. He is a thief. He is a murderer. And he has never paid for all the crimes he committed.'

Hereward felt sickened. He could not argue with this man at all. His thoughts flew back to the desert night when Maximos had told him there was no escape from days long gone. Now he feared that was true. First there had been Drogo, then Ragener, now this. There was a price to pay for everything he had done, a trail of blood that led from his own actions to some poor soul or other. And though he had tried to make amends since those times, the ghost of the man he had been would haunt him until his dying day. How many other wounded souls waited to meet him?

Holding out his arms, he said, 'There is nothing I can say

that will ease your pain. I am not proud of what I was. Many suffered . . . many. I deserved to be killed as a wild dog would have been. But then I met a man of God upon the road and he tried to teach me all the things I had never learned – friendship, justice, care for the weak, sacrifice. Where I succeeded, it was because of him. Where I failed, it was my own weakness. There is nothing I would wish more than to wipe away the stain of those early days. All I can do is try to live my life now as I should have done then, and hope that when God judges me, he will not find me wanting.'

Wulfrun snorted, unmoved.

'If you wish to take my head now, I cannot stop you. But I will tell you what a good man taught me. Vengeance only wounds the one who wields it. Do not let it eat into your heart. Walk away. Live your life, enjoy your days, and your friends, and those who care for you. This course will only doom you.'

The guardsman drew his sword once more. Juliana glared as the blade swung high, but it wavered there as the warrior weighed his actions. Hereward knew what raced through the other man's head. His lust for vengeance had consumed him for so long he could not easily shrug it off.

'You cannot do this,' Juliana snapped, her face wintry. 'You have sworn an oath to me.'

Wulfrun frowned, not understanding.

'Did you hear what I said? This warrior and his men now fight for the Nepotes. For the first time since we were brought low, we have allies. Victor Verinus can no longer trample us under his feet. Our lives depend upon this man and his followers. You have sworn an oath to defend me,' Juliana repeated, 'and I will hold you to it. You cannot let your feelings for this man intrude. Lay down your sword.'

Hereward was struck by the pain in the other man's face. 'I have sworn an oath,' he whispered, letting his sword fall. Smothering her cold words with a smile, Juliana whispered in Wulfrun's ear, but whatever she said seemed to do no good.

His shoulders were hunched, the fire gone out of him. But she had won, and she seemed pleased by that. Turning, she took her mother's arm.

When the two women had left, Deda told Wulfrun how he had overheard Victor Verinus demanding Juliana's chastity. 'You talk of crimes,' the knight continued, 'but the Stallion's are not in days long gone, they are now, and they are unending, and they are unspeakable. We must stand together before more blood is spilled.'

'How could I ever trust him?' Wulfrun snapped, jabbing a finger towards Hereward.

The Mercian bristled. 'And how can we trust you? In battle will I forever be watching for a sword in my back?'

Now it was Maximos' turn to make the peace. He rested one hand on the commander's arm. 'Set aside your hatred, for now. Deda is right. We must ensure Victor Verinus commits no further crimes. We must protect my family . . . my sister.'

Wulfrun clenched his fists. He could not deny what Maximos had said, but still he fought with himself. 'My oath is to the emperor, and Victor Verinus is in his favour. And my oath to Juliana . . .' He bit off the words.

The Mercian understood the guardsman's torment. One man could never serve two masters, but he had sworn to do so before God. Hereward hoped he would not regret those vows. 'In war, we find our enemy, and then choose our allies, and not all of them are friends,' he said.

After a moment, Wulfrun nodded. 'Very well. But there will come a time when this battle has been fought. And then we will end this between us with honour, and one of us will die.'

And with that, he whirled and marched out of the door. Yet barely had he crossed the threshold when a thin girl with lank red hair stepped into view. She must have been waiting outside until the raised voices had died away. A beggar, Hereward guessed, but she showed nothing but confidence in the way she scanned the hall.

Maximos scowled. 'Be away with you, witch. The Verini are no longer welcome here.'

The girl was unmoved. 'I bring you news of al-Kahina,' she said. 'Come now, lest she lose her life.'

CHAPTER FORTY-SIX

Golden shards shimmered on rippling black water. Oars dipped, splashed. Hollow echoes whispered back from on high. Across the vast vault of darkness, three pools of light drifted as the flat-bottomed boats crossed the abyss. Ghosts of marble columns marched out of the gloom into the illumination of the swinging lanterns and disappeared into the gulf behind. The world seemed to be holding its breath.

Hereward knelt in the prow, watching the way ahead. He could see nothing; it was blacker than a moonless fenland night. When he cocked his head, all he could hear were the distorted rumbles and beats of lapping water and falling droplets. In the chill air, the smell of wet stone was sharp in his nose.

He smiled. After so long, they were close.

Behind him, Kraki rowed, slow, steady. Sighard and Salih ibn Ziyad squatted astern. No one spoke. Twelve of them there were in all, but that was more than enough if the girl had been right. Somewhere ahead, through a ragged hole in a stone wall, Meghigda waited in her cell. Once they had her back, they could take this war to Victor Verinus' door.

At first, Maximos had called the Stallion's daughter, Ariadne, a liar. Then, when Hereward had become convinced of the truth in her eyes, the Roman had refused to come. Salih had bared his teeth and half drawn his silver dagger before the others had restrained him, but Maximos would not be persuaded. Hereward could only guess that at the last his troubled feelings for the woman he had once loved, and then abandoned, had proved too much. Either that or he could not face the edge of Meghigda's tongue in front of the men he had come to call brothers.

Once he had sent word for the men to accompany him, Ariadne had led the way through the deepening shadows like a wolf-child, lean and loping. As the sun slipped behind the hills they had found themselves heading south-west, past the grand homes of wealthy Romans with the vast dome of the Hagia Sophia looming high overhead. Here they had come to a basilica surrounded by a colonnade with lush gardens alive with the music of the birds' evensong.

Through doors and darkened corridors she guided them, until they came to a steep flight of stone steps leading down into the cistern which collected water channelled from far outside the city. And there she had left them. As they stood on the stone platform where the three boats were moored, Hereward and his spear-brothers had marvelled at the construction. Never had they seen such a wonder. But once they were out on the water, all thoughts returned to Meghigda.

Behind him, Hereward could sense Salih ibn Ziyad's brooding presence. The Imazighen wise man had barely spoken a word since they had left the house of the Nepotes. Only one thought burned in his mind now: saving his queen. The price that would be paid for her suffering would come later.

As they swept past one of the spectral stone columns, a woman's shriek rang out from deep in the dark ahead. Every man on those three boats jerked alert. Hereward stiffened, his blood running cold. He had heard agony in that cry.

The boat rocked as Salih half stood. 'Row faster,' he urged, 'or we will be too late.' His voice crackled with desperation.

The Mercian pushed aside all thoughts of what might have caused that shriek. But everything he had heard about Victor Verinus told him to expect the worst.

Another shriek rang out, and another, and then a long silence that left Hereward praying for another scream.

Now they had no need for subterfuge. The boats ploughed through the black water. Echoes of the splashing oars and Hereward's exhortations became a constant rolling thunder. Soon the gulf of darkness fell away and the lantern-light shimmered across a dripping stone wall. 'There!' Salih called, pointing to a gaping hole in the masonry.

As soon as the boats crashed against the narrow platform, the spear-brothers leapt out. While three men moored the craft, Hereward snatched a lantern and led the others through the ragged gash. Drawing Brainbiter, he prowled into the catacombs. The English warriors pressed close at his back, eyes darting into every tunnel they passed.

'If Meghigda is dead, there will be blood,' Salih hissed, 'and agonies unimaginable by man.'

The Mercian believed him.

His men were unnerved by the silence, he could sense it. If Victor Verinus waited at the end of the passage, there was no doubt that he could hear their approach. Lowering the lantern, Hereward peered ahead. In a chamber at the end of the tunnel, the light of a guttering candle danced. He sniffed the air. The iron scent of blood wafted on the draught. He hoped Salih could not smell that reek, for he feared the wise man would not be able to control himself.

'Be ready,' he whispered.

His warriors raised their weapons, their eyes searching for even the hint of movement in the gloom.

When Hereward stepped into the candlelit chamber he hunched low, ready for any attack. But none came. A body lay face down on the filthy floor, blood puddling around the head. The throat had been slashed. The thumping of his heart eased when he saw that it was a man. But it was not Victor Verinus. The victim was smaller, older, the skin of the arms like parchment, the thinning hair white. And this was a wealthy man too, his tunic woven from fine cloth and heavily embroidered.

Hereward's eyes darted to the only other person there. A woman sat on the dirty straw of a cell, behind bars of iron reaching from the floor to the rock overhead. The door hung open. The Mercian furrowed his brow when he saw that it was not Meghigda. Long black hair framed a face as hard as flint. She was grinning, taunting silently. As he watched, she opened her mouth and shrieked, drawing up a play of agony from deep inside her. When the scream died away, she grinned once more, her gaze challenging him.

Salih ibn Ziyad lunged. His silver dagger glittered in the flickering candle-flame. When Hereward swung up an arm to hold him back, the wise man roared, 'Who are you? What have you done with my queen?'

The woman only grinned.

'Stay your hand,' the Mercian commanded. He peered back along the passage, his thoughts whirling. 'Maximos was right not to come. This is a trap.'

'But what kind of trap?' Guthrinc muttered, looking round.

'I do not know, but we should not tarry to find out.' Hereward levelled his blade at the woman. 'Stand. You will come with us. And once we are away from this place, you *will* answer our questions, mark my words.'

With a shrug, the woman eased out of the cell and joined them. The Mercian felt uneasy that she had obliged so quickly.

'Make haste,' he urged. 'I would not be down here any longer than need be.'

As the spear-brothers streamed into the passage, Salih snarled, 'Then that dog still has Meghigda.' His voice crackled with fury, but his eyes showed only desperation.

As the men clambered into the boats, Hereward spoke his thoughts aloud. 'Victor Verinus knew we would come here.

He wanted us to come. And he made sure his daughter would bring us.'

'She tricked us?' Kraki growled.

The Mercian shook his head. 'You could see she spoke true. She was as much a pawn as we were.'

Even when they were in the boats and rowing hard across the cistern, the warriors could not rest. Eyes darted around. They listened for any sound among the whispering echoes. They knew, as well as Hereward did, that the Stallion's game was still to play out.

'We are simple men,' Sighard protested from the stern. 'Give us an axe or a spear and we will show you the fire in our hearts. But we are not prepared for this city of plots and whispers, words as sharp as blades and shadows and trickery.'

Kraki glanced back. 'I miss the smoke-filled halls of Eoferwic, and the rain dripping through the thatch. I miss the simple pleasures of mead and hearth-fire. But this is the world we have inherited now. It is just another battlefield. We learn the rules or we die.' He held Sighard's gaze until the younger man nodded his acceptance.

But as they drifted out of the dark towards the landing platform, booming echoes resounded, so loud that they could not hear themselves speak. The sound of running feet on stone steps. The crash of axes upon shields, the rattle of mail-shirts.

Warriors flooded out from the steps and formed a line three deep along the stone platform. Crimson capes swirled in the lantern light. A wall of shields, cold eyes gleaming over the edges. The Varangian Guard waited in silence.

'Do we fight?' Sighard gasped.

'We will be slaughtered.' Glowering, Kraki sat back on his bench and scanned the row. 'They are many, we are few.'

'Row back, then.'

'To what end?' the Viking growled. 'There is no way out. We would be waiting for death to claim us.'

Sighard shook his head. 'What do they want? We have done no wrong.'

Hereward searched for Wulfrun among the ranks, hoping that conflict could be averted, but could see no sign of him. On the edges, archers trained their shafts upon the three boats. The Mercian sensed his men looking to him. He showed a confident face. 'Keep your weapons down,' he called.

But as the boats bumped against the platform, the woman leapt out and ran to the guard's commander. 'They murdered Jacob Scleras,' she called, pointing at Hereward. 'Cut him down because he is one of the emperor's trusted advisers.'

The Mercian felt his heart sink. Now he could see what Victor Verinus had planned. 'He was already dead when we found him—'

'Lies!' the woman shrieked. 'I saw it with my own eyes. And they say this is part of some greater plot. They threaten us all!'

Hereward tried to protest, but the archers only tightened the strings of their bows. The commander pointed his sword at the English. 'Out of the boats, now,' he demanded. 'Do not think to fight. You will be dead before you have taken one step.'

Once the guard had seized all weapons and surrounded the spear-brothers the commander pushed his way forward. He was smaller than the others, with ratty features. 'I am Ricbert,' he said. 'You are . . . ?'

'Hereward of the English.'

The commander frowned as if this name meant something to him. 'We received word of a plot against the emperor . . .'

'Victor Verinus,' the Mercian hissed.

Ricbert gave nothing away. 'We were told you would be here to slay another man who stood in your way, as you have killed so many others in recent days. The rest of your men wait for the order to rise up. But it is too late for that now. The Varangian Guard will hunt them down like dogs. This plot has been broken, like every plot before it.'

At the foot of the stone steps, Hereward glimpsed a slight

figure watching from the shadows. It was Ariadne. 'Run,' he cried. 'Warn my men! You will be well rewarded.' The girl did not hesitate. He heard her feet pound up the steps, and though two members of the Guard gave chase, she was younger and faster and not encumbered by mail and shields.

The Mercian felt the edge of a sword bite into his throat. Ricbert stepped forward and looked up into his eyes. 'It will do no good. We are the Varangian Guard. We will not rest until your men are captured or dead.' He looked round his men and commanded, 'Take them away from here and prepare them for execution.'

CHAPTER FORTY-SEVEN

The blade stabbed towards the heavens. Victor Verinus looked along the notched edge of his sword, turning it slightly so that the candlelight danced along the steel. The hilt was carved ivory capped by a gold dragon, the blazing eyes inlaid rubies.

Ragener watched his master's admiring nod and felt a pang of envy. Surely he too deserved a weapon as fine as that. But the woman seated upon the bench in front of him showed only contempt. Meghigda's face was swollen and bruised from the beating he had inflicted upon her. Blood crusted her nostrils and one eye had half closed. But still she refused to bow her head.

'I am al-Kahina,' she murmured through split lips. 'You can break my body, but you can never crush my spirit.'

Ragener cracked his knuckles across her head once more, then waited for Victor to voice approval. When the Roman said nothing, did not even look his way, the sea wolf silently vowed to try harder still.

Meghigda spat a clot of blood on to the marble floor. Her cold, murderous gaze fell upon Victor and then rose to Ragener himself as he prowled round her. 'My life means nothing,' she uttered. 'My fight will be carried on. If not by me, then by some other brave soul who raises my standard.'

'You *are* nothing,' Ragener snarled. 'Bow your head.'

'Never.'

'You would rather die?'

'There is no victory for you in my death, only in my surrender.' She showed a bloody grin, and Ragener felt uneasy at what he saw there. 'My life was given up long ago, when I was a child, and my days yet to come were stolen from me by those who slayed my mother and father. After that, every day was a gift. Every day was used to fight, against men like you, who would steal the joy from others. Strike me again. Cut me, burn me. There is nothing you can do to bring fear into my heart. Kill me and know that you have lost. Your own death will come soon enough, and I will be waiting in hell to greet you.'

Ragener gripped her throat and squeezed, but she held her chin up and her eyes still burned with contempt. He glanced at his master once again, but Victor only admired his blade.

'This sword was given to me by my father, and it was given to him by his father, and so on,' the Stallion mused. The sea wolf thought there was an odd note of wistfulness in that voice, unexpected at such a moment of victory. 'This is how we do things here,' the general continued. 'So that we never forget that days long gone still shape our lives, and the days yet to come. There is a skein to all things, one that we cannot see. Lines drawn from then to now. One thread is pulled there, another life is lost here.'

Lowering the blade, he weighed it on the palms of his hands. 'I wielded this sword at Manzikert, the scene of our most crushing defeat, when so many of our men from the western and eastern *tagmata* were slaughtered. It has always been a part of me. With it, I have killed the bravest men, the fiercest warriors. I forged my mind in the furnace of battle, made myself better than the weak and sickly child who would receive the back of his father's hand for his failings.'

Ragener narrowed his good eye. Victor seemed to be talking to himself. He could not understand why his master was not slaking his thirst with the finest wine instead of musing over ancient days.

'Strength, you see. That is what this sword means,' the Stallion continued. He laid the blade on the table next to the candle. 'Without strength, you are nothing.'

'I am strong,' Ragener ventured. 'My body might have taken more blows than most men could bear, but my heart is strong. My fire burns bright.'

Victor seemed not to hear him. 'Every death . . . every drop of blood spilled by this blade . . . led to this night.'

The sea wolf flexed his fingers tighter still.

'Our empire has grown weak. The glory of our long gone days has been frittered away. Once, when we whispered, the world listened. And when we roared the world quaked. Now we have an emperor who is little more than a boy. He mewls, he dribbles, he spits his food. Now we are a people who count the grains of gold in a coin while our enemies creep ever closer to our walls. If my father were here now . . . if I had not stabbed this sword through his breast when he was too weak to raise a hand against me . . . he would be sickened by the weakness he would see around him. Constantinople is in the grip of an illness. Only death will wipe it away. Then we can heal, and grow strong once more.'

A sound rustled out across the chamber. A whisper. A prayer. Filled with regret, or hope, or defiance, Ragener could not tell, but he did not look down.

Victor prowled to his window, closing his eyes as he inhaled the sweet scents rising from his night-garden. After a moment, he murmured, 'The Varangian Guard is distracted. Hunting down the rest of the English. Thinking this plot has been caught in good time and the emperor is safe once more. And thus I am free to strike. When the emperor dies, I will be far away, with those who will attest I had nothing to do with the slaughter.' He smiled to himself. 'Whipped curs, broken to my will.'

'And the Verini will hold power,' Ragener murmured, 'and I will be raised up.'

'The Verini,' Victor mused. 'All but my brother.'

'Nathaniel?'

'My other brother. Karas.' The Stallion's eyes flickered down. For the first time, Ragener thought he glimpsed some weakness. Unease? Fear? Could it be? 'His land lies to the east. But once he learns what power I wield, he will have no choice but to come and bow before me. No doubt. No doubt.'

Desperation rose up in Ragener and his hand jerked involuntarily. He heard the snap of Meghigda's neck. 'She is dead,' he said. The queen's head lolled forward. 'Ah,' the sea wolf continued with a shrug. 'It is what it is. I did not mean to kill her, but she defied me. She thought I was nothing. And now she is nothing.'

He removed his hand from Meghigda's throat and gave her a gentle shove between the shoulders. She toppled from the bench and sprawled across the marble floor. The Hawk rested the tip of his boot on her side and rocked her, just to be sure.

She was dead.

Now Victor deigned to glance at him. The general looked irritated, not because the woman was dead, Ragener knew, but because here was another inconvenience, and he needed none of it on this night of nights. 'She has served her purpose. When you brought her to me, I knew she would have some use, and so it presented itself. A lure for the English. A chance to drive the Varangian Guard away from where they could do harm to my plans.' He fluttered a hand. 'Do not leave the body here. Dump it somewhere where the dogs can eat it. She will be forgotten soon enough, and no trouble to us.'

Ragener turned up his nose as he looked down at the still form. They said she was a queen, a warrior, but she had died as easily as any woman he had killed. And yet her final words hung over him. Fear flickered in his heart and he found he could not look into her face.

'When you are done, go to Justin. He waits for you,' the Stallion continued. 'Prepare him to take the crown tonight. It should have been Arcadius, but that was not to be.' He shook his head. 'But first find my finest cloak and some gold to wear at my neck. I would be well dressed for what is to come.'

The sea wolf nodded, realizing that when Victor had set a price on Meghigda's head it had not been out of grief, or vengeance. Only fury that his plans had been disrupted.

The Stallion clapped his hands together. 'And now I am triumphant. There is only the waiting. All that is left is to claim the spoils of battle.' Ragener saw a hungry look cross his master's face. 'How fitting that tonight of all nights the fair Juliana will be mine.'

Once the two men had stepped out of the chamber, Ariadne crept in and threw herself across the fallen form of Meghigda. Tears streamed down the young girl's face and grief burned in her heart. Part of her wished she had not returned to her father's house en route to warn the English. But the queen would still be dead. Every word had echoed through to her hiding place in the other room, and when she had heard Meghigda's neck break it had taken all her strength not to cry out in despair. She was surprised by the heights of the desolation she felt. But in the time she had watched over the queen, and listened to her words, she had felt a rare thing grow in her heart: hope. Hope that there was more to life than the miserable existence that was her lot, more than pain and suffering. Hope, too, that there were better people in the world than her father.

Ariadne raised her red eyes up to the heavens and made a silent vow. Meghigda and all that she represented would live on. Hope would not die with her.

CHAPTER FORTY-EIGHT

'Meghigda is dead. They have left her body near the church of the Forty Martyrs.' Choking back a sob, the red-headed girl plucked at the flesh of her bony wrists. 'My father has won.'

Rowena felt her heart go out to the urchin. Ariadne was her name. She looked so frail and poor, and now consumed with a terrible sadness. But then the girl pulled herself up, her face hardening. Rowena was shocked by the transformation. 'She will live on in me,' Ariadne said. A fire lit her pale eyes. 'We cannot let it end here.'

'We can do nothing.' Simonis Nepa levelled a wintry stare at the girl. From the courtyard at the back of the silent house, a cool breeze blew.

'The woman is dead,' Juliana repeated. 'And Victor Verinus has won.' She held her mother's gaze for a long moment. Rowena tried to decipher that odd look. As their tormentor ascended to even higher power, were they afraid that he had not yet plumbed the depths of the agonies he would inflict on them?

'He has won? Won what?' she asked.

Ariadne rubbed at her cheeks to dry the tears. 'I do not know the nature of his plot. But he has arranged for your friends, the English, to be captured by the Varangian Guard – some of them at least. I must warn the others. Tell me where they are—'

Rowena grabbed the girl's shoulders. 'Captured, you say? Is my husband with them?'

'The Norman? He is.'

'It is too late for them,' Simonis said before Rowena could ask for help. 'If the Varangian Guard have taken them, they must believe your friends were plotting against the emperor. They will be executed on the morrow.'

'No. I cannot accept that.'

'We can do nothing,' Simonis repeated.

Rowena could see there was no point arguing. Mother and daughter seemed resigned to whatever fate awaited them.

'My father is coming here,' Ariadne said, as if to confirm all their thoughts. 'To claim his spoils, he said.'

Juliana and Simonis clutched each other's shoulders, their gazes locked. Trying to find strength, Rowena thought. 'The time has come,' Juliana murmured. 'There is no backing out now.'

'We must defend ourselves,' Rowena began.

Anger flared in Simonis' face and she lashed out, striking Rowena across the cheek. 'Do not speak to me,' she snarled. 'Your duty here is done.'

Rowena was stunned by the change in her mistress. But as she eyed Simonis' icy features, she felt realization dawn upon her. Until this moment, she had only seen the face that Simonis had wanted her to see.

'Did you hear my mother? Leave this house, and do not return,' Juliana snapped.

Nodding, Rowena turned towards the door, but her mind was racing. If Victor Verinus was on his way, there was much she could learn here. When she heard the mother and daughter leave the courtyard, she whispered, 'I do not accept this is an ending.'

'Nor I,' Ariadne said with defiance. 'What will you do?'

Rowena weighed her response. In the past she had been too headstrong, she saw that now. She had thrown herself into danger without considering the consequences, and had paid a harsh price. However much she wanted to race to the Varangian Guard and plead for Deda's release, she had to keep a calm head. 'I must know what Victor plans,' she whispered, glancing back to be sure that Simonis had not returned. 'You must warn the rest of Hereward's men. They are good at hiding, especially if Herrig the Rat is with them. Then we shall see.'

She told Ariadne where the English warriors waited for their leader, and the girl slipped away. Rowena crept into the dark house. From a far corner, she could hear the women talking. They were bathing. How strange, she thought. In the chamber near to where she hid, Kalamdios' mewlings reached a high pitch. He seemed to sense something was amiss.

The door on to the street creaked open. Rowena shivered despite herself. She would never admit to fear, but Victor made her skin crawl. He looked at her as he looked at every woman, with a hunger that seemed as if it could never be sated. Once Simonis had led Victor through to the chamber where Kalamdios sat on his wooden throne, she crept from her hiding place and moved softly to the door.

Candles flickered all around the chamber. It looked as if Simonis had prepared it for a ritual, Rowena thought. Kalamdios was agitated. His eyes rolled, his mouth worked furiously and his fingers snapped and plucked at the air. In front of the master of the house, Victor stood tall and proud, his iron-grey hair hanging around his shoulders. A smile played across his lips as he studied the two women who stood before him. Juliana could only stare at the floor. But Simonis bit her lip as she held the gaze of the visitor. The Stallion paid no heed to Kalamdios at all.

'Tonight I am triumphant,' he said, 'and Constantinople enters a new age. When my son wears the crown, our strength and pride will be restored. In the days when you fought against me, did you ever think I would be standing here on the cusp of such power?'

Simonis forced a smile. 'There was never any doubt you had the strength to succeed.'

Victor laughed. 'How different the world would be if you had had the strength to defeat me, eh, Kalamdios?' He glanced at the hunched master of the house. 'Your weakness has cost you everything you built. In the end, it has cost you the greatest prize of all, the thing you wanted as much as I did. Your weakness, Kalamdios. Never forget that as you sit there, wishing that you had died that day when I plunged the blade into your head.'

When Kalamdios' mewling became reedy, Victor only laughed. He turned back to the women.

'Now I can take whatever I want.'

Simonis gave a hesitant nod.

'And I want you,' he continued, looking down at Juliana. 'You must watch this, Kalamdios, and watch carefully. I am taking your daughter from you as I have taken everything else.' He nodded to the mistress of the house.

With trembling fingers, Simonis eased the dress from her shoulders. It slipped to the floor and she stepped out of it, naked. Rowena could see no shame in her face. She must have suffered this hardship so many times it had become little more than any other chore.

Stepping forward, the mother hooked her fingers under the shoulders of Juliana's dress and let it fall away. She too was naked beneath. She lowered her eyes. 'Do you like what you see?'

Victor could not contain his grin. Reaching out with his large hands, he squeezed her right breast and thumbed the nipple. With unnecessary roughness, he pawed down across her belly to the soft hair, and then slid his hand between her legs. Juliana flinched.

Rowena turned away, unable to watch this grotesque display

a moment longer. But then she heard the Stallion say, 'Before the dawn, the emperor will be dead, and I will leave here to control an empire. Does that excite you?' Only the hope that he might reveal more of his plans drew her back. She had to be strong, as strong as Victor claimed to be.

She watched him raise Juliana's chin so she would look into his eyes. 'You give yourself freely?' he asked. 'I do not rape women. Only the weak have to seize by force what the strong take by will alone.'

'I do,' Juliana replied, 'in recognition of the power you wield. Do you give yourself freely?'

Victor threw his head back and laughed. 'You have some fire in you. I knew you would not disappoint me.'

With a shrug of his shoulders, his tunic fell to the ground. Then he grasped his member and worked it erect. He displayed himself for a moment, smiling, before he placed his hand on Juliana's head and forced her down.

Rowena felt sickened. What would Wulfrun do if he knew the woman he loved was being stripped of her innocence by this monster? But then, as she watched, she began to frown. Juliana curled both hands around Victor's cock and pushed it into her mouth. Deeper, and deeper still, she went, until Rowena winced, unable to comprehend how the girl did not choke. Victor closed his eyes in ecstasy. Simonis watched, impassive. Kalamdios twitched and puled.

But all Rowena could think was that this was no chaste child. Whatever Juliana may have pretended to Wulfrun, she was exhibiting all the skills of a Frankish whore, and ones that only came with long experience.

The monastery was still. Only the sighing of the wind in the roof broke the silence as Neophytos hauled his bulk along the corridor. At the door to Nathaniel's chamber, he pressed his ear to the wood and listened. Soon the sacrist would be required in the church, where the emperor would be praying for all those who lost their lives at Manzikert, and no doubt for the old emperor who had lost his head. But there was still time. With chubby fingers, the eunuch wiped the sweat from his brow and pushed the door open.

Nathaniel sprawled on his bed, naked. His eyes were wide and staring, but he still breathed, though shallowly. The boy sitting beside him jerked alert and smiled.

'Here, boy. Now leave us,' Neophytos said, pressing a coin into the lad's palm. Once the young one had slipped out, the eunuch picked up the fallen goblet from the pool of wine. He sniffed it, wrinkling his nose at the bitter edge to the scent, then nodded.

'Our appetites destroy us, Nathaniel, one way or another,' he said in his sing-song voice. From his pouch, he removed a lump of grey metal and set it to heat in a spoon upon a lantern flame.

The door opened and a hooded figure slipped in. He sat upon a stool in one corner, keeping his head down.

'Pay no heed to him,' Neophytos said with a smile. He leaned over the sacrist and pressed two fingers against the pulse in the older man's neck. 'You live,' he said with a nod. 'You can hear. You can see. You can taste and smell. But you cannot speak and you cannot move. Why, you are quite like my uncle Kalamdios.' Neophytos allowed himself a satisfied smile. These days, he took his pleasures where he could.

Once the lead had melted, he took the spoon and dribbled the contents into Nathaniel's ear. There was no scream, of course, and no widening of those staring eyes, but Neophytos thought he saw an odd light in them. He enjoyed that too. Leaning down, he kissed Nathaniel on the forehead, and said, 'And so, for you, the night draws in.'

'You will know soon enough when the emperor has fallen,' Ragener said as he paced the chamber. No sounds drifted through the monastery at that hour. They might have been alone in the world. He eyed the moon-faced boy, Justin, as he perched on the edge of the small bed. He looked as calm as if he were just awaking from a deep sleep, not someone who was about to take on the burden of the crown.

The sea wolf opened the door a crack and listened. How long until the blood flowed? His heart thumped in anticipation, but his elation was tinged with anxiety. This was the night when his life changed. The misfortune that had dogged him from when he was a boy would lie behind him. He would be raised up.

'Will my father come to me?' the boy asked in his dreamy voice.

'When all who stand against him have fallen, and not before. He will come to save Constantinople from anarchy, not be seen as the man who caused it.'

The boy nodded, staring blankly at the wall. Ragener knew there were some who found Justin unsettling, but he had always felt he had much in common with the lad. Perhaps they could be friends. The emperor and his chief counsel.

As he turned back into the chamber, the door slammed against his back. The Hawk stumbled forward. Before he could steady himself, the flat of a blade clattered against the base of his skull. Stars flashed, then darkness.

When Ragener came round a moment later, he saw another boy looming over his charge. It was Leo Nepos, scion of that family which Victor always spoke of with contempt. He wielded a blade almost as big as himself, its tip pressed against Justin's neck.

'You shall never be emperor,' Leo was saying. 'I will take your head first.'

The Hawk tried to scramble to his feet, but his head still spun from the blow. As he pitched forward again, he saw Justin grip the blade with both hands, pressing it away. Though the other lad dragged the sword back, carving through soft palms, Justin showed not a glimmer of pain. His face remained as still as a mill-pond.

Shocked by what he saw, Leo hesitated, and that was enough. In an instant, Justin transformed into a wild beast. Snarling and spitting, his features contorted. Throwing aside the blade, he leapt on the other boy, tearing wildly with clawed fingers. Red lines ripped across Leo Nepos' face.

When the boy had been sent to end Justin's days, no one could have guessed what would be unleashed, Ragener thought as he staggered to his feet. He could not have guessed himself.

Before he could draw himself up, the girl, Ariadne, darted in. A knife shimmered in her hand. Throwing herself upon her brother's back, she cuffed him across the back of the head with the hilt of her blade. Dazed, the fire went out of him.

'You are your father's daughter,' Ragener slurred.

But Ariadne turned to him, her eyes blazing. 'I am not,' she spat. 'I am al-Kahina, slayer of devils. This night you will live. But know that one day, when you least expect it, I will come for you. And then I will take your other eye, and your hand, and your feet as well, and I will leave you in the filth of the street where you belong.'

Ragener shivered. Those very words had been uttered by Meghigda in the cell in the catacombs. How could this girl have known that – unless the spirit of the Imazighen queen now possessed her? He staggered back, crossing himself.

Hauling Leo to his feet, Ariadne thrust him into the corner. 'For all that he has done, he is still my brother,' she said, waving her knife towards Justin. 'I cannot stand by and let you end his days.'

Leo lowered his blade. 'If he leaves here . . . if he leaves Constantinople . . . he can live.'

For the briefest moment, Ariadne's face softened. Ragener thought he saw something pass between her and the Nepos boy, but then she whirled and thrust Justin towards the door. 'Take him away from here,' she said to the Hawk, her voice and her eyes cold. 'Take him to my uncle in the east. Karas will care for him – they are of a kind. Take him . . . and wait for me.'

Ragener felt gripped by a terrible fear. Grabbing Justin, he dragged the boy out into the silent corridor. 'Run,' he urged. 'Run. This night is going to hell.'

The candles flickered. Shadows danced across the chamber as Victor threw his head back in ecstasy. Kalamdios whined like a sick dog. The naked women were silent.

Rowena crouched in the shadows. She could barely bring herself to spy any longer, but she still hoped that Victor might utter something, just a word or two, that would give her information she could use to save her husband.

While her daughter worked upon her knees, Simonis crossed behind him. Pressing her breasts against his skin, she kissed him upon his shoulders and his neck and caressed his broad chest with her slender fingers. When he moaned a little, she lifted a goblet from a table beside Kalamdios.

'Let us give you more pleasure than you can bear,' she whispered in the Stallion's ear.

Reaching around him, she eased the goblet to Victor's lips. He slurped the wine, the red liquid cascading down his chest, soaking Juliana's hair. When he had had his fill, he smacked his lips. With another kiss upon his neck, Simonis tossed the goblet aside.

Rowena could not understand how the women could give themselves willingly to such a beast. She knew full well the price that had to be paid when such sacrifices were made, whatever the end.

Linking her arms with Victor's, Simonis pulled her hands behind his back and locked them. At first she was gentle, but then she yanked them tight. Rowena could see that Victor enjoyed the restraint. His smile became a grin of pure pleasure.

But then a shadow crossed his face. Rowena leaned forward, puzzled. The Stallion's eyes opened, and he moved his lips as if trying to speak, but no sound came forth. When he staggered a step, Simonis supported him.

'The wine is strong,' she breathed in his ear.

Juliana looked up at her mother, Victor's cock still deep in her throat. Those wide eyes, those once innocent eyes, smiled, Rowena thought. And then Juliana bit down.

Rowena recoiled, her hand flying to her mouth. She might well have cried out, but if so it was lost beneath Kalamdios' wild mewlings, which had whipped up to fever pitch. And now Victor did make a sound, but it was only a long, terrible groan like the closing of a tomb.

Sickened, Rowena pulled back. She could not bear to watch, but hearing the noises that issued from that bloody chamber was just as bad. Soles flapped upon the marble floor; a convulsion. A grunt from Simonis as she held her prisoner fast. And then a sound like tearing silk. Rowena tried to smother the vision that flashed across her mind but she could not deny it: Victor Verinus was a stallion no more.

She listened to the sound of a large form slumping down, and then Juliana coughing and spluttering as she spat out the contents of her mouth. Mother and daughter laughed. Kalamdios made a wheezing, barking noise that seemed almost joyful.

'And so we have taken from you all that you valued.' Rowena glanced back into the chamber. Victor lay with his head in Kalamdios' lap. Simonis was kneeling beside him, whispering in his ear. 'You are dying now. Soon your blood will have drained away. You cannot speak, but you can hear, man who is no longer a man. And you should know how badly you have failed. You thought yourself so clever with your plots and your plans, your taunts and your torments. But you underestimated the Nepotes.'

'Poor Victor. You never guessed, did you, nor even suspected?' Juliana breathed, running her fingers through the general's lank hair.

'Maximos murdered your son, not that queen. She witnessed

his crime, but through love she never spoke out. And now she too is dead,' Simonis murmured, enjoying twisting the knife even at the last. 'That was always the first part of our plan. To take away your best hope for emperor so you would be forced to rely upon that boy . . . that monster, Justin.'

Victor shook as if he had a fever. Rowena watched the pool of blood around him gleam in the candlelight.

'And Maximos killed the English warrior in the street outside this house, so they would join us in the fight against you,' Simonis continued. 'From that moment, all that you hoped for was slipping through your fingers. Then we only had to wait for you to do our work for us. Murdering the emperor's closest advisers, who could be replaced by our own. And then murdering the emperor himself. When he dies at the hands of your men tonight, it will not be Justin who seizes the crown, it will be Maximos. He will be the hero of this night, and he will be the new emperor. And the Nepotes will rule Constantinople, and the Verini will fade away, never to be remembered.'

'He goes now, Mother,' Juliana said. 'Quickly.'

As Simonis clamped her hands on Victor's head and forced his mouth wide, Juliana pressed something into her father's hand. His fingers twitched and spasmed, but she held them tight and manipulated them towards their dying tormentor's mouth.

Rowena heard his groans become stifled. She winced at the grunts and gasps as he choked upon his own flesh. But after a moment they grew weaker and weaker, and finally they were done.

Victor Verinus was dead.

Racked with horror, Rowena clawed her way out of the chamber and scrambled towards the door to the street. She knew now that the Nepotes were capable of anything. If they found her there, if they suspected for a moment what she had witnessed, her life would be over.

As she stumbled out into the cool night, a figure stepped

towards her. In her shock, Rowena cried out, clasping her hands to her mouth to silence herself.

But it was only Alric. 'You must come with me,' he urged, looking around as if he feared for his own life. 'I know Victor Verinus' plan. Tonight rivers of blood will be spilled.'

CHAPTER FORTY-NINE

Black rats fought over crumbs of bread. Cloaked in the gloom in the corner of the piss-reeking cell, ringed tails lashed the air, claws raked, fangs were bared. Hereward sat on the filthy straw, his back pressed against the cold stone, and watched the frenzy. The hungry vermin had turned on each other in a moment to get what they most desired.

Beneath the Boukoleon palace, where not long before the Varangian Guard had dashed the hopes of the English, the low-ceilinged cell was large enough to accommodate Hereward, his men, Deda and Salih ibn Ziyad. Through a grille in the solid door, wavering light washed from a single torch in the corridor. For men used to seeing in the black fenland nights, it was enough.

The Mercian glanced around the faces of his spear-brothers. In twos and threes, they sat whispering, some laughing. They did not look like men who had been told they faced certain death when the sun came up. Only Salih sat alone, brooding. Head bowed, wrapped in his black robes, he looked like a battlefield raven waiting to feast.

Hereward felt the weight upon his shoulders. All his men's hope of a new dawn had been placed in him, but he had led them only to this, as he had led them to defeat at Ely. They deserved better. And now they expected him to find some path out of this plight.

'No one blames you for what happened. You have done only the best for us, but sometimes fate decrees that even the strongest man's will is not enough.'

Hereward jerked his head up at the words. It was as if his very thoughts had been read.

Sighard stood in front of him. 'You are our leader, Hereward, but this is not your burden alone.'

'Then why are your brothers so spirited?'

'Would you have it any other way?' Sighard squatted. 'Turn your thoughts out, not in. We are all warriors. There are days when you fight better than you ever have before, and the sod turns under your foot and you fall before a weaker man's spear. You know that. And you know that death waits for all of us, and he can come on a summer's day as readily as a winter's night. How you meet him . . . that is the mark of a man.' He smiled. 'Clear your head of the doubts that nag you. You know what I say is true.'

'I promised you gold and glory—'

'You promised us the chance of gold and glory. And you gave us that. We are all thankful. We could have died at Ely, but you helped us live. And in Afrique, and here in this pit of vipers. We owe you all we have. And if there was mead here we would drink to you, aye, even as we walked to our death.'

The Mercian felt warmed by Sighard's words. For so long he had been a solitary wolf in winter woods. Now he had brothers who would die for him. Who accepted his word without question. And who accepted the failures alongside the victories. He could ask for no more from this life. 'We still live,' he said with a firm nod. 'And so we still fight.'

Sighard grinned. Glancing around, he leaned in and whispered, 'One more thing. The blackness was eating my heart. I wished only to die. But you would not let me. You . . . and

Kraki . . . you made me fight when I had laid down my arms. I owe you my life. That I will never forget.'

When Sighard had returned to the others, Hereward thought on what he had said. They had reached their lowest ebb, but they had been here before and fought their way out. Given a chance, they would do so again.

When the door ground open, he was ready. But as he jumped to his feet, he paused. Wulfrun stood framed in the dancing torchlight, his helm tucked under his arm. Hereward thought that the commander looked as if he had been told of the death of a loved one. 'Follow me,' he intoned, and spun away.

The English glanced at each other in surprise, but they did not need to be told twice. Grinning, they stumbled over each other to get out into the corridor.

Wulfrun waited with Ricbert, the guard who had seized them. He heard the smaller man ask, 'You are sure of this?'

'No,' the commander said. 'But this world has been turned on its head. If we run with dogs instead of lions, so be it.'

He led the way up steep stone steps and into a chamber that looked out over the night-garden. 'Take your weapons,' he commanded, sweeping his arm towards a jumble of axes, spears and shields in one corner. Thinking it was yet another trap, the English hesitated until Hereward plucked up Brainbiter and slid it into its sheath.

'What has brought this change of heart?' he asked.

Sliding his helm on to his head, Wulfrun said, 'Victor Verinus is dead. How, I do not yet know. But his plot has not died with him. The Varangian Guard are abroad in the city, searching for your men, and far from where they are needed. Victor's men lie in wait to slaughter the emperor and any of his advisers who stand with him.' He paused, seemingly gathering his strength. 'And those who killed the Stallion will wait for Victor's plan to unfold and, blameless, will then seize control.'

'Who murdered him?'

Wulfrun moistened his lips. 'The Nepotes.'

337

'The family of your woman.'

Wulfrun would not meet Hereward's eye. The commander sent Ricbert out and a moment later the aide returned with Alric and Rowena.

'They pleaded for your worthless lives,' Wulfrun said, his face like stone, 'and I listened.'

'The Verini planned to attack the emperor at the monastery as he prays for those who died at Manzikert,' Alric said. 'The Varangian Guard would not be allowed upon the sacred ground during those prayers, even if they had been near. And thus the emperor would be undefended.'

'How did you learn this?' Hereward asked.

Smiling, Alric tapped his head with his good hand. 'Sometimes I have brains of mud, but this day God blessed me. The poisoning of the sacrist had been weighing heavily upon my mind. But with Nathaniel in that role, he could place others of a like mind around him. Together they could allow Victor's men into the monastery and hide them away until they were needed.'

Ricbert glanced at Wulfrun. 'My spy who died upon the altar . . . he must have had news of this plot.'

'It seems many of us have mud for brains,' the commander muttered. 'I should have seen this unfolding . . .' He caught himself, not wishing to show weakness. But then his features darkened. 'I have bad news. Victor Verinus did not die without bringing more misery into this world.'

Wulfrun led the way into another chamber. A body lay upon a table. Hereward felt a wave of sorrow when he recognized Meghigda. He could see that her neck had been broken. In death, the troubles that had weighed upon her features had been replaced by a look of peace.

Salih ibn Ziyad cried out as if a blade had been stabbed through his heart. Remembering the agony of grief he had felt when his wife was killed, Hereward winced when he saw the raw emotion burn into the other man's face. Salih fell to his knees in front of the table, his hands clasped and his head bowed. From his mouth flowed a babble of words in his own tongue, each one filled with passion.

'As a leader, she had no equal,' Hereward said, 'and as a warrior too. She was brave and honourable. Is this truly what Constantinople is – a place where nothing good can survive?'

'There is a sickness here,' Wulfrun agreed, 'but honour will shine through. I believe that above all else.'

Rowena broke away from Deda's embrace. 'Maximos could have saved her at any time. He killed Victor's son, not her, but Meghigda never betrayed him. Yet he remained silent unto the end.'

Hereward flinched. 'Maximos?'

''Tis true,' Rowena said.

Wulfrun cursed under his breath. 'Plots upon plots. I was tricked by that bastard Maximos' grins and slapping of backs.'

'As were we all,' Hereward snapped. He swallowed his anger, for now.

But Salih rose up like a wraith from the grave. 'Maximos' days are numbered,' the wise man hissed. 'He will pay for this.' He rested one hand upon the hilt of his silver dagger and swore an oath in his own tongue.

Beckoning to Hereward, Wulfrun led him out of the chamber. In the corridor, the commander said, 'We have our differences, you and I. But now I am asking for your aid. Help me save the emperor's life. Without the spears of your men, he will certainly die.'

For all that the other man hated him, Hereward felt only respect for Wulfrun. To live by a code of honour in a city like Constantinople was worthy of any praise. 'Very well.'

Wulfrun looked surprised at the response, but he nodded. 'If I know Victor, the men he had in place will be savage. We are few and they will be many. I have sent word to the Varangian Guard, but they may not return in time. This course may only lead to all our deaths.'

The Mercian rested one hand upon the hilt of his sword. 'I am sick of running like a dog, sick of hiding. Let us fight like brothers, shoulder to shoulder. And if we die this night, so be it. We will not be alone in hell.'

CHAPTER FIFTY

The full moon hung over the gleaming dome of the Hagia Sophia. Outside the monastery of St George, the street was a river of silver in the stillness of the evening. Shadows flitted across it, as silent as ghosts. The air was fragrant with the perfume of Constantinople's gardens and peace lay across the roofs, but as the English closed upon their destination their thoughts were only of blood.

When the warriors were crouching by the low wall along the monastery's front, Hereward heard a low whistle, and the rest of his men streamed from a dark passage between two grand houses. Hiroc the Three-fingered looked relieved as he knelt beside his leader. 'The red-headed girl, Ariadne, said you would be here sooner or later. I thought it might be a trap. God knows, you cannot trust any of the lying curs in this city, but . . .' He clapped the Mercian on the shoulder, allowing himself one of his rare smiles.

Once the new arrivals had been informed of the task ahead, Hereward sent Alric to the monastery doors. Victor's men would be guarding the entrances in case the Varangian Guard returned, he guessed. But the monk returned a moment later, shaking his head. 'They are barred,' he whispered.

Hereward watched Wulfrun glower. The commander was afraid time was fast running out. The emperor was inside. Soon he would be alone in the church, praying before the altar. An easy target for a knife.

Crooking a finger at Herrig the Rat, the Mercian sent him scurrying across the approach to the monastery. Even in the moonlight, he was little more than a smudge of darkness as he weaved like his namesake, low and fast.

'What can he do?' Ricbert sniffed. 'Make himself as small as vermin and wriggle under the door?'

Hereward gave a tight smile, but said nothing. When he reached the monastery, Herrig paused only briefly, scanning the walls. Then, finding cracks and crevices invisible to most eyes, he began to climb.

Wulfrun and Ricbert marvelled as the scout scaled the walls with a speed that belied the difficulty of the ascent. 'He will fall and break every bone in his body,' Ricbert said with astonishment. 'Does he have no fear?'

In the fens, Hereward had seen Herrig claw his way up a soaring ash tree and leap from branch to branch on adjoining trees with scant regard for the danger. Nothing seemed to frighten him. The courage of madness, Kraki called it.

Herrig reached a window on the first floor, clambered over the edge and disappeared into the dark. The warriors waited, breath tight in their chests as they listened for any sign of discovery. Finally, the door swung open. With a gap-toothed grin, Herrig the Rat beckoned them forward.

When Hereward loped up to the door, the scout opened his hand. Two bloody fingers nestled in his palm. 'For my necklace,' he whispered, jangling the string of mementos of the Normans he had killed.

One of the dead men lay just inside the door in a pool of blood. His throat had been slashed. Hereward guessed the guard had never even heard Herrig creeping up on him. Holding up a hand to bring his men to a halt, the Mercian cocked his head. The monastery was silent. 'Lead us to the church,' he murmured to Alric.

But as they crept along the corridor under the light of sizzling torches, he heard footsteps drawing closer from somewhere ahead. He twirled a finger and his men pressed into doorways. The closer they could get to the church before they were discovered, the better it would be for them. But their hiding places were poor, and if whoever was approaching had sharp eyes they would be seen in an instant.

As the Mercian crouched in a doorway, his hand upon the hilt of Brainbiter, he saw Salih ibn Ziyad still walked along the corridor. The wise man seemed to have been in a dream ever since he had been forced to leave Meghigda's side.

The footsteps were drawing near to a turn in the corridor. When Deda stepped out to intercept the wise man, Hereward dragged him back. There was no time. 'Be ready,' he whispered to his men as he watched Salih stride towards the turn.

But at the last, the black-robed wise man slipped into a doorway. The shadows swallowed him. An instant later, a man rounded the corner. He was unmistakably one of Victor's cut-throats. His brow was low, his tunic shabby and stained. As he prowled forward, he gripped a double-edged sword with a notched, stained blade and no decoration upon the hilt. Hereward watched as the guard's gaze fell upon the ill-concealed English. His eyes widened and he opened his mouth to raise the alarm.

From his hiding place, Salih ibn Ziyad lunged. His silver dagger flashed. Blood glittered in the torchlight and the man plunged to his knees, clutching at his throat. The wise man was already moving on before his victim was dead.

Hereward darted along the corridor to catch up with him. Consumed by his need for vengeance, the other man could not be trusted to take care. But barely had he rounded the corner when the Mercian realized his fears had become redundant.

Deep in the monastery, a bell tolled. The first of Herrig's

victims had no doubt been discovered. And as the sound of running feet echoed on all sides, he knew the time for subterfuge had passed.

Catching Deda's wrist, he hissed, 'Keep the monk safe. Take him away from the fighting.' The Norman nodded, putting one hand in the middle of Alric's back and urging him through a doorway. For a moment, Hereward and the churchman held each other's eyes, and then the English warriors swept into a tight knot, their shields locking into place. The Mercian barely had time to realize that Salih ibn Ziyad had disappeared before Victor Verinus' men began to rush towards them from both ends of the corridor.

Hereward scowled. 'Once the plotters hear this din, they may well throw caution to the wind and strike the emperor down.'

'Then you should go, now,' Kraki growled beside him. 'Leave us to fight these dogs.'

'Abandon my brothers? Never.'

The Viking peered over the lip of his shield and snorted with derision. 'Look at them. They may be savage . . . cutthroats and thieves . . . but they are not fighting men. They run like children at play. Do they think they will knock us flat on our backs with one blow? Where is the skill, eh? Where is the battle-plan?' He eyed the Mercian through the holes in his dented helm. 'No. We will rid ourselves of these jolt-headed fowl in no time. When you see your chance, run.'

Hereward knew that Kraki was putting on a brave face. Their enemies might not be seasoned warriors, but by sheer numbers alone they could discourage any resistance. Victor Verinus must have known this. If he had amassed his own army of axes-for-hire, suspicions would soon have been raised. But a few coins pressed in the palms of low men in the inns and markets bought him all he needed: enough fodder to slow any resistance until the emperor was dead. 'Very well,' he grunted. 'But I know you only want the glory for yourself.'

'Glory? I want to show these bastards they should never spit upon the English again.'

On every side, the wave broke upon the shield wall. Swords and axes rained down. Lit by the ruddy glare of the torches, snarling faces hove into view. The Mercian's ears rang from the tumult of yells and curses, but soon he began to hear shrieks and screams too.

'Stay your hands,' he called to his men. 'Keep a calm head.' Bracing his shoulder against the shield, he decided to let these disorganized fools exhaust themselves a little before the battle proper began. When he was sick of the crash of steel on wood, he bellowed, 'Now.'

Reaching up, he stabbed Brainbiter over the lip of the shield and into the furious face of the man hacking wildly at him. The attacker spun back, trailing a stream of blood. Another stepped into his place, but this time Hereward glimpsed a shadow of unease on his opponent's face. He attacked with caution, leaping back whenever the Mercian lunged. Hereward grinned. Kraki was right – these curs had no plan. They were not brave. They feared too much for their own lives. Perhaps they could be held at bay.

Spears thrust through the gaps in the shield walls. More shrieks rang out as the iron tips rammed into unprotected bellies and groins.

With a roar, Kraki cleaved a man's head in two. 'That is why I wear a helm,' he bellowed.

The stone floor became slick with blood. But still more of Victor's men ran to join the fight. 'Let them come,' Sighard cried. 'The sooner they get here, the sooner they die.'

Kraki snorted back a laugh. 'What is this I hear? A warrior, not a mewling babe? I will ask the monk later if this is a miracle.'

Peering through the swirling bodies, Hereward caught sight of Wulfrun and Ricbert. They were fighting back to back, in silence, their faces like stone. No effort was wasted as they cut down those who came at them. For a moment the Mercian was puzzled by the space they had carved around them until he realized that few of the Verini men were attacking them directly. Their crimson cloaks were unmissable, and no doubt designed to be so, a clear sign that here were members of the fearsome Varangian Guard whose reputation was unparalleled across Constantinople.

One day these city curs will fear us the same way, he silently vowed.

'Now I have done all the hard work, I will leave you to clean up,' he said to Kraki. 'Be ready to close the wall.' The Viking only grunted.

When he saw a gap in the line of enemies, Hereward put his shoulder to his shield and rammed his way forward. On either side, men fell away from the force of his charge. Yanking aside his shield, he thrust his blade into the stomach of the startled rogue standing in front of him. With a wrench, he tore open the belly and then ducked down to let the cascade of guts and gore splash over him. Slicked in blood from head to toe, he knew it would make it harder for his enemies to tell if he were friend or foe. In the thick of battle, that momentary confusion was often the difference between victory and defeat.

His horrific appearance seemed to terrify his attackers. From their wild eyes, he guessed they thought him mad, and perhaps they were right. Slashing right and left, he cut a path easily through the ranks to Wulfrun and Ricbert. They too looked at him as if he were some wild beast.

Hereward grinned. 'To the church. Let us see which of these dogs are brave enough to give chase to a devil and two of the emperor's Guard.'

If Wulfrun was pleased by this alliance, he did not show it. He swung his axe down into a man's neck, almost cutting through to the breastbone, then stepped aside as the blood spurted. When his foe fell away, a clear path along the corridor appeared.

The three men raced away from the churning battle, praying they were not too late.

CHAPTER FIFTY-ONE

The emperor knelt in front of the altar. Head bowed, tears streaming down his cheeks, he was mewling like a child. The blade of the axe bit into his bare neck. One drop of blood trickled down his pale skin and spattered on the cold stone floor.

Like all of Victor Verinus' men, the one standing over Michael was a rogue. Filthy-clothed, with lank, dirty hair, his eyes were bovine, his jaw was slack and he was missing an ear. A ragged scar ran from his forehead across his left eye and down to his jawline, no doubt the result of some drunken brawl. He moistened his lips. This man had killed many times before, but never an emperor, Hereward could tell. The magnitude of the crime troubled him.

A halo glimmered around the executioner, as if he were an angel sent from God, not some devil. The church was suffused with the glow of a hundred flickering candle-flames, the light reflecting off the sea of gold that seemed to cover every surface. The sweet aroma of incense hung in the air. The service to honour those who died at Manzikert must have been well under way when the assassin revealed himself.

Around the altar, the finance minister Nikephoritzes and the emperor's closest advisers cowered. The abbot and a few of the senior monks whimpered in prayer, but no man was close enough – or brave enough – to move.

As he scanned the nave, Hereward saw one other, a hooded man watching from beside a pillar against one wall. He did not move, did not show even the slightest hint of dismay at the slaughter that was to come.

Raising his sword, Hereward took a step forward. Wulfrun's hand fell upon his arm. 'Hold,' the commander whispered. 'Do not provoke him.'

'If we stay here, the emperor dies,' the Mercian hissed. He watched the rogue twitch, gathering his nerve. One blow of the axe would be enough and then he could make his escape through the door behind the altar.

The assassin seemed to reach an accommodation with himself. He swung the axe up high. Nikephoritzes cried out.

At the rear of the altar, the heavy oaken door creaked open. As Deda and Alric eased in, the rogue jerked round. His weapon trembled above his head. Wulfrun and Ricbert seemed gripped by the shimmering blade, but Hereward saw his moment.

As the Mercian raced along the nave, the Norman sized up the situation in an instant. Levelling his sword, he commanded, 'Do not move,' and then repeated the order in the Roman tongue.

The assassin hesitated, his dull wits turning slowly. By the time his decision had alighted upon him, Hereward was already leaping up the steps to the altar. In mid-flight, he swung his sword in an arc. So powerful was his blow that the blade cleaved through sinew, gristle and bone. The axe tumbled to the floor. The head flew up, turned once, and came down upon God's table. For a moment it rolled from side to side, and then came to a halt, looking blankly over the fools who had been led such a dance by Victor Verinus.

The emperor shrieked as blood cascaded upon him. When he staggered to his feet, he found himself staring into the crimson-stained face of the man who had saved him. Whatever he saw there, he all but shrieked again. But then Nikephoritzes and the other advisers were at his side, babbling with relief that Michael yet lived.

'Do not tarry,' Wulfrun boomed as he strode along the nave. 'There are many enemies abroad in this monastery. Take our emperor to a safe place and guard him well until I can come to you.'

A circle of greying men folded around the callow youth and swept him past Deda and Alric and out of the door.

'Fortune has smiled on us,' Ricbert gushed as he raced to his master's side. 'Though I would not have wagered a single coin of my own upon this outcome, the emperor has survived.'

'We are not done here yet.' Hereward looked along the nave. Head lowered to hide his features, the hooded man was walking towards the door. 'Hold.' The Mercian levelled his sword. 'Reveal yourself, Maximos.'

The hooded figure paused, his back still to the altar. But he knew, as all there knew, that he could no longer hide his identity. Turning, the Roman stripped off his hood.

Hereward felt his anger glow like hot coals. He had called this man friend. They had walked the hard road together, and fought shoulder to shoulder. And all of it had been built on lies. 'Did a word of truth ever pass your lips?' he asked in a cold voice.

'Do not judge me.' Maximos' voice cracked.

The Mercian was surprised to see emotion twist the other man's face. For a moment, he looked as if he had been stabbed through the heart.

'When you found me, I was a prisoner,' the Roman continued, 'but in truth I have been shackled since I was born. A captive of my blood . . . a captive of days long gone. All I have done . . . all I have been instructed to do . . . has been leading to this night.' He spat on the flagstones. 'You cannot begin to understand what it means to be Nepotes. No man can.'

'We are all bound to what has gone,' Hereward said, unmoved. 'But those chains only imprison us if we let them.'

'Do not judge me!' Maximos raged.

Wulfrun jabbed his sword towards the Roman, his face like stone. 'You would have watched our emperor die. And then you would have seized the crown.'

'I have committed no crime.' Maximos raised his chin in defiance, but after a moment a tremor ran through him. 'No crime,' he repeated in a hollow voice, 'this night.' Tears stung his eyes. Hereward could see that months – years – of long-submerged feelings were bubbling to the surface in the heat of that night's events. 'My friend, Arcadius . . . No, we were more than friends. I loved him as I had loved no other. And I killed him. Stabbed him in the side and watched his life-blood flow into the sand as he pleaded for mercy. And I loved Meghigda too, and I betrayed her. And now she is dead. But my blood demands I be the man you see before you. I tried to run . . . with Arcadius . . . but though miles lay between me and Constantinople, still I could feel the weight of those shackles. I will never be free of them. For if I were, I would not be Nepotes. I would have betrayed my father, and his father, and all the fathers before him. And I am a good man! I betray no one . . . except myself.' He gripped his forehead as if he were on the brink of madness.

'The death of your friend and the woman you loved,' Hereward began, 'was a price worth paying to earn . . . what? A crown. And more enemies than you could ever imagine.'

'I had no choice,' Maximos replied in a small voice. 'I was born to achieve this. I was shaped to achieve this. I have no other life, though God knows I searched for one.' He winced at the self-pity in his voice, and his eyes blazed. 'You think me proud to stand here? I have destroyed myself by degrees. I care not if you run that blade through me now.'

'This plot was your doing?' Wulfrun demanded.

Maximos spat. 'I am nothing. A tool. I do what I am told. That is the Nepotes way.'

'You have been plotting for a long time,' Hereward said. 'Is that not so? Before your father was wounded. And after your mother . . .'

'The Nepotes stand or fall together.' Maximos' voice was like winter.

'We shall see if you are guilty of any crime,' Wulfrun said. 'I have many questions—'

'No.'

The commander whirled at the voice. Juliana stood in the doorway at the foot of the nave. There was steel in her smile, no longer sweet. The candle-flames made her blonde hair shine, as though she were filled with light. Behind her, Simonis was the night to her daughter's moon, her face dark with disappointment. This day had not turned out as planned.

'Juliana, this is not the place for you.' Wulfrun strode along the nave. The young woman skipped to meet him, clasping her hands on his arms. Hereward watched Wulfrun flinch at the unseemly display, but he seemed incapable of resisting. And in that moment, the Mercian knew that Maximos was right – the Nepotes stood together. Kalamdios, Simonis, Neophytos, aye, and Juliana too, this plot had been shaped by all of them. There could be no other explanation. He studied the younger woman's face, seeing the hardness there. How well she had worn her mask. How easily the lies and the manipulations had slipped from her tongue. Only Maximos had resisted that hunger for power. But in the final reckoning, he had been too weak.

'I came to tell you of our good fortune,' Juliana gushed, her eyes sparkling. 'Victor Verinus is dead. Have you heard? We no longer live under his shadow. And all that he stole from us is now ours once more, and all that was his too. The Verini are dead or scattered and there is no one here in Constantinople to lay claim to it. Is that not wonderful?'

352

'We can speak of these matters later,' Wulfrun said, easing her hands off him.

Juliana giggled. 'You are always so serious. The Varangian Guard are here, my love. They have joined forces with the English, and Victor Verinus' men have been put to the axe. This plot is no more. Rejoice. All is well.'

The plot is no more, and the Nepotes have failed . . . this time, Hereward thought. After all that Rowena had whispered to him before they left the Boukoleon palace, the Mercian felt astonished by the depth of the young woman's cunning. He could see not even a hint of deceit in her innocent face. How much did Wulfrun suspect, he wondered? How much of what he guessed was he denying to maintain the play that this was the sweet woman who had won his heart?

'Maximos, you must come with me,' Wulfrun commanded. 'There is more to this plot than Victor Verinus intended. I would know what part you played.'

'My love.' Juliana breathed the words and smiled, but the flint in her features was finally clear. 'Oaths are a grave matter, are they not? You would never betray your oath to your emperor, would you?'

The Mercian frowned, trying to read the truth among those sly words.

'You would never betray any oath,' the young woman continued. 'Those words bind you to a course, for all time. You would never make an oath lightly and recant when you realized the burden it placed on you?' Shaking her head, she raised her eyes and her hands up to the vaulted roof. 'Here, in the eyes of God, in his place? No. I know you would never do such a thing.'

Wulfrun's shoulders sagged. Hereward realized Juliana was speaking of the oath the commander had sworn to her, no doubt in a moment of weakness. She had him fast.

The commander turned to Maximos. They held each other's gaze, and, for a moment, an understanding seemed to pass between them. Hereward saw the same haunted look in both faces. 'You speak truly – you have committed no crime,' Wulfrun said in a flat tone. 'Go now. Return to the house of the Nepotes and enjoy your good fortune.'

Maximos nodded, but showed no sign of relief or joy. As he left, Simonis slipped an arm around his sagging shoulders. But when she whispered some words in his ear – no doubt ones she intended as comfort – he only became more hunched. Still smiling, Juliana blew her love a kiss and skipped after her kin.

For a long moment after the Nepotes had gone, Wulfrun faced the door, his head bowed. Hereward left him there, knowing that no words could ever console him.

CHAPTER FIFTY-TWO

29 August 1072

The drums pounded a steady beat. Grinning figures plucked a stirring melody from stringed instruments as women whirled in dance around them. Chunks of lamb sizzled on glowing charcoal, the mouth-watering scent wafting on the breeze. On the slopes of the seventh hill, carousing folk thronged through the streets around the Golden Gate. The celebration was in full flight. Another plot had been crushed. Constantinople endured.

High on the polished marble walls, the spear-brothers looked down upon the festivities. Barely more than half remained of the exiled war-band that had set sail from Yernemuth months before. But though they had plumbed dark depths, they were the stronger for it.

Hereward shook his head, barely comprehending what he was seeing. 'Only yesterday these very same men and women were bemoaning their ruler's weakness.'

Guthrinc nodded. 'Aye, fill a man's goblet with wine and put meat in his belly and he will cheer the Devil on his throne.'

The Mercian's brow furrowed as he peered into the heart of

the crowd. The Nepotes dispensed good cheer to any and all. Kalamdios sat upon his wooden chair, a lopsided smile twitching on his lips. While Simonis and Juliana hung wreaths of pink mullein flowers round the necks of easily flattered men, and Neophytos the monk folded his chubby hands together and beamed, the boy Leo showed off his newly learned swordplay to the other lads. Only Maximos watched the proceedings with a face that looked as if it had been carved from stone.

All of their hands were stained with blood, Hereward thought. He imagined Juliana, Simonis and Neophytos coming together after Victor Verinus had inflicted his vengeance upon them, each one of them filled with bitterness and loathing, each one of them helping to build the plot that would bring down first the Verini and then an emperor.

Deda followed his friend's gaze. 'I have seen cunning and cleverness in my days, but never as much as this. If their plot had gone as planned, they would be raising their goblets over the emperor's dead body. Now they have paid for a feast in his honour.'

Deep in his throat, Kraki growled. 'Putting smiles on the faces of any who might suspect them, while they sharpen their daggers for another day.' He spat over the edge. 'The fens were a dismal, rainy place, but at least we could tell who our enemies were there. Life was simple. You fought, you feasted, you fucked, and then a new day dawned. Now I waste my hours trying to tell friend from foe, and sniffing my food for poison.'

Along the wall, Hengist was dancing around a statue of some old emperor riding in a chariot pulled by an elephant. Beside him, Sighard marvelled at the magnificence of the defences, the triumphal arch, the large, square towers that seemed to soar up to the azure sky.

'If we had these walls at Ely, we could still be pissing on King William from the top,' Kraki muttered as he peered down the vertiginous drop.

'They keep the enemies out,' Guthrinc said with a nod, 'and they keep the enemies in.'

For all the soaring music Hereward could only hear those drums. They sounded to him like the thrum of a thousand feet marching to war. 'New enemies, new rules, new weapons, new battlefields,' he said as he looked across the rooftops to the magnificence at the heart of the city. 'We have been beaten down, but we have not been broken. We have faced threats we could never have dreamed of back home in the fens, and we have prevailed. There is gold and glory here as we always thought, and it is still within our grasp.'

Flushed from the heat, Alric clambered up the stone steps.

Kraki cupped his hand to his mouth and bellowed, 'Do you want me to give you a hand?'

The spear-brothers threw their heads back and laughed at that.

When he emerged on to the wall, the monk wiped the sweat from his brow and called, 'I may have only one hand, but I at least have the wits to use it.'

Guthrinc guffawed, slapping the Viking on the back. Kraki scowled, but Hereward could see it was only a play. The Mercian nodded. There were worse places to be.

'He comes,' Alric said when he had hurried over. His smile faded. 'Are you sure you can trust him?'

Hereward shook his head. 'But I have faith, monk, as you taught me.'

A moment later, Wulfrun stepped on to the wall. Under the brim of his helm, his eyes were as cold as ever. Ricbert was a step behind, and five other members of the Varangian Guard followed, their hands resting upon the shafts of their axes.

Around him, the Mercian sensed a darkening of the mood. Kraki and Guthrinc stepped in close to his shoulders, their fingers clenching around their weapons.

Coming to a halt, Wulfrun searched Hereward's face for a long moment, weighing him. Seeming to reach some kind of conclusion, he removed his helm and tucked it under his arm.

'The emperor is pleased,' the commander said.

'Pleased,' Guthrinc repeated. 'For saving his life. He is not a man given to wild joys.'

Wulfrun kept his gaze fixed on Hereward. 'When you had the chance, why did you not flee Constantinople?'

'I made an oath to my brothers that we would find a new life here, glory and gold. We cannot return home – there is no future for us there.'

'So you will risk your own neck to carve out a life here?'

'We will earn our life here, as we earned it in England – with a blade and a strong right arm. And I will lead my men to that goal.'

Wulfrun nodded, seemingly turning over each and every word. He was a hard man to read, Hereward thought, but the hatred that had burned in him before seemed to have ebbed. Perhaps that was even respect he saw in the commander's eyes.

'And would the emperor reward us with places among the Varangian Guard?' he asked.

Wulfrun thought for a moment and then shook his head. Hereward simmered. Even now, after all they had done, they were being denied. But then the commander added, 'It would mean nothing if any man could join our ranks. You must prove yourselves first.' He looked around the faces of the spear-brothers. A faint smile played on his lips. He seemed pleased by what he saw there.

'What would you have us do?' the Mercian asked.

'Doom is drawing towards this city,' Wulfrun replied, his voice clear. 'Few believe that to be so, for Constantinople abides.' He swept his hand along the defences. 'These walls are strong. They will never fall. But when death stands at the Golden Gate, then they will believe. News has reached me of the Turks building their army in the east. Great battles lie ahead. Rivers of blood will be spilled. Are you ready?'

'We are always ready,' Kraki said with a shake of his axe.

'Good,' Wulfrun replied. 'Then you will prove yourselves in the army, and you may yet earn a place in the Varangian Guard, and the gold and the glory that come with it.'

'If we live,' Hereward said.

'If you live.'

When the Mercian looked around his spear-brothers, he could see the answer in their faces. 'Show us a war and we will win it for you,' he said.

'Very well. Arrangements will be made.' Wulfrun walked away a few paces and then turned back. 'Nothing you have endured will compare to what lies ahead. May God smile upon you. You will need all his help.'

As Hereward watched Wulfrun leave, he felt a pang of pity. The commander was the real victim here. His misplaced love for Juliana would cause him much suffering in addition to the misery Hereward himself had inflicted upon him.

Once the Varangian Guard had left, the spear-brothers clapped their arms around each other, and laughed. They had purpose now, and battles to fight. After the long journey from England, when all had seemed lost, that was enough. As they made their way down the steps in search of mead, Hereward turned back to watching the crowds. Alric stepped beside him.

'There is some justice in this city after all,' the monk said.

Hereward watched the Nepotes finish dispensing their favours and begin to make their way back along the streets to the centre of their web. At first he thought to laugh at his friend's statement, but then he glimpsed something that gave him pause. 'Justice comes in many forms,' he said, 'and sometimes while you look towards the light, it waits in the dark.'

Alric eyed his friend, puzzled by this cryptic statement. But Hereward did not explain. He was too busy watching a shadow separate from the crowd and begin to follow the Nepotes, who smiled and chatted, oblivious of what lay at their backs. Death, it looked like, Hereward thought. Death, waiting in silence.

Swathed in black, Salih ibn Ziyad took slow steps but he did not deviate from his course.

Hereward watched the steady progression of the Nepotes and the shadow that followed them and nodded. No man could escape the fate he had forged by his own deeds. Judgement Day always came.

Author's Notes

And so we leave England's shores behind, for now, at least.

Over the past three books, we've had a taste of some of the hardship, conflict and upheaval that Hereward and the English probably experienced in the period following the Norman Conquest. Viewing events through that prism, it's easy to forget that at the same time great things were happening elsewhere. The world was in a state of flux, with new powers rising, and old ones falling into shadow.

For me, the Byzantine Empire was one of the most interesting places to be in those waning years of the eleventh century. For hundreds of years, Byzantium had been a great world power with Constantinople its shining jewel. The city's commanding position at the point where west meets east allowed huge wealth to flow into its coffers from the Mediterranean and Asia.

But catastrophe struck in 1071 and the fortunes of Byzantium began to turn. The Imperial Army was unexpectedly defeated by the Seljuk Turks at the battle of Manzikert in Armenia. The emperor, Romanus Diogenes, negotiated peace terms with the sultan Alp Arslan. But on his return to Constantinople he found that his enemies had replaced him with a new ruler, Michael, who refused to meet the terms of the peace treaty. And so the long period of wealth and stability ended. Inside Constantinople plotting was rife, with different factions battling to seize the crown. And outside the great walls, the snubbed Turks began to cross the unguarded frontier and flood into Anatolia. Soon they were within striking distance of Constantinople itself.

Intrigue and struggles for the future of an empire no doubt made Constantinople a dangerous place. But this didn't seem to deter the English. A great many fled the rule of William the Bastard, certainly many of those who could afford to uproot themselves. We know from the historical record that a huge number of fighting men left England to work as mercenaries abroad. The warrior skills of the English and the Vikings were held in high regard across Europe.

And Constantinople was the destination of choice.

The emperor's feared elite force, the Varangian Guard, commanded huge respect and were extremely well paid. In Constantinople itself, they were celebrated with a degree of adoration that warriors had never experienced elsewhere. In many eyes, they were the X *Factor* winners of their day, only with worse hair and more talent, albeit for killing. They were given their own district in the city, the Vlanga, with fine houses, and the gold they earned gave them a sumptuous lifestyle. Women crowded around their streets, trying to get a look, a touch, give a token, or more. The majority of the Guard were English or Vikings. If you had spent the last few years near-starving on the slopes of Ely, with King William's army threatening to end your days, wouldn't you want a shot at riches and fame?

This is a great canvas for the ongoing story of Hereward and his men. We don't know for certain what happened to the hero of Ely after its fall – there are competing theories – but it's very likely that those warriors who escaped the slaughter would have gone east in search of gold and glory.

One final word on place names. You'll have noticed that not once was the word 'Byzantium' used in this book. That's because it's a name imposed by latter-day historians. At the time, this was still considered the Roman Empire, and the people who lived within its borders called themselves Romans.

I also took the decision a long time ago to refer to Constantinople only by that name. Every place in the world at this time was called more than one thing, depending upon who was speaking. But in storytelling, clarity is paramount. I could have had the English calling the city Constantinople and the Vikings calling it Mikkelgaard. And the same with Ceuta/Abta/Sabta. But that could lead to confusion. Better to choose one name and stick with it, I think. (As, no doubt, the mercenaries of the time would have done. If all your comrades in arms were saying they were on the way to Constantinople, would you bloody-mindedly insist on calling it Mikkelgaard? I doubt it.)

Even greater drama lies ahead for Constantinople and the Roman Empire: war on several fronts, conspiracy at home. I'd quite like to see how Hereward and the spear-brothers deal with it all . . .

James Wilde

ABOUT THE AUTHOR

James Wilde is a man of Mercia. Raised in a world of books, he went on to study economic history at university before travelling the world in search of adventure. Unable to forget a childhood encounter – in the pages of a comic – with the great English warrior Hereward, he became convinced that this great fighter should be the subject of his first novel. *Hereward* was a bestseller and two further successful novels, chronicling the life and times of the near-forgotten hero, followed. *Hereward: Wolves of New Rome* is the fourth book in the series. James indulges his love of history and the high life in the home his family have owned for several generations in the heart of a Mercian forest. To find out more, visit www.manofmercia.co.uk